Dead Ahead

Lynn Emery

Lazy River Publishing

Lynn Emery/Lazy River Publishing
P.O. Box 74833
Baton Rouge, LA 70807
www.lazyriverpublishing.com

Publisher's Note: This is a work of fiction. Names, characters, places, and incidents are a product of the author's imagination. Locales and public names are sometimes used for atmospheric purposes. Any resemblance to actual people, living or dead, or to businesses, companies, events, institutions, or locales is completely coincidental.

Book Layout & Design ©2013 - BookDesignTemplates.com

Dead Ahead/ Lynn Emery -- 1st ed.
ISBN 978-0-9997628-2-0

Joliet Sisters Psychic Detectives
Spirited Sisters
Dead Wrong

LaShaun Rousselle Mysteries
A Darker Shade of Midnight
Between Dusk and Dawn
Only By Moonlight
Into The Mist
Third Sight Into Darkness

Chapter 1

They Be Creepin'

Charmaine stood at the front of a crowd of gawkers. A screwball bunch of crime-scene junkies by the looks of them. She didn't get it. If Detective Harrison of the New Orleans Homicide Division hadn't pulled the "You freakin' owe me" card, Charmaine would still be at home sipping tea. She'd sworn off liquor—well, cut down at least. When she got shoved from behind, she spun around to cuss the fool out. Her sister Jessi grinned back at her.

"Jeez, what a funky scene. You got a strange way of spending a Monday morning. What's the big 911 you kept texting me? I barely had time to finish off Dre." Jessi cackled when Charmaine's mouth turned down in distaste. "Don't get all holy-roly on me, church lady."

"Harrison. Pretty much threatened to expose our past indiscretions if I didn't show." Charmaine pulled a long face at the memory of that phone call.

"Fuck him. He can't out us without getting himself in trouble. His boss will ask awkward questions about us. Let's go get some breakfast. Not lunch. Hell, it's only ten. We'll call it brunch." Jessi turned to leave. She swore when Charmaine yanked her back.

"He says Scotty would get some blowback as well. They'd yank his liquor license, step up sanitation inspections of his kitchen."

"Shit." Jessi blew out a loud breath into the humid October early morning air.

She didn't have to say more. Jessi knew Charmaine would do anything to protect her friend. Scotty was more than a friend. He had become part of their family over the years. Never mind Scotty was a big boy, literally, and could handle his own business. Bonds forged in the streets held as strong as blood. Sometimes stronger.

"I can't figure out why Harrison called me to a murder scene. He hates our 'ghost busting bullshit,'" Charmaine said, quoting his favorite description of them as psychic investigators.

"Yeah, well, we take on regular cases, too. He's just ticked we got state-licensed. We're a legit security firm. Thank you very much, asshole Detective Bryan Hezekiah Harrison."

"Hezekiah? C'mon." Charmaine gaped at her sister.

"I would never shit you, sis. I did a background check on him. Bet it was the name of a grandfather or something. He uses only the initial on official documents."

"Jessi!" Charmaine shook her arm hard.

"Hey, hey. I paid two hundred dollars for this Tracy Reese." Jessi yanked free from Charmaine's grasp. "Well, Art did.'"

Charmaine blinked at her. Jessi wore a sleek, silky blouse over black slim pants. "Nice purple color."

"Eggplant, darlin'. So, stop messin' with my look," Jessi sniffed.

"Harrison's gonna mess with more than your look if he finds out you're digging for dirt on him," Charmaine hissed, careful to keep her voice low. She looked around to see if anyone was trying to listen in. "He's a friend. Remember?"

Jessi's sniff turned into a snort. "He's a cop. Remember? They like locking us up for the least little reason. Don't let that uncle act fool you."

"He's helped us out more than a few times," Charmaine countered.

"Yeah, and y'all damn well better put some respect on my name."

"Oh shit." Charmaine jumped almost a foot in the air at the deep voice over her shoulder. She landed with a hand over her heart. "Don't sneak up like that. I almost caught a heart attack."

"How did you..." Jessi scowled at him.

"A dead body makes for a pretty good distraction," Harrison replied with a chuckle. His black-coffee eyes twinkled for a moment. One second later, amusement faded from his chocolate-brown face as he led them into the murder scene. He nodded.

Charmaine and Jessi followed his gaze. A trail of blood across hardwood floors disappeared down a hallway. Crime-scene techs and another plainclothes detective delicately stepped around the room. One held a camera, clicking away to document the gruesome details. The Uptown home on Octavia Street was recent construction, but then so was a lot of

New Orleans post-Hurricane Katrina. A tile foyer led into the living room. A wide door led to the dining room. Late October afternoon sun slanted through floor-to-ceiling windows.

"The décor isn't helped by postmodern gore," Jessi mumbled. She started to walk away to get a better look.

Harrison pulled her back. "Meet me outside."

"I wish y'all would stop jerking me around." Jessi glared at him and Charmaine. Then she did a precision about-face left.

Charmaine shrugged an apology at Detective Harrison with a weak smile. Then she followed her sister's path across the small concrete front porch and down the steps.

"We already processed the front yard and this," Harrison said, his large hands sweeping out as he walked. "So, Officer Ward will let you through." He pointed to a slender uniformed white policeman, who nodded in acknowledgement.

"He's cute. Red hair, freckles." Jessi's irritated frown melted into a warm smile. She waved the fingers of her right hand at Officer Ward. He nodded again with an impassive expression.

"Focus," Charmaine snapped.

"I am focused, girl. He's built underneath that shirt. My first redhead."

"He's on his job, not paying attention to you. Which is what you should be doing." Charmaine pinched Jessi's right arm.

"I like a challenge. Pinch me again, see what happens." Jessi switched back on, annoyed, as she frowned at Charmaine.

"If y'all can lay off the sibling rivalry for a minute..." Harrison huffed in frustration. He stared at the house. "I don't like this one bit."

"Yeah, bloody murder ain't all that cuddly, especially on a Monday. But then, job security for you. Right?" Jessi popped a square of gum into her mouth and chewed.

Harrison ignored her comment. "We got three witnesses claiming some kind of ghost came out of nowhere. Next thing, their friend lets out a blood-curdling scream."

"A spirit doesn't have physicality. I mean, it can't touch a person." Charmaine looked at the house, arms crossed. "Drugs?"

"Recreational weed. We're still looking. They might have cleaned up before we got here, though." Harrison rubbed his forehead as if massaging a headache. He faced Charmaine and Jessi a few seconds later. "So, do your thing."

"Pardon?" Charmaine blinked at him.

"Look, don't play dumb. Before a bigger crowd gathers, I'll let you close to my witnesses. Let me know if they're lying." Harrison pointed at Jessi. "You, wave your magic wand or whatever you do. Find out if ghosts, goblins, or, God forbid, a vampire is close by."

"Does this ensemble say 'Van Helsing' to you? Like vampires are real," Jessi retorted.

"Keep it down, damn it," Harrison shot back in a hoarse whisper. He looked over his shoulder. "The last thing I need is my boss getting word you two are involved."

"Excuse me, but we're not involved," Charmaine put in before Jessi could give a more colorful reply. "*You called us.*"

"Yeah," Jessi added. She gave him a head-to-toe look of scorn.

"They're not clients or even remotely connected to one of our cases," Charmaine said. "So, unless you can come up with a better reason for us being here—"

"We're going about our merry business." Jessi smirked at him, but it faded under his withering gaze.

"I talked to the DA in your favor about that last case. You know, the rich family with murderous habits. You didn't tell me certain facts. And yeah, I can get you in deep shit without getting any on myself." Harrison raised a thick forefinger in the air. "Not to mention your less-than-legal computer hacking to gather info on folks, Jessi."

"I use paid databases like any legitimate professional in the investigative..." Jessi's voice trailed away. "Damn. Can't count on those dumb cop stereotypes when you need 'em."

"I don't care if you tell anyone about my middle name, by the way." Harrison gave a wolfish grin at Jessi's look of wide-eyed surprise.

"Points for the detective." Charmaine made an invisible mark on a pretend scoreboard.

"Threats between friends ain't cool," Jessi complained.

"Look, let's get along for once. Shall we? I'm just as exposed here. We need each other. So, before my boss swoops in to look over my shoulder..." Harrison blew out a breath.

Charmaine looked at him. "Yeah, well, Jessi is right. Going hardball doesn't exactly make us receptive. But like you said, we need your help in the department sometimes—"

"Aw, man," Jessi blurted.

"Well, it's true," Charmaine replied with heat.

"Fine." Jessi let a sigh drag out to express her dissatisfaction. "Tell us what's going on."

"I can't share details of the crime yet, at least not all of them," Harrison said, holding up a wide palm.

"This shit is unbelievable. He calls us out here but won't tell us key information." Jessi shook her head.

"Hell, you're the voodoo-hoodoo psychics. I shouldn't have to tell you anything," Harrison snapped. His raised voice drew unwanted attention from those nearby. "No ma'am, there is no danger to anyone in the neighborhood."

Charmaine laughed. "Pretending we live here? I can't afford to walk down this street. Houses start at six hundred thousand dollars."

"You're right, so we don't have time to argue. As professional paranormal investigators, you gotta be a little bit interested in knowing more." Harrison tilted his head to one side. "Not your usual place for a haunting. Is it?"

Charmaine looked at the stylish, pale-blue contemporary cottage. "Go on."

"Here we go," Jessi breathed.

Harrison switched to narrator mode. He gestured for them to follow. They went down the alley, a narrow driveway wide enough for a vehicle. "We put the witnesses in the garage in back. They had a late-night Sunday get-together. Four friends. Hipster dishes from the new neo-Creole cuisine restaurant on Canal. A little weed with dessert, and boom. A demon from the depths of hell crashed the party."

"Everybody hold up." Jessi stopped dead in her tracks. When Harrison and Charmaine stopped as well and looked at her, she jammed both fists on her hips. "How we gone get paid?"

"Say what?" Harrison blinked at her.

"We don't do freebies," Jessi said with a pointed look at her sister. "Not counting elderly ladies that always remind you of our granny, no matter how different they actually are."

"Mrs. Loranger was an isolated situation. I didn't know she had a habit of killing her husbands." Charmaine turned to Harrison, whose mouth had dropped open. "Only two, that we know of, and one might have been an accident. It's kind of a long story. That was in St. Tammany Parish, so you wouldn't know about it."

"And she was the great-aunt of a retired justice of the peace. Lived in a little community called Goodbee. Whole thing got hushed up. Favor to him. She's in a private psych hospital," Jessi said.

"Right. State and parish forensic beds are few and far between. She's probably going to spend the rest of her days there. Incompetent to stand trial. They say it's dementia, but I don't think she was ever screwed on too tight. If you know what I mean." Charmaine was about to go on when Jessi cut her off.

"But back to my question. Who's paying our fee?" Jessi crossed her arms to wait, feet planted as if she wouldn't move another inch.

Harrison tsk-tsked in disapproval. "Whatever happened to civic duty?"

"Are you going to blood-soaked murder scenes without a paycheck? Hell no is the answer," Jessi clipped before he replied.

"Listen to me, young lady..." Harrison pointed a forefinger at Jessi's nose.

"Oh, please. Don't try the daddy act with me. Never had one, and if I did he wouldn't order me around." Jessi brushed past him on her way back to the street. The cute redheaded police officer blocked her path.

"Excuse me, ma'am. Need to talk to Detective Harrison," Officer Ward said.

"Sure." Jessi stepped close to him and proceeded the dancing act. He went left, and so did she. He stepped right, and she matched his move.

"Sorry," Ward murmured.

"You're smooth on your feet. We should go to the club, so you can show me." Jessi winked at him. She chuckled when he blushed pink.

"If you're through waltzing around, Ward?" Harrison called, his deep voice an irritated rumble.

"Right, uh..." Ward drew himself up to squeeze past Jessi, even though there was plenty of room. "There's a guy out here says he has information on the murder. But I don't know. He looks like a wacko if you ask me."

"Then get a statement and get rid of the nut," Harrison snapped.

"Thing is, he's got a card says he has authorization from headquarters to shadow officers. Kind of like a ride-along. I checked, and Chief Addison says to give him full cooperation," Ward quoted, reading a text on his cell phone.

"Trying to deal with a damn murder and now this bull—"

Harrison stomped forward, muttering. Jessi and Ward jumped off the cement drive to give him a clear path. Jessi, Ward, and Charmaine stood together, exchanging glances. Jessi's smoldering gaze settled on the policeman. Charmaine made eye-rolling an Olympic event at the obvious seductive act. For his part, Officer Ward's defenses seemed to be wilting under the heat. He gave Jessi a slight smile.

"Don't stand around like statues. Get out here," Harrison yelled.

"Sir." Ward reacted first by jogging toward his voice.

"Yeah, whatever," Jessi wisecracked. She followed with a hip-swaying stroll.

"We're working, so stop acting like a cat in heat," Charmaine said over Jessi's shoulder as she walked behind her.

"Who's acting? I'm gonna let that cute cop take me into custody," Jessi quipped with a giggle.

"Horny and corny. Great," Charmaine muttered.

"Since when did you get so judgy?" Jessi halted suddenly.

Charmaine bumped into her. "Hey, a little warning. That guy looks familiar." She dug into her crossbody bag until she found her slim tablet. She opened the case and swiped through several pages. Then held up the screen so Jessi could see.

"E.J. Locke, author of fantastic fiction and nonfiction on macabre crimes of the nineteenth century," Jessi read. She switched her gaze from the tablet screen to the man. "He looks a bit crazy in his photo. So, he's a patient at your clinic?"

"Of course not. E.J. Locke is one of my favorite authors. His Father Cable series is like a modern classic. He's also an expert in religious studies, fusing the horror genre with the psychology of belief." Charmaine felt genuine awe.

"You sound like his publicist," Jessi teased. She snatched the tablet out of Charmaine's hand and read. "Right. I thought so. Some slick hype."

"Well, the man happens to be brilliant so the 'hype' isn't all talk. And we get to meet him." Charmaine elbowed Jessi aside.'

"Hey! Don't make me slap your silly..." Jessi stopped mid-warning.

Harrison and Locke stood toe-to-toe in what sounded like a not-quite-cordial discussion. Locke was a good inch shorter than Harrison. His short brown hair framed a middle-aged white face. A young woman beside him with long blond locks kept trying to point a compact video camera. Officer Ward blocked the lens with one hand each time. The woman glared at him. Meanwhile, police officers led staff from the coroner's office to the house.

"I'm telling you, Officer Horace—"

"*Detective Harrison.*" Harrison frowned at Locke.

"Right. My apologies. There are forces at work in this crime that—" Locke broke off when the woman whispered to him. "Excuse us a minute."

"Gladly," Harrison shot back. "Ward, get rid of them. And make sure Miss Rasta doesn't take any film of my crime scene. I don't want this poor woman's next of kin to see her address on one of those tabloid websites."

"Got it." Officer Ward strode over to stand between Locke, the camerawoman, and the victim's house.

Seconds later, Locke and the woman darted around Ward before he could react. They made a beeline for Jessi and Charmaine. Harrison signaled to Ward, who blocked their progress toward the sisters.

"What part of 'go away' confused you folks?" Harrison growled. "We have an active investigation. We can't do our jobs if we have to deal with thrill-seeking reality-show types."

"I see. So, we should ignore the fact that you have two well-known paranormal detectives on the scene. Apparently called in by you, Detective Harper." Locke eyed Charmaine and Jessi in turn.

"*Harrison*, damn it." Harrison seemed flustered by his quick identification. He darted a glance at Charmaine.

"Listen, um, detective. We can keep this between us. Your superiors don't need to know about the Joliet sisters being here. To be honest, they weren't too thrilled with letting me observe police activity firsthand. Having friends in even higher places helps. So, it appears we have the same goal." Locke spoke in a soft, confidential tone.

Harrison fumed for a few beats as he looked from Locke to the sisters. He clenched his jaw and said, "No filming."

"Agreed," Locke replied quickly, despite a squawk of protest from his camerawoman. "We can get footage later."

"She needs to delete any images taken already," Ward added. "You were standing on private property. I saw you. Without permission from the owners..."

"She's dead, dude," the young woman spat.

"Her next of kin didn't consent. You could be in legal trouble," Ward said. Before she could answer, he plucked the camera from her hands and pressed a button. He held it to her. "There we go. All taken care of."

The young woman yanked it from his hand. "I'll sue you for assault and destruction of private property."

"I was just looking at it and accidentally hit a switch while explaining the law to you," Ward replied with a smile. "Sorry."

"Nazi," the woman hissed. She took a step back.

"I'm Jewish, ma'am," Ward said mildly and continued to smile at her.

"It's all right, Becca. I said we can get footage later," Locke said, his tone terse. He frowned a warning at her.

Another plainclothes officer strode up. "Sir, the witnesses are getting antsy. I've got their statements. Any reason they need to stick around?" The detective squinted at Harrison. Then he looked at the others with a question in his dark eyes.

"Follow the coroner to get more details on the victim's condition, manner of death, etcetera," Harrison said with a wave of one hand. "I'll finish up here."

"If you say so."

"Yeah, Detective Gautier. Fifteen years of experience and seniority say so," Harrison spoke in a calm yet forceful voice.

Though Detective Gautier didn't look cowed, he gave a sharp nod and left. He side-eyed Jessi, Charmaine, and Locke as he strode away. The camerawoman gave Gautier an appreciative once-over as he walked off. Charmaine filed away Becca's thoughts that she could get information while having fun with the buff cop.

"Harrison suspects Gautier was assigned to him to keep tabs," Charmaine said low to Jessi.

"Yeah. I didn't need to read minds to figure out they're not exactly pals," Jessi whispered back.

Harrison eyed them with suspicion as he gave instructions to another police officer. He brushed away Locke's attempts to listen in. Jessi nudged Charmaine and nodded toward Becca. The camera jockey snapped photos on the sly. Locke did a great job of distracting Harrison and the other officers. Finally, Harrison joined Jessi and Charmaine again with Locke right on his heels.

"I want you two to come with me. Not you." Harrison raised a palm like a traffic cop at Locke.

"Is this your version of being cooperative?" Locke waved the card from the chief of police.

"I don't care whose ass you kissed, mister. Or who kissed yours, for that matter. I won't compromise a murder investigation. I doubt the family of our victim would be too thrilled if I did." Harrison jerked a thumb for the sisters to follow him. When they were a few feet away he muttered, "So go suck yourself."

"Whew. Gotta remember that one," Jessi said with a giggle.

Harrison stopped when they arrived at the door to the garage. He faced them with a grim expression. "No graveyard jokes."

"Yes, sir," Charmaine and Jessi replied together.

"Look, these folks just lost someone they cared about. Respect their grief. Add to that, they're genuinely rattled by *something*. I want to know if it's the mind-altering substances or... you know."

"Real spirits. Gotcha," Charmaine replied with a serious tone.

"Jeez. Those two words don't even sound right together," Harrison muttered. He opened the door and led the way.

The former garage had been converted into an apartment. They entered the living room, which flowed into a modern kitchen. A bright dining room sat to the right. Charmaine guessed the door led to a bedroom with a bath. Decorated in brick-reds, shades of gray, and turquoise, this garage would probably rent for more than Charmaine's mortgage payment. A man and two women huddled together in the dining area. The witnesses sat on the window seat of a bay window. One of the women sniffled as they tried to comfort her.

Harrison spoke low. "The victim is, was, Amanda Morrell. She runs an interior design and antiques shop. She's the fourth generation of—"

"The Morrell family of New Orleans. Her paternal third great-grandfather owned a custom shop in the Vieux Carré in 1793, give or take a few years. He immigrated from Haiti during the revolution. He managed to escape with most of the family fortune intact. He'd inherited two sugar plantations." Charmaine blinked as Harrison and Jessi stared at her. "I'm not that good. Pulled it up on my iPad."

"Right," Harrison said, drawing out the word. He gazed at Charmaine as though spooked, despite her explanation. "Anyway, her pals are Timothy Acker, Leslie Crandall, and Demi Draper."

"The brunette looks familiar," Jessi mumbled. Her salon-perfected eyebrows pulled together as she gazed at the woman.

"Demi Draper. Her father's a big-time export and import guy. Mostly electronic parts. He's also a customs broker. Don't ask me to explain it. Bottom line, all three of them come from money. They went to the same fancy private schools until college," Harrison said. When the man stood and came toward him, Harrison put on a muted smile. "Mr. Acker—"

"How much longer will we have to stay cooped up in here? Sarah and Dem are close to totally losing it. Just thinking about poor Amanda lying dead a few feet away." He wound up to continue but stopped when Harrison placed a hand on his shoulder.

"I understand how difficult this is for you," Harrison said.

"I doubt that," Sarah Crandall shot from her place beside Demi. "This is just another day at the office for you. Another murder. She was our friend."

"Amanda," Demi whimpered. She buried her face in both hands.

Sarah Crandall stood and shrugged off the lace shawl around her shoulders. "I've had enough. Unless you're going to charge us, we're leaving."

"Maybe we should be patient a little longer, Sarah" Acker said. He twisted his hands together. The mention of criminal charges seemed to dampen his burst of rebellion against authority.

"Hi. Jessi Joliet, and this is my sister, Charmaine. Look, the cops don't care about your *party favors*. Finding out who killed your friend is their top priority." Jessi put on an open, caring expression.

"Who are these people?" Sarah said to Harrison.

Harrison jumped in with a quick side glance at Charmaine. "We use them as special consultants on select cases. They're experts on unusual phenomena."

"You mean because we saw a ghost or whatever it was." Acker crossed his arms and gave a shudder.

"Like psychic detectives?" Demi said through a wad of tissues.

"Yeah, something like that," Harrison admitted with obvious reluctance.

"Don't be ridiculous," Sarah blurted. She looked at Acker. "Timmy, your wild imagination gets even more weird when you smoke weed. It's obvious what happened."

"Really?" Harrison looked at Sarah with interest.

"Some street thug must have broken in and killed Amanda while trying to rob us," Sarah said.

"Except there's nothing missing. I still have my father's 1952 Patek Philippe, my credit card and..." Timmy held up his wrist to show the watch in question.

"Just as obviously he or they must have been scared off before they could finish ransacking the place. You've seen the house. Furniture turned over, the painting over the wall safe hanging crooked. And who the hell still keeps valuables in a wall safe? The thieves didn't need to guess where to look." Sarah blew out a sharp breath. "Sitting ducks."

"I don't know how you can blame Amanda." Demi went from tearful to pissed off. She stomped over to Sarah. "You're just mad because Ethan chose her over you. Pretending to still be her friend so you can spy on them."

"She's welcome to that lying snake. I'm so over *him*," Sarah replied with fire in her violet-blue eyes. She tossed her silky blond hair over one shoulder.

Demi sneered at her. "So, I guess you won't be running over to his place to offer him solace in the form of a blow job."

"Seriously, you two?" Timmy yelled. "Amanda was brutally murdered almost in front of us, and you're having a cat fight?"

"Listen, we're here with an open mind to get all the details from last night," Charmaine broke in to steer them away from more volatile exchanges.

"Yeah," Jessi added. "No matter how weird and way out there they might sound to anyone else. Char and me are good at getting to the bottom of anything odd. That way the police can do their jobs without wasting time on what doesn't exist."

"So, you uncover fake supernatural events? Finally, somebody is making sense," Sarah said.

"Uh, yeah, we... Tell us what happened. I know you giving statements to the police over and over. We're paying attention to a different angle," Charmaine said.

"We were celebrating Sarah finishing up her Ph.D. in economics and business management at Cornell. She got back from an international study trip abroad last week." Timmy nodded at Sarah.

"I spent three months in Africa, New Zealand, and China," Sarah said with pride.

"Us mere mortals are in awe," Timmy drawled. "I'm an accountant. Demi works for Amanda's father in... What exactly is your job again, Dem?" Timmy looked at her.

Demi glared when Sarah snorted. "I've only been there six months. I'm in marketing."

Charmaine picked up on the hint of more to that story, but let it go. For now. "Okay. You all came over for dinner."

"Right. Well, we had planned on going to The Club but changed our minds," Timmy answered.

"The Club?" Charmaine looked at the three friends in turn.

"The Southern Yacht Club," Sarah explained. "Demi is always our guest, of course. We're legacy members."

"Stop it, Sarah," Timmy warned with a dark look.

"No worries. The fact that her father is practically my grandfather's *employee* is annoying. I completely get it," Demi said with a careless shrug of one shoulder.

"You nouveau riche, sniveling—" Sarah lunged at Demi.

Jessi stepped between them and blocked a slap aimed at the brunette. "Show some respect for Amanda's memory."

"Sorry," Timmy said on behalf of the two still-fuming women. He pushed them farther apart. "They're just upset by everything that's happened."

"Uh-huh." Jessi gave Sarah an evil squint until she literally backed into a corner to escape. Then she stared at Demi with a puzzled frown.

"So, you came here for dinner and..." Charmaine prompted. Detective Harrison seemed content to give the sisters leeway.

"We talked and everything. A couple of other friends joined us, but they left around ten last night. I'm not sure what time it was, but the lights started flickering. And that's when I saw it. Looked just like the stories said."

"You must have smoked or sniffed something a hell of a lot stronger than we did, Timmy," Sarah retorted and shook her head.

"I know what I saw. The grunch. That's who killed Amanda."

Chapter 2

Nah

Tuesday morning, Charmaine hurried through her morning routine. She stuffed a slice of toast in her mouth, grabbed her tote bag, and made a dash for the side door. Her office phone rang. She tried to ignore it, swinging open the door anyway. The insistent trill yanked on her last nerve.

"I should have dumped that damn landline a long time ago. Just 'cause it was Mama Etta's phone number."

Charmaine continued to mutter oaths, regrets, and threats against whoever existed on the other end of the call. She dropped her tote bag. Since she'd neglected to zip it closed, its contents spilled at her feet. Worse language burst from her lips as she stepped across the mess. She crossed the hallway into the room she'd added for her office. Then she grabbed the cordless handset.

"What?" she barked. Then she remembered to be professional since it was her business line. "I mean, Joliet Services. How can we help?"

"Be at my office this afternoon. Four o'clock. It's not a request," Harrison said. A click and dial tone announced he was in no mood for discussion.

That sealed it. Charmaine had to go through her Tuesday morning at the counseling clinic battling a foul mood. As usual, seeing her first client served as an attitude adjustment. The latest clinical director and a few colleagues usually didn't earn her patience. Her clients always did. She loved everything about being a mental health social worker. Struggling to pay for college and then to get her master's degree had been worth it.

"I told that no-good landlord. I said, 'I know what you're up to.'"

"Mrs. Lirette, we've talked about this more than once," Charmaine said.

The woman, dressed in three layers of colorful clothes, gave a sharp nod. Theo Dora Lirette looked a good fifteen years older than her forty-eight years. A hard life had aged her.

Yet Charmaine could still see the pretty woman she had been. Her mousy-brown hair was stuffed under a threadbare pink beret. Too much rouge on her pale cheeks made her look like an elderly Raggedy Ann doll.

"Don't be so formal. And I already know what you're going to say, Miss Social Worker," Theo Dora said with a stubborn purse of her bright-pink lips.

"You missed your appointment with Dr. Vega last week."

Charmaine cocked an eyebrow at her. The long-acting injection of an anti-psychotic medication helped stave off her paranoia. Dr. Vega, a psychiatrist, sent Charmaine notices if patients skipped doses. At least Theo Dora had only missed one so far.

"I was busy. Lots to do."

Theo Dora fumbled in the oversized knit bag she carried everywhere. It was stuffed with her prized possessions. Charmaine didn't have to imagine what her house looked like. She'd visited the rundown row house. One of those pickers from The History Channel would have a blast sorting through it all. Stacks of wacky cheap things lived alongside antiques Theo Dora had scrounged. Charmaine was just happy that most in the neighborhood thought it was all junk. Otherwise, Theo Dora might be targeted by local addicts and hurt.

"Let's go over your Wellness and Recovery Action Plan. Okay?" Charmaine pointed to the battered spiral notebook peeking out of Theo Dora's bag.

To her relief, Theo Dora agreed. The WRAP plan, written in Theo Dora's own handwriting, listed the signs that she was heading for a crisis. Even in her most paranoid state, Theo Dora would recognize her neat script. That way she couldn't claim the CIA or FBI had planted the information to trap her. For the rest of their hour, Charmaine and Theo Dora went over what she should consider doing next. Theo Dora finally used Charmaine's office phone to make a new appointment with Dr. Vega. Of course, that he was just down the hall made it convenient. Still, letting Theo Dora make the decision was important.

"Surprise, surprise. He can see me in twenty-minutes." Theo Dora gave Charmaine a knowing look. "You don't have me fooled, young woman."

"I'm guilty of plotting to help you live your best life," Charmaine replied.

Theo Dora patted the back of Charmaine's hand. "Um-hmm. You can write that the patient showed insight and hasn't completely gone off the rails. Must toddle off. I don't want to keep handsome Alejandro waiting."

Charmaine laughed, though she was right. Dr. Vega was fine. "I know he'll be pleased to see you, too."

"Oh, I saw that article in the paper. Are you and your sister going to help the police catch the grunch? I was out near Bayou St. John and saw the grunch myself. Been seeing them for years." Theo Dora spoke in a conspiratorial whisper.

"Theo Dora—"

"Don't you worry." Theo Dora put a forefinger to her bright, thin lips. "I won't say a word to your boss."

"I appreciate your discretion, but—"

"Outsiders don't understand our culture. I mean, she's from Iowa." Theo Dora shrugged as if she didn't need to say more.

"My side gig isn't exactly a secret anymore," Charmaine said with a laugh.

Theo Dora clicked her tongue. "True natives know there's more to our city than meets the eye. But all these newcomers? They think

talk of spirits, voodoo, and supernatural creatures is just tourist claptrap."

Charmaine's smile faded. Theo Dora had a
point. Beth Parker might have moved to New
Orleans, but she hadn't embraced the local flavor. She'd dropped more than a few subtle
hints of disapproval. As it happened, Charmaine and Jessi hadn't had a high-profile paranormal investigation case lately. Not since
Beth had taken the position eight months ago.
Charmaine had a feeling their working relationship was about to be tested.

"So, you've seen the grunch." Charmaine
didn't ask a question. Of course, a woman
prone to hallucinations would see one of the
city's more colorful urban legends.

"With all the development for the last
hundred years, you can't expect them to stay
in The East," Theo Dora said, referring to New
Orleans East.

"Right. Okay then. Dr. Vega awaits."
Charmaine stood.

"Before I go." Theo Dora dug out a tattered stack of newspapers. "For you, dear.
Don't worry about giving me credit as a con-
tributing consultant."

"What is this?" Charmaine took the papers
and looked through them.

"Contemporary accounts of those poor souls. Well, they became quite menacing, so it's hard to feel much sympathy for them. That poor girl. Torn limb from limb." Theo Dora shook her head.

"The rumors are exaggerated," Charmaine murmured as she continued to read.

"My Great Aunt Millie maintained an extensive archive of local legends. She was even more loopy than I am. Runs in the family, I'm afraid. Though my younger sister and brother seemed to be untouched by the madness gene." Theo Dora's mouth turned down into a sour expression.

"Hmm."

Charmaine didn't comment further. She'd met them both, though briefly in two family sessions. They weren't exactly pictures of stable mental health themselves. The feuds between the siblings were epic, almost Shakespearean.

"Anyway, my other Great Aunt Grace, Millie's oldest sister, told me she'd spoken to one. It was back in the late 1930s, I think. She went out for a walk along Old Gentilly Road. Don't ask me why. Anyway, one actually stalked her, but she talked her way out of getting chopped up. Well, according to her. Not sure you can count on her to be accurate," Theo Dora said.

"Right." Charmaine glanced up at her and then scanned another article.

"More likely, she spread her wings for him, if you get my meaning. Grace was a bit of a slut, to be frank. Didn't do the family reputation much good, I can tell you." Theo Dora tut-tutted a reproach of her long-dead relative.

"I can only imagine. Wait a minute. You think your great aunt had sex with a creature that lived in the swamps?"

"Well, after all, they were human beings. After a fashion, I suppose. And she did have exotic tastes, from what grandmother said," Theo Dora replied, her tone matter-of-fact.

"But... your grandmother died when you were a teenager." Charmaine had no trouble remembering Theo Dora's childhood anec-dotes. Their weirdness explained a lot about her and her siblings.

"Grandmother always stressed that family history is very important." Theo Dora smiled.

"Childhood stories that included the sexu-al habits of your ancestors." Charmaine blinked hard while wrapping her head around it.

"No graphic details. Certainly not. Anyway, the articles will get you started. Most of what you find on the internet is nonsense."

"There isn't a lot. Not factual, as you said, so thank you very much. Detective Harrison would love talking to you," Charmaine muttered as she went back to reading.

"Really? You think I could talk to a him? He's quite a good-looking man." Theo Dora brushed the layers of sweaters and patted her hair.

Charmaine snapped out of her reverie. "Wait, no. I didn't mean—"

There was a knock. Dr. Vega stood in the doorway of Charmaine's small office. "I'm feeling quite neglected, Mrs. Lirette."

"Hello, doctor." Theo Dora beamed at him. She stood up to leave, then paused. "Just kidding, dear. I'll leave the handsome detective to you. I wouldn't want my other gentleman friends to get jealous."

"Okay."

Dr. Vega favored Charmaine with an amused grin. His Latin-lover face reminded her why Theo Dora suddenly got distracted. The man made a white lab coat look sexy. Charmaine smiled back at him, remembering their brief affair. They had enjoyed each other, and then it was over. No drama. Still friends. No one at the clinic had a clue.

"Thank God for staff turnover," Charmaine whispered.

She turned her attention back to the articles on her desk. Charmaine read until the end of workday and headed to see Harrison. His office was in the NOPD District One headquarters on North Rampart Street. Or as Jessi called any police station, enemy territory. Her sister stood in the lobby, all attitude as she watched the comings and goings.

"Any idea why we've been summoned?" Jessi said by way of greeting.

"Nope." Charmaine let out a slow breath, an attempt to push down the knot of anxiety clogging her chest.

"I solemnly swear I haven't done anything that would get me or you arrested." Jessi continued to scan their surroundings.

"I feel so much better," Charmaine retorted.

Detective Gautier strode across the lobby with a hand outstretched. "Good afternoon. Thanks for coming by."

Charmaine accepted his handshake. "No problem."

Jessi followed her lead. Once she let go of Gautier's hand, she smiled at him. "Of course. We enjoy responding to show-up-or-else invitations."

"Detective Harrison is on edge lately. Having so many unsolved cases doesn't help. I hope to assist him in changing that. This way." Detective Gautier nodded for them to follow as he walked deeper into the station.

"I'm sure you will," Charmaine replied with a side-eye at Jessi.

"Um-hum." Jessi looked from Charmaine to the detective.

"Sorry if he was a bit abrupt. The Morrell investigation is being heavily scrutinized."

Detective Gautier led them through security. Then they took an elevator to the fourth floor. Harrison's office faced North Rampart. To Charmaine's surprise, it was neat and tidy. Despite the subtle inferences from Detective Gautier, Harrison didn't look harried at all. He put down a coffee mug with "Superhero Dad" on it in bright-red letters.

"I'll take it from here. The lab called about the Jefferson results. Check on that, please," Harrison said.

Detective Gautier's expression flickered to a frown that vanished fast. A mild mask dropped into place. "Sure thing."

"Email me the results. If it's what I think, you might be able to pick up our suspect tonight." Harrison watched the young detective leave, then shut his office door. "Ladies."

"Why are we here?" Jessi dropped into a dark-brown, vinyl-cover chair.

"Yeah. I thought you didn't want anyone to know you called us in." Charmaine strolled over to a side table and poured coffee into a foam cup.

"You're entirely too comfortable in my office," Harrison said with sigh. He went back and sat at his desk.

"Shit, you've dragged us over here enough," Jessi quipped. She picked up a silver-framed photo on his desk. "Cute kids, by the way."

"Put that down." Harrison whisked it out of her hand.

"Fine. We'll skip the small talk. Why the fu—"

"Jessi," Charmaine cut in. Then, holding her coffee, she settled into the chair next to her sister. "Something has happened. Something significant enough that you wanted us to show up at District One. But you don't want the ambitious Detective Darian Gautier to be in on our little talk."

"You should take that fortune-telling act on the road," Harrison replied with a snort.

"You know damn well she ain't actin'." Jessi grinned at him.

Harrison cleared his throat. He glanced at Charmaine and then away. "Yeah, well. Since spooky is your specialty..."

Jessi heaved a sigh and looked at her cell phone. "Look, I've got a five o'clock class. Get to the point."

"You graduated last year," Harrison countered.

"I'm doing postgrad work to become a paralegal. And yes, I qualify. No felony convictions on record. Now back to the subject." Jessi crossed her arms.

"As if I didn't already have questions about the legal profession," Harrison teased. Then his face pulled into a scowl. "Timothy Acker, aka Timmy to the society crowd, is insisting that a supernatural creature killed Amanda Morrell. He talked to that crazy author who showed up."

"E.J. Locke," Charmaine interjected.

"Yeah, him. And, big surprise, the media got hold of it. Locke swears he didn't talk. Anyway, our deputy superintendent asked me to consult you. And no, he doesn't know you were at the crime scene." Harrison gazed at the closed door to his office.

"Which means Detective Gautier can't use it as leverage. And you get credit for being one step ahead." Jessi grinned at him. "You lucked out, bruh."

"Maybe. Or the Deputy Super will feel threatened I thought of it first. Doesn't always do to outshine the boss," Harrison muttered. Then he smiled. "One bright spot? Murphy is ticked off I'm getting direct orders from the top."

"Well, well, well. We're officially on the case." Charmaine sipped coffee.

"Whoa, slow it down. You're not going on the books as police consultants. No way." Harrison shook his head.

"Who. Will. Pay?" Jessi enunciated each word as if talking to a toddler. "No money, no honey, as we used to say in my former profession."

"Locke agreed to hire you. Find out his interest in the case and report to me. The guy shows up at my murder scene. Then he uses his connections to latch onto my investigation. Makes me wonder." Harrison's dark eyebrows pulled together.

Charmaine leaned forward with interest. "Yeah, like, did he know the victim? Where was he at the time of the murder?"

"You two don't need to know what leads we're following," Harrison clipped. "Locke wants you to investigate the supernatural angle. The police don't chase goblins and spirits, at least not for now, thank God."

Jessi shrugged. "Cool with me. Long as I'm getting paid, I give less than a shit what the po-leece do."

"Our investigations need to be parallel. They're obviously intertwined. We should share information," Charmaine protested. She glanced from Jessi to Harrison.

"A real human being killed Amanda Morrell. I don't care what some self-important writer of scary books says. As long as chasing shadows keeps Locke out of my way, I'm happy." Harrison pulled out a business card and handed it to Charmaine. "Here's his contact information. He's eager to hear from you."

Charmaine accepted the larger-than-normal embossed square. "Speaking of over-sized egos."

The thick, black card sported silver print. One side had a slick publicity photo of Locke. A gushing review quote beneath it hailed him as a master of page-turning novels. The other side listed his website, email address, and the name of his literary agent.

"Why didn't he hire us directly?" Jessi asked.

Harrison's handsome face twisted into an expression of disgust. "He wants to be kept in the loop from the NOPD. Locke likes showing folks he's a big-timer. Treating me like I'm his damn secretary and messenger."

"You want us to keep him busy. Far away from the official murder investigation." Charmaine squinted at him.

"Like I said, command from on high," Harrison replied. His scowl changed into a sly smile. "If he's too distracted chasing invisible butterflies? Well, I consider it lagniappe."

"As long as his checks are good, I'll take him out to the middle of Lake Pontchartrain if that's what you want," Jessi replied with a chuckle.

"Do me a favor and 'accidentally' shove him overboard," Harrison joked. "By the way, did you get a whiff of anything... undead at the Morrell murder scene?"

"Not a peep. And why is this Locke guy so interested?" Jessi looked at Harrison.

"You tell me. Meanwhile, I'm going to find out who's feeding him info from inside the department." Harrison tapped his ink pen on the desk.

"So, you don't believe he's getting psychic messages." Charmaine laughed at the sour look the detective gave her.

"He hasn't told me, and I haven't asked him. I don't believe in ninety percent of that crap," Harrison replied with a wave of one hand.

Working with us has made you a believer in the other ten percent. Progress." Charmaine grinned at him.

"We don't *work* together. You two keep stumbling into crime cases, which is shady enough, by the way," Harrison shot back.

Charmaine and Harrison exchanged good-natured barbs about who got in whose way. Harrison pointed out his official status meant he was always right. Charmaine maintained he owed Joliet Investigations gratitude for helping him solve unique crimes. Jessi's voice brought both up short.

"Hello, Mr. Locke. I'm Jessi Joliet of Joliet Investigations. You wanted to meet with us about the Morrell murder. No, this evening isn't a good time. Let me check with my partner." Jessi tapped the screen of her cell to mute the call. "Is Thursday at six in the evening good for you, Char? I'm free."

"Hmm, that'll give us a day to dig into his background," Charmaine said as she pulled the tablet computer from her bag. She swiped to open her calendar app. "Yeah."

Jessi nodded and unmuted her phone. "We'll be there Thursday. Thank you for the business. Bye-bye." She ended the call and looked at them. "While you two were blah-blah-blahing, I took care of business."

"You get a gold star," Charmaine quipped.

"Look, I'm going to class. Y'all may have time sit around chitchatting, but I got things to do." Jessi stood and brushed long faux locks over her shoulder. They hung down to her waist.

"Excuse me, Miss All-Business. She's right, though. I have another client to meet. I want to grab some dinner before. Bye, Detective H." Charmaine followed Jessi to the door.

"Another ghost-busting gig, huh? No, on second thought, I don't want to know. Better not wind up with a dead body." Harrison stood as he glared at Charmaine.

"A simple haunting that is likely her imagination. That's what we find in most cases," Charmaine replied mildly.

Harrison's grunt of skepticism followed them out his door. The detective was sure big trouble always followed the Joliet Sisters. Charmaine and Jessi agreed to meet at her house Thursday for the drive to Locke's home. Thursday afternoon, Charmaine waited for her sister. She sat in her home office going over background material on E.J. Locke. Jessi used her key to let herself in the back door into the kitchen.

"Hope you got some food. I'm starving. Didn't get a chance to eat lunch." Jessi didn't pause for Charmaine to reply.

"You gone start bringing groceries to this house, much as you eat over here," Charmaine yelled back.

Ten minutes later, Jessi strolled in with a plate of steaming food. "Man, I love Jolof rice. Dating that guy from Ghana paid off in more ways than one. How is he?"

"Kosi is fine. He finished up his MBA and went home to run the family business. And no, just because his people are rich is not a reason to follow him. Besides, his parents have his wife all picked out." Charmaine continued to tap the wireless keyboard of her all-in-one desktop.

"How medieval. I bet he'd put a ring on it," Jessi said around a mouthful.

"You'd lose money. Kosi is an obedient elder son. He was just having a good time with a loose American girl," Charmaine murmured.

"If he said that, then to hell with him. Snooty mofo."

"No, *I* said that. I'm not looking for a husband."

"I never said you had to *stay* married. Two words: divorce settlement," Jessi said with a chuckle.

"Okay, I'll help you find a rich man to marry and then milk dry."

"I have another master plan. How'd the meeting with the new client go the other night?" Jessi drank from a tall glass of lemonade and patted her mouth with a napkin.

"She's a nice woman in her thirties with an overactive imagination. Mostly stress from a recent divorce. Though her house on Race Street could have a spirit or two," Charmaine said.

"Uh-huh, lower Garden District. Fancy."

"A two-story built in 1868."

"Hell, that's considered new construction in New Orleans," Jessi said with a laugh.

"I gave her seven big herb bags to cleanse the place of negative energy. Easy $200 consult." Charmaine shrugged. The bags contained mostly sage with a few other fragrant herbs added. Smudging, or burning sage to clear negative energy or spirits, had a long tradition. "Huge mansion, so I'm gonna need to stock up again."

"And if it doesn't work..." Jessi gazed at her sister.

"Go over there to check out the place. If you don't find anything, I'll recommend her to a therapist. Her ex-husband and his lawyer put her through the wringer. Another reason why marrying money ain't always a great idea." Charmaine swung her chair around and rocked back. "Let's go over what I've found out about Locke."

"Cool." Jessi ate another forkful of rice.

"He bought a house in New Orleans in 2009. Before that he was living in Kotonah, New York. Suburb outside New York City. He was a successful accountant to the rich and famous for twenty years. He wrote his first best-selling horror novel in 2002. He came here as a volunteer to help rebuild after Hurricanes Katrina and Rita. I won't go into all the details of how he was inspired by legends of New Orleans." Charmaine sat straight again to look at her computer screen.

"Please don't," Jessi retorted. "We'll suffer through his pitch when we meet. Anything shady?"

"Not so far, but it's early. Amanda Morrell," Charmaine said, switching topics.

"Yeah. Privileged, drug use, and I don't know about those friends of hers. They went from grieving to being at each other's throats mighty quick." Jessi finished the last of her meal and put the plate aside.

"Right. Import and export business, the Morrell family and the Drapers." Charmaine rocked her chair as she thought.

"Nah, no drug smuggling for them. They don't need the money or the risk. Demi's family mostly deals in electronics and rare minerals used in high-tech devices. The Morrells deal in agricultural products, sugar, and farming equipment. Some of it's pretty high-tech, too." Jessi grinned when Charmaine raised an eyebrow at her. "Yes, big sis. I completed my assignment to find out more about the victim and related persons of interest."

"You're racking up the gold stars." Charmaine grinned back at her. "Too bad you broke up with the professor, and Diamond got tired of her boyfriend from an old-money family. We lost two sweet sources of inside gossip on the society pages set."

"Hey, life goes on. Don't worry, I've still got sources," Jessi said.

"Your ghost-informant network might not help. Most of them died back before the twentieth century. You need to find some younger spirits, girl." Charmaine got up and went to kitchen. "Bring your dirty dishes," she called over her shoulder.

"Hey, I take what I can get. It's not like I can go to a supernatural supermarket and order up what I want, ya know."

An hour and several arguments later, they arrived at Locke's condo on St. Charles Avenue. The lobby featured clean lines, wall murals, tall, leafy plants, and twenty-four-hour security. Jessi gave a low whistle as they walked to the desk. Moments later, Locke's personal assistant, Miss Rasta, as Harrison called her, emerged from the elevators. Except her braids were gone. Her dark hair was styled in loose curls. She led them up to his fourth-floor luxury home.

"Thank you so much for meeting with me," Locke said as he shook their hands with vigor.

Jessi extricated herself from his firm grip. "You're paying us, so yeah. We're here."

"Nice to see you again, sir," Charmaine said in her most cordial tone. She meant to give Jessi a scowl to communicate she should behave, but Jessi was too busy scrutinizing every corner of the fancy place. When her sister turned around to ask an insolent question about his income, Charmaine spoke up fast. "How can we help?"

"Please, call me Eli." Locke flashed a smile at Charmaine. "Let's get you something to eat and drink."

He crossed the open floor plan from the living room to a spacious kitchen. Two trays of food were on the huge island, along with wine and soft drinks. That caught Jessi's attention. She let out a cry of approval as she hot-footed over to the goodies. Fifteen minutes later, they sat in the living room, nibbling and exchanging small talk. His personal assistant, whose real name was Becca, hovered, making sure Locke's wine glass stayed full. Locke told them about himself, some of which they'd found out from their own searches online. As Jessi pre-

dicted, Locke went on and on about the inspi-
ration New Orleans had on him.

"My first novel, about the mystery sur-
rounding Edgar Allen Poe's death, was quite a
success. But once I visited New Orleans I knew
my next book would be set here." Locke started to go on when Jessi cleared her throat loud
enough to cut him off. She wiped her fingers
with a napkin and cocked her head to one side.

"Very interesting. So, to business. What's
up? Why did you offer to hire us?"

"What she means is—"

Locke raised a palm. "No need to explain.
I've rambled on long enough. In fact, my novels play a large part in what is happening."

"Sorry, what is happening?" Charmaine
blinked at him.

"Murder, Charmaine. More than one in
New Orleans," Locke said.

Jessi gave a soft grunt. "Uh, yeah, the violent crime rates in this city ain't exactly a secret."

"You don't understand. I'm not talking
about common street crimes. Tourists getting
robbed and shot. Drug deals, burglaries, or
armed robberies gone bad," Locke said.

"I never understood why people say that.
It's not like burglaries or robberies are good

before somebody gets killed," Jessi quipped. She drank wine.

Locke went on. "I'm talking about the most unique case you'll ever investigate. Circumstances and events the famous Joliet sisters are uniquely qualified to unravel."

"Amanda Morrell's murder," Jessi said.

Locke leaned forward. "And more."

As the daylight faded outside, Becca had turned on mid-century-styled lamps around the room. Locke's voice pitched low as he continued talking about dark forces. Combined with the soft lighting, the atmosphere had slowly changed. Charmaine felt as though they had wandered into the performance of a third-rate mystery production.

She worked hard to mask her annoyance with the theatrics. "Not to be rude or anything, but I don't see—"

"I mean *my* murder. By creatures I created in the pages of my novels," Locke said.

Chapter 3

Say What?

Friday at seven in the morning Jessi and Charmaine nursed steaming cups of coffee at Li'l Dizzy's Café. Both wanted to report to Harrison before they started their day. Charmaine had appointments at the clinic, while Jessi had three classes before her part-time job. They watched him scoop up scrambled egg whites with grits. He savored the food, slurped coffee, and sighed.

"Can't believe you're eating that stuff." Jessi nodded at his plate.

"Promised my wife and oldest daughter I'd eat healthier. Egg whites aren't so bad once you get used to them. A side of fried catfish would help, though." Harrison gazed at plates laden with food carried by a passing waitress.

"You poured on the butter and salt. Not to mention toast piled with jelly," Charmaine said.

"At least I'm trying." Harrison gulped the last bit of coffee and sat back. "So, E.J. Locke is a nutcase who believes his own made-up stories. My bosses are listening to the dude. I'm gonna need more caffeine."

Charmaine got the attention of their waitress and got him a refill. She waited until the woman poured and left. "We'll deal with him. Once we show him it's all in his head, then we can get back to Amanda's murder."

Harrison sat forward and lowered his voice. "You said there was nothing supernatural going on."

"Not that I could tell that first sweep," Jessi agreed.

"Then you two won't be getting back to anything when it comes to my investigation. Any questions? We clear?" Harrison squinted at them in turn.

Charmaine huffed. "Yeah, but—"

"Uh-uh, no buts. I'm finally able to deal with normal murders and assaults without all of the woo-woo-woo." Harrison made B-movie ghost sounds as he waved both hands. "I plan to keep it that way."

"Amanda's friend Timmy wasn't lying or seeing things because of the drugs," Charmaine added to cut off Harrison's next point. "Which tells me something unusual happened in that house."

"What do you know about the grunch?" Jessi asked him.

"That it's a dumb urban legend, like a lot of nonsense sold to tourists. Which is all I need to know," Harrison said with a snort. He gazed at Jessi and then Charmaine. "Okay, I'll bite."

"So, one story says Marie Laveau castrated the devil's baby, but he escaped into the bayous outside the city over two hundred years ago. It escaped and split into two creatures. The grunch. Since then, they've eaten generations of people along deserted roads." Jessi laughed at the eye roll Harrison gave her.

"Another story says a group of lame and disfigured people were so badly treated, they escaped into the swamps around New Orleans. This was about two hundred years ago as well. Inbreeding led their offspring to be even more weird-looking, you know, birth defects. But they learned to survive. They take revenge on us normal people whenever they can," Charmaine said.

"First of all, the stories had these things living in the swamp, Harrison said, pulling out his wallet. "You might notice New Orleans has developed a bit since the 1700s. There are no swamps and bayous nearby anymore. And second, creepy-looking creatures roamed the streets, and nobody noticed them? Seriously? A load of bullshit from some weed-smoking, pill-popping privileged white kids with more money than morals. Thanks for an entertaining breakfast, though."

"You agreed to meet us for a reason," Charmaine said, her tone sharp enough to make him glance up at her.

"Yeah. Normally, you would dismiss any of our theories about the supernatural over the phone. But here we are talking about this stuff in the flesh." Jessi's arched eyebrows went up.

"And you're a busy man. So..." Charmaine gazed at him steadily.

Harrison fidgeted with his wallet for a few seconds. He pulled out bills after gathering up all three tickets. "Breakfast is on me, so don't worry about it. I had to get an early start anyway."

"Harrison, give up the deets. Something strange has come up about the Morrell murder, other than Timothy Acker talking about the grunch," Charmaine pressed, ignoring his attempt to change the subject.

"Here you go, ma'am. Delicious as usual. No change necessary," Harrison said to the waitress with a broad smile. He watched the woman move off. Other diners left as well, probably to jobs around the city. He heaved a sigh and looked at Charmaine.

"We gone find out anyway," Jessi put in.

"Another murder with bizarre circumstances," Charmaine blurted out.

"Stop rooting around in my head. You're not authorized to access sensitive police information." Harrison stabbed a forefinger at Charmaine.

"Sure, charge Charmaine with felony mind-reading. I want to hear you explain it to your bosses and the district attorney." Jessi grinned when he transferred his dark scowl to her.

"Always the smartass." Harrison shook his head at Jessi. Yet his sideways smile was more like a tolerant big brother.

"So, the other murder case?" Charmaine prompted. She knew Harrison was playing for time to come up with a dodge. "The one near Wright Road."

Harrison's face turned grim again. "Damn it, Charmaine. We found the homeowner dead in his master bedroom. Place on Cardenas Drive. Well, his wife found him. The lady next door saw someone creeping around the back-yard that night. Poor guy interrupted a burgla-ry, most likely. House was a mess, with drawers emptied and a few items missing."

"Hey, that's New Orleans East, where the grunch used to prowl, according to the sto-ries," Jessi said.

"Which isn't even close to Uptown. Unless you're gonna tell me the grunch drive to their victims now." Harrison heaved a sigh when Charmaine stared at him, arms crossed. "The neighbor claims the person had a strange, shuffling kind of walk. She caught a glimpse of a scary face. All scarred, she says, and it had huge hands with... claws. It's ridiculous. I sus-pect the woman is a bit nutty. A lot of that go-in' around."

"Any connection to Amanda Morrell or Locke?" Charmaine frowned.

"None. Just a coincidence." Harrison's cell phone buzzed, which interrupted what he was about to add. He pulled it out and left the table to talk.

"We need to do our own research to see if they're connected. The police settle on the simple explanation," Charmaine said. "Not a criticism. They've got their hands full. We have time to dig deep."

"Right. I'll go talk to the neighbor on Cardenas." Jessi took out her cell phone and did a quick search. Yeah, it's already been reported in the news. Got the address."

"Good. Meanwhile, we'll prepare for our next meeting with Eli Josiah Locke," Charmaine murmured.

****

Saturday at five-thirty in the evening they arrived at a grand old Victorian on Prytania Street. The two-story home had been updated with fresh paint. The top half of the rust-orange front door had a huge window with leaded glass. Other windows were trimmed with a turquoise blue. Steps led up to the porch with a swing seat hung from the ceiling on one side.

"How lovely," Jessi said, pitching her voice to imitate an upper-class old New Orleans accent. "The guy has two expensive homes.

Those books must be pulling in some sweet cash."

"He's sold movie rights in the US to four of them. Had a play based on another in England. It was a hit, too. There's talk of a television miniseries as well." Charmaine parked her Chevy Cruze in the driveway beside a Volkswagen. A black BMW was farther up the drive.

"His trusty sidekick is here, I see," Jessi said as they climbed the steps. "Let's try to get rid of her. She's in the way."

"I don't know. She could be helpful," Charmaine replied as she pressed the doorbell. A Westminster chime echoed inside. Minutes later, a gray-haired black woman came to answer.

"Good evening. You the Joliet sisters, right? I'm Viola." She ushered them in. "This way. I'm gone bring y'all refreshments in a minute. Make yourselves comfortable. Mr. Locke and Miss Ann, I mean Miss Becca, are in his office working."

Jessi grinned at her accidentally-on-purpose slip of the tongue. She nudged Charmaine and the sisters exchanged a look. Charmaine knew what Jessi was thinking. Viola didn't have much use for Becca. Even better, she might be a source of inside gossip.

Viola led them through the foyer to a second living room, smaller than one on the opposite side of the hall. A baby grand piano sat in a far corner. Chairs and small sofas were arranged in tasteful order. A crystal chandelier completed the sumptuous look.

Jessi turned in a circle, taking it all in. "Wow."

"Two million at least," Charmaine said. "Even with all his money, a condo and a Garden District house is a bit much."

"The condo belongs to a friend." Locke spoke from an open archway, causing both sisters to jump in surprise. He strolled in with a wide smile and shocked them again by kissing each on the cheek. "So glad you could come."

"Uh, thanks." Jessi blinked at him. "But you did hire us, so..."

"I stayed at my friend Milo's for a while to get away. Ghosts don't move out just because you renovate an old home. A fact you must know all too well." Locke went to the piano, played a few notes standing up, and then wandered to one of the windows. He stood with his back to them, staring out.

"Here you go." Viola pushed in a wheeled serving cart. Fancy appetizers on platters were on the top level. A pitcher of tea and a variety of soft drinks were on the bottom.

"Whoa, you didn't have to cater the meeting for us. But I'm glad you did." Jessi met her halfway to help.

"Oh, no. I won't have restaurant food in my kitchen. Not while I can cook," Viola said. "Now you sit down."

"We can serve ourselves," Jessi insisted.

Viola ignored her as she piled a plate with tiny meatballs, a couple of finger sandwiches, and three drumettes. She put them on a small round table and pointed for Jessi to sit. She repeated the serving twice more. Locke and Charmaine sat down as well.

"This is a full meal, ma'am. Thanks." Charmaine breathed in the aromas of spicy sauce from the meatballs.

"You're busy career women. I figure you don't get to eat so grand all the time. Might as well fill up on Mr. E.'s dime." Viola winked at them. "Now, dig into that bread bowl full of my spinach and crab dip. Then have Mississippi teacakes for dessert. My great-grandmother's recipe."

"Viola takes good care of me, even if she does get sassy every now and then." Locke put on a fake scowl.

"I'll be in the kitchen if you need me," Viola replied.

"No need, dear. I'll put away anything left. Becca will help. You go relax."

"If you're sure. I can make it to my women's ministry meeting after all," Viola said as she looked at her wristwatch.

Becca walked in and paused at the serving cart. "Hello."

"Serve yourself," Viola said to Becca over her shoulder.

Locke gave a small sigh but didn't reprimand his housekeeper. "I have a bit of tension in the house every now and then.

"I'll clean up before I go. My meeting isn't until seven. They give time for working people to get there, you know." Viola left with a genial smile for everyone, except Becca.

Jessi swallowed and stood. "I'll look around for a bit."

Charmaine nodded. She watched Jessi take her glass of peach tea with her and head off on the path Viola had taken. Jessi would use whatever time she could to get information from Viola. Then she'd do a self-guided tour of the house. Becca frowned after her. She seemed about to follow Jessi, but Charmaine intervened.

"Join us, please. I'd like your take on the, um, issues Eli is having," Charmaine called to her. She smiled when Becca turned.

Becca glanced at the archway through which Jessi had vanished. Then she looked at Charmaine and smiled back. "Sure. Though I won't be much help. I haven't seen anything."

"Becca and Viola think I'm being silly, but I know what happens when I'm alone in this house. Viola has her own apartment in the east wing. Quite separate and private. I'm being targeted by the entities I created." Locke drank whiskey, having ignored the tea and soft drinks.

"I offered to stay here for a few weeks. To reassure Eli." Becca gazed at him.

"Generous. And brave, considering," Charmaine remarked. Becca had designs on being the third Mrs. Locke. The desire radiated from her like heat from the marble fireplace in one wall.

"Lana stayed over for several weekends. Not a peep. They're after *me*, and no one else. That might change at some point. I don't want anyone taking the risk."

"Lana probably scared even the monsters away," Becca said with a tight smile.

"Lana is?" Charmaine looked at Eli.

"Lana Salcedo Reilly," Becca replied.

Charmaine noted Becca's effort to keep her expression neutral. The meow came through in her tone anyway. Lana was a roadblock to Becca's plan to lock down Eli Locke's affection. Given his other connections to local elites, Lana was no doubt a socialite as well. Charmaine looked at Eli, waiting for what she knew would come next.

"We've been seeing each other for over a year. Lana says ninety percent of the ghost stories and legends told about New Orleans are nonsense. But they're good local color, especially for tourists. Even owning a home here doesn't make me a resident in the eyes of her inner circle." Locke laughed at the clannish nature of New Orleans natives. Then he grew serious again.

"Back to the ghosts," Charmaine said.

"Not just ghosts. Other kinds of creatures. I wrote two novels featuring the grunch as monsters. My publisher wants me to write at least three more. You know, make it a series. We have interest from one of the streaming services for a video series." Locke got up and poured more whiskey in his glass. He knocked back half of the contents and sat down again.

"This has really got you shook." Charmaine studied him for a few seconds.

Locke exhaled noisily. "I'm not losing my sanity. What I'm going through is real. Lana is starting to act a little... distant. Becca looks at me strange. Oh, don't deny it. I'm not a fool."

"Eli, you're one of the most stable and brilliant men around. I'm sure you believe what you're experiencing. I know there are unexplained phenomena in the world. It's just so—" Becca seemed to struggle for the right words.

"Bizarre, I know. I know how it sounds, Becca," Locke finished for her after a few seconds. "Thanks for the support. No, I mean it. You have your pick of jobs. You didn't sign up to work in the middle of my version of *American Horror Story*." Locke put his glass down and rubbed his forehead. When Becca crossed to him and put a hand on his shoulder, he covered it with one of his own. "My rock."

"Always," Becca murmured.

Becca fussed over Locke. She fixed him another drink and coaxed him to eat something. Charmaine watched them for a few moments. Then she switched her attention to the rest of the room. Nothing. Not a hint of anything supernatural. Not that she had Jessi's ability to commune with creatures on a different plane of existence. That's one of the ways Jessi talked about them. Charmaine teased her that it was a fancy way of saying ghosts and goblins.

"Feeling better?" Charmaine said after a few seconds. She glanced at Becca, who nodded.

"I'm fine," Locke said. "Really, it's just... I'm afraid that I might be responsible for that poor woman's death." He drank more liquor.

Jessi's voice startled them all, as they hadn't noticed she'd returned. "You heard about the other guy they found dead?"

"What?" Locke blinked at her.

"His neighbor says a weird-looking dude was creepin' around the guy's house." Jessi walked in. She had a small plate laden with more food. "Viola got skills when it comes to cooking. Umph, umph, umph."

Charmaine shot a heated look at Jessi, but it was lost on her. Jessi was too busy savoring the selection of cheeses she'd stuffed in her mouth. "The cops think it's more likely a burglary that turned bad."

"There ain't no *good* versions of a burgla-
ry. Like I said before—"

"My point," Charmaine cut in, her tone ra-
zor sharp. Jessi shrugged and kept eating.
"There is evidence the second victim interrupted someone who'd broken in."

Locke blinked hard. "You said 'second victim,' as if you believe the two murders are
connected."

"I don't know any such thing," Charmaine
replied fast.

"Ms. Joliet, Charmaine, the police contacted you about the second crime. Which means
they put some credence in reports of a creature being seen near the man's home." Locke
rubbed his jaw. "My God, it's happened again."

"Eli, calm down." Becca leaned into him,
an arm around his shoulders. She glared at
Charmaine, then Jessi. "Maybe you should
leave. We've had a long day, and talk of murder doesn't help."

Jessi licked a thumb and put her now-
empty plate on the table. "Your boss called us,
Becky."

"Becca," the woman clipped.

"That's what I said," Jessi replied in a mild
tone.

Locked pushed free of Becca's hold on him. "No, no. I find talking to Charmaine comforting. You don't totally dismiss what I'm saying, do you? You've seen fantastic things in your investigations."

"Some of the stuff online is really blown out of proportion," Charmaine began. She stopped when Locke leaned across and placed a hand on her arm. "But yeah. We've dealt with paranormal forces that were real."

Locke's grasp tightened. "I can feel you're on my side."

"Mr. Locke," Charmaine said.

"Eli," he corrected.

"Eli. We do investigate all reports for our clients. But if there's nothing there, we'll tell you," Charmaine explained.

"Yeah. We have a scientific approach. None of this corny séance bull." Jessi pointed using a toothpick, then stuck it in her mouth.

"So, you do believe me." Locke gazed at Charmaine with more than business interest.

"We're open to all possibilities." Charmaine patted his hand. Then she moved her arm from his grip. "Ahem. To that end, I think we should spend some time here."

"Stay the night," Locke said, still looking at her.

"What? Eli, I hardly think they would consider such a thing." Becca eyed Charmaine with new suspicion.

"Matter of fact, it's SOP with us," Jessi put in, a twinkle of mischief in her brown eyes. "Standard operating procedure. Oh yeah. We do supernatural stakeouts all the time. Right, sis?"

"Examining the site of possible paranormal activities does give us valuable information. Firsthand observation is the best data," Charmaine replied, more interested in Becca's reactions than the stakeout.

"Great. I'll fix up the extra master suite. No need to bother Viola. She'll be leaving soon. I don't like to make her work long hours just because she lives in." Locke stood and pulled up Charmaine with him. He gazed into her eyes. "How do you like your eggs?"

"Say what?" Charmaine glanced from him to Jessi and back again.

"Breakfast. I'm going to cook for us," Locke said.

Charmaine noticed for the first time he wasn't bad-looking. A touch of gray on one side of his brunette hair made him look intellectual, not old. His hazel eyes had hints of green. His body was toned. "I love a good omelet."

"I make a killer asparagus and cream cheese omelet." Locke smiled at her.

"Sounds delicious."

Jessi looked at Locke for a few seconds before she turned to Charmaine. "Um, y'all need a minute to negotiate details about our stay, in private?"

"Eli, can I talk to you a minute? In your office." Becca's voice held an unmistakable edge.

"I'll make sure fresh towels and linens are out. Viola can spend the night with her sister. Less outside interference while we're investigating," Locke said to Charmaine.

"You know, I could leave my equipment and leave you two alone. Both of us don't have to stay," Jessi offered.

"Don't be ridiculous," Charmaine said before Locke could respond. Then she looked at him and Becca. "Jessi is a channel. Recording them is fine, but she can talk to apparitions."

"Alternative forms of electromagnetic energy with a biological origin," Jessi put in.

"I'm sure Jessi will do her thing and allow you to do yours," Locke said. "Teamwork. Right?"

"Too true, Eli. We don't live in each other's pockets." Jessi winked at him.

"Your office, please?" Becca insisted.

"Be right back," Locke whispered and winked at them.

Jessi watched them leave. She faced Charmaine. "Ha!"

"I swear, Jessi." Charmaine shook her head and walked away to examine a painting on the wall.

"We can find out a lot by seeing beyond the masks people wear." Jessi lifted a forefinger as if lecturing to a class. "For example, it's obvious Becky—"

"Becca," Charmaine corrected in a dry tone. "And stop it."

"I don't do anything by accident. I'm a professional investigator. As I was saying. *Becca* has a thing for old Eli. Whether she's really in love with him or a gold digger? Not conclusive yet. More observation needed. However, her passion isn't returned by our client. Just as obvious since he has a girlfriend. Not to mention he's got an eye on tapping your goodies, too."

"Real professional," Charmaine retorted.

"So, Eli isn't the settling-down type," Jessi continued, ignoring her dig. "Which gives Becca motive to scare the shit out of him. He comes to depend on her more. She's hoping they grow closer and he falls hard for her. Combine loyalty, hero worship, and hard spanks on the bottom in the bedroom. Strong mojo, honey. Men over forty love that stuff."

"Oh really?"

"I should know. Satisfying paying customers was my business at one time," Jessi said without a trace of embarrassment.

"Uh-huh." Charmaine raised a palm to cut off more theorizing from her sister.

Raised voices floated toward them. One female, the other male. They didn't have to guess or use psychic skills to know what was happening. Solid walls prevented them from catching it all. Still, the muffled anger came through loud and clear.

"See? Motive. We need to look into Ms. Rebecca, aka Becca, Hanson's background, girl." Jessi poured herself another glass of tea.

"Agreed. I'll play the flirtation game with Eli, see if he lets slip this is all a PR scheme to sell books. He could be planning to leak a story to the press, especially about hiring us. Except..." Charmaine's voice trailed off.

"Yeah, he's already rich from his books. Not to mention sales of movie and television rights. But money and influence are strong drugs. Powerful men seem to always want more. Out-of-control egos for days. You'd think they would be satisfied with making millions, having people throw themselves at their feet to serve them. All the perks of being rich and famous." Jessi sat down and crossed her shapely legs encased in denim leggings.

"Never enough, eh?" Charmaine brushed her fingers over the fabric of an antique settee.

"Nope." Jessi gave a small laugh.

"Humph." Charmaine decided not to pursue how Jessi knew so much about such men. They'd never discussed the details of her former sex work, and likely never would. "What about Viola? She could have a motive."

"Nah, I don't think so. First, she seems to genuinely like the guy. With housing prices in New Orleans, she gets to stay in a nice place for free. She lost the family home in Hurricane Katrina. Five generations had lived there, but they never did successions through the years."

Charmaine nodded, understanding. "Which meant none of the living relatives had clear title. Or homeowner's insurance."

"Yeah, what a mess. She lived in the house after her mama died, who'd lived in it with her kids and Viola's grandmother. Viola has two sons who decided to stay in Atlanta after the hurricane. Her daughter is in Lafayette. But she loves New Orleans." Jessi shook her head. "No, Viola isn't just grateful; she has real affection for him. Though she did hint that he's a 'rascal.' I'll tease out what she meant once we get to know each other better."

"Okay, but it's strange Viola isn't scared to live in a haunted house. Well, hang out with a guy who's haunted. Hmm, can a person be haunted? I need to research. I'll bet the Third Eye Association will have info in its archives." Charmaine tapped in a note to remind herself. The Third Eye Association, a closed society of people with paranormal abilities, maintained a huge physical and digital library.

"No weapon formed against her will prosper, and not today, Satan," Jessi said. She laughed when Charmaine looked at her with a questioning expression. "She's a Black southern church lady to the tenth power, honey. No demon would dare set foot across her threshold. She done prayed up that place. Any crap that old devil tries with her will fizzle right on out. Praise His holy name! I'm quoting her exact words."

"Could be an act."

"Then she deserves an Oscar. You can spend some time with her for a read, but I didn't detect a false note." Jessi yawned and patted her midsection. "I'm stuffed. You take the first shift. I don't think my eyes will stay open even if I try."

"No problem," Charmaine murmured.

"Besides, Eli will be happy to have alone time with you." Jessi smirked when Charmaine glared at her.

Eli walked in before Charmaine could shoot a tart response. "Well, we have the house to ourselves. Perfect for an investigation. Though I can't guarantee anything will happen."

"Becca's gone? I'm surprised she didn't stick around for the fun." Jessi glanced at Charmaine and away to avoid more daggers.

"She's had a long day and the stress got to her. Viola has gone to her church meeting and will spend the night with her sister." Eli clapped his hands together. "So, let's get to it. Any equipment you want me to help set up?"

Jessi stood and stretched. "Thanks for the offer, but my stuff is portable. Easy to carry. I prefer to arrange it myself. Be right back." She left.

"Her gear is in my trunk," Charmaine explained. "Nice art. Mix of old and contemporary work. Is that a Salazar?" She pointed to a nineteenth-century painting of a woman wearing a tignon.

Eli blinked in surprise. "You're familiar with early Louisiana artists, I see."

"You mean for a girl who grew up in public housing in the Seventh Ward. Yeah, I actually read books, too. I've read several of yours, by the way." Charmaine smiled.

"I didn't mean... Damn it, planted my foot firmly in my mouth on that one. Not the way to impress a lady." Eli held up the cut-glass whisky decanter as an offer.

"Wine would be nice—red, please. But not too much. Have a keep a clear head for tonight," Charmaine replied. "No worries. It's true though. Poor girl makes good. Courtesy of a hurricane."

"How so?" Locke went to a vintage cocktail bar in the far corner. He returned with a glass for her. Then he poured another whiskey for himself.

"With all the generous folks willing to help after Katrina hit, I got money to finish college and graduate school. I'm a licensed therapist." Charmaine watched to see his reaction.

"You can tell if your clients are seeing ghosts or just plain crazy. Impressive," Locke replied. He sat in the chair next to her. "Have you decided which category I'm in?"

Charmaine made a show of scrutinizing him. "The jury is out."

Locke gave a deep, throaty laugh. Then he leaned close to her. "I like you, very much."

"Okay, let's get this party rockin' y'all," Jessi said as she walked in. She glanced from Locke to Charmaine. "We ready?"

"Absolutely." Charmaine jumped up.

She gave Locke a look full of promise. He smiled back in answer as if they shared a secret. Charmaine read him like a book. Locke had full confidence in his seduction game. Money, good looks, and local connections. The combination served him well. But not with Charmaine. He was cute, but she had no time to play with him.

"I brought three anemometers since this place is big. Viola says you've seen ghosts in three locations. Good thing I packed heavy. Figured I'd need more than the usual since you have this vast estate." Jessi grinned at Locke. "Charmaine, you set up one in here. One in Eli's office and one upstairs in the master suite." Jessi got busy pulling devices from her rolling duffle bag.

"I'll show you where it is, Charmaine," Locke said. He waited for Charmaine to place the first anemometer at Jessi's direction, then led her to his office down the hall. "What is that thing?"

"It was originally invented for meteorological purposes, to detect wind and measure its velocity. We use it to detect rushes of air and cold spots. Signs of paranormal activity," Charmaine said. Her speech came strictly from what Jessi told her. Otherwise, she wouldn't have known an anemometer from a thermometer.

"Science and the supernatural. Sounds like the name for a great reality series," Locke said as he pushed open the sliding door to his office. The heavy, dark-oak doors moved apart smoothly, hardly making a sound.

Charmaine forgot the smart remark she was about to make. The library had a wall with a floor-to-ceiling built-in bookcase. Locke's wide antique desk made of teakwood dominated the otherwise airy room. Another wall unit behind it had a writing table with Locke's computer. He could easily turn from the big desk and use it. More books were on shelves above. A combination of light and dark woods created a stunning contrast. On another wall were photos of Locke with A-list celebrities, local and national. A smaller desk on a far corner had a computer and another phone for Becca.

"Wow." Charmaine gaped at the setup.

"I'm glad you like it. I added on to the house and expanded my office-slash-library."

"With these windows and that view I'd never get anything done. Not that I intend to write a book," Charmaine added with a laugh.

"You should. With your experiences you could have a best seller. Plus, a television spin-off would be great."

"We're not going the whole corny route." Charmaine gave a laugh. Locke's face had turned white as he stared at her. "I didn't mean you and your books are... What's wrong?"

"Going to kill." Locke's mouth worked like a goldfish out of water. His finger shook as he pointed to something over Charmaine's shoulder. Then he fainted, hitting the floor with a solid thump.

Chapter 4

Dead on Arrival?

Charmaine whirled around to scan the room but saw and felt nothing. She strained to hear even a whisper. Nothing. Locke groaned, a reminder that her client lay passed out at her feet. Since she didn't see blood, Charmaine chose to make a quick spin around the room.

"Jessi. Get in here!" Charmaine yelled.

Seconds later, she heard footsteps muffled by the carpeted runner on the staircase. Jessi entered the room at a dead run and skidded to a halt on the hardwood floor. She took in Locke on the floor, her sister trotting around in a circle, and then did her own inspection.

"Hey you, freeze. Yeah, I see you, buddy. And that ghost axe ain't gonna hurt nobody." Jessi stabbed a finger at what looked like an empty corner of the office. "What? The devil got your tongue?"

"Jessi, who the hell are you... Crap. You see something." Charmaine went to Locke when he moaned louder.

"A puny ghost playing around. Oh, oh. Look, dude, I didn't mean that as an insult." Jessi's mouth fell open. Her gaze went from the floor to the ceiling. "Oh. Shit. It's growing."

Charmaine struggled to help Locke to a sitting position. He grabbed for her shoulder but got her right breast instead. "Hey, watch the hands. Being unconscious is no excuse for... Jessi, stop playing with your new friend and help."

When her sister didn't reply, Charmaine let loose an angry string of curse words. Books and porcelain figurines flying through the air cut her off. A rumble like an approaching freight train shook the room. Jessi hand-held an anemometer, which beeped wildly as the bottom of the drapes lifted from the floor. Papers from Locke's desk swirled into a circle at a dizzying speed. A clap like thunder made them both cringe. Jessi seemed to be screaming at the entity, but Charmaine couldn't make out the words. Charmaine let go of Locke, ignoring the way his head bounced on the antique carpet. She rushed out to the formal living room. Jessi's duffle still sat on the floor. Several agonizing seconds passed as Charmaine fumbled around inside it, then let out a whelp of relief when she found Jessi's latest tool. The Disrupter, at least that's what Charmaine called it, looked like a big smartphone. She ran back to Locke's office with it.

"Damn. Damn. Damn." Charmaine tried to figure out how to turn it on.

"Oh no you don't. Settle your ass down, or I'll—So you think I'm playing?" Jessi batted away a file folder that came at her.

"Do something!" Charmaine yelled at Jessi and threw device to her.

She turned back to help Locke. What she saw made her heart bounce in her chest. His left arm stretched over his head as something pulled at him. Locke's eyelids fluttered for a few seconds. Then he came awake, shifting into full-blown panic. His lips formed the words "Help me." The sound of his voice seemed to be sucked away by a vacuum. Charmaine's ears popped at the change in air pressure. A force dragged Locke a few inches. The man panted in frozen terror. A wet stain spread across the front of his expensive pants as he lost bladder control. Before she could make a move to him, Jessi's cry spun Charmaine around.

"Get off me." Jessi batted at an opponent only she could see. Then she put a hand to her own throat.

"Aw hell no," Charmaine growled.

She started for her sister, but Locke's croak of torment made her look at him again. For a painful few seconds she stood rooted to the floor. Then she decided. Charmaine ran to Jessi and snatched the device from her.

"Press the green button, then the orange one on the left," Jessi croaked.

"To the left. To the left," Charmaine muttered.

She gasped with relief when the top part, a dark screen, lit up. A thin green line grew longer as she held down the orange button. An object slammed into her back. She glanced down at the leather-bound book as it dropped to the floor.

"Don't release, no matter what gets thrown at you," Jessi panted, waving both arms.

"You mean..." Charmaine ducked to avoid a small, decorative antique lamp. She felt the air when it whisked a few inches by her head. Jessi raced past her out of the office. "No, no, no! Don't leave me in here by my—"

Charmaine dodged a trio of ink pens, another book, and a letter opener that embedded in wooden bookcase. But she held onto the Disrupter for dear life. Jessi strode back in holding a box with a wand attached at the end of a cable. She swept the room with it and then aimed. An odd, sweet odor descended on the room. Charmaine's nostrils twitched.

"Stay focused, sis," Jessi warned. "Don't let up until you hear the ping."

"The wha?" Charmaine puffed out. She strained against the sensation to sneeze and cough at the same time.

"Just hold on."

The room went still. Noises stopped as though some invisible hand had flipped a switch. The Disrupter did indeed "ping," twice in fact. Charmaine looked at Jessi, who nodded. Then Charmaine released the button. She stumbled to the leather captain's chair behind Locke's desk and dropped down. Jessi leaned against a wall with one hand for support as she panted.

Jessi stood straight and flexed her arms for a few moments. Then bent forward with both palms on her thighs. "Whew, that was fun."

"Please. Oh God." Locke whimpered almost incoherently.

"Shit, our paying customer." Jessi sprang to his side. She winced at his damp slacks but felt along his body all the same. "Don't think anything's broken. No open wounds, either. Let's get you a change of pants."

Charmaine joined Jessi, getting on the other side of Locke. Together, they managed to help him stand. He wobbled on still-weak legs. Then they walked him to the stairs. Locke let out a cry of distress. He pulled free of the sisters and covered his soaked fly with both hands.

"I can make it on my own," he rasped.

"You're still shook up. Maybe we should come with," Charmaine said.

He shook his head hard at her, then used one hand on the railing to pull himself along each step. He hopped up the last two and walked fast until he disappeared. They heard a door slam. After a few seconds, the sisters faced each other. Jessi put a hand over her mouth and bent double.

"C'mon, Jess. It's okay. Your devices worked. It's over. We saved the guy's life and..." Charmaine stopped.

Jessi's shoulders shuddered as she failed to smother giggles. "He peed his pants. Mr. Horror, Master of the Macabre, couldn't handle a little breeze and a few flying objects."

"Stop it." Charmaine glanced up at the second-floor landing. "He might hear you."

"I can't." Jessi sat on the stairs. She slapped the fine wool runner with one hand.

It took five minutes of Charmaine fussing before Jessi recovered from her bout of uncontrolled laughter. Charmaine yanked Jessi off the stairs and back into the fancy living room. A reminder of how much money they'd miss out on if Locke fired them did the trick at last. Jessi went to the downstairs powder room. She returned and wiped her eyes as she sat down.

"Sorry. It was just..." Jessi gulped the last wine from Charmaine's glass.

"Get it together *before* he comes back in here," Charmaine snapped.

"He was so smooth, so in control. To see him passed out in a pool of piss." Jessi stifled a giggle that threatened. "It's okay. I'm good."

Charmaine looked toward the door to make sure they were alone. "He paid over three thousand dollars, a retainer for us to work exclusively for him. For at least a month. Non-refundable. If we solve this thing in a week?"

Jessi got up and poured more wine in the glass. "You just got my mind right, sis."

Locke came through the archway dressed in fresh clothes. His deep-blue slacks and long-sleeve tee-shirt even looked expensive. To his credit, he'd regained most of his confident demeanor. He went to straight to the whiskey.

"What an adventure." Locke's jaunty tone might have been meant to distract from the slight tremble in his hands. "Sorry about... you know."

"Your reaction was totally normal. Ghosts have that effect on folks," Charmaine said.

"Yeah. We're used to it though." Jessi finished off the wine. Then she picked up a drumette and gnawed on it. She noticed Charmaine glaring at her and put it down.

"What you saw is no ordinary ghost. Have you heard of the Axeman of New Orleans?" Locke gulped the amber liquid. He seemed to need fortification just saying the name.

"Um, maybe." Jessi looked at Charmaine for a hint and got none.

"A hit horror television series featured the Axeman as a character back in 2013. Set in New Orleans?" Locke prompted when neither replied.

"We don't watch much television," Charmaine explained with a slight smile.

"The Axeman first attacked in 1910, but his first victims weren't killed. No, the true blood bath began in 1913, an Italian named Maggio. The phrase 'beaten to a pulp' fits. The blows to his head were so powerful, his brains splattered the scene. That was just one victim. More followed." Locke closed his eyes when he gulped more whiskey.

"You're saying the ghost we saw was this Axeman of New Orleans?" Charmaine felt a chill when Locke nodded in response.

"The guy must have been something else when he was alive. He expanded when I called him out. Like the ghost version of that big green superhero. You know the one that goes bonkers when he loses his temper and—" Jessi broke off when Charmaine shook her head hard and drew a finger across her throat. "What?"

"Fortunately, we came prepared. You probably won't have any more appearances tonight," Charmaine said.

"Probably? Not very reassuring." Locke put the glass down.

Charmaine read him loud and clear. "We'll drive you to the condo if you like. I'll go upstairs with you to pack a bag."

"Not necessary. I won't be forced from my own damn house." Locke's gaze skittered around the room despite his brave words.

"My man Eli," Jessi burst out. She stood. "Show this Axe guy he can't float in here and take over. Notice how he got outta here fast when I tapped his ass? Yeah, we're not gonna let him push us around."

"My office is a mess. And you look shaken, Charmaine," Locke said.

Charmaine let out a slow breath. "We had a fight on our hands for a minute, but we're all safe. That's what matters."

Jessi held her gadget out to show him. The device dangled from a leather strap looped around her wrist. "The strap is one of my modifications. Can't be dropping your weapons during a fight, or in case you have to run."

Locke took hold of it. "Looks like a big cell phone."

"Cool, right?" Jessi grinned with pride.

"The Disrupter," Charmaine said.

"The proper name is electromagnetic field neutralizer, or EFN for short. They're sold to protect people worried about the effects of radiation from electronics. You know, cell phones, remote controls, whatever. Me and my friend adapted this bad girl to zap ghosts," Jessi said with enthusiasm.

"Like an electronic pest repellent," Locke said.

Jessi looked offended. "I'm talking serious science. Ghosts and other so-called supernatural beings are energy, electromagnetic waves. Since those waves can be detected, they can be neutralized. My friend Logan is a rocket scientist. Well he's a biophysicist helping NASA—"

Charmaine broke in. "Jessi, please. Eli doesn't want a lecture on electrical impulses."

"The bottom line is we got your back. No seances and phony stuff folks sell to tourists in the French Quarter." Jessi gave a snort of scorn. She went to her duffle bag. "You got some serious shit goin' down. Calls for extraordinary action."

Jessi talked to herself in a soft voice as she pulled items from her bag. Locke didn't ask any other questions. He still looked jumpy. He picked up the whisky decanter but put it back down again. Then he stood and walked around the room. Charmaine allowed him space to wind down from their harrowing experience. She did a quick search for more details on the Axeman, bookmarking the sites to read later.

"I'm guessing you wrote a book on the Axeman?" Charmaine asked after Locke sat again.

"Four. Fiction and a true crime title. Caused quite a stir, the nonfiction book, I mean. I followed clues after extensive historical research. I believe the killer might have been a member of a prominent local family. Two descendants sued." Locke's color had returned. He used a toothpick to stab a meatball. "Sales shot up."

"And the lawsuit?"

"Dismissed. They appealed, of course. Nothing beats free publicity." Locke chewed. He looked relaxed at last.

"Yeah, but the legal fees," Charmaine countered.

Locke shook his head. "Worth it. They wanted me to settle—the family, I mean."

"But you were happy to go to court. Made the media coverage last longer."

"National interviews. Happened around the time of the popular television series I mentioned. Wonderful timing, right?" Locke smiled at the memory. "Signed my second rights deal with Netflix six months later."

"Nice return on investment then," Charmaine drawled.

"Excellent, as a matter of fact. But I didn't make up what I wrote. I had documentation." Locke wiped his mouth with a paper napkin. "I know what you're thinking."

"You're telepathic, too?" Charmaine joked.

"They have a motive for making my life miserable. But they can't create a ghost. And I seriously doubt they'd murder a complete stranger just to get back at me. Makes no sense."

"You're right. It doesn't *if* you assume the two are connected," Charmaine replied. Her gaze swept the room. "Had any repairs or renovation done lately?"

"I had the security system upgraded a few months ago. Why?" Locke blinked at her with a confused frown.

Charmaine continued her examination. She didn't see any out-of-the-ordinary wiring or appliances. "Interesting."

"What is your next move?" Locke asked, breaking into her thoughts.

"Jessi is probably rigging up her version of a home shield to keep out any more spirits. I promise you she's thrilled. Gives her a chance to use it for the first time." Charmaine smiled at him. The sound of Jessi humming a popular R&B tune confirmed Charmaine's assertion.

"So, I'm the guinea pig. Whatever you did earlier worked. If her shield operates on the same principle—"

"It does," Jessi put in as she strode into the room with a brisk, all-business air.

"She tested it. We wouldn't put a client at risk. And we'll be here tonight."

Charmaine put a hand on his shoulder. When Locke pulled her into a tight hug, Jessi paused from tapping her instruments. She did a bump and grind with her hips, an impish grin stretching her full lips. Charmaine glared at Jessi when she turned her back to them. Her shoulders shook with laughter.

"Thank you so much for being here." Locke firmly pressed his pelvis against Charmaine's. His growing "gratitude" became obvious.

"Uh, sure." Charmaine extricated herself from him. "I need to help Jessi adjust... things."

"I'll put bottled water and snacks upstairs in the bedroom. The spare room, I mean," Locke said. He nodded at Charmaine.

Jessi looked from him to Charmaine. "I'll stay downstairs. You take upstairs. That way we'll have both floors covered."

"Great plan," Locke blurted before Charmaine could reply. He gave Charmaine's arm a quick squeeze before heading off.

Charmaine spun to face Jessi. "Very funny, Jess."

"You're welcome. Go on and enjoy the perk. You have before," Jessi said, one salon-shaped eyebrow raised.

"Only once before. Twice. Okay, three times," Charmaine added as Jessi continued to stare at her. Then she grinned. "Oh, shut up and do your damn job with the gadgets. I'll make another sweep to look for wires or anything out of place."

Jessi's soft giggles followed Charmaine as she crossed the hallway. Bluetooth tech made setting up sound and video devices easier. Still, a projector or speaker had to be present in the room. She checked to make sure the house didn't have intercoms. Such a system could be hacked to send ghostly voices through the house. Or to only one room.

Twenty minutes later she found Jessi in the kitchen. Eating.

"We ate already. Sheesh." Charmaine gave her sister a playful slap on the butt as she passed.

"I promised Viola I'd clear up," Jessi said around the last bite of a meatball. "You know we always followed Granny's rule. Don't let good food spoil or go to waste."

Charmaine leaned against the long kitchen island, arms crossed. "Kinda cold in here. Wonder if he'd mind if I raise the thermostat?" She looked around.

"Most folks don't like strangers messing with their A/C. I'm sure Eli will be happy to warm you up. All. Night. Long." Jessi rolled her hips.

Charmaine aimed a swat at Jessi and missed. "Seriously. What do you think?"

"He didn't fake the fainting spell or wetting himself. And unless they have some major advanced equipment, there's no fake haunting setup. I doubt we missed something between both of us searching." Jessi loaded the fancy stainless steel dishwasher.

Charmaine watched Jessi for a few minutes. "Speaking of Viola, I'm surprised all the talk of spirits hasn't spooked her more. I get she's got her faith in God and everything, but still. I know plenty of church ladies who wouldn't take the chance. Plus, they wouldn't approve of Eli stirring up the devil with those books."

"She's not like your judgmental folks," Jessi drawled, referring to Gems of Heaven, the latest church Charmaine was test-driving—as far as Jessi knew.

"I'm back at St. Mary Baptist." Charmaine ate a cheese snack cracker from a box.

"Since when? You were all into Gems of Heaven and High Potentate of the Heavenly Father Pope John Paul Bates." Jessi sat on a stool at the island.

"*Bishop* Bates is a pretty nice guy. It's just they turned out to be too fundamentalist for my taste. But back to Viola. Don't you think it's odd she hasn't seen anything?" Charmaine frowned.

"So-called hauntings can be specific to a person or place. Also, we know some people are simply not sensitive to the extrasensory world. Viola is very practical, down-to-earth. Aside from her buying into the whole religious mythology—"

"Don't start, Jess."

"I was very respectful of her beliefs. Anyway, I'm not sure I could take her if she decided to thump my ass," Jessi said with a laugh.

"Never underestimate a pissed-off church lady," Charmaine joked.

She didn't remark that Jessi seemed to really bond with the older woman. Jessi rebelled at any hint she was sentimental. Nevertheless, it was clear they'd become pals despite their differences.

"So, our game plan—be alert for more paranormal partying and develop a cleanup operation." Charmaine dusted cheesy cracker crumbs from her hands over the sink.

"The Axeman was real. Based on descriptions of his crimes, he had some powerful rage. That kind of intense emotions don't always dissipate once the person dies."

"Why would he come after Eli? Most of his victims in life were Italian immigrants. Doesn't make sense."

"Or explain why the grunch would have it in for him. You know, I get a feeling that Eli hasn't told us everything," Jessi said, her voice low even though they seemed to be alone.

"Girl, if we had a dollar for every client that lied to us," Charmaine said with a grunt. "I'll

check the second floor again. You can doze off.
I'm too keyed up to sleep right now anyway."

Jessi yawned. "Good idea. I maybe ate too
much. Stuffed the carbs, too."

"Ya think?" Charmaine shook her head.

"Yell if you need me. Of course, if I hear
joyous screaming I'll mind my business." Jessi
winked at her.

"Shut up."

Outside of Eli's less-than-subtle attempts at
seduction, the night was uneventful. Charmaine managed to get enough sleep to not be
tired the next morning. Eli invited her to
"sleep in" with him, but she declined with
great diplomacy. To his credit, Eli didn't push.
By eight o'clock they were on their way home.

"Bishop what's-it must have had an influence. You're not usually so shy when a good-
looking dude offers you a good time in bed.
Lord, deliver me from celibacy," Jessi said, pretending to pray.

"I'm gone ignore your blaspheming, girl.
Wow, what a beautiful day." Charmaine
breathed in the breeze from her open car window. "You know, we could go check out the
second murder victim's neighborhood this
weekend. What about today after lunch?"

"Yeah, more people will be at home for us to talk to." Jessi looked at her. "You wanna meet up around two your place?"

"Sounds good." Charmaine agreed.

"That gives you plenty of time to get your holy ghost shout on at St. Mary's," Jessi joked.

"I'll need every minute of those hours to lift you up in prayer," Charmaine shot back.

****

By two-thirty that afternoon, the blue skies held a mixture of white-and-gray clouds. They arrived in the New Orleans East subdivision of attractive brick homes. Jessi drove them in her Jeep. They cruised up and down streets, taking in the neighborhood. A few residents strolled along the sidewalks. Others tended flower beds or mowed lawns. After making a couple of circuits, they headed to Cardenas Drive. Yellow tape lined the neat front lawn of the modest-yet-attractive ranch-style home.

"His wife and two kids are still at his mother's house not far away in Little Woods," Jessi said, reporting her findings.

"I don't blame them. The cops should have taken down this crime tape by now." Charmaine looked at her.

"They're through, but the folks from Xtreme Clean haven't gotten to the house yet. They're kept busy these days," Jessi said, her tone grim. The crime-specialty cleaning company stayed busy.

"Yeah. Your friend Shaunice still work for them? She might give us some good info."

Jessi parallel-parked in front of murder victim Rayvon Woods' home. "I'll call her tonight. So, together or split up and talk to neighbors on both sides?"

Charmaine got out of Jessi's Jeep and stood on the sidewalk. "Let's go see if the witness is home. The one who saw somebody in the backyard that night."

"I got her phone number and called her. Mrs. Gladys Grayson is expecting us." Jessi nodded in the direction of a redbrick home down the block. "Let's look at the backyard first, though."

They walked to the front door of the Woods home, but, as expected, the door was locked. Charmaine led the way around to the backyard. A chunky pit bull behind a fence in the yard next door barked warnings at them. Jessi eyed the dog and moved away even though a chain-link fence separated them. Minutes later, they walked the perimeter of the yard, then moved in until they both stood in the center.

"Too bad we can't get in the house," Charmaine said.

A tall man took turns shushing the dog and staring at them. "Can I help y'all?"

"Hi. We're helping the police and the family figure out what happened. We're just taking a look around," Charmaine said.

"Okay." The man didn't look convinced. He looked them up and down. "You workin' for District Seven?"

"We're private investigators," Charmaine replied with a smile that wasn't returned.

"I'm keeping an eye on the place for Taletha, Mrs. Woods. All quiet since Ray died. Nobody been around except you two. Unless you got some ID or something from the police saying you should be here, move on." The man's blunt manner left no room for discussion. "The family doesn't need any more articles written about 'em."

"We're not reporters, sir. Honest," Jessi said. "Someone was seen lurking around the yard that day. Did you—"

"I gave a statement to the police. If y'all working for them you can get it," the man said.

"We don't work *for* the police." Jessi squinted at him.

Charmaine cleared her throat as she nudged Jessi. "We consult with them at times on special cases. A neighbor says there was something odd about the person she saw."

"There's always something odd about a strange dude trespassing," the man said flatly. He patted the large head of the pit, who looked from the man to them.

"That dog would love for him to give an attack command," Jessi said in an uneasy undertone to Charmaine.

"Mrs. Grayson says this person didn't look exactly... human," Charmaine pushed on.

The man blinked a few times, then laughed. "You mean Gladys got y'all chasing after a boogie man? Like I told that other woman, Gladys can't half see and she's got a wild imagination."

"Other woman?" Jessi said.

"Yeah, white with big hair. Dressed like a hipster. What my girlfriend calls 'boho chic.'"

"Becca," Jessi and Charmaine said in unison with twin frowns.

"I get it. Y'all are ghostbusters. Wasting your time. When Gladys pulls out her Bible and starts talking about the end of the world, you'll figure it out."

"Great. A religious fanatic," Jessi muttered.

"Don't take any pictures or video. Mrs. Woods hasn't given permission for any of that. I better not see anything on TV or on some supernatural reality show, either." The man gave them a pointed look.

"We specialize in unusual phenomena," Charmaine said.

"Fancy way of saying you looking for a story to cash in. Like I said, there's nothing to see. So, you can leave now." The man raised his left hand to reveal the cell phone in it.

"Thanks for the friendly chat," Jessi said.

"You're welcome," the man called back with a tight smile.

Jessi tugged Charmaine by one arm. "C'mon before he decides to open the gate and let that set of fangs loose on us."

"Let's hope Mrs. Grayson is in a better mood," Charmaine muttered.

She gave the man a genial good-bye wave. He stayed put to watch them. He disappeared inside once they were on the sidewalk out front. Charmaine was sure he continued to observe from a window, though. They went past his home to the address of Mrs. Grayson, the next house east of the murder scene. Ten minutes later, they sat in a cozy living room surrounded by photos of smiling children. Some were in sports uniforms. Others showed girls and boys dressed up, posed to look their best.

"I have nine grandchildren. The oldest two are in college, first year. Time flies, as the saying goes. I got Sunday dinner on the stove if y'all hungry." Mrs. Grayson hovered, eager to play hostess.

"No thanks," Charmaine said before Jessi could reply. She ignored the annoyance radiating from her sister.

Mrs. Grayson looked younger than her sixty years, with skin a golden honey color. She smiled as if sensing the sibling tension but said nothing. She sat down in one of two chairs that matched the sofa. "How can I help, children?"

"We're looking into the more… unique aspects of the tragedy next door," Charmaine said.

"You mean the devil that came out the swamps. You've heard about the grunch, right?" Mrs. Grayson went on without waiting for an answer. "Well, you know the stories say they lived out here when New Orleans East was more swamps, bayous, and forestland, over a hundred years ago. We have lots of land set aside for conservation. The Bayou Sauvage National Wildlife Refuge, for one."

"Yes, ma'am." Charmaine started to go on.

"I'll bet James told you not to believe anything I say. I saw you talking to him. Worse than his bite. Him and the dog." Mrs. Grayson chuckled at her joke.

"Yeah, well, I'm not going to test that theory by going close to the fence, let alone inside it," Jessi joked.

"James is alright. Good father, too. Though he needs to marry his girlfriend. The Lord instituted marriage for a reason." Mrs. Grayson glanced at their hands as if looking for wedding bands.

"So, you actually saw someone crossing Mrs. Woods's yard that day?" Charmaine said to steer her back to the subject.

"The grunch were society's outcasts. Most of them with physical or mental defects or disabilities. A shame the way people born different were treated in old times. I have a nephew with Down syndrome. My youngest sister's boy. He's got a job. I'd put down my Bible and whip anybody trying to harm Leo." Mrs. Grayson wore a fierce expression.

"Mrs. Grayson." Charmaine was the one growing impatient for once.

"Yes, yes. Back to the creature. It was dragging one leg, though that didn't slow it down much. Any body parts missing from poor Mr. Woods?" Mrs. Grayson cocked her head to one side.

Charmaine gasped at the gruesome turn to their conversation. "Excuse me?"

"Some of the grunch were known to take parts off their victims for trophies. Of course, other stories claim they would eat them. Nonsense. They used them for satanic rituals or spells." Mrs. Grayson nodded.

"Uh." Charmaine searched for words. She glanced at Jessi for assistance.

Jessi sat forward. "So the legends say. There's another story about a goatlike creature."

"Yes, called a grunch as well. I don't think it's true. Sounds too much like those silly Bigfoot sightings, if you ask me." Mrs. Grayson shrugged as if dismissing such wild notions. "But the grunch being society outcasts has a historical basis. There were settlements of people out here during the early days of New Orleans."

"A lot of this area had scattered communities and villages in the eighteenth and nineteenth centuries. Folktales about those days are common," Charmaine prompted. Her hint of skepticism had the desired effect.

Mrs. Grayson looked at her. "More than the tales folks are telling. I know some are saying Rayvon's past finally caught up with him, but—"

"Hold up," Jessi broke in. "What about his past? We heard he was a building contractor."

"His latest profession, and he ended up doing something shady in every one of them. No, the grunch are real, and one of them got him." Mrs. Grayson paused with great drama. "I know some of their descendants. I can make a call, so you can meet them."

Chapter 5

Stranger Than Fiction

Monday began overcast, a dull, gray sky empty of cheer. Sluggish, humid air made it seem as though fall, with cooler temperatures, had abandoned the city again. Charmaine and Jessi went about their usual day. Charmaine had one of their grandmother's favorite blues tunes on their minds. Stormy Monday, indeed. By noon, dark gray clouds moved in. Thunder rumbled; rain poured. The mood of the city turned sulky. All day, Charmaine caught snatches of dismal thoughts from random people. By the time she left the clinic, she felt lower than an earthworm. Jessi felt the same, based on the texts they exchanged. They agreed liquid refreshment might help. Scotty's café and bar would provide the tonic they needed. They hit the door with the five o'clock early-evening regulars.

Jessi slapped a hand on the polished wood of Scotty's bar. "Set 'em up and keep 'em comin'."

"You two are going to get something hot and solid in your stomachs first," Kat, Scotty's cousin from Memphis, replied with a determined note in her voice.

She came across as less intimidating and more like an older sister. This despite the orange waist-length braids, piercings, and being six feet tall. At thirty-nine, she thought of Scotty as her baby brother. She'd blown into New Orleans for a visit three months ago and to get away from a bad breakup with her latest girlfriend. Instead, she ended up staying to help Scotty when he lost his bartender. But with troublemakers, the cordial attitude could switch to "takes-no-shit" in seconds.

"I was going to order. Don't be pushy," Jessi shot back.

"Look, if you want to end up splattered across a street, that's your lookout. But I'm not having Scotty lose his license 'cause you can't make good decisions." Kat was blunt as ever.

"Gee, thanks for caring," Jessi said and gave a snort.

"Hey, Kat. The usual for me, too."

Charmaine accepted a brief hug across the bar. She followed Jessi to a corner booth. A crack of thunder and the sound of rain pounding the roof came seconds later. More people filtered in for the traditional Monday red beans. The smell of buttery cornbread, onions, and sautéed Cajun sausage gave Scotty's place a homey atmosphere. Still, the weather appeared to dampen the mood.

"Mondays," Charmaine muttered. "We may need to reschedule our visit with Penelope Fayard."

"No way. You're just getting creeped out by Mrs. Grayson's spooky stories. Gotta admit the lady sent chills up my spine even. But I'm eager to meet the descendant of a real-life grunch." Jessi's expression brightened. She grinned at Scotty when he walked up and plunked a tall mug of beer down.

"Hey, hey, y'all. What's up?" Scotty glanced over his shoulder, checking to make sure his staff didn't need help. Only then did he sit.

"We're going to see the grunch," Jessi piped up. She took a sip from the mug of Stella Artois.

"The goat-headed monster that rips folks apart? Don't even think about asking me to run point as a bodyguard." Scotty let out a sharp whistle.

"See, that's the alternative legend, the New Orleans version of the Chupacabra. It lives on Grunch Road, a remote section of New Orleans East. Or it was a hundred years ago or more. A lonely stretch of road that ended with gravel, mud, and shells not far from a bayou. Lovers foolish enough to slip off there for a bit of nookie would disappear. The only clue to their disappearance? An eerie howl in the night." Jessi's voice rose, the lights flickered, and a roll of thunder rattled the building.

"Wow," a woman nearby breathed out. She made the sign of the cross.

Jessi relaxed against the chair back. "Good thing I don't believe that bullshit. Yay, dinner is served."

The lights shone steadily, and the entire dining room seemed to exhale a sigh of relief. Scotty's waitress approached. She balanced a tray with two plates of steaming red beans. Cornbread muffins sat on a smaller plate alongside tall glasses of sweet tea. She appeared unfazed by whatever atmosphere had existed. She was too busy doing her job as more people filtered in from the rain. Once she'd arranged their orders, Elisia scurried off to greet a couple.

Scotty leaned toward Jessi. "Scaring off my customers will get you banned."

"They shouldn't be eavesdropping on other folks' conversation." Jessi bit into a corn muffin and grinned at him.

"The other legend is that a group of people shunned by the rest of society moved into the wild swamp and forestland around New Orleans. We're talking over a hundred years ago. Maybe two." Charmaine picked up her fork to eat but stopped.

Scotty leaned back when Elisia brought him dinner, a steak with grilled zucchini on the side. A bottle of fancy water completed his meal. "Shunned?"

"Because they had medical issues like dwarfism, cleft palate, and more. In the old days, folks thought they were cursed. That their parents must have committed some kind of awful sin," Charmaine said.

"Or they were in league with Satan," Jessi added.

"Anyway, the 'grunch' got sick of being treated like crap. They formed their own community, or so the story goes. After years of inbreeding, their descendants were born even more deformed until they were monsters." Charmaine shrugged when Scotty grunted his skepticism. "Hey, I'm not saying I believe it. But apparently they exist."

"Keep your voice down. We swore on a stack of Bibles to keep Ms. Fayard a secret," Jessi whispered.

Charmaine glanced around. Satisfied no one paid attention to them, she nodded. "Mrs. Grayson made us promise to be discreet. Without a stack of Bibles," she added with a look at Jessi.

"I understand, too," Jessi said, ignoring the gibe. "They weren't just shunned. Many were beaten and worse. No wonder she's obsessive about privacy."

"Imagine if word got out there's truth to the legends. I bet reporters would show up. Her life could turn into a waking nightmare," Charmaine said, careful to keep her voice low.

"I've heard the stories. You sure this is a good idea?" Scotty looked at Charmaine with a frown of concern.

"You know we can handle ourselves in a tight spot." Charmaine patted his arm and smiled.

"I also remember y'all needing to be rescued a couple of times."

"Her first name is Penelope. She's probably a middle-class working mom juggling soccer practice and PTA meetings," Charmaine joked.

"Those stories are too crazy to be real anyway," Scotty agreed.

They shared a laugh and enjoyed their delicious meal. Scotty's menu was among the best in the city. Nothing fancy. Just old basic New Orleans soul dishes most days. Though there was the occasional foray into haute Creole cuisine. Their talk turned to local events, mutual friends, and family. All quite normal. The bad weather only made the atmosphere in Scotty's place feel cozier. A bright and welcoming port in the storm, so to speak.

Two hours later Jessi guided her Jeep along Chef Menteur Highway. The rain had not let up. Flashes of lightning caused them both to startle every few minutes. Their snug feelings from Scotty's seeped away the longer they drove.

"Sheesh, how much farther?" Charmaine muttered with a shiver.

"Turn left in a quarter of a mile," the mechanical female voice piped up from Jessi's GPS app.

"This place seems a long way from Mrs. Grayson's. Bad weather makes the ride seem like forever," Jessi said.

"And a helluva lot less pleasant," Charmaine replied, thinking of the sunny Sunday they'd spent with Mrs. Grayson.

"Look at these solid middle-class houses. Like you said. She's probably a sports mom or grandmother. The most dangerous she gets is yelling at the coach when he calls a play against her grandkid."

Charmaine exchanged a look with Jessi as the houses became older, more neglected. Jessi steered the Jeep onto Peltier Road. Their virtual guide announced their destination was ahead, and then that they'd arrived. Thick shrubbery almost obscured the front of the house. A dim, yellow bulb in a floodlight helped, but not much.

"At least it's not raining so hard now," Jessi said, forcing cheer into her tone. Thunder rumbled as if to counter her attempt at the bright side.

"Let's get this over with." Charmaine didn't move to get out despite her words.

"We can handle one little middle-aged lady. Now c'mon." Jessi got out of the Jeep without waiting. She strode to the front door with confidence.

Charmaine scrambled out of the seat belt with a soft curse. She didn't want to sit outside in the dark car alone. Jessi was knocking on the peeling painted wood when Charmaine caught up. Seconds ticked by. Jessi pressed the doorbell button. They didn't hear a bell echo inside, so she knocked harder.

"Guess the doorbell isn't working." Charmaine peered around in an attempt to see more. Faint outlines in the dark made her feel they were being watched. She fished a small flashlight out of her bag. Charmaine sighed in relief when the light revealed stone garden gnomes.

"She's probably hard of hearing, bless her heart," Jessi said. Still, she glanced over her shoulder as if wary of their surroundings. She took out her cell phone. "Wait a minute. She said to text when we got to the front door."

Another minute passed after Jessi's text. Then they heard scuffling. Heavy curtains inside a window to their right twitched. More scuffling. Mumbled voices. Finally, the door cracked open. Weak light did little to reveal who looked out at them.

"You Jessi, that your sister? Nobody else with ya?" a gruff voice queried.

"Jessi Joliet of Joliet Investigations. And my sister, Charmaine. I called ahead. Mrs. Grayson said—"

"Yeah, yeah. Gladys."

The gruff voice didn't sound too fond of Mrs. Grayson. The door thumped shut. Clicks and clacks of locks being undone came seconds later. The door swung open wider to reveal a hulking figure in murky light. The screened storm door was unlocked, and the figure gestured with one hand for them to come in. Charmaine tried to read the person. Lightning cracked the sky overhead. Thunder rolled so loud both sisters jumped.

"'Bout to rain some more. You comin' in or not?" The figure turned and headed off as if not caring one way or the other.

"See? No big deal." Jessi opened the door, shoved Charmaine ahead of her, and let it bump shut behind them.

"Who's that?" a female voice called from the interior of the house.

"Them," the gruff voice replied.

Charmaine swallowed against a rock of anxiety in her throat but followed the figure. She turned right down a hallway. The figure appeared silhouetted in an open doorway. Another gesture with a beefy arm urged them forward. They passed a door behind which they heard the strains of a commercial jingle.

"I sure didn't think it was the pizza delivery guy," the female replied with a throaty chuckle. "Well, come on in. Y'all might have all night, but I don't." More laughter.

"You asked like you didn't know they was comin'," the gruff voice, now more recognizable as male, shot back.

Charmaine, more fascinated than scared, followed the tall figure. She blinked in surprise. The den looked larger than she would have guessed from the outside. Tidy furniture spread out across the den. Three tables made the room appear to be more a meeting area. Two other women, one black and one white, and a wiry Asian man sat at one table, playing cards. They stopped at the same time as if choreographed to act in concert. They stared at Charmaine and Jessi. Then, one by one, they put down their cards and stood. When Charmaine started muttering in a barely audible tone, Jessi glanced at her.

"What are you saying?" Jessi whispered.

"I'm praying hard that a soccer mom shows up," Charmaine said.

They both jumped when the door bumped closed. The hulking figure stood before it. Though the room was dimly lit, Jessi and Charmaine gasped when they gazed at the person. His left cheek bulged out. That whole side of his face looked lopsided, like dull-pink melted playdoh. The mouth twisted to the right.

"Have a seat. JoJo will pour us some coffee. I'm Penelope."

Penelope Fayard, one of the two women who'd been playing cards, stepped forward. She nodded instead of offering a handshake. Charmaine estimated Penelope was maybe five feet   tall. She had a large forehead, plump, short limbs, and a limp. She was dressed in a sweater and blue jeans. Her brown hair was swept up in a thick topknot. Penelope waved a hand, and the other woman and a man nodded. The woman, turned off a radio, playing blues music. She and the man sat on a small sofa. Then Penelope pointed to two matching chairs. Jessi gulped, looked at Charmaine, and sat. Charmaine joined her.

Penelope watched them with an amused sideways glance. "Calm your nerves, children. We don't bite most days."

Her companions laughed loudly. The black woman shook her head. "Shame on you, Pen."

Penelope turned around a chair from one table and sat facing them all. "Gladys says I should talk to you about our community."

"Mouth of the south Gladys should mind her own business," the hulk mumbled. Then he left.

"Don't mind JoJo. Gladys was a friend of my mama's since junior high. She stuck up for mama when she was bullied. She's a church lady now, but back in the day she could kick ass." Penelope grinned at them with a wink.

"Did people know about your family being the grunch?" Charmaine blurted out. She flinched when Jessi kicked her ankle. The frowns on their hostess' and friends' faces confirmed her faux pas. "Sorry."

"We don't use that word. Ever." Penelope's amused mood was gone.

"Ever," the other woman echoed. The man merely grunted his disgust.

"We're sorry. You're all descendants of... the community?" Jessi asked.

All three nodded. JoJo returned with a tray, cups, and a coffeepot. He served them with the practiced dexterity of a waiter. Tea cakes had been artfully arranged on a platter with a floral pattern. JoJo poured coffee for Charmaine and Jessi. The others served themselves.

"Pen's pastries, cakes, and cookies are sold in stores throughout Louisiana, Mississippi, and Alabama," the woman said. She bit into one and sighed in appreciation.

"I'm sure they're wonderful. We're still full from dinner. You know how red beans fill up the belly," Charmaine chattered, nervous to make up for her earlier lack of finesse.

"I'll give you some to take home." Penelope sipped coffee. "So, how can we help you?"

"We?" Jessi gazed around.

"For the last hundred years or more, we've had our own governing council. I wouldn't be talking to you if we had voted against it. Gladys means well, but JoJo has a point. She is a bit of a chatterbox," Penelope said.

"Humph, a bit," JoJo retorted.

"We're the Pines Village Community, though that's not a legal name. Most of us still live in New Orleans East. Some in St. Tammany Parish," the woman said.

"Pines Village was the first community out this way," the man put in.

"It's not really a location name, hasn't been for decades. Now it refers to us as a group. We're family, though not related. We encourage marrying outside the group." The woman looked at Penelope.

"Yes, that part of the legend is true. Cut off and shunned, for a few generations folks married cousins. Some children were born with severe problems, though not all."

"My daughter just finished her Ph.D." The woman wore a proud, almost defiant expression.

"Some of the younger people live in the outside world. That's what we call folks that move beyond our traditional neighborhoods. A lot of us haven't moved far from the locations of our ancestors' original camps. We won the land, you see," the man said. He looked at JoJo, who slipped out at some invisible signal.

Jessi stared after JoJo. "Okay."

"He's going put tea cakes in a bag for you to take. And he'll probably wash dishes even though I told him not to." Penelope smiled. "JoJo is the mother hen of our group."

"Oh." Charmaine exchanged a side-eye with Jessi.

"People judge us by how we look. Which is why we still mostly keep to ourselves. JoJo manages day-to-day operations at the bakery we built. Our accounts only know him from phone calls. My handsome son and grandson handle field sales and deliveries. They're what you would consider normal." Penelope put down her cup.

"Several of us own businesses." The woman started to continue bragging but stopped when the man shook his head.

"Back to the reason for your visit," the man said. Power seemed to have shifted from Penelope to him.

"Right. A couple of recent murders have been committed," Charmaine said.

"Nothing to do with us," the woman hissed. She clamped her lips together when the man raised a palm.

"Let them tell it," Penelope said. "Go on, child."

"Um, witnesses claim to have seen... odd-looking characters near the scene of both crimes," Charmaine finished and cleared her throat. She drank coffee in hopes a jolt of caffeine would steady her nerves. The entrance of another, younger woman didn't help. She felt surrounded.

After a few seconds of heavy silence, Jessi spoke up. "Look, I know you don't like the word, but folks are saying grunch killed these two people."

"A lot of us young people in the community don't mind. We even got some grunch rap artists," the young woman said. She laughed when Jessi's mouth dropped open. "I got some CDs I can sell you. We be hustling always."

"Lord have mercy," the older woman said.

"The Lord ain't never answered all them prayers, auntie," the young woman retorted. "You want us to snitch on some of our relatives or friends. That it?"

"We're not police," Jessi said.

"You're here because you assume we're a bunch of psycho serial killers. You believe the old stories about our ancestors. Well, I don't blame 'em if they killed a few so-called normal people back then, the way they was treated." The younger woman scowled at Charmaine and Jessi as if lumping them in with their tormentors.

"We're not accusing y'all of anything," Jessi put in. "But if you have any reason to think—"

"We don't," the older woman snapped. She stood. "I may have been outvoted by the full council, but that doesn't mean I have to listen to any more insulting accusations."

"Cool down. They're just following leads like any investigator would. Gladys swears they're not cops," Penelope put in.

"She's *your* friend, not mine. And JoJo is right. She sticks her nose in our business way too damn much for my taste." The woman marched out, brushing past JoJo as he returned.

He blinked at the others around the room. "What did I miss?"

"They think somebody from our group is skulking around killing people," the younger woman said mildly. She picked up a tea cake, then sat down to eat it.

Charmaine shivered when JoJo turned his ruined face to her. "We're just reporting what we were told. We certainly haven't come to any conclusions. Definitely not saying anyone here—"

"Tore a man to pieces and ate his flesh?" JoJo broke in.

"What?" Jessi looked around.

Charmaine put a hand on her arm. Despite his grisly words, Charmaine read him and the others in the room. A jumble of thoughts told her they were afraid for their loved ones, anxious about possible persecution from the police, and lurid media stories. Not one of them had thoughts of hurting anyone, including Jessi and Charmaine.

"You know somebody at the coroner's office," Charmaine stated. JoJo shifted his weight from one foot to the next. He looked away.

"Ain't sayin'. But I know what I'm talkin' about." JoJo sent Penelope a sharp glance then slipped from the room again.

"Jessi and I aren't trying to cause trouble for you." Charmaine felt her phone vibrating through the leather of her crossbody bag. She ignored it.

"Hell, I'm still wrapping my head around the fact y'all really exist," Jessi said. "Look, you should want to help us figure this damn thing out. There's a horror writer itching to make some coins on a story about the community."

"Eli Locke. Bastard," Penelope spat.

"You know him?" Charmaine frowned when her phone started up again. The buzzing sounded like a nest of angry wasps were in her purse.

"Not well." Penelope looked at her companions. On some silent signal they filed out.

"Well enough to know you don't like him," Jessi said.

"Before he wrote a book, he did a radio show in New York. In his spare time. He was an accountant. He inherited property in the city. As values went up, he made good money.

He wasn't the struggling writer he makes out. Anyway, ghost stories were more of a hobby back then. He said there was richer material in the South, especially New Orleans. He partied here a lot," Penelope said.

"Excuse me a minute. I gotta return an urgent call," Charmaine said. She held up her phone so only Jessi could read the screen. Then she hurried out.

Jessi smiled at Penelope. "A friend is having health problems."

"Yeah. *Right.*" Penelope didn't return the smile.

Charmaine heard muted voices in another room. She avoided that direction, instead going down the hall until they grew faint. She checked a small living room to make sure it was empty. Then she dialed Detective Harrison's cell number.

"Hey, I—"

"You have to meet me now. Shit is poppin' all over," Harrison said.

"Why are you calling us like we're nine-one-one?" Charmaine whispered.

"This kind of stuff ain't our thing. Not by a long shot. I'm playing it off to my boss as a bunch of drunk tourists partying. I don't know how much longer I can keep it up. Hold on. I'll be there in a minute. Tell them to calm down," Harrison grumbled.

"What's going on?" Charmaine glanced around. Footsteps came closer but then faded in another direction.

"Ghosts, vampires, you name it. All over. The French Quarter. Tremé. Magazine Street. Just meet me at my office. One hour. Oh hell. Hey you. Stop!" Harrison shouted at someone. The call ended.

Charmaine stood staring at the lighted screen of her phone for a few seconds. Excited voices pulled her attention back to her surroundings. She hurried down the hallway, concerned about Jessi being alone. Everyone huddled around a television. "Sorry I had to leave."

"Shhh," the wiry Asian man said, a finger to his lips. He then pointed to the forty-six-inch LCD screen. A male reporter walked toward a house as he spoke.

"Extraordinary events are unfolding even as we speak. There have been multiple sightings that frankly sound impossible. Take a look for yourselves," the reporter blinked into the camera.

Then the screen switched to another scene. The video seemed to have been shot earlier in the day, before dark. A woman dressed in a housecoat stood with her back to the camera. She gestured wildly, making her bright-red hair bounce.

"I know what I saw. I've seen her portrait. It was Madame LaLaurie. She was carrying a whip and chains. I heard the tortured screams of her victims."

"That's crazy," Jessi said and was shushed into silence.

"This witness, who did not want to appear on camera, is adamant about her account. Last night, WWL received calls from other viewers. People who claimed to have seen ghosts, the grunch, and other fantastic legends roaming the streets of our city. Even more disturbing, a gruesome murder occurred in the lower Garden District, a couple hacked to death in their homes. Reportedly, the wounds match those inflicted over a century ago by the Axeman of New Orleans. Sources insist the serial killer is back. The police have declined to comment, saying only that they're following up on reports. This is..." The reporter's words were partially drowned out by screaming behind him. He hastily signed off with a promise of more details as they became available. JoJo used the remote to mute the audio.

Charmaine stared at her text messages. She had six from Harrison, four from Eli. She even had one from Becca. "So that's what Detective Harrison meant."

"She's talking to NOPD about us," the other woman said with an "I told you so" look at Penelope.

"No. Definitely not. He doesn't know we're here or about you," Charmaine said quickly. She hit the button to close the screen and shoved the phone into her purse.

"You know about us, I'm sure, from searching online. We conduct confidential investigations into what some folks call paranormal phenomena. Most of our cases have a scientific or fairly routine explanation. Like y'all." Jessi shrugged.

"You don't know anything about us," the unnamed woman hissed before Jessi could continue.

"We don't buy into the stories," Charmaine put in.

"You should," JoJo rumbled from behind them.

Jessi and Charmaine spun to face him. Penelope and her friends stared at them in silence. Charmaine realized they'd been so focused on the television, she hadn't noticed a shift in the mood.

"Are you saying..." Jessi's voice trailed off.

"Nothing," Penelope snapped. "We're ordinary citizens who simply want to be left alone."

"You people have done enough to us." The black woman faced the others. "I sure as hell intend to bring this up at the next assembly. I got a family to protect."

The others exchanged quiet words with Penelope. They spoke in a code for several minutes. The Asian man appeared to reassure her. The other woman's tone was sharp, argumentative. Penelope clipped back to assert her authority. Then they filed out, leaving only Jo-Jo and Penelope behind. When the door closed, he took up a position next to Penelope. He stood with his hands folded. Nothing he did implied a threat. Still, his imposing size and tight expression didn't inspire warm fuzzies.

"You've probably already guessed this meeting is over," Penelope said, no rancor in her tone.

The door cracked open a bit. Penelope smiled at a child of about ten. The little girl had two thick, sandy-brown braids down her back and smooth café au lait skin. She came into the room wearing a shy smile. She held two packages of treats. She handed one to Jessi and one to Charmaine. She spoke to Penelope in Creole French and skipped off again.

"My great niece. She lives in Delacroix with her grandmother. Her mother... has troubles. Look, we're struggling to hang on like a lot of folks. We had some stability before Hurricane Katrina. Not a lot, but still." Penelope sighed. She stood and went to fill her cup with coffee. JoJo started to help, but she waved him away. Penelope took a bottle of whiskey from a cabinet, poured some into her cup, and held it up as an offering.

Charmaine shook her head. "No thanks."

Jessi wore a look of regret. "Sounds like we're gonna need clear heads for the next few hours."

"I'm sure Club Mellow will be open. Your pal Scott will be happy to give you any drinks you'll need," JoJo said in a dry tone. He smiled when Charmaine looked at him.

"But how did you know..." Jessi cast a side glance at her sister.

"You think we survived this long living in complete isolation? Thanks for the heads up.

Have a safe drive into town." Penelope sat and drank from her cup.

"We didn't come here to warn you. There's no threat," Charmaine replied.

"Isn't there? It's already started. You saw the news. It's only a matter of time before the old stories get trotted out," JoJo said.

"Just like you found me, some smartass with a YouTube following will show up on my doorstep. For all I know, you've led them here already," Penelope said.

"No, of course not. No one knows we're here." Charmaine sat next to her. "Okay, all cards on the table. Someone hired us to track down what's going on. He's scared out of his mind. Ghosts are haunting him."

Penelope exchanged a glance with JoJo and both laughed. "Girl, please. The only time Eli Locke isn't lying is when he's not talking."

"He—" Jessi stopped when Charmaine clutched her arm.

"I'll tell you who's after Locke. The people he jacked on investments that turned out to be shady," JoJo snapped.

"Or nonexistent. Eli was a shyster financial advisor. He danced right on the line between illegal and simply low-down. He advised peo-ple, got high commissions, and when the investments went bust? They were left broke." Penelope gave a grunt of disgust.

"The district attorney or AG couldn't prove insider trading or connect him to the investments. A few other people were charged. Not him. After Hurricane Katrina he bought abandoned properties. Made a sweet profit off people's misery," JoJo added.

"Then he had a couple of best-selling books. So much for crime doesn't pay," Penelope said.

"We saw a ghost at his house. At least I did. The Axeman," Jessi blurted out. She winced when Charmaine jabbed her in the kidney with an elbow. "Hell, they know a lot already."

JoJo and Penelope exchanged a glance. JoJo left and returned a few seconds later with the Asian man. They huddled with Penelope. A whispered discussion followed. When a third white man entered, he nodded at them before joining the others. Jessi pulled Charmaine into an opposite corner of the room.

"We need to get out of here and meet Harrison," Jessi said low, her back to the group.

"Yeah. But we also need their cooperation. They know more than they're saying." Charmaine peered around her to find Penelope staring at them as she listened to her friends.

"No shit. I didn't need telepathy to figure that out." Jessi walked off before Charmaine could stop her. "Okay, y'all. Here's the deal. We got to leave. Urgent business elsewhere. Blah-blah-blah. So—"

"Fine. Get out. You came looking for us. Remember?" JoJo tossed back. Everyone except Penelope muttered agreement.

When Jessi put both hands in her pockets, JoJo and the Asian man pulled out small pistols. The black woman they'd thought had left pushed through the door behind them. She held a Glock pistol in one hand. Penelope raised an eyebrow at them all.

"You don't need to finger weapons in your jacket, young lady. You're outgunned and outnumbered anyway. Everybody relax. I said put the hardware away," Penelope snapped when her companions didn't move.

The men hesitated for a few beats but obeyed. The woman behind slipped the Glock into a concealed holster. Jessi slid both hands out of her pocket with care. She gazed at the woman when she pulled her floral blouse and sweater down again.

"Damn. Can't even tell she's holding. I got to get me one of those. Hot pink and black lace, too," Jessi said.

"Great. More charges on the company credit card," Charmaine muttered. Then she walked over to Penelope. "Thanks."

"We're willing to help so nobody else gets hurt. On one condition," Penelope said.

"Which is?" Charmaine said before Jessi could object.

"Don't tell your detective pal or anyone else about The Community. You two have street credibility in certain circles." Penelope's shrewd gaze lingered on Jessi. "You sister has to say she agrees. Out loud."

"We both agree." Charmaine squinted at Jessi.

"Yeah, okay," Jessi said.

Penelope chuckled. "Jessi, you don't really have a problem with it. You just like to be defiant."

Jessi smiled at her. "I also get a teeny bit annoyed when guns are pulled on me."

"Not that you weren't prepared to do the same," JoJo said. His returning smile looked downright menacing.

"As you said, you have to go. We'll be in touch."

Penelope flicked a finger, and the woman who'd held the Glock swung the door open. Charmaine and Jessi were ushered out by JoJo. They walked ahead of him without glancing back at his forbidding face. Both exhaled in relief when they made it across the threshold and stood in the front yard. Steady rain had returned, so they dashed to their vehicle. Once in the Jeep, Charmaine looked at Jessi.

"Notice two things. We didn't get names for most of them."

"Yeah. They didn't look surprised by the wild news story. I think the stuff they're not telling us includes answers about what's going on," Jessi said.

"Plus, how do they know all that about Eli?" Charmaine blinked hard as she performed mental gymnastics to figure out the twists and turns of the case.

"My guess, Locke doesn't know about The Community. He would have bragged about knowing real grunch. Heck, he would have signed a movie or reality show deal by now." Jessi started the engine.

"Don't drive off just yet." Charmaine strained to pick up thoughts as the Asian man and black woman came out of the house. They looked at the sisters with suspicion but kept on to separate vehicles.

"Well?" Jessi prompted.

"Nothing except... She's singing a nursery rhyme. The guy is reciting a poem in... Vietnamese, I think. They know how to block a telepath." Charmaine looked at Jessi.

"Shit just got real," Jessi breathed.

"Not more real than an epidemic of supernatural creatures running rampant all over the city," Charmaine replied in a dry tone. A blast of her ringtone reminded them about Harrison. "Drive."

Chapter 6

Peek-a-BOO!

Charmaine and Jessi thanked the uniformed cop who had led them to the courtyard of District Five. Harrison paced. He held a cell phone to one ear. He took turns talking and puffing on a cigar. A few concrete tables were scattered around. A couple of other cops were having a break from their stressful jobs. Or at least they were trying to. Random curse words in a booming, gravelly basso made it hard. Harrison let loose again when his phone rang.

"Sir. I know. Lots of drugs on the street make people crazy. We got it under control. Well, um, sure. Control might not be exactly...

Right." Harrison looked at his phone with a frown. "Bye to you, too, *sir.*"

"Don't throw it, dude. That phone must have cost the taxpayers a cool seven hundred dollars," Jessi drawled.

"Worth it if I could aim it at Murphy's head." Harrison referred to his immediate boss. He appeared to be considering throwing the cell phone anyway. Instead, he growled deep in his throat and puffed on the cigar.

"Mrs. Harrison probably won't like you smelling like an ashtray when you get home." Charmaine aimed her composed observation well.

"Yeah, well." Harrison's ire went down a notch at the mention of his wife. He put out the cigar but didn't throw it away. "Seen the news? Of course you have. Everybody in the damn country has seen it."

"Hey, it's coming up to Halloween. Folks are partying in anticipation of the Voodoo Festival. You know how wild stuff gets. Lots of ghost excursions and smart operators firing up the imagination of tourists," Charmaine replied. She patted his shoulder in sympathy. They sat together at a table.

"Throw in gallons of booze being guzzled, and street pharmaceuticals. Somebody is gonna report Bigfoot is tap-dancing in Jackson Square," Jessi joked.

"Umph, I wouldn't be a bit surprised," Harrison said. He took a deep breath and let it out.

When he coughed, Charmaine went to a vending machine they'd passed in the hallway. She came back with three cans of soda. She put a Barq's Root Beer down in front of him. He grunted his appreciation. Then she gave Jessi a bottle of orange soda. The Barq's Red Cream Soda was for her. All three drank in silence, basking in sympathetic contemplation.

"So, you want us to sort out the crazies from the real goblins, right?" Jessi looked at him, head to one side.

"Your sister's the mind reader. Why don't you tell me what I'm thinking right now," Harrison said to Charmaine.

"You ordered me to stay out of your head."

Harrison let out a gruff hoot of laughter. "Oh, now you decide to do what I say. Bullshit."

"Okay, so maybe it's not as easy as looking into another person's brain." Charmaine started to go on when Officer Ward, the redhead Jessi found so tasty, stood in the door.

"Another one, sir. I'm going out to a coffee shop on Magazine Street called The Daily Grind," Ward called. He left when Harrison waved him on.

"Time's a-wasting, detective," Charmaine goaded.

"Most of the reports haven't turned out to be anything too unusual. Full moon, you know." He pointed at the sky. The giant reddish-orange disc overhead almost seemed to nod agreement.

"A Hunter's Moon, also called Blood Moon and the Dying Grass Moon. The theme is death," Jessi said. She shrugged when Charmaine and Harrison turned to stare at her. "Helps in my line of work to know stuff like that."

"Anyway, the moon isn't to blame for people acting a fool," Charmaine prompted. "Let's stick to the facts."

"Charmaine is the one talking about facts, and you're spouting superstition. We are indeed living in strange times." Jessi giggled for a few seconds. She blinked when both Harrison and Charmaine glowered at her. "Sorry, go on."

Harrison let out a slow breath. "Six reports are the usual stuff for New Orleans. A couple came from tourists who went on one of those cemetery tours. Apparitions appeared out of tombs. Cold, clammy hands gripping them on the buttocks. Nonsense."

"I know a few horny spirits. Not surprised one bit," Jessi whispered close to Charmaine's ear. She pressed her lips together when her sister shushed her.

The detective, wrapped up in thoughts of his own, seemed not to have heard. He went on. "You're right. In the other cases, drugs or alcohol were involved. Sometimes both. Not reliable. But then there's the murder."

"Yeah, the report we saw mentioned it," Charmaine said. She waited for him to continue.

"Got to be personal. Damn. The way they hacked their way through 'em." Harrison shook his head and drank more soda.

Charmaine read him clearly. The detective made plans to drink something much stronger once he was off duty. She got a glimpse of the horrific details and his musings about the nightmares he'd have for days. "That bad, huh?"

"And don't you start with the Axeman of New Orleans bullshit. Whoever killed that couple won't skate by because of dumb-ass talk about some nonexistent boogeyman." Harrison struck the table with a fist.

"Yeah. The last thing we need is bunch of serial killers roaming around New Orleans. Like in Baton Rouge," Jessi retorted. She had a healthy disdain for the capital city, like many natives of New Orleans.

"I said it was personal, so kill the talk about serial killers," Harrison thundered and rose from the concrete bench.

Jessi chuckled. "I see what you did. Kill, serial killers. Good one—"

"I wouldn't," Charmaine mumbled aside, tugging on Jessi's jacket sleeve. She studied Harrison's granite-like expression. The storm gathering in his dark eyes promised an explosion.

"Okay, okay. Everybody done lost their sense of humor. Sheesh, don't get your tighty-whiteys in a twist," Jessi replied. She stood as well. "We're on the same team."

Harrison rubbed his face with a palm. He looked at Jessi, a hand on her shoulder. "I'm sorry. Long hours. Not enough sleep, and pressure from all sides. Including from up the command chain. The local politicians have gotten in the act."

"Apology accepted." Jessi nodded. "We'll start looking into all of the reports. Might as well separate the bogus crap from the real thing."

"I printed out the details." Harrison glanced around. He pulled a single sheet out of one pocket of his slacks and handed it to Jessi.

"We'll look this over later." Jessi slid the paper into an inside slot of her jacket.

"Thanks." Harrison let out a long exhalation. "Better get back on it."

"We'll call you when we find out something," Charmaine promised. "Hey, Brian. We got this. Me and Jessi will deal with the supernatural BS. That way you can do good old cop work." She smiled at him.

"Yeah. And catch the psycho bastard that made two kids orphans," Harrison said. He nodded when Charmaine and Jessi winced at the grim reality of his words.

"Damn," Jessi breathed.

"That reminds me. What have you found out so far? You mentioned being tied up when I called. Please tell me you've exposed Locke for the useless drama queen he is." Harrison put both hands on his trim waist.

"More silliness from Eli. Nothing of interest." Charmaine cleared her throat.

Harrison studied her for a few beats. "But you'd tell me if you found something."

"Sure. Absolutely," Charmaine replied.

"Lying through your teeth. Never mind. I don't want to know."

"You really don't," Jessi blurted out and yelped at Charmaine's sharp elbow-poke in the ribs.

"Please St. Expedite, get me answers so I can stop this crap show soon," Harrison muttered. He gave them a final wave as he exited in time to meet one of his officers halfway. The female officer didn't bring good news by the looks on both their faces.

A half hour later they sat in Charmaine's cozy kitchen. Bags of Chinese takeout littered the table of her eat-in dining nook. The Five Happiness restaurant on South Carrollton Avenue had delivered. Savory smells of beef with garlic sauce and kung pao shrimp filled the air. They'd acquired a surprise visitor as well. Kat, Scotty's bartender-slash-cousin, gratefully accepted an offer of shrimp toast and fried potstickers. After small talk and silent munching in appreciation of the Five Happiness magic, Jessi tapped the table with one chopstick.

"To what do we owe this pleasant, though unexpected, visit?"

Kat sipped from her paper cup of tea. Then she wiped her lips. "Right. Um, I want to hire you guys. I know you're super tied up, but it's about Scotty," she added when Charmaine started to speak.

"You've got our attention for damn sure now," Jessi said with a side glance at her sister.

"He won't tell you himself, and we gotta keep this just between us. It's about his former employee Rochelle. She's low-key stalking him." Kat frowned.

Jessi blinked at her for a few seconds before she burst into laughter. "I was about to take you serious."

Charmaine studied Kat. "She's not kidding around, Jess."

"No, I'm not. Y'all might not know she had a thing for Scotty," Kat replied.

"Honey, all his buddies knew. Any woman who showed even a hint of checking out Scotty got her special treatment. She hated Charmaine with a burning passion. You know how Scotty lays out the red carpet for Char when she shows up," Jessi said.

"Oh, stop," Charmaine said.

"It's true. I don't know why y'all don't quit all the brother-sister pretending and just hook up," Jessi said. She dodged the balled-up napkin Charmaine threw at her.

"Ignore the high school antics, please. Go on," Charmaine said.

Kat gave her a knowing smile. Then it faded. "I heard about the drama she brought to the place on a regular basis."

"Scotty finally let her go. The last straw was when she threw cola in a woman's face. She got mad 'cause the woman flirted with him," Charmaine added.

Well, it's turned into a full-on obsession. A kind of 'If I can't have you, nobody will' kind of thing. That shit gets dangerous, in my experience. I had my own crazy ex-girlfriend nightmare," Kat said.

Charmaine tapped a polished fingernail on the table surface. "Sounds like girlfriend needs a firm talking-to with a side of attitude adjustment. I'll look into it."

Kat pulled a check from her pocket. She slid it across to Charmaine. "Good. Here you go."

"Keep your money." Charmaine pushed it back.

"Hold up, y'all. We're talking about Scotty. A man who can kick ass every day of the week and twice on Sundays. He doesn't need protection. And I'll bet he'd be pissed if—"

"That's why he won't find out." Charmaine looked at Jessi and then Kat.

"I was about to say the same thing," Kat agreed. "But I'm gonna leave the payment here. Y'all got expenses. I can afford it. I checked her address in the employee files. She's moved, and her phone number has changed to unlisted. I did a credit check, too." She handed papers to Jessi.

"Hell, you should work for us after Scotty hires a permanent bartender," Jessi said as she took the pages and read them.

"Y'all know I sold real estate, right? I'm still a licensed broker. Made good in the local market and in Atlanta." Kat shrugged when Jessi looked up at her. "Yeah, I plead guilty to accessory to gentrification. I've got five properties that do short-term rentals."

"I ain't mad. A woman's gotta do what a woman's gotta do. Hard to make coin out in these mean streets. Especially for a black woman." Jessi took the check and tucked it into her jacket.

"We don't take payment for helping friends," Charmaine objected.

"You need to dig deeper to find her. Which means access to paid databases and legwork. Get dirt on her for leverage. She and her husband have a habit of ordering expensive furniture and then skipping out. I'm guessing they got more skeletons," Kat said.

Charmaine frowned. "They have three kids. I don't want to do anything that might hurt them, too."

"Hey, their parents shouldn't be thieving scam artists. Anything bad that happens is on *them*, Char. Don't start with the good-girl guilt-trip," Jessi retorted. She went back to reading the report. "They have good taste, though."

Jessi and Charmaine's cell phones played competing ringtones. They looked at their screens. Then at each other, eyes wide. Kat kept eating as they scrambled to excuse themselves. They raced to Charmaine's office and closed the door.

"Hey, Harrison. What's up?" Jessi asked, picking up first.

"Hi, Eli. How... Okay, calm down. You're talking so fast I can't understand—" Charmaine looked at Jessi.

"Uh-huh. Yeah. We'll get over there. No, we won't talk to... Hello?" Jessi blinked at the phone in shock for a few seconds. Charmaine looked at her, mouth open.

"We gotta go," they said at the same time.

"Eli says someone, something, has followed him to that condo, the one where we first met with him. Even with your devices, he was scared to stay at his house." Charmaine pulled Jessi by the hand.

Jessi yanked her to a halt. "Harrison says they've got two crime scenes. One of the police officers has been injured by 'unknown assailants.' He wants us there now. Items are still flying around."

"We can't be in three places at once, Jessi. Eli could end up dead," Charmaine exclaimed.

"Harrison needs our help. He's a pain in the ass, but he's had our backs more than once. Plus, somebody could get hurt at these two places." Jessi waved her phone.

"Text him back. Explain Eli's message is life or death." Charmaine swung the office door open. She collided with Kat's tall frame.

"Y'all got a lot goin' on, I'm guessing. Can I help?" Kat looked from Charmaine to Jessi.

"Not unless you're good at wrangling spirit thugs," Jessi replied. She marched to the long table in the hallway and grabbed her bag.

Kat followed. "My great-aunt lives in a little place called Patoutville in Iberia Parish. She taught me a few things, helped me clear out a couple of houses I owned. One tenant, a woman, moved out in the middle of the night. Called me screaming about cold hands grabbing her breasts."

"Yeah, well, we're talking about more than a ghost who likes to feel up people. As in two dead bodies so far." Jessi faced her.

Charmaine appeared ready to leave. "I put the food up. Locked the back. Let's go out the side. I'll set the alarm."

"She takes time to clean up while hell breaks loose across town," Jessi joked to Kat.

"Five seconds to throw bags and boxes into the fridge. You might try learning a few simple housekeeping techniques. Let's move," Charmaine yelled over her shoulder.

"Kat's going to follow us. She's got experience ghostbusting," Jessi called back.

"I hate that word. Ghostbusting. Wait, Kat did what?" Charmaine faced them both. Then she blew out a breath. "No time. Tell me later. Don't blame us."

"Blame y'all?" Kat went out first.

"When you freak out and have nightmares for the next few weeks," Charmaine shot back.

"I'm driving. You're too timid," Jessi pushed Charmaine past her Cruze and to the Jeep parked next to it.

"You mean observe traffic laws to avoid ending up dead." Charmaine got in the Jeep despite her response. "Wait a minute. Which one do we go to?"

Jessi and Kat stopped at the same time. "Eli is more defenseless than the police. Plus, he's paying us."

"Works for me," Charmaine said.

"Whoa. You must be doing something right with real estate." Jessi looked at Kat's BMW X2 SUV with appreciation.

"We don't have time to chitchat," Charmaine yelled.

Minutes later they were weaving in and out of city traffic. Jessi made good use of her car horn, urging people to get out of her way. Charmaine gripped the passenger-door handle and said a prayer. She saw Kat's silver BMW one car behind. Fifteen minutes went by as they negotiated a stalled car, red lights, and a streetcar crossing. More worrying; messages from Eli had stopped. They finally arrived at the condo. Flashing police lights made Charmaine's heart thump until her chest hurt. Five minutes of arguing with a female cop delayed them from going up. Then Eli hurried over to them. He was wrapped in an expensive-looking jacquard throw, and beads of sweat rolled down his flushed face.

"I know what you're going to say. But I brought one of the devices with me. I didn't know Becca would be foolish enough to follow me. Who's that?" Eli blinked hard as he looked past Charmaine and Jessi.

Kat strode up to join them seconds later. "Katarina Davenport. Evening, everybody. Call me Kat."

Everyone, including the police officer, took a minute to gaze at the six-foot-tall newcomer. Only then did Charmaine and Jessi notice her striking appearance. Dressed in a black shirt with the long sleeves pushed up to the elbow and black jeans, Kat looked impressive. Like she could take charge of any situation. She smiled at them. The female officer raised one eyebrow at Kat.

"We're here to help," Kat said with a small nod to her.

"They work for me," Eli confirmed, going with the flow.

"Um, Kat is... consulting with us. Busy night," Charmaine said. "What's going on?"

The officer turned to Charmaine. "Sorry, but this is a crime scene. Nobody goes in. You witness anything that happened here tonight?"

"No, but we're investigators." Jessi used her serious professional tone as she squinted at the cop.

"Good for you. Nobody but NOPD officers can go in. Here's my card. In case you hire security staff, I can work off-duty." The officer handed her card to Kat.

"At least tell us what's going on." Charmaine said.

The officer gazed at Charmaine for a few minutes. "You're those psychics been in the news. That case in Jefferson Parish. I get it. He says he didn't do it. A spirit did. That's some strong stuff he's on."

Everyone turned to stare at Eli, the obvious question hanging in the night air. Eli backed away until he bumped into another policeman. Then Eli looked up at the third-floor balcony. He pointed, his mouth working with no sound coming out. His eyes rolled up until only the whites showed. He collapsed with a high-pitched whimper. They looked up and saw nothing but the building.

"Harrison is right. Drama queen," Jessi said with a snort.

****

Harrison arrived and checked in with the police officers who would be conducting the investigation. Becca had been sent to the hospital. Eli lay on an ambulance gurney with an emergency medical tech tending to him. For over two hours, Harrison let Jessi and Charmaine cool their heels outside, waiting. Literally. The fall night air chilled them, as one of the first cold fronts had moved through. Charmaine hugged herself, pulling her sweater tight.

"Wish this darn thing had buttons. Should have paid attention to the weather forecast," she muttered.

"We've had a few other things to worry about. We haven't had a chance to interview the first set of witnesses. Now this." Jessi nodded toward the condo building.

"Yeah. You think famous author E.J. Locke is causing what the reporter called our 'rash of supernatural sightings'?" Charmaine made air quotes with her fingers.

Jessi snorted. "Give me a break, Charmaine."

"He really believes it, Jess." Charmaine nodded toward the emergency medical vehicle. Both doors were open, giving them a view. Eli seemed to be more alert and talking to the tech.

"Does he?" Jessi turned to Charmaine. "We got witnesses saying he's a white-collar criminal."

"He hasn't been convicted, so technically he's not a criminal. Strictly speaking." Charmaine blinked when Jess cocked her head to one side. "Why are you looking at me all funny?"

"You're trying to justify giving him some. You think the guy is sexy. Look at him. He squeals and passes out like a little bitch at the first sign of trouble." Jessi pointed to Eli to underline her argument.

"Aw c'mon. We're used to paranormal entities wreaking havoc," Charmaine countered.

"Wreaking havoc, she says. You're talking like a character in one of his corny-ass novels."

"I'm just saying. Most of our clients go into shock. Not to mention a giant, murderous spirit wielding an axe is a reason to scream." Charmaine shivered when a breeze chilled her more.

"Yeah, well. You got a point. I thought about running my ass outta there for a second. I've never seen a spirit get bigger like that. Damn." Jessi shook her head at the memory.

"And he's not making up all the sightings around town. We didn't find any kind of setup in his house to fake a haunting," Charmaine said.

"Plus, who has the time, technical skills, and money to put equipment in different locations?" Jessi frowned as she appeared to go over the logistics. She shook her head again.

"So, we agree. We're not talking about a serial hoaxer on the loose." Charmaine looked at Jessi.

"Which means we have a citywide infestation of electromagnetic energy bursts," Jessi replied in grave tone.

"Huh?"

"The technical term is what me and Logan came up with. We're still brainstorming scientifically accurate terminology," Jessi said with a grin.

"Lord have mercy," Charmaine breathed.

"God is not a proven construct." Jessi laughed at the murderous scowl Charmaine aimed at her. "Hey, I'm an ex-stripper-slash-hooker with a college education, the most dangerous cynic you can find."

"We'll discuss your path to damnation later," Charmaine clipped. "Ghosts and poltergeists are popping up all over New Orleans. How in the hell do we de-haunt an entire city?"

Harrison's approach cut off the rest of their conversation. "Your boyfriend is asking for you, Charmaine. What he needs is a good lawyer."

"Eli wouldn't hurt Becca. I mean, he depends on her for so much in his business," Charmaine added when Harrison raised both dark eyebrows at her.

"Yeah, well, maybe they had a fight. The condo looks like a tornado hit. His friend is gonna be pissed at all those broken vases and ruined artwork. And no, I can't let you go in." Harrison lowered his voice and turned his back to a group of NOPD officers, uniformed and plainclothes. "Look, I may be a deputy commander over homicide cases—"

"Becca's dead?" Jessi and Charmaine yelped in unison.

"Louder. I think folks in Texas and Mississippi might have missed that," Harrison hissed between clenched teeth.

"Sorry," Charmaine whispered. She peeped over his shoulder. The group of officers seemed oblivious to them.

"Rebecca Hanson isn't dead, but she's beaten up real bad. I'm checking to see if your boyfriend—"

"He's not my *boyfriend*. I wish people would quite assuming I screw anything with a pulse and a penis," Charmaine complained.

"Okay, your client, then. We're going to find out if Locke has a history of violence, against women in particular. Could be they were fighting about you." Harrison pointed at Charmaine.

"Why would they..." Charmaine pressed her lips closed.

"Becca wants to be more than his personal assistant. Anybody who spends time watching her around Locke can see it," Jessi said.

"Bull's-eye. Maybe she threatened to expose his shady past." Harrison stared hard at them both. "Yeah, I know about his questionable investment-advice history. From the looks on your faces, so do you. Who told you?"

"We're private investigators. Finding out stuff is what we do," Jessi spoke up before Charmaine could.

Harrison glanced back at his colleagues and faced them again. "If you hold back on evidence of a crime, don't expect help when your ass is in a sling. Got it?"

"So far there's nothing to connect his time as an accountant to what's happening now," Charmaine replied with confidence.

"Yeah, none of his dissatisfied former clients are dead. So, they're not haunting him," Jessi added.

"Somebody he scammed could be taking revenge in a very creative way. I mean, look at the guy. He looks scared shitless." Harrison gazed to where Eli still lay on the gurney. "Wait, who's she?"

"By the way she's fussing over him, I'd guess that's his fancy girlfriend." Jessi took out her smartphone. "Lana Reilly. Twice widowed, once divorced. Hot on the Uptown social scene."

"Hmm, you've got competition. Good-looking, well-preserved, middle-aged sexpot," Harrison teased.

"Forget open mic comedy night, detective," Charmaine shot back. She studied the well-dressed woman. She wore her blond hair swept up in a top bun. Her clothes were pricey, and her manners all Garden District "ladies who lunch."

"Hopefully, she'll calm him down so we can get a halfway decent statement out of him."

Jessi turned to follow their gazes. "Guys who run scams are excellent actors. Better than any of the pros in Hollywood."

"Yes, and because they're sociopaths they can lie without emotion. They have no empathy, no guilt. They'll strip every penny from a seventy-year-old grandmother without losing sleep," Charmaine murmured.

"Well, at least you haven't gotten totally lost in his charms," Harrison quipped.

Charmaine grimaced at his bad joke. "Ha-ha."

Harrison's look of humor faded. "I'm hoping Becca regains consciousness so we can interview her before..."

"They don't think she'll survive her injuries? Oh my God." Charmaine shivered, but not from the cold air.

"Damn, that was some beating." Jessi snapped her fingers. "I'm gonna sweep the place."

Harrison watched Jessi jog toward her jeep. "You can't go inside," he yelled after her.

"She's going to use one of her gadgets out here. Of course, it's better if we're inside, but she might be able to get a reading even at a distance." Charmaine glanced up at the building.

"Look, I don't care what kind of hocus-pocus y'all do. I—"

"Jessi works with a friend who is a bio-physicist. She also hangs out with an astro-physicist, a top medical research grad student, and now lawyers. Pretty impressive, actually. Though I still believe in the spiritual world. Not that scientific research and theology are mutually exclusive."

"Skip the college lecture," Harrison broke in before Charmaine could continue. "What I was gonna say is you two have work to do. I want to know what the hell is going on in my city."

They watched Jessi approach the building. She stayed just outside the yellow crime tape. Moments later, Kat strolled back over to join them. Charmaine made the introductions as Harrison strove to be polite. He didn't like the addition of a new outsider.

"I thought you'd gone home," Charmaine said to Kat.

"I'm leaving in a sec." Kat's gaze slid sideways to Harrison and back to Charmaine. "Just wanted to say Scotty found a regular. So, call if you need me." She nodded and strolled off.

"What's up with her?" Harrison watched her leave.

"Jessi and me can't be everywhere at once. We sure as hell need an extra set of hands with everything going down." Charmaine let out a long sigh as she looked at the scene.

"You got her from a temp agency for ghostbusters?" Harrison popped a slice of gum into his mouth.

"Cute. Kat's a friend who also happens to have experience with paranormal episodes. She's a real estate broker, and old houses are frequently inhabited by spirits. Especially in New Orleans." Charmaine smiled when Harrison grimaced.

"Bunch of nonsense," he grumbled.

"And yet here we are, with you asking us to fix your ghost problem," Charmaine said.

"Keep that little fact as low-key as possible. Still, I have to admit *something* is going on. The popular theory in the department is some new street drug that drives folks crazy." Harrison glanced at his colleagues. Uniform officers had managed to disperse a curious crowd.

"Plausible, with the way synthetic weed and bath salts make people act. You may have caught a break. No embarrassing news stories about ghosts outsmarting the NOPD." Charmaine stifled a smile when he glared at her.

"We're on top of keeping the peace, okay? I won't lie to the media. If they buy into one theory, that's on them." Harrison heaved a sigh. "You're right, though. Reporters are already doing stories on the dangers of drug abuse instead of spirits. You and Jessi staying out of the headlines would be a nice change."

"Joliet Investigations places a high priority on discretion and privacy for our clients," Charmaine replied with a straight face.

Harrison grunted. "Uh-huh. Just get out there and stop the ghosts, or whatever name you got for 'em, from scaring the public. Man, can't believe I just said that." Harrison shook his head and walked away.

Jessi jogged over to Charmaine. "Hey. My readings aren't definitive. Too much energy around. The cops are on edge. Plus, the scene of a violent act generates a spike in disturbance. Emotions from the victim and the perpetrator. Eli could have attacked Becca."

"Because she threatened to snitch on his dirty past? He doesn't seem like the type. I know, I know. There is no 'type' when people get desperate enough," Charmaine said before Jessi could counter her point. "And no, I'm not saying Eli couldn't have done it because I think he's cute."

Jessi packed away the EMF detector in her shoulder bag. "I didn't say a word. What's our next move?"

"Kat hasn't left. She pretended to go so Harrison wouldn't give us grief." Charmaine nodded to where Kat's car was parked on a side street.

"I don't know if she's ready. Hell, we weren't ready our first time on a case with ghosts." Jessi followed when Charmaine walked toward Kat's BMW SUV.

"All she's gotta do is visit a couple of witnesses, gather info, and report back to us. We'll follow up. That way we'll know if we even need to chase down these other sightings. Agreed?" Charmaine said.

"Sounds like a plan to me. I don't wanna spend the night or the next twenty-four hours running around town." Jessi yawned.

"Yeah. First time I ever hoped drug use on the rise was an explanation. If we're having an outbreak of murderous ghosts..." Charmaine looked at her sister.

Jessi stopped walking and pulled Charmaine by one arm to stop her as well. "Then we got a serious problem."

"Poltergeists with the power to take physical action against the living," Charmaine added.

"Scary shit for sure."

Chapter 7

Dead 2.0

After a quick conference with Kat, who they officially hired as a temporary contractor, Jessi and Charmaine set off to the worst sighting. The murder of a local couple had similarities to the over one-hundred-year-old Axeman crimes. Harrison had filled in the terrifying details. Few locals even knew about the bloody local legend. New Orleans recorded so many violent crimes that a reporter's mention of it didn't capture much attention, yet. They arrived at the cottage-styled three-bedroom home on Florida Boulevard. The crime tape and police cruiser looked out of place in a neat, upper-class neighborhood.

Jessi parked her Jeep and yawned. "Maybe we could have waited. It's almost one o'clock in the morning."

Charmaine peered through the windshield. "Gruesome as it is, the sooner we can examine a site after intense activity the better."

"It happened almost twenty-four hours ago. I doubt a few more will make a big difference. My bed is calling to me," Jessi complained.

"We don't want to be rude and not show up after Harrison asked Officer Ward to stay."

Jessi perked up. "Ricky's here? Well, let's not keep him waiting."

Charmaine watched Jessi exit the driver's side with renewed vigor. "We're here on business."

"Yeah, of course," Jessi said without looking back.

Officer Ward met Jessi halfway down the paved path leading to the house. "Hey, great to see you again. Wish it was over a beer and dinner instead."

"I like Chinese and Greek food. Indian, too." Jessi smiled at him.

"Then we won't have a problem agreeing on where to go." Officer Ward grinned back.

He stepped closer. "I'm off after I finish my shift here. Three whole days. Been doing a lot of overtime with the craziness going on."

"Let's go with Indian first. Nirvana on Magazine Street. I like it good and spicy," Jessi replied.

Officer Ward gazed at her. "I—"

"I don't mean to interrupt this fascinating chitchat. Actually I do, because it's almost two in the morning and I want to go home," Charmaine clipped. She looked from Jessi to Officer Ward.

He cleared his throat. "Right. My partner will stay out here in case reporters show up." He nodded to the police car. A black woman police officer waved to them but kept talking on her cell phone. "Don't worry. Annette is cool."

"Okay. Let's get this over with." Charmaine looked at Jessi with concern. "Has the house been cleaned yet?"

"The crime cleaners will be here at seven. Sorry, but there's still a lot of dried blood. Over here; I brought these for you." Ward led them to a small duffle back on the sidewalk. He pulled out masks, disposable rubber gloves, and shoe covers.

"Maybe we should get hazmat suits, too." Charmaine eyed the house with dread.

"The forensic team collected most of the brain matter and..." Officer Ward broke off when Charmaine gasped. "Yeah, guess you could do without certain details."

"No, no. It's just I wasn't prepared." Charmaine stood straight. "I'm ready. Hey!"

Charmaine and Officer Ward realized they were alone. Jessi had climbed the six steps to the front porch. They exchanged a quick look and scurried to catch up with her. Jessi wore gloves. She'd put the mask strap over her head, but it hung around her neck. She paused at the front door for a few seconds before she crossed the threshold. Charmaine held her breath without knowing why. Lights over the porch and inside made the house look bright and inviting.

"Jess?" Charmaine started to follow, but Officer Ward put a restraining hand on her arm.

"Maybe we should let her, you know, do her thing. She explained a little how you two work as a team." Officer Ward's gaze never left Jessi.

"Been getting to know each other, huh?"

"I know about her last career, if you're wondering," he added.

"You're a mind reader, too," Charmaine murmured.

"My grandmother thinks I inherited a sixth sense. Nothing to any of it."

A crash and thump inside the house cut off their conversation. Jessi shouted a stream of colorful epithets. Then she yelped. Running footsteps pounded across hard-surface floors. Charmaine and Officer Ward rushed forward, the policeman in the lead. They skidded to halt in the living room and saw... nothing.

"Let me handle it. Y'all hang back a minute," Jessi shouted from deeper inside the house over more thumps.

"I don't like the sound of this, Jess," Charmaine yelled back. She turned to Ward. "Let me go in first."

"No way. If anything happens to y'all, Harrison will rip me a new one. My job is protecting the public. Remember?" Officer Ward lifted a foot to follow Jessi.

"Stop!"

Charmaine used every ounce of mental energy to push into his mind. She'd never tried it before. In fact, she'd never thought to do such a thing. Her reaction came as more of an emotional reflex than a conscious decision. A jolt shook her body like an ice-cold steel rod up her butt. She rocked back on her heels. Her vision went hazy for a few seconds. When the daze cleared, she swallowed against queasiness. Officer Ward stood quietly with a slight frown of confusion.

"I'll stay here?" Officer Ward gazed around as if looking for the source of his uncertainty.

Charmaine nodded. She scuttled down the hallway before he connected his mental muddle to her. She checked in the kitchen and bedroom.

"Jessi. Jess, answer me," Charmaine hissed low as she hot-footed down the hardwood floor. "Why am I whispering?"

A series of deafening crashes reminded her. Maybe she could avoid stirring up any more spirit pests than necessary. Hopefully, Jessi would keep whatever bumped in the night occupied. And that she packed her unique brand of ghostbusting heat. More noise made Charmaine pause. She peered into a bedroom decorated in pink, purple, and lavender. Her heart ached for the little girl it belonged to, now dealing with loss. Jessi's voice shook her back to her target.

"Yeah, well, I don't want to hear your bullshit excuses. Stop whining and tell me what's going on," Jessi said.

Charmaine strained to hear, but the attempt made fatigue slam into her. Using her psychic ability to affect Officer Ward had drained her, it seemed. Her mind felt fogged up, unable to push again. For some reason, she'd heard spirits on a previous case. She hadn't been able to duplicate the experience. Mainly because she had no clue how or why it had happened. Jessi continued what appeared to be a one-sided conversation in an empty room.

"Two people died. They left behind kids. You know what having your parents snatched away is like."

Charmaine followed Jessi's frustrated voice around a corner to the short part of the T-shaped hallway. The eastern section ended in a master suite. The stench of death lingered. Blood spatter remained on the walls, area rug, even the ceiling. Yet Charmaine managed to drag her attention away from the grim signs of violence.

"Your ghost boyfriend is here? I thought he 'lived' in the Garden District. Hey, Lucas. How's tricks?" Charmaine waved at the air and immediately felt foolish.

"You're not my *boyfriend*, so wipe that goofball grin off your face. And don't change the damn subject." Jessi glared at her.

Charmaine shrugged an apology. "Lucas, Jessi is right. We've got two little ones left behind who will deal with trauma for a long time. The least we can do is get justice for them."

"If you don't start spitting useful info I'm going to rock your spirit world. You know I can. You know I will," Jessi said, vicious intention dripping from each word.

Minutes passed with Jessi nodding, asking a few questions low, and nodding more. Charmaine's legs felt weak. She looked around until she saw a comfortable-looking chair. She eased down into it with a sigh, content to let Jessi do her thing. Moments later, Jessi strode over.

"You don't wanna sit there. The mother was sitting in that chair when the attack started. Look, a big stain on the—"

Charmaine leapt from the chevron white-and-blue upholstery with a cry. "Oh God."

"Don't freak. She died in the master bath," Jessi said and turned around to examine the room.

"Charmaine's throat went tight. Tears came to her eyes. "Just imagine the terror that poor woman felt."

Jessi swallowed hard. "Yeah. At least the kids didn't see."

"Small comfort, but it's something. And they weren't hurt." Charmaine worked hard to glimpse a small shred of bright side.

"Anyway, Lucas is able to range farther from his locus. He's not the only one. Something has amped up spirits all over New Orleans. And more are coming. The murderous force of the most brutal dead is being conjured up. His words, not mine." Jessi's arched brows bunched together with concern.

"You mean someone or something is making a lot of dead walk the streets? Lord have mercy." Charmaine sat down hard on the edge of the king-sized bed.

"No ordinary living being could do what's being done. The word is out on the street among his kind. A new day is coming where the dead will walk in the world. Meaning they will take over. Right, Lucas." Jessi let out a snort.

"What's he saying? I can't hear anything but a faint rustle in the distance," Charmaine added before her sister could ask.

"He's scared. Even my threats haven't shaken loose a lot more. He wants to help, but spies are everywhere. Hey, no one else is here. Don't worry," Jessi said to him.

Charmaine sprang to her feet. "Yes, there is. Your other boyfriend. I better check on Officer Ward."

"Shut up, Charmaine," Jessi spat. She turned back to empty air. "None of your business. Don't you even think about... Hey!" She sprinted through the door.

"Oh no. I had to open my big mouth," Charmaine said.

She pushed past her tiredness and ran after Jessi. Furniture bounced around. A roar shook the house. The female officer came to the front door. She gaped at the commotion without entering. When a framed print flew across the room she jumped, then pulled out her two-way handset. The sound of rushing wind sucked away her words. Charmaine turned back to find Jessi bent over Officer Ward, who clutched at his throat. Jessi's hands covered his as she shouted. The female police officer slammed against the front door, her face plastered against the glass. Eyes wide with terror, she fought to get free. Charmaine struggled with each step she tried to take toward her. A boom seemed to signal the end of the world.

Then she saw it. A looming shadow, like a dark stain, moved across the ceiling. She dodged in time to avoid the crystal chandelier of the living room coming down. Popping noises, like gigantic firecrackers, came a second before the lights winked off.

Panic propelled Charmaine back to her sister. Adrenaline flooded her body as she managed to reach Jessi's bag. She fumbled for agonizing seconds until her hand closed on something hard. Not caring what it was, Charmaine pulled it out and pressed every button she could find. Blood on Jessi's hands made Charmaine scream and hold down on a green button with all her might. A hand, or claw, clutched the back of her sweater and smashed her into the large leather sofa.

"No, you mofo. I'm not letting up," Charmaine yelled in defiance.

She held onto the device while she dodged flying objects. A vase clipped her forehead a glancing blow. Charmaine's eyelids fluttered from the pain, but she kept fighting everything, including the urge to drop the device and go to Jessi. Papers swirled with dizzying speed like a dust devil. Like a winter storm, a final blast of icy air swept through the house and then died away. The darkness grudgingly lifted enough that Charmaine could make out her surroundings.

"Ricky! Breathe. Breathe, damn it!" Jessi pumped the handsome officer's chest. Then she pinched his nose and covered his mouth with hers.

Officer Ward wheezed and then coughed. "Jeez, this is one helluva first date."

Jessi cried out in relief and rested her head on his shoulder. He wrapped both arms around her for a few seconds, then gently lifted her up. Charmaine grabbed Jessi's hands to search for wounds.

"Something gouged Ricky," Jessi said, her voice muffled against the cloth of his uniform shirt.

"But I'm okay." Officer Ward extricated himself from the grip Jessi had on him. "Annette must be going nuts out there, wondering what the hell is happening."

"Annette!" Charmaine yelped.

She threw the gadget at them before running to the front door. A wide smudge on the pane gave the only testimony to poor Annette's plight minutes before. The street lights along Florida Boulevard were out. Charmaine, her eyes adjusting to the dark, searched the wraparound porch. Then she ran down the driveway to the courtyard behind the house. The cop sat on the ground, holding her head in both hands. Charmaine spend a few minutes reassuring the officer, who was not injured as far as she could tell. Flashing lights and sirens announced the arrival of police. Only then did Charmaine pick up a chorus of voices. When a new cop arrived, Charmaine left him to assist his colleague. Neighbors came outside to consult each other about the power outage. Mixed in with what she heard, Charmaine's head filled with troubled thoughts.

Jessi and Officer Ward joined her on the front lawn. "Annette is okay, but confused and scared. I told her the burglars must have come back.

"I didn't get a chance to call it in. Guess it was one of the residents," Officer Ward said.

"Or twenty. Smell that? Burning wires like an electrical short or fire." Jessi looked around at the ground.

"Power surge. A squirrel got into a transformer. No, a tree limb fell on a power line," Charmaine said.

Officer Ward turned to Charmaine. "You know because you're psychic, I guess."

"No, that's going to be your explanation if anyone asks," Charmaine said, gazing back at him.

"You mean lie." Officer Ward shook his head.

"Okay. Fine. Tell these upper-middle-class families with two-point-five kids and a dog that an evil supernatural force did it," Charmaine replied.

Officer Ward blinked at her. "Wind has been kinda strong all day."

"Ahem. Yes. It has," Jessi added.

None of them looked surprised when Harrison strode up. "Well?"

"We're thinking a big limb from a tree hit somewhere on this power grid. Whew, it's windy out here," Jessi piped up.

"Sir—"

"Don't bother. I've worked with these two enough to know what's what. Go coordinate with the other officers," Harrison said in a brisk voice.

"On it." Officer Ward gave Jessi's arm a squeeze. He seemed about to kiss her cheek but checked himself.

Harrison turned to Jessi and Charmaine. "Give me the *just-between-us* version of what happened at the site of a double homicide."

Charmaine and Jessi looked at each other, then at Harrison again. "Well," they both started.

"Here we go." Harrison blew out a sharp breath.

"Something in the house tried to stop us from examining the place. I mean with our usual tools. The good news is my EMF meter, anemometer, and bioelectric neutralizers have been modified with memory. Up to six readings are stored until I delete them or take a seventh reading," Jessi said.

"Your what?" Harrison gaped at her.

"Paranormal 'entities' are another form of energy. In fact, my friend Logan, who by the way was named one of the top 'Under-thirty scientists to watch' by *Science In the New Age* magazine..."

"I. Don't. Care," Harrison yelled. He pulled a hand over his face. "Skip to the bad news."

"I never said there was bad news," Jessi protested.

"You two are mayhem magnets. Now tell me what I can't repeat to my command when asked," Harrison said with a tired sigh.

"A force like we've never experienced hit us like an out-of-control eighteen-wheeler. Furniture flying, chandeliers dropping from the sky, the works," Charmaine said, then regretted her candor when Harrison covered his face with both hands. "That's about it."

"You left out the part about Ricky getting choked by a ghost. Lucky for us Charmaine used my strongest neutralizer," Jessi added with a sharp nod. "What? He asked for the full story. He needs to know what we're dealing with."

Harrison dropped his hands. "In other words, we're not sure what happened. Either vandals, burglars, or curiosity-seekers broke in.

"Sounds good to me," Jessi said with a grin that brought another deep sigh from Harrison.

"Who called? Officer Ward was, um, too busy to request backup," Charmaine said.

"Alarm from the house is monitored. It sends a signal to the alarm company if the power is cut or surges to a certain level. This address is flagged. Dispatch notified me fast."

"Good looking out, detective." Charmaine cleared her throat when he rolled his eyes. "Anyway, it's possible they were killed by someone who broke into the house."

"We won't know for sure if that theory will fly. The insurance company will compare the inventory list on file with what's left in the house. But not until forensics does one last walk-through. Then the cleaners will do their thing." Harrison stared at the house.

Jessi followed his gaze. "Everybody has computers, tablets, big-screen televisions. Easy to spot that stuff is gone. Not that we had a chance to look before shit started coming at us like bullets. Let's find out now."

Harrison grabbed Jessi's arm and yanked her back. "No way. Fade into the crowd before my boss shows up. He's on the way."

"You expect us to blend here? Look around. We'll be specks of brown in a sea of milk, if you know what I mean." Jessi waved to the crowd that had gathered to ask the cops questions.

"Just do it," Harrison spat through clenched teeth.

"You have enough to handle. We don't want to be an additional source of stress," Charmaine said in her best career-social-worker, smoother-of-troubled-waters tone.

"Too late. Now go." Harrison glared at them.

"We'll check in with you later." Jessi blinked when he growled in response. "Leaving now. Bye."

Charmaine pulled her along as they both jogged to Jessi's Jeep. They ignored curious stares as neighbors watched them go. More than a few saw Jessi and Charmaine as suspects. Jessi had been on target. They could not easily melt into the crowd. Minutes later, Officer Ward waved them on so they could drive away and not be stopped by other cops.

"We still have the other sites where incidents happened. And contact info for other witnesses." Jessi said.

"Harrison didn't order us to stay away from his investigation," Charmaine added, following her train of thought.

"Not that we would have obeyed like good little girls anyway." Jessi and Charmaine nodded at the same time and smiled.

****

Hours later that day, Charmaine and Jessi met up. They went to three addresses where more supernatural sightings had been reported. They were frustrated when witnesses backed away from statements about ghosts or spirits. Most didn't want to admit they'd been intoxicated. Either that or skeptical cops had ridiculed them into denial. Still, Jessi's instruments told the tale. Residue, faint but still there, showed up on her EMF meter. They headed home after leaving the last of the three addresses.

"The levels are above what you'd expect from electronic swag. We had to really work on my tools though," Jessi said, referring to her scientist pals. "So much interference in this techy age."

"Humph" was Charmaine's distracted response.

She steered the Chevy Cruze. toward their friend's home for lunch. Diamond had invited them via text to her place for homemade chicken salad. They arrived at the home on Louisiana Avenue and parked in the narrow driveway behind Diamond's red Kia Soul. Moments later they were in the bright kitchen overlooking a small backyard. They engaged in chitchat for several minutes over lunch.

"So, I got another music video gig. All that pole dancing paid off." Diamond kicked a leg up to illustrate her flexibility.

"Girl, yaasss! Work your moves. I'm so proud of you all up in the classy side of stuff.

No trap hip-hop mess with rappers on a shoe-string budget." Jessi slapped palms with Diamond.

"Don't knock their game. Some of the biggest stars started out in the projects," Charmaine said.

"Jessi is right, though. You gotta pick and choose, recognize who's got the cash to pay. A lot of girls are dancing for free or for burger-and-fries money. I have to think of my baby's future," Diamond said. "Still, I help out promising artists."

"Yeah, don't give too much away for pocket change, though. Some of these fools forget who they owe once they make it," Jessi said with a nod.

"What y'all working on? C'mon, spill. I've been watching the news. I know y'all all up in that wave of ghosts running wild around here." Diamond pushed a plate of sandwiches on famous New Orleans French bread toward them as inducement to talk.

"Girl, it's crazy. Like somebody flipped a horror movie switch to let 'em out all at once." Jessi dug into a sandwich. After a bite, she moaned in pleasure and gave Diamond a thumbs-up sign.

"Is that possible?" Diamond blinked at her and then looked at Charmaine.

Jessi laughed. "Diamond, you too funny. I was just joking."

"New Orleans has three hundred years of history. Not to mention mediums, voodoo priestesses, and psychics drawn to the place," Charmaine replied with a shake of her head.

"And cemeteries. Hotbeds of restless spirits," Jessi added. "Nah. New Orleans don't need no help in the ghost-population department." She chugged a glass of mint tea and sighed.

"I thought you didn't call them 'ghosts.' " Diamond sipped from her glass as well.

"Easier for civilians to understand. Trying to explain the science behind electromagnetic manifestation just messes with their minds. People cling to their superstitions." Jessi gave Charmaine a sideways glance.

"Thousands of years of doctrine to support God is real. Carl Sagan said, 'Science is not only compatible with spirituality; it is a profound source of spirituality.' "

"Stephen Hawking summed it up nicely. Now that we understand the science of things, we don't need a great mythical creator. I'm paraphrasing. Nice word I learned in college."

Jessi smirked at her sister and popped a potato chip in her mouth.

"Please, Lord, no. Not another religious debate over lunch." Diamond giggled. "I just said—"

"Yeah, yeah. We got it." Jessi rolled her eyes while Charmaine giggled along with Diamond.

"Anyway, our client is convinced he's the reason for the ghoulish outbreak," Charmaine said. "He writes horror novels. The guy is convinced he's writing his fictional monsters into existence."

"Well, that's crazy," Diamond replied.

"Yep." Jessi helped herself to a second sandwich. She munched on chips with gusto.

"Everybody knows you have to do a summoning spell to make 'em come. You would have to have a powerful conjure woman or man, though. I mean, with all that's going on." Diamond spoke casually, as if discussing gardening techniques.

"We haven't detected any spikes leading us to a source. We'd know if a powerful psychic was operating in the city." Charmaine went still in the act of pouring herself more tea. She put down the glass pitcher and looked at Jessi. "Wouldn't we?"

"Oh yeah. I guess. I mean, unless she found a way to mask herself," Jessi said with a frown. "Naw. The Shadow Squad would have alerted me by now."

"They don't perform like trained puppies in a circus," Charmaine said.

"And they have their own agendas. Have you asked them?" Diamond got up, grabbed a bag of chips, and refilled the bowl.

Jessi stopped chewing and looked at them both. "Um."

"Lucas hinted that *something* unusual was going on." Charmaine looked at Jessi. "Maybe he was talking about more than a new spirit."

"It doesn't take much to spook Lucas," Jessi said. Then she sighed when Diamond erupted in more giggles.

"That's a good one, Jessi. Let's come up with more paranormal puns. I'm taking another English class. They'll be so impressed when I—"

"Don't even, Diamond. When are you going to graduate, anyway? You should have enough credit hours by now," Jessi said.

"I wanted Indyah to have her own room and a yard to play in. So, work came first. Financial literacy and business management classes helped me get this house. That and shaking my bootie to the video beats," Diamond quipped. "Getting a college degree is going back on the front burner soon. My great-aunts and granny been nagging, so don't you start."

"Good for you." Charmaine smiled at her.

"I'm pretty proud of myself, too. Back to your ghost problem. You better pin down Lucas. Use your womanly charms on him. He's hot for your lady parts." Diamond grinned when Jessi glared at her in annoyance.

"Stop calling him my boyfriend," Jessi snapped.

Charmaine broke in before Diamond could continue teasing Jessi. "Okay, let's not return to the fourth-grade playground. Jessi, find Lucas in one of his favorite haunts and do whatever it takes to make him open up."

"Gee, thanks for the original suggestion," Jessi mumbled.

"Damn it."

A soft trill announced texts had come, so Charmaine pulled out her phone. She read for a few moments while Jessi and Diamond took girlfriend-styled jabs at each other. The news added more complications.

Jessi stopped joking around with Diamond and pointed to the phone. "What's up?"

"Kat says Rochelle is at it again. Sanitation inspectors went to Scotty's café because of an 'anonymous' complaint. A window at Scotty's house was busted when someone tried to break in. And his new Range Rover was keyed. One of his neighbors scared off the person last night, but he didn't get a good look at m." Charmaine read the main points, skipping the curse words sprinkled in calling Rochelle colorful names.

"I hope he called the police," Diamond said. She huffed when Jessi gave a cynical snort. "Hey, it might scare her into getting some sense."

"Scotty wouldn't press charges. I'm more worried about him trying to handle it himself. At some point he'll lose his cool." Charmaine frowned with worry at the possibilities.

"Yeah, and the cops don't care about the tricks of a crazy ex-girlfriend anyway. Especially since there isn't any evidence she's responsible," Jessi put in.

"She was his girlfriend?" Diamond gaped at them.

"One hot hour on a cot in the storeroom ain't the basis for calling her a 'girlfriend,' " Charmaine quipped, forming air quotes. "I'm going to track her butt down and have a woman-to-woman with her."

Jessi wiped her hands on a napkin and stood. "Nah, sis. This is a job for some street talk. You've gone full bougie in the last few years. You ain't got it in ya."

Diamond nodded with a grin. "Take me, take me! My Aunt Teresa can get the baby from preschool today. She's retired and loves spoiling Indyah."

"You're a single mother with obligations. You can't go around threatening folks and end up arrested," Charmaine protested.

"We're going to point out some unpleasant realities that might happen if she keeps actin' a damn fool." Jessi winked at Diamond.

"Otherwise known as threats. Listen—"

"Don't sweat, Charmaine," Jessi broke in. "We'll handle it."

Charmaine started to say more when her cell played a hip-hop sample from a Big Freedia track. "Damn, it's popping off all over."

"Now what?" Jessi stood, legs apart as if ready for battle.

"Penelope says she wants to talk. She didn't go into details," Charmaine added before the question in Jessi's mind came out.

"I don't know why she couldn't call or text it out." Jessi frowned at Charmaine's phone as if it was to blame.

"There's something she wants me to see." Charmaine put her phone back in her purse. "She wants me to meet her at an address in New Orleans East tonight."

"Sounds too much like a setup. We can see Rochelle later. I'll go with you," Jessi said.

"Rochelle is on a rampage. Go check on Scotty first. Make sure he's not on the edge of doing something that will get him in trouble. Then deal with her. And keep it legal. I can't afford to spend my teeny-weeny savings bonding y'all out of lockup." Charmaine stood. She slung the strap of the crossbody bag over her head.

Diamond worked fast to put the plate of sandwiches in the refrigerator. "I'll be ready in a minute. Going to change into yoga pants and sneaks."

"What are you going to do?" Jessi asked Charmaine.

"Try to sort through our case and finally get answers that make sense. I'm serious, Jess. No trouble." Charmaine pointed a finger at her sister.

"You know me. She don't start nothin', won't be nothin'." Jessi held both arms out.

"Oh Lord. I—" Charmaine's phone buzzed again, and she took it out. Detective Harrison wanted to know if they'd found out anything. "I gotta go."

"It's gonna be alright." Jessi patted Charmaine's shoulder and went down the hall to find Diamond.

"Yeah. Sure."

That night at seven o'clock, as agreed, Charmaine pulled up to a dingy house on Flake Avenue. Fading daylight didn't make it any less intimidating. Vacant lots on both sides made the house look isolated. Jessi's words about a setup echoed in Charmaine's mind like a warning bell. Still, she marched forward. Penelope didn't seem like the sort to go in for violence. Unless, of course, she thought her family and community were at risk. Charmaine reminded herself that they'd said nothing to give the woman reason to think so. She climbed the two chipped steps to the porch. Before she could knock, the door swung open. JoJo, the tall disfigured man, loomed over her. He gestured for her to come, turned, and tromped off without waiting for her. He seemed to know she'd feel less nervous if he wasn't behind her. With a deep breath in and out, Charmaine entered the house. She wasn't encouraged to find Penelope and two angry-looking women waiting for her in a cramped living room.

"You wanted to know more about Eli Jeffry Locke. They can tell you," Penelope said, skipping a greeting.

"He's a lowdown, murdering bastard," one of them said in a flat tone.

Chapter 8

Questions, Questions, Questions

Charmaine rubbed her temples in an attempt to ease the throbbing. Stark thoughts stabbed into her head like huge hypodermic needles. Dazed, her brain worked hard to get re-oriented. Who, what, when, and where. She repeated the words that were a common method to clear mental confusion. JoJo had caught Charmaine before she slumped to the floor. The "grunch" hovered around as they plied Charmaine with herbal tea and sympathy.

"What I told you about blurting out stuff?" a gravelly female voice said.

"Hell, I didn't know she was a delicate little flower," the second woman retorted.

"She's a sensitive, a telepath. The real deal. I didn't believe it until now," Penelope said. "Now, hush and give the girl space to breathe."

"That means her sister can see spirits and more. What if they're the ones causing all this confusion?" JoJo asked.

"Wait a minute."

Charmaine suddenly felt vulnerable as the mood seemed to shift against her. She tried to get out of the stuffed chair she was in. Yellow spots floated around her. She gulped when dizziness hit again. A strong hand pushed her back into the floral upholstery.

"Easy, girl," JoJo rumbled.

"We're psychic investigators, not instigators," Charmaine managed to get out. She blinked hard to banish the haze. A cup appeared in front of her.

"Drink more of this. It's not going to hurt you. Nothing but lemon balm tea with peppermint. Calms the nerves and settles the stomach. You're queasy, right?" Penelope said.

"Uh-huh."

Charmaine felt so out of whack, she took her chances and drank the tea. Moments later she did, indeed, begin to feel better. JoJo and the other two women murmured to each other with side glances at Charmaine.

"My friend was born with a veil. Her grandmother and mine were friends. I still miss her." Penelope sighed.

"Where is she?" Charmaine drained the last of the tea. The taste of lemon and honey lingered. The wave of nausea gone, she could appreciate the delicious flavor.

"Damita died young. She had lots of medical issues. That's one part of the legends that's true. Most of us are born with defects or problems. Anyway, she'd get a strong reading sometimes like you and get sick to her stomach." Penelope took the cup from Charmaine.

"Thanks for the tea." Charmaine eyed the three others, still deep in a muted conversation. About her.

"They think since Eli Locke is paying you, that you're helping him," Penelope said after a while with a sharp nod at her companions.

"Helping him do what?" Charmaine looked at Penelope.

"Your phone's been buzzing like a little beehive." Penelope pointed to Charmaine's crossbody bag.

"Oh." Charmaine pulled it out. Jessi had sent six texts and left three voice messages.

Charmaine tapped in reassurances she was okay. When her phone rang, she answered and hastily convinced Jessi no one was forcing her to say she was fine. "I'll call you later."

"Where's your mama and daddy?" Penelope wore a maternal expression.

"Mama lives in Missouri City, Texas, now. She's got a new husband, a preacher. We thought she'd died during the hurricane. My daddy is MIA. Jessi's is in prison and..." Charmaine caught herself before she revealed more personal information. She looked at Penelope with wide eyes.

The little woman wore an elfin smile. "Not supernatural, exactly. I just have a natural way of inspiring folks to confide in me. I worked in a circus for five years, billed as the 'Little Fairy Fortune Teller.' Most folks wouldn't even remember they told me all their business. Putting the rest together was easy." Penelope shrugged as if to say, "No biggie."

"I think you *do* have some psychic ability," Charmaine said.

"I'm through being a carnival freak-show attraction. I run a business now, a very successful one at that. We help others start their own businesses, too. With the internet, we don't have to be subjected to stares, name-calling, and the like. We employ those rejected by your world," Penelope said.

"We're part of the same world, Miss Penelope," Charmaine replied.

"Oh yeah? Tell that to the folks who won't hire us. The teachers who mistreat our kids. The landlords who won't rent to us." Penelope shook her head. "Not much has changed since our ancestors fled old New Orleans two hundred years ago."

Charmaine thought about racial oppression. Remembered they way she and Jessi had been treated for being different. She couldn't come up with a convincing argument against Penelope's view. "But you've learned how to make a way out of no way."

Penelope grinned at her and winked. "Like you and your sister."

Charmaine smiled back. JoJo and the other two women rejoined them. They weren't convinced Charmaine could be trusted, let alone be an ally. She didn't have to read their minds. Suspicion was written in their expressions and radiated from them like heat.

"Eli Locke hired me to find out why supernatural characters in his books are coming to life. Nothing else," Charmaine said before any of the three said a word.

"He knows why," the gravel-voiced woman spoke first.

"You don't really think it's a coincidence they're all from *his* books, do you?" the other woman chimed in.

"Stephen King is more famous than him," JoJo said.

"Anne Rice. Better writers by a country mile, too, if you ask me," the gravel-voice woman added.

"But you don't see their characters strolling down Canal Street. Gotta ask myself why that is," JoJo said.

"Easy. EJ Locke is doin' it," the gravel-voiced woman said, providing the logical conclusion. The other two nodded.

"They have a point," Penelope added.

"We haven't found evidence or motivation for Eli to cause the spike in sightings. We searched his house. No equipment to fake ghosts. And he can't be all over the city at once. The coordination required, the expense. I don't see it." Charmaine shook her head at them, but they were unmoved.

"Then you got a limited imagination. He killed Pen's sister. I don't care what the police in New York said, or the district attorney," the gravel-voice said.

Charmaine gazed at Penelope, who nod-
ded. "If you tell me the whole story, I'll tell you
what I know so far."

****

Later that night Charmaine relaxed on Jessi's sofa. She nursed a cup of strong after-
dinner coffee. Jessi like Louisiana brew with
the biggest kick. Diamond sat in a matching
chair with Indyah on her lap. The four-year-
old played a game on her mother's
smartphone. Much to their surprise, Jessi had
cooked. Her simple meal of burgers and fries
had been pretty good. Frozen potatoes, pre-
made beef patties, of course.

"Lord, it's almost nine o'clock. Hurry up
and finish giving us the new four-one-one. I
got to get Indyah home soon. It's way past
time she got settled in her own bed," Diamond
said.

"Don't rush her, Di. She still looks shaky."
Jessi plopped down on the other end of the
sofa.

"Stay-up-late time," Indyah piped up. She
became animated at the prospect.

"Not on a Wednesday night, baby girl. You're not going to give me grief about getting up tomorrow," Diamond replied.

"I'm fine," Charmaine said to Jessi.

"You didn't eat much, and I know it wasn't 'cause my food wasn't good," Jessi replied.

"Delicious," Diamond agreed. "You're going to make a great housewife one day."

"You done lost your everlasting mind," Jessi shot back, All three shared a hearty laugh at the idea of Jessi being domesticated.

"The details might get a bit too grown-up for little ears," Charmaine said with a nod at Indyah.

Diamond stood, both hands under Indyah's armpits. "Okay, mama's girl. Go watch Nickelodeon for a minute on T-Charmaine's tablet. Then we're going home."

"Yaay, *The Loud House.* Yaay, SpongeBob!" Indyah yelled.

"You gonna have that baby's brain turn into mush watching that crap," Jessi called after them.

Seconds later, Indyah sat cross-legged on a dining room chair. Charmaine's nine-inch tablet played videos, to the child's delight. Diamond scurried back to the living area, dropped down, and gazed at Charmaine expectantly.

Indyah gurgled encouragement to her Nick.com friends in the background. Jessi leaned forward to listen as well.

"Locke has been married twice. The first time when he was still in college. The second time to a member of the so-called grunch community," Charmaine began.

"Whoa, the grunch are real," Diamond interrupted.

"They don't like being called 'grunch,' especially by outsiders," Jessi admonished. "Though their younger generation have made it their own. They think of it sorta like saying grunge, punk, goth, or street."

"Keep some respect on their name. Call 'em *The Community* if I have to meet them," Diamond said, and then turned to Charmaine again. "Go on."

"So, his second wife was Penelope's sister. She did their version of passing in the majority world. She didn't have obvious physical abnormalities and hid her background. Got an MBA, moved to New York in 2001, and got a great job. Long story short, she met Locke. They had an affair for about eight months and got married. She disappeared six months before the first allegations about Locke's shady business practices went public. They're sure he killed her." Charmaine frowned at the cold cup in her hand. She went into the kitchen to get something stronger.

"Notice she's not calling him Eli right now," Jessi stage-whispered to Diamond.

"I hear you," Charmaine called from the kitchen. She stared at the coffeepot for a minute. Then she poured herself a glass of merlot instead. She returned to the living room sofa to twin gazes that followed her until she sat down. "Where was I?"

"Locke is a stone-cold wife-killer," Diamond said.

"Allegedly," Jessi put in, a forefinger raised.

"Right. No body has been found to this day. She had a history of bipolar disorder and going ghost. Penelope's mother was so upset that the community hired a private investigator. He found her online blog that had posts about feeling lost, depressed, and worthless. She'd talked like that before she'd disappeared." Charmaine sipped wine.

"He could have signed on to her account using her password, left that as a trail, and made sure her corpse would never get found." Jessi looked at them.

"Or pointed the police to her blog, knowing it would cover him," Diamond added.

"Plausible hypotheses. No evidence. The NYPD and the New York DA were right. All they could do was question Locke and let him go," Charmaine replied.

"Hmm. Motive?" Diamond looked from Jessi to Charmaine.

"Again, her sister believes Lydia, that was or is her name, uncovered his dirty dealings," Charmaine replied.

"Let me guess. The private detective found evidence Lydia may have uncovered the truth." Jessi said.

"That's why I pay you the big bucks, partner," Charmaine quipped, which brought a grunt of derision from Jessi. "But yeah, Lydia worked for a private equity firm. Two of their senior advisors were among several people who noticed something fishy with Locke."

"And her sister thinks Lydia tipped them off?" Jessi asked.

"She worked with Locke on one of his projects and brought wealthy investors to him. Then she vanished. Locke insisted anything she said was suspect, the rantings of a disturbed mind," Charmaine said.

"Her blog and history of mental illness backs up his version," Jessi put in.

"Boom." Charmaine lifted her wine glass and drank.

"But you don't like all these coincidences," Diamond said.

"Amanda Morrell, the first victim, finished school in New York and knew Locke. Why didn't he tell us?" Charmaine frowned at the rich red liquid in her glass.

"Then his assistant ends up beat half to death. The women in his life either have really bad luck or..." Diamond looked from Charmaine to Jessi and back again.

"Yeah, but what about the other three murders? Are we saying he killed those people, too? I don't see connections." Jessi said.

"Then we need to find them." Charmaine put the goblet down with a thump on the coffee table.

"Before somebody else ends up in intensive care or worse," Jessi said. She closed her eyes and pretended to rub an imaginary crystal ball. "I see another late night of snooping in our future."

****

At midnight, Charmaine and Jessi stood in the St. Louis Cemetery No. 1. Both hugged themselves against the brisk October night. The temperature had dipped down from a pleasant seventy-four that day to around forty-eight degrees. The wind swirled leaves and debris from florals left on graves around their feet. They waited for Lucas to show up. At least Jessi did. Charmaine came to keep her sister from hanging around tombs in the dead of night by herself. Not the Jessi cared. She'd reminded Charmaine how many times she'd done it before to meet up with members of her Shadow Squad, a group of ghostly inform-ants. Charmaine reminded her how many times she'd gotten in trouble doing so.

"Lucky for us we have ancestors buried here. We get a special pass to visit." Jessi rubbed her hands together and then stuck them back in her sweater-coat pocket. She pulled the fur collar up higher around her ears.

"Yeah, but the Archdiocese didn't mean at midnight to chitchat with dead people." Charmaine glanced around as if expecting a priest to swoop down in retribution.

"We're on serious business, not to collect souvenirs or scam thrill-seeking tourists with a fake séance. Organized religion is an even bigger scam, if you ask me," Jessi said, winding up for a familiar monologue.

"Except I didn't," Charmaine cut in before she got going. "Focus on the reason we're here. I don't want to hang out in this City of the Dead longer than necessary."

"Me either. With somebody stirring up nasty energy, anything could happen," Jessi murmured, looking around.

"Oh gee, thanks for mentioning that *after* you talked me into coming. We could have gone to that mansion in the Garden District where Lucas used to work—"

"Where he was enslaved, forced to support a brutal system that allowed slave owners to enrich themselves," Jessi said, going into her other favorite topic to expound on at length.

"Preaching to the choir." Charmaine tugged her faux leather jacket tighter against her body.

"Okay. We knock on the front door of the rich people and say, 'Excuse us. We're going to sit in your living room until our friend the ghost shows up. Coffee would be lovely, thanks.'"

"We could wait outside," Charmaine countered and stamped her booted feet to warm up.

"To get shot by NOPD as prowlers. Look, Lucas will come, we'll get the info, and leave. So, cool your jets, as Uncle Buddy used to say," Jessi said, quoting their oldest maternal great-uncle.

"Brr, that won't be a problem with this wind," Charmaine grumbled. "Easy for Lucas to take his sweet time. He doesn't feel the cold."

"We could change places if it bothers you so much, miss," a male voice said over Charmaine's shoulder.

She jumped two feet in the air. When her boots hit the ground, Charmaine scrambled behind Jessi. "I can hear him again. Clear. Too clear."

"Damn, interesting how your ability to hear Alt Energy beings comes and goes." Jessi wore a quizzical frown. "Hi, Lucas."

"Hey, Jess. I'm glad you could make it," Lucas said, as if they'd dropped by a late-night wine and cheese gathering.

"I'm here freezing my butt off because you insisted. Now let's skip the polite conversation and get on with it," Jessi snapped.

"Such an attractive derrière, too. I wouldn't want it to freeze off as you put it," Lucas said, a sassy smile implied in his tone. "But as you say, we'll 'get on with it.' There's something you should see."

"Perfect, a grave stroll at midnight," Charmaine muttered. Still, she followed Jessi, who she assumed was following Lucas.

"You can't see him yet?" Jessi whispered.

"Only hear him. And what do mean by *yet?*"

"I figure if your sensory perception is developing, at some point you'll see them, too," Jessi whispered back. "We're in uncharted waters here, as Logan's doctoral advisor puts it."

"Are you discussing me with those geek freaks? I'm not a lab rat." Charmaine drove home her annoyance by poking a finger in Jessi's spine.

"Stop it before you get slapped," Jessi hissed over her shoulder. "You should want answers as much as us. We—"

"Here," Lucas said, his smooth baritone voice soft on the wind.

Charmaine blinked at what looked like empty air. Then she followed Jessi's gaze to where it seemed Lucas was pointing. A white tomb gleamed bright beneath the moon in a clear indigo-blue Louisiana sky. Charmaine gasped as she clutched invisible pearls. Jessi stomped a foot.

"You kidding me? Marie Laveau's tomb. You got us out here risking carjackers, drug dealers, and drive-bys for a tourist trap," Jessi shouted. "If you had a neck I could grab, I'd choke you, Lucas."

"I do not waste your time on nonsense tales told to entertain childish minds," Lucas replied mildly.

"Right. You just wanted to show me a bunch of junk littered around a grave," Jessi shot back.

"If you stop having a temper tantrum and observe, you'd see why I brought you to this place. See there?"

Lucas's insistent tone brought Jessi up short. She studied the area of ground at the foot of the tomb. "Hmm."

"Oh, Lord. This is not good," Charmaine said, reading her sister's thoughts. "Someone is trying to raise spirits."

"*Non, mes petites*. Someone is trying to *raise the dead*," Lucas replied.

The solemn pronouncement seemed to bounce off the headstones and statues around them. A strong breeze picked up at that moment, which produced a moaning sound. Charmaine bumped up against Jessi. She looped arms with her.

"Let's go, Jess," Charmaine breathed from a tight throat.

"Don't be silly. We need to get a good look as this superstitious BS somebody playing at," Jessi said, unbothered by the creepiness of the scene.

Charmaine gulped. "Lucas, you'd tell us if any *dead folks walking* were close by. Right?"

"She hasn't been successful so far, but there have been... consequences," Lucas replied.

"Ah, someone will surely suffer the agonies of hell for such sacrilege," an accented female voice hummed. Except for the forbidding words, the voice sounded silken and musical.

"May I introduce the Widow Paris?" Lucas said.

"Bonsoir, little ladies. Though I prefer Madame Glapion. Considering the extraordinary circumstances, a more informal address between us is in order. Call me Miss Marie. I am older than you, after all." Marie Laveau followed her self-introduction with robust laughter.

"I know all about you," Charmaine stammered. "Your first husband, Jacques Paris, disappeared. You then lived with Louis Glapion until he died around 1855, and—"

Marie laughed again. "Child, no one living or dead knows *all* about *moi.*"

"Yes, ma'am." Charmaine swallowed hard. She clamped her lips together.

"I'm surprised I haven't seen you before. All accounts would indicate you were a powerful force in life. I would expect your energy flow would remain," Jessi said.

"Ah, you are the one who does not believe in God," Miss Marie replied, a note of reproof in her voice.

"Jessi, Madame," Lucas said.

"I'm Charmaine, um, Miss Marie. Don't worry. I'm working on her." Charmaine yelped when Jessi jabbed her in the side with a sharp elbow.

"Lovely name. I believe I have a tenth niece christened Charmaine," Miss Marie said.

"Give me a freakin' break. Enough tea ladies' front-parlor chatter. After two hundred years you show up. Why?"

"Show some respect to your elder, by about two hundred years, in fact," Miss Marie clipped. "I know much that you could learn, though tethered to this dismal patch of earth."

"She can't roam freely like me. We're not sure why," Lucas explained.

"*Eh bien*, small matter to me. I knew all that happened in the best boudoirs of old New Orleans without leaving my courtyard. Even now my sparrows flock to bring me news," Miss Marie said.

"Not so bad. We get plenty of admirers. The tourists," Lucas added, his comment directed at Charmaine.

"Right," Charmaine replied. She smiled in the direction of his voice.

"So, what am I supposed to be looking at?" Jessi cut in with impatience. She waved a hand at Miss Marie's tomb. "I see bunches of dead leaves, a necklace, a bowl of black powder. A couple of dolls in coffins. Real cute."

"Sage and other herbs. The amulet is from the Fon people. Beautiful, *oui*? The dolls are made of corn husk dipped in myrrh oil," Miss Marie replied.

"And the powder, Madame?" Lucas asked.

"Each is unique, created by the one using it based on what they're trying to do. Set on fire, I think, to increase the power. I would guess the usual, but there is something bitter mixed

in. Some kind of poisonous weed. Fools!" Miss
Marie made a spitting sound. Her voice re-
treated as she let out a string of old Creole
French.

Charmaine jumped. "What's wrong?"

"Madame, non, non. It will be all right. The
Joliet sisters are here," Lucas said. He continued in Creole French as well, his voice fading.

"Something upset her is all. Turns out the
Voodoo Queen is more drama queen," Jessi
replied with a nervous laugh. She turned in a
circle to scan the area.

"Everyone stay calm," Lucas said, his voice
close by once more.

"Pfft, I'm always calm," Miss Marie protested. "I don't like bunglers."

"Ahem, Madame means to say someone
has tried to bring her back," Lucas continued.

"Instead, the idiot has set in motion the
means to help the devil have his way. Spirits
that should have been left resting have been
raised. Oh, that Père Antoine was here to help.
Like all saintly souls, he has the eternal peace,"
Miss Marie said.

Charmaine could almost see her making
the sign of the cross. "Madame Glapion was a
very devout Catholic. I'm sure you've earned

peace as well with all the wonderful good you did, nursing the sick and more."

"Such a sweet child, Lucas. I'm glad you brought her here. Are you in the true faith, dear one?" Miss Marie said.

"I'm a Baptist."

"Pity," Miss Marie replied.

"Well, one of my grandfathers was Methodist. But we were raised in the Baptist church. Now I attend churches that are part of the Full Gospel Baptist Fellowship and—"

"She doesn't know what the hell she is, to make a long, boring story short. It's all nonsense," Jessi cut in.

"So, how do you explain us?" Miss Marie asked, amusement in her tone instead of rebuke.

"Geophysics, biophysics, math, and history. Not myths and fairy tales."

Miss Marie laughed like a wise grandmother indulging naive children. "Now who speaks nonsense?"

"Ahem, can we get back to the reason for this visit," Lucas said before Jessi could clap back.

"This is your show, so get on with it," Jessi clipped. She cast a side-eye in Miss Marie's direction. A soft chuckle made her let out a hiss.

"Someone is calling on spirits. I've found at least six of these in the last day or so." Lucas's already whispery ghost voice grew softer.

"Calm your nerves, child," Miss Marie said to him.

"Yeah, Lucas. What are they gonna do? Kill you?" Jessi grinned.

"Seriously, Jess," Charmaine snapped.

"I'm just sayin'." Jessi shrugged, showing no sign of regret.

"There are worse things than death," Lucas replied. All sound seemed to die away at his ominous declaration.

Charmaine glanced around to check for threats. "Maybe we should speed this up."

Jessi's grin vanished. "Okay, so what's different? You can't swing a dead black cat in New Orleans without hitting somebody who dabbles in the supernatural. Most of them are fakes. Some honestly believe they have supernormal abilities when they don't."

"*Oui*. It was so in my day as well. Harmless amateurs. But now..." Miss Marie's tone made them all look at the assortment of items at her tomb again.

"Okay, you've seen these items before," Jessi said. She glanced at Charmaine when Miss Marie didn't answer and seconds ticked by.

"My grandmother told me stories about a notorious *hougan* in Saint Domingue," Miss Marie began. "He lost control of a loa he called up. Well, only the foolish think they can control a loa. More likely, he thought to use one and send it away. Arrogance can have deadly results, *mes petites*."

"A word to the wise. We'll remember," Charmaine murmured.

"Ah, but you try to banish or how to say it... redirect spirits. For this one with the sharp tongue, they find her attractive. Why, I don't know. Bad-tempered little thing." Miss Marie tsk-tsked, much to Jessi's annoyance.

"We've both been through tough times because of our abilities," Charmaine said fast, before Jessi could offend.

"Èskize mon. I know only too well about hardships. *Mais oui*," Miss Marie replied with a sigh. "I shall be more tolerant of the child's moods"

"I'm a grown-ass woman," Jessi said, though her voice was low and some of the fire gone.

"Madame Glapion is well over two hundred years old, or would be if alive," Lucas whispered. "I think she has a right to call us all children."

Miss Marie continued as if she hadn't noticed their side conversation. "Life was hard for *gens de couleur.* And women? *Mon Dieu,* terrible!"

"Sorry to say not much has changed, Madame," Charmaine said.

"So, someone has made the same mistake as this voodoo priest back in the day," Jessi said. "Maybe it's him."

"*Non, non.* He died when Maman Catherine was young. I don't think she'd borne her first child yet. Still, the damage he did with one reckless act brought destruction for years. I fear the same will be true in this place."

"His energy has returned, then," Jessi advanced.

"Or someone has conjured him up," Lucas said. His voice grew faint, no more than a swish of feather. As if he would fade away to escape the danger.

"We're not going down the superstition rabbit hole," Jessi replied in her best crisp, rationalist tone. "Someone has tried to harness electromagnetic energy for her own purposes."

"Energy?" Miss Marie's puzzlement came through clearly.

"Someone called up his spirit or ghost. If he was powerful and left such a strong effect in this world then..." Charmaine said. She shivered when a cold breeze stirred leaves around their feet. She and Jessi turned in a circle to scan the immediate area.

"*Mon Dieu*, that would be a bad thing. A very bad thing," Miss Marie breathed.

"Here's your chance to live up to your reputation, show us it wasn't all hype." Jessi smiled at the spot where Miss Marie must have stood.

Charmaine jabbed Jessi in the ribs with an elbow. "So disrespectful. I'm sorry, Miss Marie. Jessi likes to provoke people."

"Oh, I understand her better than she knows. So, you expect me to join this... what does she call it, Lucas?" Miss Marie asked.

"Shadow Squad, Madame," Lucas said, his voice somewhat stronger.

"*Oui*, your Shadow Squad of informants. I used such methods in my time. However, I'm no mere tool, a source of gossip like some servant girl." Miss Marie sniffed.

"What else have you got to do for eternity?" Jessi quipped.

"Ah, ma cherie. You'd be surprised," Miss Marie replied, a wealth of humor and mischief in her voice.

Chapter 9

A Ghosts of a Chance

"What the hell do you think you're doing?" Scotty paced back and forth in front of Charmaine's desk in her home office.

"Answering questions way too early in the morning on an empty stomach, for one," Charmaine shot back.

"This ain't a joke, Charmaine. Explain why," Scotty demanded.

"Oh, I don't know. Helping out a friend being stalked by a psycho ex, maybe?" Charmaine yawned. She hadn't planned on starting her Thursday morning with drama. Scotty had other plans.

"Rochelle ain't my *ex* anything," Scotty thundered. He stopped, hands on his narrow waist.

"I see why she's addicted. You're gorgeous when you're pissed off." Charmaine gave his muscular frame an appreciative head-to-toe gaze.

Dressed in a lightweight, dark-green sweater over jeans, his six-foot-two brand of handsome dressed up any room. Charmaine continued to look at him. She wondered why she kidded herself. The tingle she felt had nothing to do with thinking of him as a brother. Maybe she'd just gone too long without a good, solid episode of sweaty sex.

Scotty blinked hard, his gaze on the pale-pink lace covering her cleavage. Her t-shirt and coordinating lounge pants weren't exactly Victoria's Secret seductive. Still, he swallowed hard as if thinking in the same vein as Charmaine. "I'm used to handling my own business."

Charmaine heaved a deep sigh. She secretly enjoyed the way he blinked fast at the rise and fall of her full breasts. "Okay, maybe I overstepped."

"Yeah, you could say that," Scotty said, still staring at her.

"But a man fighting back against a woman is at a distinct disadvantage. Rochelle could easily claim you're the one attacking *her*. She'll play the defenseless, weak female victim being menaced by a man with a history of violence. And military hand-to-hand combat training." Charmaine stood from the chair behind her desk. She walked to him.

"You could get arrested, too," Scotty said. Anger had melted from his voice.

Charmaine placed a palm on his chest. "We just talked to her. Well, Jessi and Diamond did."

"You mean threatened. She called the bar, yelling I sent ghetto hit-women to get her," Scotty said. His gaze shifted to Charmaine's thick, natural hair halo.

"If those two wanted to hurt her, Rochelle would have been calling from the trauma center," Charmaine joked. She turned and let him watch her walk away. "You want some... coffee? You must, since you come busting up in here at seven in the damn a.m."

Scotty caught up with her and grabbed her arm. He spun her around to face him. "Don't swish off from me. This is serious."

"Believe me, I know," Charmaine said, her face tilted up a few inches from his.

The kiss, long and full of passion, came as no surprise. And she let it happen. Scotty moaned soft and deep in his throat. She felt the flow of his thoughts. His mind roiled with surprise at his own actions and delighted at the taste of her mouth. Charmaine guided both his large hands to her breasts under the t-shirt.

"No bra. Have mercy," Scotty gasped as his fingers brushed her skin.

"No mercy," Charmaine replied.

Clothes flew off as though caught in a Louisiana tornado. All of the pent-up sexual tension they'd denied broke the dam of restraint. Charmaine threw every bit of erotic intensity she had on him, leaving the poor dude panting her name like a mantra. Released from the fiction of platonic friendship, more than sex happened. Emotion shook Charmaine to the core. Two hours later, they lay tangled together. They'd moved from the thick imitation Moroccan rug on her office floor to Charmaine's bed. She tried to pull free and slide from the smooth sheets, but Scotty held on.

"Don't get scared on me," he murmured.

"What are you talking about?" Charmaine tugged against his firm grasp for a second and then gave up.

"You think I can't read you like you read other people? We've been too close too long. I know why you like jumping from guy to guy. Safety. Control."

"You're not psychic or a therapist." Charmaine pushed against him and he released her.

"I'm not here to hurt or own you, Charmaine," Scotty said.

"And I'm not scared of either. You want your eggs scrambled or over-easy this time?"

Charmaine padded into her en suite bathroom before he could answer. She took a shower and dressed again. Scotty lay staring at the ceiling the entire time. He didn't say a word as she headed to the kitchen. Seconds later, she heard the shower and him thumping around in the bedroom. He emerged ten minutes later with a men's shaver in one hand. He placed it on the table in her breakfast nook.

"You seeing somebody special that stays over?" Scotty eased his bulk into a chair, elbows propped on the table as he looked out the window.

"So, you're going straight into jealous-lover mode. I'm disappointed." Charmaine banged the skillet hard on the stove.

Scotty sighed and rubbed a large hand over his face. "I didn't mean... Look, we can agree to see other people until we decide—"

"Decide what? That we want to register at Dillard's and post happy couple photos online?" Charmaine tossed out the half pot of coffee. "That's going to taste bitter after sitting for two hours. Might as well start over."

"Like you want to erase what happened between us this morning, I guess. Run away from the past. Don't talk about it, and it didn't happen." Scotty sounded more sad than angry with her.

"Look, I've talked out my past more than you. Therapy, remember? Plenty of times. So, don't try that fucking mind game with me. You have no idea what—" Charmaine swallowed hard.

"Yeah, I do. But I'm not going to fight with you," Scotty said calmly. He got up, grabbed the glass coffee pot, and rinsed it out. Then he set about making a fresh pot.

"Don't know what you're talking about," Charmaine muttered. She gave him an angry side-eye. Then she got eggs and sausage from the refrigerator.

"A big knock-down, drag-out to give you an excuse to push me away. Ain't gonna happen." Scotty got two plates out of one overhead cabinet.

Jessi let herself in through the side door into the kitchen just as he finished. "What's not happening? Fill me in on what I missed. Morning, all. So sweet of you to start breakfast for me."

"Morning." Scotty spoke over one shoulder as he got another plate and cup for her.

"Hey." Charmaine concentrated on cracking eggs into a bowl.

"I walked in on a serious-ass discussion. I know what it's about, too. Might as well get it all out on the table." Jessi dropped her leather tote-styled bag on the floor in a corner.

"What happens in my house is my business. Just keep out of it," Charmaine blurted out with force.

"Okay, but..." Jessi blinked at her in bewilderment. Then she looked at Scotty.

"You do know Rochelle could press charges against you two? Diamond has a child at home to consider. How y'all think you can roll up on folks with threats and shit is beyond me," Scotty said.

Jessi continued to look from him to Charmaine for a few seconds. Then she cleared her throat. "I'd say 'outlined her options' is a more accurate description. We pointed out that her behavior might give her husband ammunition in the custody battle. Obsessed woman with violent tendencies won't play well in court."

"You're willing to ruin her life by helping him take her kids. Real nice, Jessi." Scotty shook his head as he went back to helping with breakfast. He put slices of bread in the toaster. Then he sliced the sausage links in half.

Charmaine stopped stirring the eggs in her nonstick skillet. "I can do it. Have a seat and keep fussing at Jess."

Scotty pushed away her attempt to take the knife from his hand. "I've got the grill plate ready. Just relax."

"I'm fine. Unbothered and chill as hell. My kitchen, my rules," Charmaine insisted.

"You're gonna let the eggs scorch." Scotty nodded at the stove. He went back to his task when she hissed and spun around. "Y'all was wrong for that, Jessi."

"Look, Rochelle put herself in this position. Not us. You're crazy if you don't think her husband would have found out. He's hired Nick Moise. Moise specializes in representing men in family court against wives and girl-friends. He's a snake, but he's a sharp snake. I know his paralegal. She happens to moonlight as a private investigator like me."

"And?" Scotty turned from the sizzling meat and crossed his arms.

"*And*, the guy hired him Monday. Took off work early for the meet. I'll bet Iesha, that's his paralegal, will be following her this weekend. If she hasn't started already." Jessi sat back and crossed her legs at the table.

"Damn, he's going to divorce her." Scotty heaved a sigh.

"Not your fault. Rochelle and him been playing around on each other for a couple of years. Things went downhill after their third kid was born," Jessi said. She got up and grabbed a slice of toast. "Where's the butter?"

Scotty went back to the grill plate. He flipped the sausages over. "What a mess."

"One you didn't create. Unhappy marriages and divorce are a sad fact of life," Jessi replied.

"I can see you're all broken up about it," Scotty retorted.

"I didn't make the world, bruh. If Rochelle's got any sense, she'll concentrate on getting a new job and being a good mama," Jessi countered.

"I thought she had a job at that new hipster Creole and Japanese fusion sushi café on Magazine Street," Scotty said.

"Got fired last week. She made going after you her career."

"Hmm." Charmaine didn't look at Jessi. Instead, she took care to scoop the cooked eggs into a warm bowl.

Jessi placed the butter plate on the table along with a jar of honey. She buttered the toast and then drizzled honey on the slices. "I'm helping fix breakfast and your life. And for free, to top it off. You're welcome."

"Yeah," Scotty said.

"Hmm, what's up with you two?" Jessi bit into a slice of toast.

"Nothing," Charmaine said fast. She put the eggs on the table and sat.

"Same routine," Scotty added. He sat in the chair across from Charmaine. They avoided looking at each other. Several minutes of silence stretched as they all dug into the food.

"Uh-huh. Yeah." Jessi continued to study them as she chewed slowly.

"So, what's happening with your case and Eli Locke? Lots of crazy developments. A ghost invasion, his assistant in a coma, and him beat up," Scotty said after a time. He glanced at Jessi instead of Charmaine.

"Not to mention the grunch are real and involved somehow," Jessi added.

"My grandmother used to scare us into behaving by saying the grunch was watching."

" 'Truth is stranger than fiction' ain't just a cliché." Jessi nodded at him.

"A lot of legends have some basis in fact. It's just the re-telling gets exaggerated or distorted," Charmaine offered.

"Yeah, so anyway, the grunch isolated themselves over a hundred years ago because of the way folks treated them. Most still live in New Orleans East, but they keep a low-pro. I don't blame 'em at all," Jessi continued.

"And you think they're in on the murders, the ghosts running loose, and intimidating Locke. Just. Wow."

"We're not sure," Charmaine said. "They're certainly a tight-knit and organized community. And they know him. Or least some of them do."

"Yeah, he had an affair with the sister of one." Jessi raised an eyebrow at him. "And it didn't end well. The woman is missing."

Scotty's dark eyebrows went up. "Presumed dead, right?"

"Some think so," Jessi said. "By the way, I couldn't find records they got married. Probably lived together common-law."

"Sounds like motive, means, and possible opportunity to me," Scotty replied.

"But if it's them, I don't get why they'd wait years to get revenge. They could have been much more direct. Made him disappear, too." Charmaine looked from Scotty to Jessi.

"Would be neater, less complicated. I don't get why they'd toss spirits into the mix." Jessi didn't let reviewing theories spoil her meal. She put a forkful of eggs in her mouth and chewed.

"Yeah," Charmaine agreed and drank coffee.

"Hmm, great food, Charmaine," Scotty said after a time.

"I scrambled a few eggs and put them in a bowl. Not exactly breakfast at Brennan's," Charmaine wisecracked.

"But still. Nice to start with—"

"You've eaten over here plenty of times. Nothing special about today," Charmaine broke in.

"Well, um, we haven't hung out in a minute, so..." Scotty gazed at her, but Charmaine gave full attention to slicing the sausage on her plate.

Jessi chewed in silence for a few seconds. Then she swallowed a gulp of coffee. "Y'all wanna tell me we're really talkin' 'bout?"

"It's pretty obvious we're talking about breakfast," Charmaine clipped.

Jessi put her cup down. "I don't—"

Scotty stood. "Well, I better get moving. I got a consulting job helping a new restaurant open. The owners are a corporate outfit based in Dallas. First time entering the market here."

"Sounds interesting," Charmaine put in quickly.

"Brings in extra cash, more than one income stream," Scotty said.

"Makes sense. Don't put all your eggs in one basket." Charmaine giggled.

Scotty burst into a too-loud chuckle. "I see what you did, but maybe you meant all in one *bowl*."

"Whatever, man."

Charmaine followed him to the door. She turned on the radio. The sound of a rowdy popular morning show blasted through. They made small talk a few seconds more as they walked, the music layered over it.

"I think we should talk about us," Scotty said low after making a trivial remark louder.

"See, this is why I didn't want to... I knew things would get funky if we, you know," Charmaine whispered. Then she gave him a playful push like she'd done before and raised her voice again. "Oh, shut up talking crazy."

"See you, Jessi," Scotty called out as he waved to her.

"Bye-bye." Jessi lifted the cup to her face, one eyebrow cocked.

Charmaine shooed him toward the kitchen door. Once he was gone, she locked it. Then she picked up his plate and hers from the table. She hummed as she hand-washed dishes. Jessi rose a few minutes later and turned off the radio. She leaned against the counter next to Charmaine.

"That was awkward," Jessi said.

"What?" Charmaine didn't look at her.

"Me busting up in here before y'all had a chance to have the 'after-hot-sex' talk. Looking at what it means, what happens next—"

"Don't be ridiculous," Charmaine clipped. She dried dishes with aggressive swipes.

"No judgment from me. Scotty's fine as hell. I knew that platonic, 'he's like a brother' crap wouldn't last." Jessi's smirk grew wider when Charmaine glared at her.

"Shut up about it."

"Ah-ha! I just remembered. Diamond owes me twenty dollars. I told her y'all couldn't hold out forever." Jessi did a little dance of triumph.

"I can't believe y'all. Taking bets on my personal life. Gee, thanks." Charmaine threw the dishcloth on the counter.

"Scotty works hard. Got his own income. Girl, we should be planning a party." Jessi poked Charmaine in the side with an elbow.

"Sex changes everything." Charmaine sighed.

"Hasn't before. Guys have come and gone, literally," Jessi quipped. She grew serious when Charmaine muttered curse words. "Okay, okay. I can see you're really worried. I get it."

"Get what?" Charmaine went back to her cleanup.

"What's between you and Scotty is way more than sex. You almost complete each other's sentences sometimes. You're scared the craziness of a relationship will happen and you'll lose him." Jessi brushed a stray tendril of hair from Charmaine's forehead.

"There won't be any craziness. Because it won't happen again, and we'll go back to normal." Charmaine threw the damp dishtowel down again with more force. "Damn it, except we can't just go back to normal now."

Jessi draped an arm around Charmaine's shoulder. "It's gone be a'ight, sis. I'm telling you."

"And how would you know?"

"You and Scotty are the most unscrewed-up people I know. And with my circle, that's saying a lot."

"Aw, thank you. I feel *so* much better after our little pep talk." Charmaine gave her a push, and Jessi pushed back. They got into an affectionate shoving match for a few seconds.

"Don't put off the talk, though. You better decide if you really want to push him back to the friendship circle or take it to the next level." Jessi put away dry plates and saucers.

"Yeah. I just need time to clear my head," Charmaine replied.

"Daaamn, it was that mind-blowing? My man Scott Edison Minor on the case!" Jessi did a suggestive bump and grind.

"Oh, shut up." Charmaine slapped her shoulder. "Since you mentioned being on the case..."

"Change of subject to keep me from dragging more details out of you."

"Jess," Charmaine warned.

"Okay, okay." Jessi held up both palms in surrender.

"What exactly did you two outlaws say to Rochelle?" Charmaine shook a finger at Jessi's nose.

"What I told Scotty, except I lied about the investigator part. And the lawyer part. And the part about—"

"I get the idea. Tell me the *real* story."

Charmaine grabbed a broom to sweep any stray crumbs from the kitchen floor. Jessi snorted but said nothing. She showed admirable restraint from the usual jokes about Charmaine's cleaning obsession.

"Right. So, far as we can find out. I mean me and Kat. By the way, she's damn good at finding info. Guess it comes from being a real estate broker and looking up facts on clients. Anyways, Rochelle's husband has consulted the lawyer I mentioned, but he's holding out one last chance to get her back. He's hoping she comes to her senses," Jessi said.

"Sounds like a good guy. I mean, I know you said he's been cheating, too. But still." Charmaine swept dirt into a dustpan and dumped it.

"Yeah. He's trying to change, looks like."

Charmaine put the broom back in a small utility closet. "So, will she? Come to her senses I mean."

"I'm beginning to wonder if she has any left," Jessi wisecracked. "The woman thinks Scotty is her dream-come-true Mr. Right. You're the psycho expert. You tell me why she's lost her damn mind."

"We prefer to be called behavioral health professionals, thank you." Charmaine frowned as she considered Jessi's blunt question anyway. "I'd have to know more of her history. Scotty may remind her of a loving father figure from childhood. He's kind, level-headed, good at business, and did nice things for her. He went the extra mile for his other employees. But because she was left in charge at times, and they worked closer than the others, she might feel special. Like he was treating her different."

"Then he made the mistake of laying some of that good Scotty lovin' on her." Jessi wiggled her eyebrows.

"That was around the time one of his friends committed suicide. I was wrapped up in the tricky case we had at the time. Shoulda been there for him." Charmaine heaved a sigh.

She went to put leftover sausage in the fridge. Jessi grabbed a piece as she passed.

"Hey, don't start with the guilt trip on yourself. Geez, anybody would think we were raised Catholic. He kept it to himself, like he does about a lot of his military days."

"I know. Still, I should have read him, noticed something was wrong." Charmaine shook her head as if banishing regrets. "Back to Rochelle."

"Like I told Scotty a minute ago, we pointed out the possible consequences. I said to her, I said, 'Look, girl. You better decide if stalking Scotty is worth losing your kids. Getting arrested and having a court-ordered psych exam ain't a good look in custody court.' Can't believe she called Scotty to complain." Jessi laughed.

"Rochelle's also had her lawyer call to warn him about sending thugs to harass her. Scotty pointed out that he had grounds to file a complaint with the cops on his client. The guy backed down once he saw Scotty wasn't intimidated. In the end, the guy agreed to talk to Rochelle about her actions," Charmaine said.

"Between our chat with her and her lawyer, maybe Rochelle will calm her ass down."

"Check to see if she has access to a gun. Pays to be safe, not sorry. Stalkers have been known to escalate when confronted." Charmaine frowned at the prospect of a vengeful and armed rejected lover.

"I'll get on it this morning before I head to the office. By the way, Kat did some checking around on Locke's local real estate holdings. Our murder victim was a contractor who renovated three properties for Locke."

"Rayvon Woods worked for him?" Charmaine blinked when Jessi nodded. "Another coincidence. And the first victim, Amanda..."

"Morrell," Jessi said. "She lived in New York and socialized in the same circles as Locke. Is it me or do you see a pattern? People who might know something about his past, either personal or business, end up dead."

"He's taking out anyone who might snitch on him," Charmaine murmured, testing out the sound of Jessi's theory. "Or one of them blackmailed him. But then he'd kill off that person. Why go after Amanda and Becca?"

"Or set loose a bunch of spirits in New Orleans. I don't see any kind of logic to it, but that doesn't mean it's not there. Too bad one of those entities isn't around to tell us." Jessi's eyes widened seconds after her last sentence.

She bounced on the balls of her feet with excitement.

"What?" Charmaine stared at her. Jessi looked the same as when she was kid about to get them both in trouble.

"We talked to Miss Marie. No reason why we shouldn't try to get in touch with—"

"Oh no. No. No. No." Charmaine shook her head hard. "Uh-uh. Forget it."

"Might as well get the story from the horse's mouth. Miss Marie can help us." Jessi ignored Charmaine's continued, almost-incoherent protests against the idea.

"You've lost your everlasting mind. I knew it might happen eventually, all the risks we take stirring up the unnatural." Charmaine waved her arms like pinwheels.

Jessi rooted through her bag. "Sounds like you're quoting Bishop Holy-Roller. Nonsense. Nothing unnatural about alternative forms of life energy at all."

"Jess, people have ended up dead. Messy dead. Painfully dead. Not slipped-away-peaceful-in-their-sleep kinda dead." Charmaine's voice rose as she spoke, maybe in an attempt to get Jessi's attention.

"Ah-ha! Here it is. I found this in an antique store on Religious Street." Jessi waved a worn small leather-bound book over her head.

"The irony of that street name probably didn't occur to you," Charmaine retorted.

"The Art of Creole Conjure," Jessi said, too enthused to hear or care. "Written in 1817. You won't be surprised to know Madame Glapion, aka Marie Laveau, is mentioned *a lot*. Gotta hand it to her. She was a boss when it came to PR."

Charmaine stomped a foot. "Jess."

"You have to stomach racism from the author. Product of his times, blah-blah-blah. Though, to his credit, he didn't believe in slavery," Jessi continued.

"You can't be serious. Meeting up with ghosts who can help us, who haven't been violent in life or after, is one thing. But you want to—"

Jessi, her dark brown eyes bright, gazed ahead into nothing. She was no longer in Charmaine's homey cottage on Esplanade Avenue. Instead, Jessi looked ahead to the adventure of her psychic detective lifetime. She nodded slowly. Then she faced her sister. "Yes. We're going to have a meetup with the infamous Axeman of New Orleans."

"The bishop is right. We're going straight to hell." Charmaine covered her face with both hands.

"Before we do, we're gonna get a preview," Jessi said with glee. She giggled hard as Charmaine let out a groan.

****

Saturday afternoon they sat in Penelope Fayard's New Orleans East home once again. Afternoon sunlight would quickly fade on the fall day. Yet the living room seemed bright enough despite the circumstances. Diamond had begged to come along, having dropped off her daughter with an aunt. Now she seemed to have lost her eagerness to meet the legendary grunch up close and personal. Charmaine sipped herbal tea to calm her nerves. They all listened as Penelope's humming came from the kitchen. The aroma of baked goodies filled the house.

"Shouldn't you wait until Halloween night? I mean, you might be able to call on the Shadow Squad and a few others for backup. You gonna need all the help you can get." Diamond twisted her hands together.

"Don't be silly. There is nothing special about All Hallows' Eve. I like the sound of that better. More poetic. Now, where is..." Jessi searched another large tote. She used it to carry a full arsenal of trade tools.

"I'm gonna start calling you The Bag Lady of New Orleans," Diamond teased. "You've got a closet full of 'em, I bet."

"Not quite, but almost. I need a variety, depending on the equipment I need for our fieldwork," Jessi replied, unbothered by the joke.

"Fieldwork. Nice description for Going-to-Meet-Our-Doom," Charmaine muttered.

"I think Charmaine is scared," Diamond said in a stage whisper. Then she imitated creepy wailing while waving her hands. She laughed when Charmaine rolled her eyes. "I'm coming along. Sounds like it's gonna be big fun."

"You must have missed the part about us trying to get through to the Axeman. This ain't Casper the Friendly Ghost," Charmaine said. She huffed in frustration and helped Jessi organize her gadgets.

"Look at all the ammo y'all going with. Jessi has kicked supernatural butt plenty of times. I trust my home girl." Diamond and Jessi grinned at each other and shared a dap. The intricate hand slaps lasted a few seconds.

"You know I takes care of biz," Jessi replied. She slung a crossbody bag over her head. "I had a local leather shop put an extra pocket here. I can slip my modified stun pistol right in. Easy access."

Jessi sprang up in a demonstration. She spun to face an imaginary threat, smoothly pulling the stunner out and pressing the button. Then she spun the opposite way to use a different device. Diamond yelled encouragement. Penelope came in with a plate of blueberry muffins. She froze in the archway leading into the living room, mouth hanging open.

Charmaine met her halfway and took it from her. "I'm really sorry, Ms. Fayard. Jessi, cut it out."

Penelope blinked for a few seconds and then burst out laughing. "Girl, you lucky I keep a low profile. Otherwise, I'd record this on my cell phone and make you go viral. Whew, Lord!" She fanned her face.

"My mean moves saved our asses more than a few times." Jessi made one last defensive sweep like a martial arts fighter. She finished in fighting stance. "Okay, that was more theatrical than necessary, but you get the idea."

Charmaine set down the muffins on a coffee table. "I'm glad y'all all happy to be facing down a crazed serial-killing spirit."

Penelope stopped mid-chuckle, her expression sober in an instant. "Oh, yeah. The murders."

"Which someone is more than willing to blame on the grunch—excuse the word," Charmaine added when Penelope winced.

"That kind of exposure would ruin our businesses. Hell, it would ruin our lives," Penelope said.

"People saw something they couldn't explain connected to a horrible event. It's natural they'd fall back on an old story," Jessi argued. "I say it's a stretch someone is trying to deliberately blame the community."

"Eli was married to one of their descendants. He's been visiting New Orleans for years and researched local history. He's written a book about them." Charmaine ticked off each point on her fingers.

"You think it's him, huh? I thought you was sweet on the dude," Jessi joked.

"He ain't *that* cute. Everybody is a suspect," Charmaine shot back.

"And besides, Scotty done knocked old Eli outta the running now," Jessi wisecracked. She put a hand over her mouth the second the last word died away. "Oops."

Diamond's head whipped around to Charmaine. "Get it, girl. He fine."

"End of discussion," Charmaine hissed with a death stare at Jessi.

"Just as well you don't get romantically involved with Locke. Lydia vanished. The Morrell girl is dead. His assistant as good as." Penelope's soft voice made the words sound even more ominous.

"Covering his tracks to keep even more skeletons locked in his closet." Charmaine said what they were all thinking.

"Y'all thought about looking into his past relationships for more bodies?" Diamond asked, looking around at the others.

"Checking out any other missing friends and lovers is on my to-do list," Jessi said. "But right now, we're going ghost-busting."

Diamond stood. "Great. I'm ready."

"You're not bringing the ghost of the Axe-man to my house," Penelope squeaked.

"Of course we won't." Charmaine patted Penelope's shoulder.

"Okay. Where we goin'?" Diamond looked at Jessi.

"To Hambrick's Haunted Funeral Home on Michoud Boulevard."

Chapter 10

Dead Man Talking

The official name of the funeral home didn't include the word *haunted*. The Hambrick family had roots in New Orleans that stretched back seven generations. However, they'd only been in the death business since the late 1930s. They were among the most prominent and prosperous black families of their day. The present generation, however, had transitioned into less-grim occupations. They didn't hide their history, yet they weren't eager to highlight that embalming and grave-digging had financed private school educations.

Located in New Orleans East on Michoud Boulevard, the last of their three funeral homes had closed in the 1970s. Many influential, local black socialites, politicians, and community leaders had ended up 'clients.' In fact, having your loved one's last rites handled by Hambrick's was a status symbol for many years. The Victorian mansion built in 1872 had been purchased by Benjamin Hambrick in 1885. His grandson converted to a full-service funeral home in the 1930s. Within five years, stories of the building being haunted began to circulate. By the 1960s, the family gave up trying to dispel the rumors. They sold the property to a company that opened it for ghost tours. It changed hands twice more and now sat vacant and newly renovated.

"You know, I think it would have been a better idea for Kat to come instead of me after all," Diamond said from the back seat of Jessi's Jeep.

"Kat had to work. Scotty's new bartender and server didn't last long. The restaurant business is cutthroat competitive," Jessi replied in a conversational tone. No one listening would have guessed she was on her way to meet a murderous ghost.

"I'm sure you could reschedule for her next day off?"

Charmaine looked at Diamond over one shoulder. "You were all hot to come along a minute ago. Who's scared now, huh?"

"Uh, it's not... I just don't wanna get in the way. Y'all got more experience than me." Diamond cleared her throat.

"You won't have to operate the machinery, Dee. Just follow our lead. Help me set up the barriers outside, and you can stay in the car. If any extra-natural energy forces come out to play, they won't break through." Jessi gave Diamond a thumbs-up gesture to encourage her.

"Probably," Charmaine put in.

Diamond leaned forward until her head poked between the two front seats. "Say what?"

"Jessi hasn't actually used her latest system, the EMF restraint devices. In theory, they would act like those invisible electric dog gates. Keep them confined to an area," Charmaine said.

"A means of protection for the public while we're working. I'm also testing a noise-cancellation or sound-dampening system. That way, we won't draw attention, either," Jessi added.

"Oh." Diamond gulped.

"Yeah, ghost-hunting and elimination can get noisy. Messy, too." Charmaine suppressed a smirk to maintain a serious expression. "But you've got complete confidence in your girl Jessi."

"Uh, right. What could go wrong?" Diamond swallowed hard again. "In a haunted funeral home with the Axeman wandering around."

"Well, we're not sure he'll show up." Jessi focused more on the task ahead. She didn't appear tuned into Diamond's anxiety.

"He could be off somewhere else. Far, far away," Diamond said, her voice tinged with hope.

"I brought artifacts I think draw him here. Items from the scenes of two crimes." Jessi jerked a thumb over a shoulder in the direction of her bag of tricks in back of the Jeep.

"How did you come by those?" Charmaine cocked her head to one side.

"A spirit in my Shadow Squad came through. She knows ghosts who lived next to the Maggio family, a couple of his victims. I got in touch with descendants. They have antiques from one of the original Italian grocery stores," Jessi replied, wheeling the Jeep around a slow-moving truck.

Charmaine looked at Jessi hard. "I'm surprised they let you have them."

"I didn't steal them. For real," Jessi added when Charmaine continued to squint at her. "A great niece sold them to me cheap. She was happy to get rid of them. Gruesome souvenirs, in her words. One woman's trash, as they say."

"Good. We don't need any more bad mojo," Charmaine said.

"With familiar pieces connected to him, I think we'll get lucky." Jessi nodded. She held up a stun gun for Diamond.

Diamond took it and shrank against the backseat again. "Yeah, lucky us."

They drove for another fifteen minutes in silence. Jessi radiated anticipation. Charmaine felt grim determination. She fidgeted with a couple of Jessi's modified "EMF disrupters," stun guns with electromagnetic wires to "shock" a spirit. If she was going to be faced with a crazed dead murderer, Charmaine intended to be well-prepared. Diamond's murmuring from the backseat sounded like a cross between street rap and a fervent prayer. She gasped when Jessi parked in front of the historic funeral home.

"King Jesus, if you can spare a couple of warrior angels, that would be double awesome. Amen," Diamond breathed.

Jessi swung the door open and hopped to the ground. "Damn, Dee. You're falling into that religious nonsense trap, too? You better put some steel in your spine, girl." Jessi jabbed a forefinger at her like a drill sergeant reprimanding a soldier.

"Okay," Diamond squeaked. She swung the rear door open, put one foot on the pavement, and cast a glance around.

Jessi slapped the belt around her waist. Two small holsters held compact gadgets. She strode to the back of the jeep. Seconds later she returned with the duffle bag slung over her shoulder. Charmaine joined them both on the sidewalk. All three stood looking at the two-story structure. White columns typical of late nineteenth-century architecture went up both floors. Both had porches facing the street. A light shone in one window on each.

"We cocked, locked, and ready to rock?" Jessi eyed them like they were her troops.

Charmaine stared at the mansion. "I guess."

Diamond swallowed hard. "Uh..."

"Y'all sure you wanna go through with this?" A male voice said from the darkness.

"Jeez!" Charmaine jumped enough distance to reach the side of the Jeep.

"Oh no." Diamond tried to run, but Jessi grabbed her right arm and snatched her back.

"Evening. Didn't mean to sneak up on y'all," the man said.

"Hey, Kareem," Jessi said and chuckled with him. "You did that shit on purpose. Relax, everybody. Kareem has a janitorial service contract to clean Hambrick's. He's gonna let us in with his keys."

"Here ya go." Kareem grinned at them. He handed Charmaine and Diamond an embossed business card. "Read my reviews online. I have contracts with fifteen businesses in the area. Satisfied customers, every one of 'em."

Charmaine scanned the card and then look up at him, eyebrows raised. "I'm sure your client here wouldn't be thrilled you're letting us in tonight."

"Nah, it ain't a problem. Y'all new to my night-cleaning crew. Right?" Kareem winked at her before he turned to Jessi. She slipped him a roll of bills, and Kareem shoved the money into a pocket of his jeans.

"Yep, this is our second job. Everybody could use extra money these days," Jessi said.

"Hashtag truth. Even better, one of the owners is hoping you up the body count, so to speak. More ghosts, bigger profits." Kareem spread his arms wide, a wide grin on his chocolate-brown face.

"They know about us?" Charmaine blinked at him.

"Let's just say he made an executive decision without stressing his partners with details. Right this way, ladies." Kareem unclipped a crowded ring of keys from a loop on his utility belt. Then he strode up the steps.

"So, your workers are inside and haven't been bothered?" Diamond looked relieved by his laid-back demeanor. She climbed the first stone step.

"We ain't afraid of no ghosts," Kareem sang, pleased at her delighted giggle.

Charmaine jerked Jessi aside before she could follow him. "I'd bet good money the owner paid him, too."

"Hey, don't hate the player; join the game. Besides, it's not out of our cash flow. Locke paid Kareem's *consultation fee.* Sweet, huh?" Jessi gave Charmaine's shoulder a slap and walked ahead.

"I can't believe you." Charmaine huffed as she trotted to catch up.

"Kareem letting us into the funeral home is a legitimate expense." Jessi turned to face her. "Fight me."

Charmaine couldn't argue with her logic. "Okay, fine. But this still feels... I don't know... skeazy."

"You need to stop being brainwashed by Bishop What's-His-Name. Who, by the way, stuffs his pockets every chance he gets. Now, c'mon. We got work to do." Jessi bounced up the four stone steps.

"The appeal for tithes is to finance a long list of worthy ministries," Charmaine called after her. Her argument reached empty air because Charmaine was alone. Feeling more than a bit foolish, she followed the others inside.

White-painted double doors had beveled glass set in the top half. Charmaine let out a hiss of surprise when she stepped into the entryway. Polished tiles in a black-and-white diamond pattern covered the floor. What must have been the front parlor was through an arched opening to her right. A matching room just as large was to the left of the foyer. A crystal chandelier lit up the interior. White artificial lilies filled a tall vase on a table in the middle.

"This isn't so bad," Diamond said.

"My people finished cleaning an hour ago. Weekends are big, so this being Friday we do the place right. Especially with Halloween a little over a week away." Kareem strolled over to a wall. "Lemme set the real mood."

He flipped a switch, and the lights dimmed until the foyer looked gloomy. Heavy, old-fashioned furniture served to heightened the effect. The artificial flowers and vase cast a creepy, long shadow. Charmaine felt a chill at the abrupt change in appearance. The stair-case, oak-stained dark, seemed to offer a fore-boding invitation to explore the upper floors. At the visitor's own peril.

"Oh." Diamond put a hand to her throat. She spun as if she'd heard a noise behind her.

"Pops and crackles ain't nothing but hun-dred-year-old wood settling. You're gonna be creaky when you get old, too. But that's a long way off, pretty woman." Kareem gave Dia-mond's hourglass figure an appreciative once-over. She wore stretch jeans, military-style boots, and a black leather jacket.

Diamond's vigilance didn't waver, nor did she notice his flirtation. "If you say so."

"I know every corner of this place. All that talk about hauntings is for tourists. Three years cleaning it and not even a cold chill." Kareem crossed to Diamond and put a hand on the small of her back. "I swear. Only thing I've heard is vacuum cleaners. You gone be fine."

"Thanks."

"They prepped the bodies in what used to be the kitchen. I'll show you. Family added on to the back around 1920." Kareem chattered as he walked away with a gesture for her to follow. His voice echoed as he failed to notice her hesitation.

"Is he kidding?" Diamond whispered as she looked at Jessi and Charmaine. Her wide brown eyes glittered with fear.

"Dee, it was a *funeral* home. Remember?" Jessi rolled her eyes and went off to explore down another hall.

"You were eager to come. Enjoy." Charmaine grinned and went after Jessi.

Kareem came back to the foyer. "Hey, you coming, sweet thing? You gonna like this. The current owners managed to hold onto a couple of the old embalming tables. Some of the equipment, too."

"Umm." Diamond didn't move.

"Or you can wait for us. Alone," Kareem added.

"Stay out here by myself, or go where the undertaker drained dead people. Some choice." Diamond quick-stepped to join Kareem despite her complaint.

"I think we cured Diamond of begging to come along on our stakeouts." Charmaine laughed at their pal's expense.

"Uh-huh." Jessi seemed to have forgotten Diamond—or Charmaine, for that matter. She strode to the center of the room, her intense focus on their surroundings. She held up her EMF detector.

Charmaine gazed at the oblong box that looked like a cell phone from the eighties. "Anything?"

"You want the answer to be no," Jessi said, her tone flat. She gave Charmaine a pointed sideways glance, then moved deeper into the funeral home.

"We need answers, but talking to an axe-swinging spirit is not my preferred option." Charmaine held up a palm when Jessi started to reply. "Yes, yes. The family rented out this fine establishment to a white mortician, and he handled the funeral of two of the Axeman's victims. At least they were thought to be. We don't know for sure."

"All of the archived documents support the Axeman killed those guys. They were Italian, owned stores in Vendetta Alley, their heads were beaten in, throats cut. Among other things done to 'em." Jessi stared at the ceiling as she spoke.

"At least now he's dead, he can't slash and bash people anymore." Charmaine faced the rows of chairs set up for wakes. They stood at the front of the room in a cleared space.

"Except we got four murder victims and poor Becca clinging to life that say otherwise." Jessi transferred her gaze from the ceiling to Charmaine.

"Okay, we've seen a lot since we turned pro at the ghost-chasing game. But our working theory plus trade knowledge says—"

"Spirits don't have the ability to affect the natural physical world," Jessi broke in, quoting conventional wisdom in the psychic investigation field. "Poltergeists being the exception."

"They have limited abilities. Not one case proves they're able to do the kind of bodily damage Harrison described," Charmaine put in. "Which means we're dealing with a very much alive killer."

"Or someone has found a way to use ghosts to kill for him. Or her," Jessi said.

"A supernatural hitman? I say someone, maybe Eli, is using the spirits as a distraction." Charmaine frowned at the loose ends waving around inside her mind.

"You're finally willing to admit Locke might be responsible. Scotty scratched that sex itch good. You ain't lusting after the rich guy now." Jessi grinned at Charmaine.

"Shut your mouth. I didn't—"

Charmaine broke off at the sound of heavy footsteps upstairs. She and Jessi looked up at the plaster medallion overhead. The hanging ceiling light bounced on its chain. Then silence. Creaking. More pounding. Charmaine expected bits of building to fall. The eerie clop-clop continued for several seconds, coming from all sides. Charmaine and Jessi looked at each other, then sprang toward the staircase in sync. They reached the first step when Jessi yanked Charmaine back.

"We need to check on Diamond and Kareem first."

"Oh shit. Diamond! You okay?" Charmaine shouted.

Jessi ran ahead to the kitchen. Charmaine started a prayer; her chest felt tight with fear.

All she could think of was telling Indyah her mama was hurt. She followed Jessi through a swinging door. A long, fluorescent light flickered, making the room look like an old stop-action film. Dark, then bright light, then dark. Diamond's mouth opened wide. Then she bent double, grappling with a lump of something. The pounding became deafening, drowning out their voices.

Jessi leaned on Charmaine's shoulder. "Help her get Kareem out of here. Going upstairs."

Before Charmaine could process or argue, Jessi raced off. Diamond grunted with the effort to move the solid six-foot-tall man. Charmaine said another prayer that Jessi had sufficient defensive weapons. She hooked both hands under Kareem's left armpit. When Charmaine jerked her head in the direction of an exit lit in green, Diamond nodded she understood. Adrenaline had to have kicked in for both of them. They managed to drag Kareem across the floor. Diamond let go of him only long enough to unlock the rear door. Once outside, the racket in the house sounded muffled. A scruffy-looking man and woman stopped rummaging in the dumpster to gape at them.

"You two. Stay with this guy. Call nine-one-one," Charmaine shouted at them through huffing in air.

"What's wrong with him?" The woman's wide-eyed gaze swept over Kareem and then back at them.

"Not sure. Think he fainted," Diamond gasped. She bent over him and placed a hand under his nose. Then she looked at Charmaine. "Breathing."

"We're going back in," Charmaine said.

"We are?" Diamond blinked hard.

"Told you we shouldn't have come over here. Place is cursed. Don't need to be diving in the trash of a funeral home," the man said to the woman.

"It's a museum, fool. I found some good stuff. Like that footstool they threw out," the woman replied with heat.

The man started to answer when the noise inside boomed until the antique windowpanes rattled. He dropped the ratty canvas sack he held. The woman grabbed onto his arm with a squawk. Lights flashed in the windows. The mansion resembled an amusement park version of a haunted house.

"I'm getting the hell outta here," the man said, but couldn't move. His female companion stood frozen in fear, her grip on him and her substantial weight pinning him in place. "Shirley, c'mon. Pull yourself together, woman."

"You'd want somebody to help you in need. It's the Christian thing to do," Charmaine said with a glare at him.

"Then let Jesus babysit him!" The man turned to go.

"Twenty if you stay with our friend," Diamond yelled at them.

Shirley blinked out of her daze. "Make it thirty."

"What?" Charmaine stood, outraged at the negotiating. When Jessi shouted from somewhere on the top floor, she ripped off her watch and tossed it to the woman. "Plus my watch."

Diamond pulled out an embroidered coin purse from her jacket pocket. She fumbled for a second, then handed the cash over the railing of the back steps.

"Don't think I won't find your ass if you leave him," Diamond said.

They left Kareem to his new caretakers and ran back inside. The door banged shut once they crossed the threshold. Diamond and

Charmaine both paused to stare at it. A heavy object crashed and made them both jump.

"Help up here would be nice," Jessi screamed.

"Kitchen stairs. This way," Charmaine said taking the lead. "Jessi and I looked over the layout of the house."

"Put both those ghost stun guns on full force," Diamond replied. She held hers out in front of her with both hands.

"Damn it. I dropped one. You go. I'll be right behind you." Charmaine ran back to the visitation room while Diamond's mouth still hung open.

Too many agonizing seconds ticked by as Charmaine searched. Finally, the 1930s ceiling light stayed on long enough for her to find the stun gun. She snatched it up and retraced her steps through the kitchen. She got to the foot of the kitchen staircase in time to see Diamond poised at the top. Seconds later she ran out of view.

"Jessi. Say something," Diamond called out.

Charmaine concentrated on pounding up what seemed like dozens of narrow steps. In fact, it went up for six steps, hooked right for six more steps, hooked right again for the final six steps. Even though the mayhem deep in the second floor continued, Charmaine had to stop for a few seconds. She leaned against one wall, sucking in air.

"I can't be too old for this so soon. I'm not thirty yet," Charmaine breathed. "I exercise. Every now and then."

"Hey, get offa me!" Jessi let out a string of profane insults.

"Sure would help if I could see... Yow-ee! Watch where the fuck you put those clammy hands," Diamond shouted.

Charmaine pushed off the wall. She swore when her palm came away sticky. Fresh paint. Then she saw the warning sign on the opposite wall. "Kareem, you could have said something," she grumbled.

"No don't," Jessi called out to someone.

"I'm coming." Charmaine raced down what seemed like a mile-long hallway.

She followed the shouts of foul language, threats, and banging sounds. Three doors down Charmaine skidded to a halt before a door frame. Diamond waved around her stun gun in wild, and what looked like random, motions. Every few seconds she'd jerked around, curse, and fire. Jessi stood across the wide room. She stared at the ceiling. Then Charmaine noticed what appeared to be an oval stain on the wallpaper above the wainscoting.

"What the—"

"Shush," Jessi hissed to cut her off, her gaze still on her target. "Tell your pal to quit messin' with Diamond. We both know I can sizzle your ass into the ether. You got five seconds."

All three of them jumped at a clap of thunder that made the hardwood vibrate beneath their feet. A slow rumble followed. Diamond blinked as she turned in a slow circle, looking around the room. Then she sat down hard on the floor.

Charmaine knelt beside Diamond and rubbed her back as she spoke. "You okay? Take slow, steady breaths so you don't hyperventilate."

"'Kay," Diamond manage to get out. She labored to stop rapid gasps of air in and out.

Once sure Diamond had begun to regain control, Charmaine switched her attention back to Jessi. Her sister had backed away from what Charmaine now realized was a shadow. The thing loomed up and looked like the outlines of a man wearing a fedora. Garbled rumbling followed Jessi speaking to the thing. At least that's all Charmaine could make out. After a few seconds Charmaine felt a stabbing chill down her back. The voice, a grating basso, hit her full-force.

"Oh. Shit. I hear him." Charmaine then had to follow her own advice to calm herself.

"You a mighty strong voodoo woman if you can hear me," the deep voice said.

"My sister is a church-going lady. Voodoo is just as much nonsense, by the way," Jessi retorted. "Back to the subject."

"You think I gotta answer your questions. You one funny n—" The shadow slipped left a bit at the crackle of Jessi's stun gun. "Whoa, whoa!"

"Name-calling gets you a zap," Jessi warned.

"You need me," the voice grumbled.

"I've figured out some of what's goin' on. So, don't overestimate your value," Jessi replied in a cool tone.

"Nah, babe. You *think* you know," the voice came back, more confident.

"Let's start with your name. The one your mama gave you," Jessi countered.

"Louie Armstrong," the voice joked, followed by deep laughter.

The sound grated on her nerves and made Charmaine shiver. "At least he's got a sense of humor. Let's hope he left his axe at home."

"Handle, girlie. Axe handle. Used it to beat 'em senseless. Cut 'em with the reaper when I was done getting 'em to talk." The shadow laughed again and held up a wicked long knife, or at least the silhouette of one.

"Thanks for clearing that up." Charmaine gulped down a lump of fear in her throat.

"I said what's your name?" Jessi demanded. She aimed the more powerful stunner at him.

"You want to get famous solving the mystery of the Axeman of New Orleans. Can't blame ya, doll. But... maybe you oughta concentrate on earning your lettuce for solving this case. People will keep on dyin'. Not that I care one way or the other. More fun for me."

"What's he talking about?" Diamond said from behind Charmaine, making her yelp. "Sorry."

"Hey, I kinda like that one. Reminds me of a brown sugar babe I used to visit in Storyville. Sorry my associate got a bit too sociable back there. You open for business, sweetheart?" The voice grew deeper as the shadow turned in Diamond's direction.

"I can tell by your faces he's talking about me. What'd he say?" Diamond looked from Jessi to Charmaine.

"He'd like to... hire your services," Charmaine said.

Diamond's fear vanished. She lifted her chin in indignance. "Couldn't afford me even if you had spendable cash. I don't have time for broke men, living or dead."

The shadowed hooted with laughter. "Plenty of hips, and sassy. Just the way I like my women. Give me a few hours. I know where real money is buried, and more than a few bodies."

"This ain't a blind date, fool." Jessi swung the stunner in an arch.

The buzz sounded loud in the room as the shadow wavered. Yowling boomed around them. Diamond yelled when assorted old chairs and other furniture shifted around the room by inches. Charmaine fought against what felt like thickened air around them. She grabbed Jessi's shoulder.

"Stop," Charmaine mouthed at her.

Jessi blinked back from rage and took her finger off the trigger. "He's still here."

"Just barely." Charmaine scowled at her. "Control your temper or we'll lose the best lead we got so far."

"We still got the grunch," Jessi replied.

"What the hell is that damn contraption?" the shadow complained. He looked less defined. Ragged around the edges.

"Guess you take me serious now, huh? Come on, Axeman. Talk." Jessi wore a smug grin. She holstered the stunner in a gesture to show he didn't scare her.

"Did I say I was the Axeman? Memory is shaky after being attacked, but I'm pretty sure I didn't." The shadow gave a laugh that ended in a rasping cough. "Damn you and that gun."

"Uncovering his identity is gravy. We need to get something solid on this case," Charmaine said fast before Jessi could respond to his provocation.

"Humph." Jessi frowned because she couldn't disagree. Then she looked at the shadow. "Quit wasting my time before I decide zapping you out of existence is in the public's best interest."

"You really think it was my idea to kill those folks? How many society dames and carpenters got whacked?" the shadow asked.

"He's got a point," Charmaine mumbled.

"Look, all I'm sayin' is use your brains." The shadow tapped his temple. "Yeah, I enjoy my work. But I don't do it for free."

"Don't be silly. What kind of currency could a..." Jessi's voice trailed off. She blinked hard.

Charmaine could almost hear the proverbial wheels grinding as Jessi considered the shadow's assertion. "No. Not possible."

"You don't work alone, either. Somebody was touching Diamond," Jessi said to him.

"I got a gang. Which means I outnumber your outfit," the shadow replied.

"Who hired you?" Jessi said, her hand back on the stunner.

"Locke. For information at first. He likes fame. Get the inside story from our side, write a blockbusting book, get tips on finding old records that prove what he's written."

"How long have you been working for him?" Charmaine asked.

"Hey, I'm no errand boy. I'm my own boss, ya know. The guy stumbled on us. This medium in the French Quarter had more skills than smarts. Didn't know her own strength. May she rest in peace." The shadow took off his fedora and placed it over his heart. Not that he had one in life or death. Then put it on again and chuckled at his own joke. "But that's a different story for another day. Or night, as the case may be."

Jessi pulled her stun gun out of the holster. "Stop the bullshit. Tell it straight or buzz-buzz."

The shadow took a step back. "You're gonna play that card once too often, sister."

"She means it," Diamond said. Then added aside to Charmaine, "I assume he's trying to lie or something."

"Yeah. Now be quiet before you say the wrong thing," Charmaine whispered.

"Thanks for the warning, sweetheart. What I wouldn't give for even a day with her." The shadow gave a low whistle of appreciation.

"Murdering psychos ain't her style," Jessi snapped.

"Quit tellin' her I'm a nutcase," the shadow snapped. Then he heaved a sigh.

"A lovesick ghost that can't focus. Jeez." Jessi rolled her eyes.

Charmaine looked at Diamond. "Maybe you should..."

"Oh. Right. Nice meeting you. Being polite can't hurt," Diamond whispered when Jessi and Charmaine gave her twin disbelieving looks.

Diamond backed out of the room while keeping a watchful eye out for more invisible threats. Seconds later, they heard her footfalls as she went down the kitchen stairs. The shadow sighed again, as if missing her already. Jessi looked at the it again.

"Quit stallin'," Jessi said, sounding like a detective from a 1940s noir mystery film.

"Like I told you. Locke went to this medium so she could get ghost stories from the horse's mouth. I charge for the goods. Even-Steven exchange only. He got more than he paid for, let's just say."

"You killed Amanda Morrell," Jessi said.

"Technically, no." The shadow's shoulders lifted in a shrug. When Jessi pointed her stunner at him, he held up both hands again. "Okay, okay. The medium put the guy in touch with another voodoo mambo, witch, or whatever you wanna call 'em. All I know is, bingo, I had a body. We set up a distraction. Her and her pals being boozers and druggies was a lucky break."

"Wait a minute. You're saying a psychic helped you possess someone's body to commit murder? But- but... that's not possible." Charmaine gaped at Jessi, who seemed to be speechless.

"I'd heard about it. Deads like me crossing for a few hours to enjoy a steak again. Or fine liquor. Sex, too. Me, I had a bigger plan. It's boring floating around a stupid funeral home. Ya know? I miss the fun." The shadow sounded pleased with himself.

"You set up shop again as a hit man," Jessi said in a flat voice. She stumbled back as if the cold truth had shoved her hard.

"I ain't the only dead bored outta my skull. What's that old sayin'? Idle hands are the devil's workshop. Yeah, that's the one." The shadow gave an ugly laugh seconds before he vanished.

Chapter 11

99 Problems

"Yeah. Sure thing. I'm gonna walk right on into my deputy lieutenant's office and lay it all out. A phantom assassination squad is operating in our great city. But don't worry, ma'am. I got two top ghostbusters on the case." Harrison spoke in a hissing whisper that rose to a shout by the last sentence.

"Who said we intend to tackle the Axeman and his murdering crew? Look, now you know. What you do with the information is on *you*!" Charmaine jabbed a finger in his chest.

"You're really pushing the limit with me, Joliet. You ran outta free passes a looong time ago," Harrison thundered. He glared down at Charmaine's finger.

"Oh yeah? Funny how you keep callin' us to get your ass from between a rock and a hard place. So, I'm not shaking with fear," Charmaine spat.

Jessi wedged herself between them. "Whoa, whoa. Everybody take a deep breath. We're attracting attention. What we got so far is only a burglary. Kareem interrupted a break-in, got hit, but he's gonna be okay."

"Y'all keep yelling about spirits and hitmen, somebody gonna sell a tip to reporters," Diamond added, looking around as if anyone in the crowd might be one.

"Or go viral on social media. Collect yourselves," Jessi said in a low tone.

"Detective Harrison has a good point. Not much he can do with info about Locke, mediums, and the ghosts." Diamond chewed on a bright-green lacquered fingernail at least one-inch long.

"Which means..." Jessi took Charmaine by both shoulders. "We have to stay on the case. Who else can stop a supernatural gang of murderers?"

"Hell to the no ten zillions times to infinity, Jess. Think about what you're saying. There is a powerful psychic out there. Somebody who's probably using Satan or one of his demons to kill people." Charmaine spoke with force despite keeping her voice low.

"Don't be ridiculous. What we have is a man or woman who has mastered alternative energy. Altered life forms given physical form again. Think of the tech that would require. Advanced physics, biophysics, maybe astrophysics." Jessi's eyes went wide with wonder.

"Who is killing people," Harrison interjected with vehemence.

"Right, right. That part, too," Jessi said with a wave of her hand. She still had a faraway expression on her face.

"You want to find them. Get your hands on whatever thingamabobs they use. Question them. All so you can prove your scientific theories. That's crazy, Jess!" Charmaine waved her arms like pinwheels. When Jessi smiled, Charmaine covered her face with both hands. "Oh Lord, help us."

"Just hold up one damn minute." Harrison broke off before saying more, a scowl on his face. "Great. All I need right now."

Charmaine looked in the direction he'd turned. Harrison's ambitious junior cop, Gautier, climbed out of his unmarked car. His laser-like gaze found them in an instant. He squinted as though putting two and two together. Charmaine knew the answer in his mind was a promotion. And deep shit for Harrison.

"Oh-oh. Detective Gautier is here to spy," Charmaine mumbled aside to Jessi.

Harrison pointed at them. "You two don't move. And keep your li'l friend from talking to anyone."

"Diamond knows how to keep quiet when cops are around," Jessi retorted.

"No wonder she's your pal." Harrison spared Jessi a last glare of warning before he strode off.

"Harrison is annoying as shit, but we don't want him replaced with that." Jessi jerked a nod at Detective Gautier.

"Yeah, but we need to dump him when all this is over. Any connection with the NOPD is never going to end well for us. I don't care how good his intentions or how nice a guy he looks like on the surface." Charmaine studied the two men talking, their heads bent together. "Wonder what he's saying to Gautier?"

"I can bet it doesn't include the Axeman or a ghostly hit team." Jessi giggled.

"This isn't funny, Jess. Real people have died. Think of that couple and their two little kids. Amanda may not have been Miss Angelic, but she didn't deserve to die. Or that guy in New Orleans East."

Jessi's amusement faded. "I'm taking it all real serious, sis. Believe me. I meant what I said. You know damn well Harrison can't put a stop to the Axeman or the other supernatural shit going down. It's on us. We have to find out who is helping ghosts get bodies and do bad stuff."

"How?"

Jessi turned to Charmaine. "The grunch. I don't care what Penelope says. Either she or some of her 'community' knows more than they're telling. You believe they don't know about any paranormal activity?"

Charmaine continued to frown at the two detectives. Then she shook her head. "No, but the Axeman didn't mention them."

"And do we believe he's telling us the whole truth and nothing but? Hell no," Jessi said with a grunt.

"Sister, we've got to get ourselves a solid plan. We've never faced this kind of tricky situation before." Charmaine dialed Penelope's landline office number as she spoke.

"As my former professor liked to say, you have mastered the art of the understatement," Jessi drawled. She looked around the room as police lights strobed outside and lit up the mansion's interior.

****

Kat looked around the living room of Jessi's partially renovated shotgun double on St. Andrew. "Nice."

"If you like early nineties stripper décor," Charmaine quipped with a grin.

"Hey, the pole is a great conversation starter at parties. Well, if I ever have one," Jessi replied and laughed.

Jessi lived in one side of the home. With proceeds from her days dancing at clubs, she had a healthy savings account. Her plan was to complete renovations on the other half for short-term rentals. Her half of the duplex was decorated in an eclectic mix of antiques and mid-century modern. One of her friends from her strip club days was also an artist. Her stage name had become her legal name, Sunny Daze. The walls of Jessi's combination living room and dining room featured four of her colorful paintings. Semi-abstract renderings of pole dancing, complete with patrons staring up at the women.

"Yeah. I really like her work." Kat gazed at one for a few seconds.

"Just because we danced or were in the life didn't mean that's all we are," Jessi said with a shrug. She looked at the paintings with appreciation. "She's had showings in San Francisco and New York in the last year."

"Cool." Kat faced Jessi and raised the beer bottle she held. "Thanks. I needed a good, strong ale. Interesting brand." The label of Ghost in the Machine featured a grinning green skull in gory glory.

"Cool, huh? We hosted a couple of cocktail mixers at paranormal investigator conventions. Always a big hit." Jessi flopped down on her sofa and stretched out her legs. She picked up her own bottle and took a pull from it. "Whew. I hope the freaks don't come out tonight."

"Since it's Sunday, maybe they'll take a day of rest," Kat replied with a grin. She sat on a chair. "Anyway, thought y'all might like a report on ya girl Rochelle."

"Aw, don't tell me she's at her crazy again," Charmaine said with a sigh.

"She's acting strange," Kat said.

"Girl, that ain't breaking news. Stalking a dude, obsessing over anyone who talks to him. Roxy has fully embraced strange," Jessi said.

"I mean she's gotten quiet. Well, quiet for her. I suspected she was up to something, and I was right. She's investigating you two." Kat pointed at Charmaine and then Jessi with her beer bottle.

"Huh?" Charmaine blinked at her sister.

"What the hell." Jessi swung her legs to the floor. "The nerve of that bitch."

"She visited LCIW for some strange reason. Mean anything?" Kat looked from Charmaine to Jessi. The Louisiana Correctional Institute for Women was one of the largest prisons in south Louisiana. Frequently simply referred to as "St. Gabriel" for the small town where it was located, LCIW had a reputation for being a tough place.

"Who did she talk to?" Charmaine asked.

"Doesn't matter. Three women we helped put there will be happy to spill dirt about us," Jessi said.

"But only one knew us as kids," Charmaine replied with a worried look at her sister.

Jessi gazed back at her. "Nobody with sense is gonna listen to Keisha."

Keisha Front was a former client who had tried to blackmail them. They turned the tables, and it didn't end well for her. At all. Charmaine rubbed her forehead, already feeling a tension headache taking hold. Keisha had grown up with them in the same hellhole housing project.

"A complication we don't need, though," Charmaine muttered. She got a bottle of beer. "Forgive me, Lord, for drinking alcohol on a Sunday."

Jessi looked at Kat. "She went to church this morning."

"Ah." Kat suppressed a smile.

Jessi got up and took the unopened bottle from her. She went to the kitchen and came back with a glass a minute later. "Drink lemonade instead so you can stay in good with the Lord."

"You play too much." Charmaine took the glass, even so. She sipped, sighed, and took a seat on a bar stool.

"Trouble from back in the day?" Kat eyed them with curiosity.

"Nothing we can't handle," Jessi said. When Kat's dark brows arched high, she sighed. "Keisha thinks she knows more than she does. And none of it can hurt us."

"Right," Kat said, drawing out the word. "So, is Ms. Front due for one of your special little chats?"

"Nah, forget it," Jessi said.

Kat nodded. "Okay. Anyway, Roxanne hasn't been stalking Scotty since y'all visited her. And... I have a suggestion."

"What?" Charmaine turned to her.

"Let Scotty handle her from here on out. I convinced him to file a police complaint about the vandalism. Turns out she's done that sort of thing before, so his report was taken as credible. Scotty is right. You guys have more to lose if getting tangled up with her takes a nasty turn."

"Agreed. Our licenses are on the line. And just when we're pulling in serious business." Charmaine gave Jessi a pointed look. "No more *talks* with Rochelle."

"Humph. Whatever." Jessi drank her beer. "Look, when you slap down hating heffas, there's gonna be blowback. Nothing we can't handle."

Charmaine shook her head and looked up. "Why can't life ever be simple, Lord?"

"Quit talking to my ceiling. It ain't got no answers," Jessi retorted. "Speaking of shady clients, maybe we should confront Locke with what we found out. Instead of talking to Penelope, I mean."

"No reason we can't do both. I'll talk to her; you go see Locke," Charmaine replied.

"I don't think you should go see the grunch alone, though."

"The who?" Kat blinked at them.

"Local legend over one hundred years old that turns out to be true. Unless you've got other plans tonight, Charmaine can explain on your way over there," Jessi said.

"Sadly, my weekend social calendar stays empty since I broke up with my girlfriend. Might as well fill it up with something interesting. When do we leave?" Kat looked at Charmaine.

"I don't need backup to talk to Penelope," Charmaine protested.

"Until we know who is behind all the murder and mayhem, everybody is a suspect," Jessi said.

"Good policy," Kat put in.

"I guess it can't hurt," Charmaine said. "Penelope is expecting me in a couple of hours, so around five-thirty this evening.

"Perfect. Maybe we can get some damn answers." Jessi looked at Charmaine, an impish twinkle in her black-coffee eyes. "And try not to stir up any more complications or drama."

"Me?" Charmaine sputtered in outrage. Then she listed all of the ways Jessi caused trouble, mixed in with a few choice curse words.

****

"Lord, forgive me. And I was doing so well, too," Charmaine muttered as she drove toward New Orleans East.

"Hey, I like to think of God as forgiving and having a massive sense of humor. All you gotta do is look around the world for evidence," Kat said with a laugh.

"I enjoy church, but according to them I'm a witch. Jessi isn't just a witch, but a loose woman who doesn't believe in God or Jesus." Charmaine gave a dry laugh. "We're doomed."

"When I came out as gay I heard those same lectures from some family members. I'm gonna burn in hell. Oh, they said it in a *nice* way. You know what I mean," Kat said.

"The old 'love the sinner and hate the sin' speech."

"I'm blessed to have found a church that accepts me for who I am." Kat looked at her. "You should come."

"I might. What's the name?" Charmaine pulled into Penelope's driveway behind a gray truck.

"One Community Unitarian Universal Church."

"Well, I guess that says it all," Charmaine said with a smile.

"Indeed it does, praise the Lord. Oh, and we have a gospel choir." Kat grinned back at her.

"Oh, I'm so in. The one good thing about Jessi always challenging my beliefs? She forced me to face the rigidness and judgments in some church folk." Charmaine unbuckled her seat belt. "But don't tell her I said that."

Kat laughed hard. "I won't. So, what's the plan?" She nodded toward Penelope's house.

"Tell her we know she's holding back. Then see where it goes from there."

"Think we'll have trouble?" Kat scanned the yard, then the neighborhood.

"Nah. Jessi's being cautious, but nothing we've experienced so far implies we will. Look, these folks have a history of hardship and survival. They just want regular lives like the rest of us." Charmaine followed suit and looked around despite her words.

"Yeah, but y'all been asking questions. And you know more about them than anyone, including that they even exist. People who feel threatened might do anything," Kat argued.

Charmaine bit her lower lip as she turned over choices in her head. Then she reached under the seat to retrieve a compact stun gun. She slid it into her sweater-coat pocket. "There. Just in case."

"Better to have it and not need it than need it and not have it. That's what my grandfather used to say. Never left home without his pistol," Kat said with a grin.

"Let's say a prayer to the universal God that peace will reign," Charmaine said and she swung open the driver's-side door.

"Amen, my sister," Kat murmured as she opened her door and got out as well.

They walked up the paved path to Penelope's front door. It opened before they had a chance to ring the doorbell. Penelope stood in a pink sweatshirt and black leggings. Without a greeting, she waved them both in. The smell of cookies in the oven filled the house. Penelope led them to her living room. Autumn sunshine filtered through white sheer curtains. Bright-colored paisley draperies of heavier fabric were pulled back from three sets of windows. The scents of cinnamon, sugar, and vanilla combined with a décor to make the home feel welcoming. Penelope's tight expression stood in stark contrast.

"I already heard what happened at Hambrick's." Penelope didn't offer them a seat. Then she pointed up at Kat. "Who's she?"

"A friend." Kat held up both palms as if showing she was unarmed.

"Humph." Penelope transferred her skeptical gaze from Kat to Charmaine. "My community gave you information on Locke. Go talk to him."

"My sister will. She's probably with him right now, as a matter of fact. Look, I appreciate y'all filling in the blanks on Locke for us. So far, we've kept you out of our investigation. I haven't mention the community at all, but—" Charmaine sighed.

Penelope's frown deepened. "What?"

"I might need to tell Detective Harrison about your sister, Lydia, and..." Charmaine held up a hand when Penelope started a vehement objection. "Let me finish. Explain to him that it could give Locke motive. Maybe he thought Amanda knew too much from those days in New York. The other crimes could be distractions to cover up."

"Go on." Penelope's frowned eased but didn't go away.

"I don't need to mention the grunch, I mean your community, or the legend. Detective Harrison wouldn't want to hear it anyway," Charmaine added with a grunt at the understatement. Harrison would likely groan in agony, after exploding.

"Yeah. Okay." Penelope went to a chair and sat.

Charmaine exchanged a glance with Kat and nodded. They sat down as well. Kat balanced on the edge of her seat as if ready to move fast if needed. Charmaine allowed Penelope to think for a few more seconds before she spoke.

"You think Amanda knew them both, Lydia and Eli, years ago. He comes to New Orleans, gets involved with the local crowd, and suddenly she's a threat. Makes sense," Penelope said. Her gaze focused on a point behind them. When Charmaine and Kat turned, JoJo stood in the entranceway.

"Hello," JoJo rumbled.

"Oh-oh." Kat stood to face him.

"No, no. It's okay." Charmaine put a hand on Kat's arm. "Afternoon, sir."

"JoJo spends most Sundays at my house after church. He's part of my family since he don't have his own," Penelope said from her chair. She didn't seem bothered that Kat assumed a defensive stance.

"Kids playing out back. Heard voices over the game," JoJo rumbled. He studied Kat for a few seconds, head to one side. Then he gave her a crooked smile.

"My daughter, son, and in-laws love college football. All football, actually. Church, Sunday dinner, and sports. Sound to you like we spend our days dancing with the devil and plotting murders?"

"But you know more than you're telling us, Penelope," Charmaine replied. "We spoke to a spirit, a real mean character from the past."

Penelope looked to JoJo and then back to Charmaine. "You talked to Sal. Salvador Rocca. That's his name. He probably acted all coy, wouldn't say who he is. Or was."

"Is," JoJo said. He strolled into the room. "Since Sal is still very much with us in the plane of existence. I'd have to argue past tense is wrong."

"You sound like Jessi. Exactly the kind of thing she'd say," Charmaine replied.

JoJo sat on the sofa, stretching his legs out in a casual pose. "Introduce me. Your other sister?"

"Hmm, no. Sorry, this is Kat. An associate," Charmaine blurted out.

"You said she was a friend," Penelope countered. Her suspicious frown dropped into place once more.

"Both," Kat put in before Charmaine replied. She smiled at JoJo. "With everything going down they needed an extra set of hands. Kat Davenport. Nice to meet you."

"JoJo Harahan. Pleased to meet you, too." The big man dipped his head to her. Then he looked at Penelope. "What about Sal?"

"Never mind him. I wanna know more about her," Penelope said and jabbed a finger at Kat.

"I'm taking a break from my regular profession, being a chef. I helped out another friend of ours working at his restaurant bar. I'm assisting Charmaine and Jessi until my next cooking gig." Kat maintain an open, congenial face as she spoke.

"You look like hired muscle. No offense," Penelope said, an eyebrow raised.

"I prefer nonviolent resolutions to any disagreements. Food, communication, and hospitality." Kat looked from Penelope to JoJo and back again.

"Extra eyes and brains, not just hands," Jo-Jo said. "You deal in spirits, too?"

"My grandmother and great-aunts told me stories, yeah. But I'm not a pro at it like Charmaine," Kat replied.

"Lot of restless souls getting outta hand," JoJo said.

He looked at Penelope. Not a word was said. No nods. No gestures. Still, Charmaine could almost hear them exchanging a kind of silent conversation. She strained to "hear" their thoughts but couldn't. More likely, they'd known each other for so long they didn't need to speak. JoJo seemed to signal he believed Kat wasn't a police officer or deception was at play.

"I bet Sal teased you along, like he knows so much. Some say he was the Axeman. Wouldn't Eli Locke love to hear Sal's line of bull? Not all that far-fetched, though. Strange, but Sal won't say. Which tells me something," Penelope said.

"What?" Charmaine leaned forward.

Penelope considered her question for a few seconds, and then shook her head. "Not sure. What'd he say the other night?"

Charmaine clicked her tongue in annoyance. "My patience is done."

"Just calm down now," Kat cautioned.

"No. I'm tired of being played like I'm Boo-Boo the Fool. I want to know how and for how long y'all been connected to Eli."

"Which you wouldn't have known if I hadn't said so," Penelope snapped.

"Fair point. We have the same goal, to keep more people from getting hurt," Kat put in, using a "Let's all get along" tone. Which fell flat.

Penelope let out a loud, emphatic snort. "Your version of good cop, bad cop needs a hell of a lot of work. What you want is to make bank from your rich client."

"Damn right," Charmaine said with force. "And you want to keep your existence on the low-low. So, yeah. We both have self-interest at play. If Locke or his assistant think giving up the community will help them, they will."

"He won't do that," Penelope said. She looked sideways at JoJo. Then she pressed her lips closed.

Charmaine squinted at her. She caught an odd snatch of uncompleted thought from Penelope. "Why—"

The Erykah Badu ringtone on her cell phone announced Jessi on the other end of the call. Charmaine ground her teeth in frustration as she glanced at the screen. The text message only flashed "911. Pick up."

Kat continued to transfer her gaze from Penelope to JoJo. "I'm a newcomer to this case, but Charmaine is right."

"Sorry, I gotta take this call," Charmaine said while she strode to the archway.

She swiped to take it but kept walking to the small dining area and the kitchen. The voices of children came from the backyard. Sounds of a football game on TV came from the direction of the den down another hallway. Charmaine went to the front yard to insure no one would walk in or sneak up while she talked.

"Bad timing. We're close to getting Penelope to spill the tea. So, this better be a real nine-one-one," Charmaine hissed, careful to keep her voice low.

"I'm going to jail. That do it for ya?" Jessi drawled.

****

A tense scene greeted Charmaine forty minutes later when she and Kat arrived at NOPD District Five. Harrison paced in a circle in the station lobby. He alternated between quiet side conversations with officers and glowering at Jessi. She met his gaze with a cool, defiant smirk.

"You okay?" Charmaine blurted out as she scanned her sister for injuries.

"Hi ya," Kat said.

Jessi waved at her. "Hey, Kat. Lemme tell you what's gone happen next. Once Charmaine gets past the mother hen act, she'll get pissed off in one, two, three..."

"What the hell is wrong with you? The last thing I need is to be dragging your behind out of trouble." Charmaine stood over her, both hands on her hips. "And mother hen, huh? Excuse me for caring about your ungrateful—"

"She's consistent," Jessi cut in.

"Girl, the safest place for you might be jail," Charmaine said, her eyes narrowed to slits.

Harrison's long strides brought him over to them in seconds. "Wait your turn. I get a crack at her first." He moved to stand between the sisters.

"Hello again, Detective Harrison. Nice to see you." Kat stuck out a hand.

Thrown off by the greeting, Harrison looked puzzled as he shook it. "Uh, yeah. Except this ain't a happy reunion. Not when I have to interrupt my Sunday football party to deal with typical Joliet Sisters mess."

"What's the problem, sir?" Kat calmly continued her efforts to diffuse three ticking time bombs.

"This one." Harrison stabbed an accusing forefinger at Jessi. "She chose to pick a fight with a mother of three *in front of her kids.*"

"Give me a break. Rochelle ain't mother of the year. She attacked *me*. Don't leave out the part where her badass little boys jumped me from behind," Jessi replied with enough fire to singe his eyebrows.

"They're ten and twelve. You're out in the streets brawling with grade-schoolers," Harrison retorted, his voice rising.

A cop in uniform approached. "Sir, everything under control here?"

"Yeah, yeah, Davis. It's cool." Harrison turned his back to them. They moved away and talked a few moments longer. Then Harrison returned. "Lucky for you the lady didn't file a complaint."

"You should have left well enough alone, Jessi," Charmaine said. She stuttered to get out more but stopped when Kat put a hand on her arm.

"Just tell us what happened," Kat said to Jessi. She took a seat next to her.

"I was going to talk to..." Jessi glanced up at Harrison during her pause. "Our client. I went through the drive-through to get an iced coffee. Rochelle rolled up behind me, car full of rowdy brats. We made eye contact. Then she jumped out of her car for the sole purpose of getting in my face."

"Okay," Kat replied, drawing out the word. "And what happened next was..."

"I got out of my car, too. She invaded my personal space and refused my polite request that she back up. Instead she chest-bumped me into the back fender of my jeep. I *defended myself.* Then her junior mafia piles out of the car, coming for me."

"I guess I need to remind y'all that we're facing bigger issues," Harrison said in a tight tone. "Like murder and crazy ghost sightings. What I don't need is you brawling with some other woman over a man."

Jessi barked a laugh empty of real humor. "The only time I fought over a man was when some trick tried to take my business. One time was all it took. Everybody was on notice afterwards."

"Great. Mention your criminal past. These cops want another a reason to lock you up," Charmaine hissed.

"Um, Detective Harrison. If I may explain." Kat looked at him. When he said nothing, she continued. "Rochelle is a former employee at our friend Scotty's place. She wanted more than a professional relationship and when he refused, she started harassing him. Jessi contacted her on his behalf, totally non-threatening, to ask that she stop."

Harrison directed a pointed stare at Jessi. "Non-threatening, huh?"

"I explained that Scotty could file a complaint, even get a restraining order. She's in a custody dispute with her husband," Jessi replied.

"You told her husband she slept with Scotty? Real nice," Harrison lectured.

"He found out on his own," Charmaine put in.

The same uniformed officer returned. He beckoned Harrison. "Detective, come see."

Harrison huffed as he swept a critical gaze at the three women. "Don't leave, 'cause we're not done."

"Don't leave," Jessi mimicked with a sneer. "Mr. Big Bad Policeman."

"Shut it. He's probably the only reason you're not already sitting in a funky jail cell," Charmaine said.

"Whatever." Jessi crossed her arms.

Charmaine pulled Kat aside while they waited for Harrison to return. After a whispered consultation, Kat left with a good-bye to Jessi. Another hour went by and no Harrison.

"I knew the way you handled Rochelle would come back to bite us," Charmaine said.

"You the one hot to protect your man in the first place," Jessi replied.

Kat's dark eyebrows went up almost to her hairline. "You and Scotty are..."

"What part of 'shut it' didn't you get? Unbelievable. No, scratch that. Coming from you, this entire mess is totally believable. Even predictable. If I had a nickel for every time I had to bail you out." Charmaine groaned and shook her head.

"You'd be just as rich as me if I had a nickel for every time I saved your ass," Jessi wisecracked. "Let me count the ways."

"You..." Charmaine seethed as she found to find words.

"Hey, hey, you two. Enough. Here he comes," Kat said, jerking her head to indicate Harrison approaching with the other policeman.

"You've definitely got a guardian angel on your side," Harrison said.

The District Five Officer Davis nodded. "Security cameras support your account. Ms. Willis physically touched you in a threatening manner first. You could file assault charges."

"I should, and on them baby demons of hers," Jessi said with an evil smile.

"Jessi." Charmaine frowned at her.

Jessi waved her off and stood. "I'm in a forgiving mood. So, we can stop wasting the time of these fine examples of law enforcement."

Harrison huffed and puffed like a steam engine for a few seconds. He turned to Charmaine. "Leave. Just. Take her home."

"On our way," Charmaine mumbled. She grabbed Jessi by the arm and tugged hard. "Not one more word."

Jessi favored the two policemen with a sweet smile and a good-bye wave. Once they were in the parking lot, she wiggled free of

Charmaine's grip. "I think that went well. Don't you?"

"You are a trouble magnet," Charmaine muttered. They got to her parked Cruze first. She was about to say more when Rochelle emerged from the police station. She sent them a "Death Rays" glare before heading in the opposite direction.

"I didn't press charges. You're welcome," Jessi yelled after her.

"Oh sure, start a brawl in the police parking lot." Charmaine slapped her shoulder to emphasize her point.

"She won't make a move. I think she's gonna really leave Scotty alone now. And..." Jessi paused for dramatic effect as she spun to face Charmaine. "I picked up a few nuggets related to our case. There were two more ghost sightings in this district and District One. Both were dismissed as nuts with nothing better to do. So, whoever is stirring the spiritual pot isn't letting up."

Charmaine forgot about Rochelle and being mad at Jessi. "Anybody hurt?"

"Nope. Just objects flying around a room in one incident. The other was a guy who swears he saw the ghost of Madame LaLaurie walking down Royal Street. He'd been smoking herb."

Jessi pantomimed inhaling from a joint. "The other is a well-known eccentric in her neighborhood. Less-than-reliable sources."

"Yeah. Except we know different. What did Harrison say?"

Jessi smiled. "Not one peep about our case. He joined in with the other cops about the full moon and crazies coming out. What did you find out from Penelope and her crew?"

"Not much, thanks to you," Charmaine snapped.

"Hey, you heard Officer Davis. I was minding my own-self business when Rochelle ran up on me with evil intent."

Charmaine let out a long sigh. "Yeah, you're right. Sorry."

"Wow. I got support from a cop, treated like the wrong party, and you apologized. Ah, let me savor the moment." Jessi hummed as if pleased with the world.

"Moment over. You never made it to Eli's to talk to him." Charmaine took her car keys from a jacket pocket.

"Yeah, but you didn't finish talking to Penelope. Maybe we should go back there," Jessi said.

"Kat's gone back. She took an Uber to get her SUV at my house. Then she's gonna meet up with Penelope again. She seemed to have connected with Penelope and JoJo."

"You think she will get something helpful out of them? Humph, maybe we ought to hire her for more cases."

"We'll talk about it later. But first let's try to get something helpful out of Eli Locke," Charmaine said.

"I texted him that I was delayed. He says I can still come over," Jessi replied.

Charmaine glanced at the wristwatch she wore. "Just before seven. See you there." She got in her car and started the engine but didn't drive off. A text from Kat stopped her. "Damn. Penelope and Eli both have some explaining to do."

Chapter 12

Plots Unravel – Maybe

"Penelope finally admitted the grunch dabble in the occult, huh? About time they stop lyin'. I knew those stories had some truth to 'em," Jessi said as they walked up the stone path to Eli Locke's front door.

"No, what Penelope told Kat was a few of them are superstitious. They don't have a good motive for summoning ghosts. They want to stay as invisible as possible," Charmaine replied.

They climbed the steps to lovely front porch, and she pressed the button. Musical chimes played inside the house.

"Yeah. Right. What if a secret is worth the risk? But then we gotta figure out the secret." Jessi frowned.

"And Penelope and her community have had over a hundred years to practice hiding," Charmaine said.

Someone approaching cut off more speculation. The outline of a figure in the leaded glass of the door seemed to float toward them. Charmaine wondered if an apparition would greet them to declare no one was home. Or still alive to answer questions. She heard Jessi thinking the same. They looked at each other, then at the figure. The oak-and-glass entrance swung open. A tall, lovely woman smiled, her beautiful honey-blond hair swept up in waves. The same woman they'd seen in the ambulance with Eli the night he and Becca were attacked.

"Good evening. You're expected, I believe," she said in a throaty voice.

"I'm Jessi and this is my sister—"

"Charmaine," the woman interrupted. She eyed Charmaine from head to toe. "Eli described you well. But then, he's a writer. Lush figure, full lips tinged with a hint of pink gloss, and mesmerizing brown eyes. Come in."

"Uh, hi." Charmaine blinked back at her, unnerved at her scrutiny and the fact that they'd discussed her.

"Oh, where are my manners. Mother would be appalled, may she rest in peace. I'm Lana Salcedo Reilly. Pleased to finally meet you." Lana extended a hand with fingernails manicured to perfection.

"Same here," Charmaine stammered and cleared her throat. The woman's smooth skin felt cool. Charmaine let go fast, pushing against the wild notion Lana was a ghost. This case had her mind veering in wild directions for sure.

"He didn't say anything about me. I'm hurt," Jessi teased as she walked past Lana.

"He did indeed, Jessi. You don't mind the instant informality, do you?" Lana had the charm-school manners fine-tuned to melt polar ice caps. Her smile widened, which made her hazel eyes look electric. Flecks of green seemed to appear in them.

"Not at all. Can't wait to hear how he described me." Jessi grinned at her.

Charmaine didn't join in the chatter. She was still thrown off by Lana. The woman epitomized the cliché "force of nature." An aura of gray seemed to surround her, the color of adaptability and keen intellect, according to Charmaine's Reiki coach. Lana's aura shimmered from bright to a muddy shade, an indication of blocking and being on guard. Charmaine brushed aside the left-field bent of her musings.

"I'm seeing things," she whispered. She started when Jessi gave her a baffled side-eye.

"What?" Jessi gave Charmaine a puzzled side-eye.

"Nothing. I'll tell you later," Charmaine replied, grateful that Lana seemed not to notice them lag behind. Then she jumped when Lana spun to face them.

"You know the way into the parlor, dears. I'll have Viola bring refreshments." Lana swept off, her floral caftan drifting about her slim figure as she walked.

"Feels like I stepped into a Tennessee Williams play," Jessi muttered. She was about to offer more commentary when Locke appeared. He gestured to them.

"I'm so glad you're here. The last few weeks have been ghastly. I'm sure you'll agree. Viola is making a fresh pitcher of rum punch. Of course, I have bourbon and red wine, if you like."

Locke babbled on as Charmaine and Jessi entered the room. He pointed to a rattan rolling bar cart. No food was in sight. Locke told them rum punch was a favorite of Lana's, that

Viola would no doubt prepare sandwiches, and more. Charmaine and Jessi exchanged a look, both with the same thought. Locke and his lady love had a head start getting buzzed. Charmaine wondered if they'd get anything useful out of either of them. Her sister's impression flowed into her head as Jessi gazed at him. Eli and Lana were more aware than they appeared at first glance.

"Thanks, Eli. I'll wait for something to eat first. I don't want that alcohol going straight to my brain," Jessi joked as she settled on his sofa worth thousands.

As if on cue, Viola entered carrying a wide tray. "I remembered your favorites. And no, I'm not working overtime. I made sandwiches for a church tea after worship today. I always make extra in case Mister Locke has Sunday company."

Lana followed her in. "Thank you so much, Viola. Eli is lucky to have a gem like you. Decent household staff is a rarity these days."

"Did she really just say 'good help is hard to find?' " Jessi mumbled aside to Charmaine.

"Shush," Charmaine whispered.

"Uh-huh." Viola appeared to share Jessi's sentiment. She gave Lana a tight-lipped smile with no trace of genuine amusement.

"No one can take her place." Locke beamed at Viola. "I practically worship each treasured step she takes in this house."

Viola turned to him with a real smile. "Go on now."

"You know it's true," Locke replied. He poured himself another drink.

"I kinda enjoy working here, too. When you're not making too much mess for me to clean up." Viola shared a laugh with Locke.

Lana's lips stretched with patrician disapproval as she gazed at them. "Well, I'm sure our guests would like to talk with Eli."

Viola's dark eyes flashed with annoyance that she masked an instant later. She turned to Lana. "I'll be in my apartment since it's my day off anyway. I'm sure you won't mind leaving the tray in the kitchen. I'll start the dishwasher in the morning."

"We will, Vi. We'll load it up so all you have to do is push the button. Enjoy your evening," Locke said promptly. He seemed not to notice Lana's blinking frown at his housekeeper's instructions. He turned to Charmaine and Jessi. "So, ladies. What news?"

Charmaine cleared her throat. Then she gave Jessi, who seemed about to burst with giggles, a warning look. Her sister clearly enjoyed the needling Viola aimed at Lana. For her part, Viola lifted her chin with a look of catlike satisfaction. Charmaine imagined she'd wear a grin at her small victory for the rest of the night.

Jessi put down her wine glass. "Someone, or more than one somebody, is calling up the ghosts. Whoever it is has skills. And we've got information that the Axeman has become the leader of a gang doing contract hits. Maybe for the same person or persons. The supernatural version of Murder Incorporated."

Dramatic to the core, Locke gasped before he gulped whiskey. Then he filled his glass again and sat down hard. "And I'm on their list? Oh my God."

"We don't know that yet." Jessi eyed him, head to one side.

Lana put on a shocked expression as well. One manicured hand flew to her throat. "My goodness. I'll have a drink, too."

Charmaine studied Lana. No telepathic insights hit Charmaine, but she also didn't believe Lana was shocked. Her hazel eyes held more shrewdness than fear. "Of course, the killers have been pretty effective so far."

"What does that mean?" Lana replied fast. Too fast. She seemed to realize her mistake.

She poured wine and spilled some. "How stupid of me to be careless."

Locke rushed forward to dab at the stain on the fine wool rug. "Don't be silly. Accidents happen."

"I've ruined your beautiful oriental rug," Lana said.

She babbled on apologies. Locke reassured her the more she babbled. Charmaine and Jessi exchange a knowing glance. Lana's performance continued until Locke poured her more wine and urged her to relax.

"It's not like the rug is worth thousands. Oh, wait; it is," Locke added with wide eyes. Then he laughed at Lana's mock-horrified reaction. "I'm teasing, love. Viola will call the rug specialist in the morning. The thing is resilient. Think of all the rowdy parties I've hosted here."

"Not to mention rowdy friends like *me*." Lana laughed as well, head thrown back.

"Hmm, you're deliciously disorderly. Never change." Locke leaned down, planted a kiss on her mouth, and took his seat again.

"I'm just rattled by the entire notion of ghosts. Eli has been trying since we met to convince me they exist. Now you say they've banded together to go after certain people.

How awful." Lana sipped from the goblet she held. Then she heaved a sigh.

"I didn't say they were after certain people," Jessi replied. She scrutinized Lana.

Lana waved a hand. "Eli suggested as much when he said they were after him. Though I can't imagine why. Unless... honey, maybe they're upset you've been writing about them. You know, exposing their secrets."

Nice save, Jessi thought. The words popped into Charmaine's mind clear as writing on a wall. Charmaine looked from her sister to Lana with interest. "Maybe."

"But why now? I've been writing about ghosts in various forms and famous criminals for the past ten years at least," Locke looked back at her. Then he turned to Charmaine as if waiting for her to solve the puzzle. Which was, of course, what he was paying them to do.

Charmaine rose and went to the tray. She picked up a sandwich. Then she took her time getting a large paper napkin before she returned to her seat. "True. So, maybe something changed recently. Think about it."

"Yes, something must be different about this point in time." Lana looked up at the ceiling, wearing a slight frown as though she'd lapsed into deep thought. An antique clock nearby tick-tocked a minute of silence.

"Thought of anything, Eli?" Charmaine prodded. She felt rather than saw Lana's spike of irritation at her use of his first name. Yet Lana's neutral expression had not changed when Charmaine turned to her.

"Not really." Eli's thick brows pulled together as he seemed to put effort into coming up with an answer.

"What was your last book about? Some New Orleans legend or other. Not that we don't have a Mississippi River steamboat full of those," Lana added with a musical chuckle.

"My current release centers around a story about the grunch I dug up a few years back. It's set in 1909 and starts off in the French Quarter. But then I take the reader back in time for background on the series of events that led to shocking murders. My editor at first wasn't sure about mixing two time periods. But we made it work." Locke wore a gratified grin. "She even used the word brilliant."

"We know you are, sugar," Lana cooed.

Jessi got up to get a second sandwich. She turned her back to Lana and Locke as she rolled her eyes. She grinned when Charmaine struggled not to giggle. "I hope you didn't put real people in the book. One sure way to piss off a descendant."

"I referred to actual historical figures of the time, but nothing that wasn't already said about them." Locke shrugged. "No one's complained before."

"Still, your publisher and agent have done an excellent job on publicity. Don't forget, it's your first book in almost two years. The media interviews have been extensive." Lana turned to Charmaine and Jessi. "He was even on CNN."

"Wow." Charmaine assumed a suitably impressed expression.

"So, Lana, you know much about the grunch legend?" Jessi asked in a casual tone. She took a bite of roast beef from between the bread slices.

"Me? No. Only the usual stories most natives have heard growing up," Lana replied.

"You're from New Orleans. Interesting." Jessi continued chewing as though her observation meant nothing.

"I lived in Houston a few years, and New York. I met Eli then, when my first husband was alive." Lana slid a side-glance at Eli, who smiled in response. "Poor John's health had already begun to fail. We came back here when the doctor said there was no hope of recovery. He wanted to die in the city he loved."

"You said first husband," Jessi replied.

"Then I married Danny Chartres. You may have heard of his family. They've been in New Orleans since the 1700s at least. Anyway, we were close to he and his wife. When Anna died, Danny and I comforted each other. We were only married two and half years. Really, it was mutual grief that drew us together. Animosity from his daughters didn't help, so we divorced." Lana sipped wine and sighed. "Yes, Ms. Joliet. I've lived."

Charmaine nodded. "You think someone may be upset about Eli's latest novel?"

Lana shrugged. "Just a theory."

Eli nodded with a grave face. "Darling, your sharp observations prove to be invaluable once again." He leaned forward, looking around at them one by one. "Ladies, what I'm about to tell you can't leave the room."

Charmaine looked at Jessi before she faced him again. "We hold everything our clients tell us as confidential."

"That's one hundred," Jessi said. She glanced at Lana.

"No gossiping with my circle." Lana made a gesture as if zipping her lips closed.

Locke drew in a deep breath, let it out, and nodded. "The grunch aren't a merely a legend. They're real. I swear it, real as you and I."

Lana blinked at him for a few seconds with her mouth hanging open. Then she began to laugh. "Oh, sweetie."

"I'm not joking," Locke shouted at her. Lana gasped as if his voice alone had slapped her across the face. Locke swallowed hard. He got up and sat next to Lana on the small sofa. "I'm sorry to be so harsh, but this is serious. I've never revealed sources to anyone before. Not even my publisher, editor, or agent. Not about them."

"I apologize for being so dismissive. Go on, dear." Lana grabbed one of his hands and squeezed it.

"Yeah, this I gotta hear," Jessi said.

Locke nodded. "Some years ago, I stumbled on a lead that led me to their community. I looked through old court records and found a criminal case from 1854. I tracked down a descendant of the woman accused of stealing fruit. It was fascinating because it mentioned the reason she'd stolen and... to make a long story short, the woman was a grunch. She was hanged, by the way. Much later, for another offense. Fascinating story."

"Hmm." Jessi raised an eyebrow.

"I know, I know. Her niece several times removed was a chatty type, lucky for me. She told me a lot that led to further research. Like a lot of legends, there is truth mixed in the fantastic. One thing did prove to be accurate. The grunch practiced magic or calling up spirits. I've always thought that part was nonsense. But..." Locke's voice trailed off. His gaze darted around the room.

"Nothing is with us." Jessi patted her leather jacket pocket.

"Did one of your devices send a signal of some kind? Eli told me about your gadgets," Lana added. She stared at Jessi's hand for a few seconds. Then she smiled. "Tell us more, Eli."

"Nothing more to tell. Not much anyway. Except I was approached by someone back in March, just before the new book was released. She claimed to be a lawyer representing a grunch descendant. Well, she didn't say grunch," Eli said.

"What did she say?" Charmaine leaned forward.

"A descendant, according to this lawyer, had concerns content in my novel might hurt his or her family. All they wanted was to live quietly. My book digging up the past might wreck all they've built. I assume the younger generations don't know the more unsavory facts about their ancestors." Eli relaxed against decorative throw pillows. "She wouldn't reveal the name of her client. And she wouldn't be specific about exactly what worried them."

Charmaine studied his body language for a few seconds. She couldn't get a clear telepathic signal from him. "But you think you know."

Eli returned her scrutiny for several beats. His gaze flickered to Lana for a split second. The woman sat still, but her hold on Eli's hand tightened. Then Lana let go of him and stood. Charmaine didn't stop looking at him. Jessi glanced at Charmaine before she followed Lana to the bar.

"All this talk of monsters and voodoo has my nerves on edge. I need more wine," Lana said.

"Slow down on the alcohol. Don't want to smash up that cool Benz," Jessi said in a mild tone.

"She's right, babe. Not to mention getting a ticket," Eli added.

"I can spend the night. With your guard puppy gone, we'll have precious time to ourselves." Lana smiled and lifted her glass in a toast.

"Speaking of Becca... " Charmaine replied.

"Ah, you knew exactly who I was talking about. Which means you've experienced her over-protectiveness when it comes to Eli," Lana said.

"Becca is an excellent employee, Lana. She takes her job a bit too seriously at times, but her work ethic is strong," Eli replied.

"She wants more than a paycheck, dear." Lana's dry tone didn't match the loaded question underlying the remark.

"Don't be silly. Becca's teenage crush will pass. In the meantime, I can count on her loyalty and hard work," Eli said, unaffected by Lana's insinuation.

"We don't own each other. I wouldn't be upset if you gave in on occasion. Quite a boost to the ego of a man almost twice her age." Lana sipped wine.

"I'm not twice her age," Eli clipped, his eyes narrowed.

Charmaine swallowed the impulse to laugh. She knew Lana was at least seven years older than Eli. He played the Southern gentleman, though, and didn't remind her. At least not out loud. Lana got the message. She drained her glass and poured more wine into it.

"What's the update on Becca's condition?" Charmaine asked, breaking the silence.

"She's coming along. 'Gradual improvement' is how the doctor described it. Her mother and an older sister insisted she return with them. Some little town in upstate New York." Eli frowned in annoyance. "I'll have to replace her. What a pain."

"I'm sure you'll find any number of nubile young things willing to serve the great man," Lana drawled in perfect southern belle sarcasm.

"So, you don't like Becca cozying up to your boyfriend," Jessi said.

"I didn't bash her around, if that's what you're implying," Lana replied. Her hazel eyes flashed yellow sparks of anger.

Jessi lifted both palms. "I wasn't sayin'—"

"Yes, you were," Lana snapped. Then she eased into a smile. "I have motive, but no opportunity. I was at Cami Weller's party for supporters of the Beaux Arts Association. Fifty witnesses will tell you we had fine food and wine until well after midnight."

"Thanks, but we're not the police. Criminal investigations are their territory," Charmaine put in before Jessi could supply one of her signature wisecracks. "Back to the grunch and your thoughts about why we should look at them."

"You don't believe me," Eli stated. "After all you've seen as a paranormal expert, you think the grunch is a made-up fairytale to frightened naughty kids."

"Well, I'm not sure about the *expert* part. Though we've seen a lot of unexplained things," Charmaine said.

"I admit the story about their origins sounds far-fetched," Eli cut in.

"To say the least," Lana added with a smirk.

Eli's jaw muscles worked as if restraining his desire to launch a verbal barb Lana's way. He turned his body toward Charmaine and leaned to her. "How many have called you crazy or frauds?"

"We don't have time to count that high," Jessi joked.

"Exactly," Eli burst out.

"Okay, but we've exposed more than a couple of phony stories or proved so-called supernatural events had normal explanations," Charmaine replied.

"Yeah. Like somebody covering up a common old crime by yelling about ghosts and goblins. The devil didn't make 'em do it." Jessi helped herself to a generous serving of red wine. She made of show of ignoring Locke's lover.

Lana frowned at her. "You're drinking from a two-hundred-dollar bottle."

"Hmm, taste like it, too." Jessi smacked her lips and grinned.

"Oh please, Lana. Jessi and Charmaine can have whatever they want in my home. The snobby upper-crust matron act is tedious," Locke barked. He stood up and stomped over to Jessi at the bar. He filled Jessi's glass, tossed a defiant glare at Lana, and sat down next to Charmaine again.

"Maybe I *will* be going home, after all." Lana put her glass down with a thump. Still, she didn't leave the room.

"Let's just all take a breath," Charmaine said in her best peacemaker voice.

"Well I—" Jessi broke off at a fiery looked from Charmaine. "Yeah, everybody relax."

Charmaine cleared her throat. "You think one of the grunch is trying to stop you. But then why would they kill Amanda, the other victims, or cause other sightings? They don't have anything to do with your book."

"A diversion to keep me from making the connection. I should have known when Amanda's young man claimed he'd seen a grunch. Instead, I dismissed it as drug use and shock, like you and the police," Eli said.

"But you've changed your mind. Why?" Charmaine asked.

Eli shook his head. "I don't know. Maybe the unconscious pieces finally clicked into place. These people must be desperate to protect their way of life. No wonder after the persecution and even violence they've faced."

Jessi walked over to stand next to Charmaine's chair. "You've talked to them."

"No, not really. I mean, my source is estranged from them. Made a new life. Things have gone too far now." Eli rubbed his mouth. Then got another drink for himself.

Lana got up and went to him. "Ragged nerves make us both irritable. Maybe that's enough talk of murder for one night."

"Unless you can give us a name?" Jessi said, ignoring Lana's hint that they leave.

"I promised not to name this person. It didn't seem important at the time, even over-the-top, to be honest. Now I understand. Had I known..."

Locke chugged whiskey and dropped the heavy tumbler. It bounced onto the fine wool rug. Lana shot a pointed look at Charmaine and Jessi as she bent to retrieve it. Then she fussed over Locke. He looked shaken and didn't object to her ministrations.

"Since you won't tell us more, there's nothing else to talk about." Jessi jerked her head at Charmaine, a signal they should go.

"Eli, reconsider. Keeping information from us ties our hands," Charmaine said.

"Internet searches, books, and even historical documents only take you so far. You can't beat first-hand eyewitnesses for authenticity." Locke's hand shook as he rubbed his forehead. "If I break one promise, I lose a valuable resource. I've signed a seven-figure contract to do three more books in the series. A lot is at stake."

Jessi spun and marched back into the room to face him. "You wanna talk high stakes? How about solving a string of murders and preventing more of 'em."

"Jess." Charmaine gazed at her sister.

"Nah, the games are over. You're right, Mr. Locke. Things *have* gone too far. A neat description of people ending up dead," Jessi continued in a relentless tone. "Your goal is to pile more money on the stacks you already got. We're worried about the bodies piling up."

"Don't you take a nasty attitude with him. You're still his *employee*. You've been paid to do a job. Get out there and do it better than you have since Eli hired you," Lana said.

Jessi brushed off her insult with a wave of one hand. She stared at Locke. "You set in motion what's happening. Now you wanna keep secrets. Makes me wonder if you really want this shit-show in motion. Maybe hiring us was a cover."

Lana marched over to Jessi and stabbed a finger toward the hallway. "That is more than enough. Get out of his house!"

"Your boyfriend hasn't answered. I wouldn't make the mistake of getting in my face." Jessi continue to look at Locke.

"Everybody stay cool," Charmaine said, careful to speak in a level voice.

"You can't blame me," Locke blurted out. "All I did was ask questions and write a book of fiction. I didn't kill anyone."

"Taking a break and starting fresh is a good idea," Charmaine said in a rush of words before Jessi could respond.

She pushed Jessi ahead of her. Jessi resisted for a few seconds but then stomped out, her high-heel boots thumping on the parquet floor. They went to where their vehicles were parked in Locke's long driveway. Charmaine glanced over her shoulder to see Locke watching them, a hand holding back the drapery. Jessi blew out a breath.

"How'd I do?"

Charmaine turned her back to the window view. "Award-worthy performance. Think the improvised good cop, bad cop act might work?"

Jessi made sure Locke saw her frown at him. The heavy fabric swished to cover the glass, hiding him from view. "Lana is real sharp. I'm not sure she bought it. Locke was too shook to catch on, though."

"Yeah, but he's a con artist, from what we've heard. He could be acting, too. Lana is something... more. Locke, I can read. Either she's blocking me or paranormal forces in the house interfere." Charmaine sighed and crossed her arms as she considered both possibilities.

"Well, the electromagnetic effects of such strong incidents as we had means there could be lingering consequences." Jessi squinted. "Or Locke could be hiding how and why he's responsible."

Charmaine turned to gaze at the house like Jessi. "He didn't refer to his source as 'he' or 'she.' I'm thinking it's a woman, though. Most of the grunch community that deals with us is female. Except for JoJo, Penelope and the other women do most of the talking."

"Yeah, and even JoJo seems to stay in the background," Jessi added.

"Another thing. Locke said 'things have gone too far,' " Charmaine murmured. "Sounds like regret. Or guilt."

"I say we have another go at Penelope about what they haven't been telling us," Jessi said.

"Hmm." Charmaine nodded and opened the driver's door of her Cruze. "Meet me back at my house."

They arrived at Charmaine's Mid-City cottage off Esplanade twenty minutes later. Charmaine had called Penelope's mobile number on the way. Her voice mail announced she'd get right back to callers. She didn't. Charmaine wasn't surprised. She and Jessi sat across from each other at the dining table in Charmaine's kitchen. They both nursed bottles of Barq's root beer.

"She's busy covering tracks and coming up with a story she hopes we'll buy," Jessi said with a snort. She reached for a bag of chips but stopped at Charmaine's frown. "What? You got plenty."

"You shouldn't put greasy snacks in your stomach this time of night. We both have to get up tomorrow morning. You'll have nightmares from indigestion," Charmaine lectured. "Don't say it. I sound like Grandma Etta Ray."

"You already know." Jessi grinned as she helped herself to a handful of onion-flavored chips. She crunched for a few seconds and then frowned at Charmaine. "I don't get why Penelope even talked to us in the first place."

"Miss Gladys, aka mouth of the South, snitched about the community. Penelope figured we'd come looking anyway. Might as well find out how much we knew," Charmaine replied.

"And send us off in another direction. We might have kept digging until we found out too much," Jessi added with a nod. "Yep. I'd play it that way myself. Still risky, though."

"Right. Unless they were counting on us being not too bright. Now they know better." Charmaine looked at Jessi.

Before Jessi could reply, a loud series of pops rang through the house. Instinct from their days in the project pushed them from their chairs. They lay flat on the floor. Charmaine looked around.

"No broken glass," she whispered after silence followed for fifteen seconds.

"Shooting in the air outside? Could be a raggedy car with a bad exhaust pipe."

Jessi started to crawl when a loud bang bounced off the walls. Windowpanes rattled. Big utensils from the canister on the counter flew over their heads. A twelve-inch carving fork embedded in a wooden cabinet door. Charmaine's set of knives whizzed by seconds later.

"Seems like the ghosts have brought the fight to us this time," Charmaine said, eyes wide.

"Ya think?" Jessi wisecracked, and then belly-crawled away.

"Don't move. They've missed so far." Charmaine tried to snatch her back. She managed to grab the hem of Jessi's sweater-hoodie.

Jessi slapped her hand away. "You want them moving in for good? We gotta act now or you'll have a new roommate."

"Crap!"

Charmaine followed, using knees and elbows. Jessi reached the chair with her bag. A glass bowl shattered against the microwave oven. They both covered their heads as shards rained down. Charmaine squeaked when blood trickled down Jessi's cheek.

"Just a scratch. Come on," Jessi yelled. She pulled out a stunner. "Where's yours?"

"Uh, uh..." Charmaine blinked a mile a minute.

Jessi checked the setting on the modified shock-pulse gun. She stood despite Charmaine's yelps for her to stay down. Jessi took two cautious steps. Something round and yellow spun toward her head, and she ducked. The ceramic sugar bowl clattered to the floor, dusting them both as if they were donuts. Charmaine's fear turned to rage. She shook crystals of sweetness from her hair.

"Oh, hell no. In here breaking up my kitchenware after all the money I spent."

Charmaine stood and scrambled to find the tools Jessi had given her. She went to the desk where she paid bills and put her mail. Before she could reach for it, the shallow drawer pulled out as if by invisible hands. Charmaine grabbed it before it flung off. Her stun gun and an EMF neutralizer fell into her open hands.

"Thank you, guardian angel," Charmaine murmured.

For a solid ten minutes, Jessi and Charmaine swept the house. The kinetic activity died down. Most of the skirmish seemed centered in the kitchen. Charmaine found her sage and other herbs in spray bottles. Jessi continued to fight while Charmaine spritzed the counteracting agents to expel negative energy. Fifteen minutes of battle ensued. Then, like a switch had been flipped, the house grew still. Almost too still. Jessi blinked a question at Charmaine, who shrugged in response. Charmaine and Jessi stood for a few moments more. They let out twin long breaths both had been holding. The sisters slumped to the floor at the same time.

"Damn it." Jessi pulled a broken chunk of pottery from beneath her butt. "Somebody gonna pay big-time. I mean that!"

"I'm gonna clean up this mess. And then, we're gone figure out who made the mistake of screwing with us," Charmaine said with a fierce frown.

Jessi gazed back at her, panting. Then she grinned. "Oh-oh. They done messed up for real. The church girl is pissed and ready for a fight. The Joliet Sisters ain't here to play."

Chapter 13

Grunch Time

Monday morning dawned as if all was right with the world. The autumn morning looked beautiful as Charmaine shuffled out to get the newspaper. Sunshine, low humidity, birds tweeting, and a hum of normal workday traffic sounded. Outside, her house looked the same. The guy next door waved as he backed out of his driveway. Nothing looked out of place. There was no evidence that a supernatural tornado had raged inside her attractive Creole cottage the night before. Back inside, Charmaine sat down in her office to read about the latest trail of mayhem beyond her four walls. She savored coffee and quiet. Thumping in another room announced Jessi was up. Seconds later, she came in holding her own mug with steam rising from it.

"Girl, you throw a helluva party," Jessi said as she plopped down into one of two chairs facing Charmaine's desk.

"Penelope hasn't called me back," Charmaine said, ignoring her attempt at humor.

"Probably hoping that visitation she arranged last night worked and you're..." Jessi drew a forefinger across her neck.

"What? No. She doesn't seem like the type," Charmaine objected.

"You sound like every neighbor or classmate of a serial killer. 'She was always a quiet, helpful person. Never would have guessed she collected human body parts'," Jessi said, pitching her voice high.

"Oh stop," Charmaine tossed back. She burst out laughing at the gallows humor anyway. Jessi joined her until they were in tears.

"It must be release from stress." Charmaine dabbed at her eyes and sipped coffee.

"Yeah. 'Cause we don't have a damn thing to be laughing about," Jessi said, still giggling despite her words. "You realize the Axeman and his crew tried to kill us?"

"And Penelope sent them." Charmaine tilted her head to one side as she let that theory percolate a few seconds. "Nah. I don't feel it."

"Look at the facts. We get info from the Axeman. You talk to her. Then we talk to Eli. Same night we're ambushed. Two plus two, girl." Jessi shrugged.

"Doesn't add up. The Axeman snitched on the grunch when he told us they were involved. Why would he turn around and do a job for Penelope?" Charmaine shook her head. "Seems like they're on opposite sides."

"Hired killers switch sides on a dime. Or maybe she offered a member of his crew incentive to start his own business."

Charmaine sighed. "Okay, but that's some complicated crime-planning. Plus, I don't see why."

Jessi sat forward. "All the work they've done for a hundred years to hide in plain sight could be trashed. We uncover one of the community committed murder and report it to the NOPD. Eli jumps on and writes another best seller. All of the persecution comes crashing down on them. Their children and grandchildren become objects of curiosity."

"Lord, when you put it that way... Nope. Still don't feel it in here." Charmaine patted her stomach.

"Stop with the gut feelings, or any feelings. Logic, hard facts, and science." Jessi lifted a finger to tick off each point.

"Penelope knows Detective Harrison is involved in our case. He'd be suspicious if anything happened to us," Charmaine countered.

"Desperate people make desperate, risky moves." Jessi clicked her tongue as she reclined against the chair back.

Charmaine put her mug down and tapped the keyboard on her desktop. "Umm, okay. Penelope and her people are one possibility. Other suspects, Eli Locke and Becca. Motives?"

"What are you doing?"

"I'm filling in a flow chart on suspects, motives, and opportunity." Charmaine continued to click away as she talked.

"Guess it will be color-coded, too," Jessi wisecracked.

"It works. Besides, my brain can't hold onto the many twists and turns this case keeps taking," Charmaine said, unbothered by her teasing.

"I'll play along. Locke has a shady past, and not just perpetrating fraud. Penelope's people are convinced he's a murderer. He's eliminating people who know where he's buried those skeletons. In one case, literally." Jessi slurped coffee.

"Eli needs to hide his felonious secrets. Check. Then we have Becca with the stalkerish crush on him. Didn't she know him in New York?" Charmaine peeped from behind the twenty-five-inch computer monitor.

Jessi snapped her fingers. "Yes, she's from New York. Well, New Rochelle, to be exact. But she worked in the city."

"First for a big literary agent, then at a publishing company. Which is how she met Locke, on the literary cocktail party scene," Charmaine added.

"So, she knows Locke has secrets," Jessi said.

"Maybe not the details. If she's crazy in love enough, she might not care. Becca will protect him, whatever he's done." Charmaine frowned at the words on the screen. "Really, though? Would a girl like Becca put so much on the line for Locke?"

"You said the operative word, crazy." Jessi snorted in cynicism about emotional entanglements.

"Yeah, love is big motivator," Charmaine murmured and tapped away again.

"You should know. Had us lean hard on Rochelle." Jessi cleared her throat.

Charmaine stood, hands on both hips. "I didn't tell you and Diamond to go full thug. In fact, I promised to let him deal with her from now on."

"Wow, having talks on handling his exes. So, y'all rockin' on the regular, huh? None of my business." Jessi hid her smirk by lifting the coffee mug to her lips.

"Then act like it." Charmaine smacked her lips in anger and plopped into the chair. The keyboard took a beating as she click-clacked more notes. Then she stopped. "I'm calling Penelope again. If she doesn't answer, I'm going over there anyway. Or to her bakery off Chef Menteur Highway."

As she put her hand out to grab the cell phone, it trilled musical bells. Charmaine blinked fast at it. Then at Jessi. The screen display showed Harrison's name, which meant he was calling from his extra cell phone.

"I don't read minds, Char," Jessi said.

"It's our favorite major crimes detective." Charmaine swiped to accept the call on speaker. "Hello there. How are you?"

"Don't ask. Get over to Tulane Medical and talk to Becca. She's feeling chatty about Locke. She won't talk to me," Harrison rumbled in a brusque tone.

"I have clinic appointments," Charmaine stammered as she toggled to look at her e-calendar. "I can't this morning—"

"Fine. Let the pain meds wear off and her mood toward Locke improve. She's going to be discharged this afternoon. I've got real leads to follow. Up to you," Harrison said.

"Well, I might could... Hello?" Charmaine glanced at her phone to find he'd ended the connection.

Jessi sprang to her feet. "He's right. Becca hasn't been able to talk for a few days. We better move fast before she changes again. I'll meet you over there. Going home to put on clean clothes. I'm not far from Tulane."

"But my appointments." Charmaine pointed to the monitor.

"Right. You gotta get other social workers to see 'em. I'll start without you if it takes a while."

"Hey, it's not always so simple." Charmaine looked up to find Jessi gone. "Sure, rearrange my professional schedule. No problem."

For the next ten minutes Charmaine sent messages to three colleagues. Thanks to technology, she switched her clients to see them without leaving her computer. Two had open spots. The other one didn't mind taking on an extra session. Then she raced to her bedroom to get dressed. As she scrambled to put on a pair of jeans and a sweater, Jessi stuck her head in the door.

"I'm taking my Jeep. On my way." Jessi hopped on one foot to get the last ankle boot on.

"Hold up. That shirt, those wool slacks. They look familiar," Charmaine blurted.

"Decided not to eat up precious time going home. Raided your closet. Not my style and a bit loose in the booty, but it'll do in a rush." Jessi grinned at her.

"Are you trying to say I have a huge butt? Very damn funny." Still, Charmaine looked at her reflection in the full-length closet mirror.

"Hey, long as Scotty likes it. Right? Anyway, I'm gone."

"Yeah, yeah." Charmaine squinted at her figure one last time.

"Speaking of Scotty, when y'all hookin' up again?" Jessi said.

"Tonight, after he—" Charmaine hissed in a breath.

"Gotcha!"

Jessi hooted and scampered off to dodge the shoe aimed at her. Charmaine muttered expletives as she dressed, left the house, and most of the way to Tulane Medical Center.

****

Jessi waited patiently in the third-floor lobby for Charmaine. She grinned when Charmaine marched by her without speaking. Detective Harrison rounded a corner before they had a chance to ask a nurse for directions. He looked like a successful businessman, dressed in a sharp navy-blue suit and pale-yellow dress shirt. His silk tie had tiny yellow diamond shapes on a lighter blue background. He could have been a CEO headed to a Fortune 500 corporate board meeting.

"I hate Monday mornings. All the weekend crap hits the fan and lands on *my* damn desk," Harrison grumbled. His version of "Good morning" left a lot to be desired.

"Thought you had better things to do," Jessi said.

"So did I. However, my boss had a different opinion. Let's get this over with," Harrison replied with a sour expression.

Charmaine looked up at him. "You said Becca didn't want to talk to you."

"I'm not going in the room. And don't tell her I'm here." Harrison frowned at no one in particular as he looked around.

"You'll be in the lobby for however long it takes us?" Charmaine asked.

"I'll be in the coffee shop. Greenberry's. Second floor."

"Great. Maybe a mocha latte will improve your mood," Jessi quipped.

"Your boss must really think Becca's statement is important to have one of his top cops just hang out." Charmaine continued to study his face.

"Don't try your magic act on me, Charmaine. I'm not in the mood," Harrison snapped. When Charmaine didn't reply or stop staring at him, he heaved a sigh. "Let's talk a minute."

He led the way to a seating area away from three chatty middle-aged white women. Harrison unbuttoned his suit jacket. He waited for the ladies to be seated in true Southern gentleman style. Then he sat heavily in a stuffed chair. Jessi lifted an arched eyebrow at him in anticipation. Charmaine blocked the incoming read from his precise cop mind. She made a practice not to use her abilities when a friend objected. And despite their spats and sparring, she considered Detective Brian Hezekiah Harrison a friend. Harrison gave her a brief smile as if he understood.

"Locke and his important pals have used their clout. The boss of my boss has, direct quote, concerns that we follow the facts. Timothy Acker and Demi Draper will be charged with Amanda Morrell's murder," Harrison said, his voice so low they leaned close to hear him.

Charmaine's mouth dropped open. "But—"

"I agree," Harrison cut in. "My gut tells me they didn't do it. But they had motive and opportunity."

"Motive?" Jessi blinked rapidly in confusion. "They're her besties."

"Amanda had an affair with Acker. He slept with Ms. Draper, who in turn rubbed her face in it. According to witnesses, they had a fight at their country club. Amanda slapped Demi silly. One of the golf pros had to pull them apart. Fists flying, thousand-dollar weaves snatched. It was a mess." Harrison shook his head.

"Hardly reason to kill but... Amanda contacted a tabloid, told them the story of Demi's mother. The headline read, 'From the Pole to a Mansion.' Seems Mrs. Draper was an exotic dancer back in the late eighties. What the upper-class would politely describe as a colorful past." Harrison shrugged.

"High-five to Mrs. Draper," Jessi said promptly. "Nothing wrong with doing an upgrade of your life."

"I can't believe that's a motive to kill, either. We're in the twenty-first century, for God's sake," Charmaine said.

"Oh, trust me. In the most refined circles it matters a lot. Mrs. Draper's social calendar is empty since the story hit. Her already-rocky marriage is imploding." Harrison looked around to be sure no one was nearby. Then he leaned toward them. "My boss didn't tell me that part. I have a few sources of my own."

"What a load of bull. She's better off without those fake friends," Jessi spat in ex-pole dancer solidarity.

Harrison shook his head. "There's more. Mrs. Draper was linked to the old Dixie Mafia. She was the girlfriend of a particularly badass gangster back in the day. Even questioned about two murders that are still unsolved. The cops in Galveston and Biloxi never found the bodies. The popular view is the victims were killed, then dropped in the Gulf of Mexico."

Jessi gave a soft whistle. "Shark snacks. Pretty effective way to make a body disappear."

"Yeah. Her boyfriend owned a couple of boat-charter outfits. Very successful, but a cover for his more lucrative business ventures. Long story short, Mr. Draper is old money and has powerful friends. He wants his daughter cleared and the bad press to go away fast."

"You mean Timmy Acker is going to be set up to take the fall," Jessi said in her usual blunt manner.

"I don't frame people or take orders from Draper," Harrison said, his deep voice rising like a threatening thunderstorm. He blinked and cleared his throat when women across the room stared at him. "I'll follow the evidence. In a new twist, Acker and Becca hooked up for a hot affair for about two months. They broke up back in February, during Mardi Gras season."

"Hold on." Charmaine frowned in concentration. "Becca is a suspect?"

"Person of interest. For now." Harrison gave her a pointed look.

"Timmy stays busy, huh?" Jessi sat back and crossed her legs. She bounced a booted foot as she considered Harrison's revelations.

"So, let me get this straight. Your boss likes the theory that Becca was Timmy's accomplice instead Demi." Charmaine frowned.

"Or maybe Acker didn't do the murder at all. It was just Becca. She has a history of stalking an ex-boyfriend. Amanda Morrell, according to sources, was sneaking around with Eli Locke at some point. They were seen together at least three times in recent weeks," Harrison said.

"Becca is possessive of him. Could be," Jessi said and turned to Charmaine.

"Which doesn't explain the other murders or the ghost sightings," Charmaine argued.

"Who says they're connected? A bunch of superstitious nuts or publicity-seeking locals. You know how the rest of the country loves all of the mystique about New Orleans. The other two murders could have been home invasions that got real violent. It happens."

Harrison laid out the alternative explanations with an impassive face. It was as though he was repeating someone else's words.

Charmaine and Jessi had a good guess whose they were, too. They exchanged a look, then both turned to him.

"Your boss wants you to tie things up with a pretty bow on top," Jessi said in a quiet tone. "That stinks."

"Big time," Charmaine added.

"And we're not going to help by throwing Becca under the bus." Jessi glared at him in defiance.

"I agree. But she's got some explaining to do. Like where was she when Amanda was killed? And, get this, she got to the murder scene before Locke and I did. My officer says she arrived at almost the same time as him." Harrison rubbed his jaw. "I hate to say it, but her part in all this raises questions."

"Well, the news she was banging Timmy is a shock. Not that we're surprised Amanda might have been involved with Eli. He seems to attract women the way honey pulls in bees," Charmaine murmured.

Jessi snorted. "Or flies buzzing around a pile of—"

"We get the image, Jess," Charmaine broke in with a grimace. She looked at the detective. "So, what do you want from us?"

"Slip in that Timmy is a suspect, and we know about their affair." Harrison glanced at his wristwatch. "In spite of command's instructions, I can't spend all day here. I have a news briefing at eleven-thirty, and I'm speaking a forensics conference downtown at the Omni. So, if we can get it moving..."

"Sure, wouldn't want to take too long setting up Becca and mess up your busy schedule," Jessi retorted.

Harrison stood. He regarded them both with a cool expression as he buttoned his jacket. "Just get as much truth out of her as you can. And don't pretend you weren't considering her as a suspect, too."

"We have bounced the idea around," Charmaine admitted, which brought a grunt from her sister. "Ignore her. Jessi hates agreeing with cops."

"You have no idea how much I'd like to ignore her, and you. You two manage to get caught up in my trickiest cases. Why is that?" Harrison's dark eyebrows bunched together in a frown of condemnation.

"Luck?" Jessi grinned at him.

Harrison blew out a breath and walked off. "I'll be downstairs. Holla."

"Well, that was interesting." Charmaine blinked at his retreating broad back. She watched as he bypassed the elevator to take the stairs.

"Real convenient for Harrison's bosses, Becca and Timmy hooking up. Then Amanda had a thing with Locke." Jessi frowned. "But..."

"Yeah. No shortage of suspects," Charmaine said to complete Jessi's thought.

"Let's go see what Becca has to say. I have a feeling your flow chart is gonna get even more complicated."

"You just said a word, sis," Charmaine agreed.

They followed signs posted on the wall to find Becca's room. The pale-blue walls almost seemed a soft white. Charmaine could see how the color would be soothing in a medical facility. Nurses and other staff moved around with hushed efficiency. A blond male RN flashed perfect white teeth and offered to help. He pointed them in the right direction. Jessi started small talk, which forced Charmaine to jab her in the ribs. His toned backside kept Jessi riveted as she watched him walk away.

"Stay on task, damn it," Charmaine snapped.

"Just 'cause you off the market," Jessi said, her gaze still on him.

"Murdering ghosts, dead bodies. Remember?" Charmaine jerked her by one arm through the door of Room 304-A.

"Yeah, yeah." Jessi followed Charmaine in, still looking back. She bumped into her.

"Shit," Charmaine blurted out. She covered her mouth with a hand when Becca's eyes fluttered.

"I'd like some water, please." Becca's voice sounded like rattling dry twigs. She waved an arm toward a pitcher of water out of reach. "Please."

"Sure thing." Jessi scurried over and filled a plastic cup. "Excuse my sister. She's naturally loud."

"Sorry," Charmaine said in a muted tone. She gave Jessi a cutting glare. "How are you feeling?"

Becca drank three long sips through a straw, taking breaths between each one. She allowed Jessi to fluff the pillows behind her. Then she pressed the remote and raised the hospital bed. She blinked at Jessi as if confused. Then she looked at Charmaine. "Oh. You two. How do I feel. Like a murdering demon straight from hell beat me up."

"They say your recovery is coming along nicely," Charmaine said. She shrugged when Jessi rolled her eyes.

Becca huffed. "You know they threatened to move me to the psych unit? All because I told the truth about what happened."

Charmaine sat in the vinyl recliner next to the bed. "You can tell us. We won't question your sanity."

"Yeah, well, that's something." Becca suffered a coughing fit.

Jessi helped her sip more water. "Take it easy. You're safe now."

"Easy for you to say. It didn't come after you," Becca breathed, her voice still weak. She grimaced, cleared her throat, and turned her face to the wall for a few moments.

"Nothing's coming after you here," Jessi said.

Charmaine shot a piercing look at Jessi. "I don't think..."

"Tulane has some of the most advanced medical tech around for diagnosis and treatment. Too much magnetic and chemical interference. Messes with what the superstitious called 'ghosts' and other supernormal entities." Jessi stepped closer to the bed with a cool and confident demeanor.

"You've swept the place with one of your gizmos?" Becca asked, her voice shaking.

"Standard procedure," was Jessi's crisp businesslike reply.

Charmaine gritted her teeth to keep in a gibe. Instead, she smiled at Becca. "Concentrate on following doctor's orders and getting better. You feel up to telling us what happened?"

Becca breathed in deep and let it out. Then she nodded. "We went back to the apartment since Eli got a bit jumpy. He kept hearing creaks and bumps at his house. Viola was gone to visit her daughter in Baton Rouge for a few days. She had her baby early. For some reason, Eli is convinced her being there keeps him safer. I cracked a bad joke. Said the ghosts were scared of her, and she never heard them anyway. That she'd be snoring as they ripped through everything."

"Including him," Jessi said.

"Exactly what Eli said. I didn't mean to... Anyway, I suggested we stay at his friend's condo. He's more relaxed there. We..." Becca's voice trailed off wistfully.

"Hmm." Jessi cocked an eyebrow at her.

Charmaine read the intimate details Jessi's intuition told her Becca left out. Eli had turned to Becca for sexual healing at least once there. The California king-sized bed in the master suite had gotten a workout. Charmaine marveled at the athleticism of a man nearing fifty. Then she shook herself away from that voyeuristic train of thought.

"And that night... " Charmaine prodded.

"We talked about his next speaking event. I wanted to stay with him, you know. Make sure he was comfortable. We both had a glass of wine, but then he wanted to turn in. I told him I'd let myself out." Becca paused.

"You were hoping to stay the night, in bed with him," Charmaine ventured.

Becca's eyes narrowed. "He's brilliant, funny, sexy, and strong. We've worked closely for almost three years, almost completing each other's sentences. So, yes. I want him. Not his money. Not his fame. Him, the man."

Charmaine slid a sideways glance at Jessi. "Okay then."

"You started sizing Eli up within five minutes of meeting him. I mean that literally, as in inches. He has to wade through women, even a few men, like you all the time," Becca said.

"But you protect Eli from us sex bandits, huh?" Charmaine's dry, cynical humor missed the mark. Becca remained serious.

"I warn off the more predatory types, yes." Becca wore a proud smile that faded seconds later.

"Eli likes the attention, so a few get through." Jessi's remark hit a sore spot.

"They were one-night stands. All of them." Becca's disdainful gaze made one thing clear. Charmaine fit the temporary-thrill category.

Charmaine gauged Becca's mood. Despite her words, Eli's flings cut deep. A thought popped into her head. Her cell phone's insistent buzzing sealed the decision to take the gamble. Charmaine knew who it was without checking. Harrison was downstairs, impatient for a result. She'd take the risk of upsetting the injured woman.

"Lana is different, very different. Looks to me like she's got staying power. Eli might even put a ring on it," Charmaine said calmly.

Jessi took Charmaine's cue. "She's got her own money, status, and let's face it. She looks good, too. Hell, some might even say she'd be an upgrade for old Eli."

"No, he wouldn't! Eli's said over and over he's done with marriage. Even if he did, he'd want a younger woman who could give him a child. She's nothing but a social-climbing—" Becca coughed hard, a hand to her throat as she panted for air.

Jessi sprang forward to pat her on the back. "Easy, girl. Don't get all freaked out on us."

"Who does she think she is?" Becca sucked hard on the straw. She brushed away Jessi's attempts to be helpful. "I'm fine."

"I'll get a nurse to be sure," Charmaine started to rise when Becca's voice cut through the air between them.

"They'll give me a sedative. You want me awake for what I'm about to tell you." Becca looked from her to Jessi and back.

Charmaine sat back down without hesitation. "Go on."

"He's with her, isn't he?" Becca swallowed hard. Her eyes became glassy with tears.

"You mean..." Charmaine looked at Jessi, unsure if she should answer, given Becca's fragile state.

Jessi swept past any such misgivings. "Lana's staying at the house with him. Viola is back, too. They seem to get on each other's nerves."

"Lana acts like the lady of the manor at times. All the time, actually," Becca said, her mouth turned down. "But Viola likes her, at least better than she can stomach *me*."

"I'm not saying she's moved in or they're planning a wedding," Jessi added to soften the blow.

"But she's there. Clinging to him twenty-four seven. The middle-aged nympho with a closet full of bustiers and sex toys." Becca's voice choked on the words.

"Wow." Jessi's eyes went wide.

"Don't get worked into another fit," Charmaine said to steer Jessi from going after the dirty details. She also didn't want Becca to have a medical emergency in the process.

"Eli has secrets. His first wife left him after he almost went to jail because of a shady deal. Most people don't know about his early marriage." Becca wore a fierce look.

"But you do your homework," Charmaine said.

Becca's mouth quirked up at one end in a smile. "She was scared of him. Though she never pressed charges for abuse or anything. But she told a few people he was capable of shutting her up about his business dealings. He was only a few years out of college. They both were, which is where they met."

"You do get the goods," Jessi murmured.

"I doubt she'd talk even if you had time to track her down. I'm mean, after almost thirty years?"

"She's probably married by now, maybe more than once," Jessi agreed.

Charmaine's therapist experience kicked in. "You dug into his background. For leverage, to hold onto him. He'll resent you for it instead of returning your feelings."

"Skip the psychological analysis," Becca hissed.

"Fine. What's the explosive revelation you have for us?" Charmaine ignored the buzzing of her phone again.

"I'm guessing you know by now Eli once had an affair with Amanda Morrell. He also made a lot of money on real estate in New Orleans and Biloxi after Hurricane Katrina. Eli scooped up properties, hired out-of-work locals to renovate them, and made a bundle. His book sales haven't been all that hot for the last two years. Until his current book, that is."

"Profiting on misery is disgusting, but it isn't a crime. Doesn't make him any different from a lot of other folks, either," Jessi said.

"A lot of hurricane victims didn't have clear property titles. His company let them think they were getting help. Instead, he ended up either their landlord or the owner," Becca replied.

"Jessi is right. Eli didn't break any laws," Charmaine replied. She stood. "Now we know Eli isn't a nice person. Thanks for the info. Get some rest."

Becca strained forward in the bed. "But he knew the murder victims."

Charmaine gave Becca a sympathetic look. She put both hands on Becca's shoulders to make her ease back onto the large pillows. "Don't get upset again. I know Eli might have kind of misled you into thinking y'all had a romantic future. Another reason he's not such a nice guy, but—"

"He knew the other man that was killed, too. And his wife," Becca said, resisting Charmaine's effort to make her settle down.

Charmaine gasped. She let go of her. "What?"

"Justin Wallace was an architect. His wife, Susan, a lawyer. They became activists to help fight for poor and middle-class black New Orleans natives who lost their properties. I believe Eli found out they were close to proving he *had* done something illegal."

Jessi stared at Charmaine. "Daaa-damn. Game-changer."

"Still think I'm just a bitter rejected woman?" Becca wore an ice-cold smile that stretched her thin lips.

After several beats, Charmaine glanced from Jessi to Becca. "We'll get back to you with an answer on that one."

Jessi chuckled deep in her throat and said to Becca, "You'll be out of a job if you keep trash-talking your boss. Which means leaving him in Lana's hot hands."

"Miss Status-Conscious won't stick around much longer. Not once Eli's connections to the murders come out. In my physically weakened and emotionally fragile state, I didn't know what I was saying. Eli will understand." Becca fell back, a hand pressed to her forehead. "Thanks for coming."

Out in the hallway, Jessi waited until the door to Becca's room swished closed behind them. She looked at Charmaine. "Becky got true female hustler moves. Is that what they teach at Mount Holyoke?"

"Girl, please. Rich women have had those kinds of moves for hundreds of years. She probably knew how to scheme and manipulate long before she got to her fancy college." Charmaine strode toward the stairwell. "Let's find Harrison before he pops a blood vessel."

"Well, he'll get top-tier medical care in minutes if he does," Jessi joked as she followed.

As Charmaine predicted, Harrison wore an agitated frown when they approached him in the coffee shop. He tapped his cell phone with quick movements. Harrison popped from his seat the second he saw them.

"I could have had open heart surgery by this time." Harrison blew out air. "Hope it was worth the aggravation."

"Thanks for the concern, but it wasn't too bad for us." Jessi grinned at him.

Harrison glowered down at her. Then he transferred his fiery gaze to Charmaine. "What did she have to say?"

"Eli knew all four of the murder victims. Becca implied he had motive to kill them. Still, she doesn't say Eli attacked her. So, I'm sure she got banged up by a ghost that turned on him. Calling up spirits is tricky. They're not trained poodles; and they have their own agendas."

"More like caged lions. A trainer might think he's got them tamed into submission and then crunch. You become a big cat snack." Jessi nodded.

Charmaine sat down. "I'd kill for a cappuccino right now."

"I'll get one. What you havin', detective?" Jessi asked before heading for the counter.

"More information so I can get on with my Monday," Harrison clipped. He sat next to Charmaine despite his irritable response.

He tapped blunt fingertips on the round tabletop as Charmaine elaborated on Becca's story. She didn't need psychic skills to know Harrison was skeptical. She could almost hear his mind working like well-oiled machinery, gears clicking. Motive, opportunity, ability. What made sense, what didn't.

"I know what you're thinking. A figure of speech only this time," Charmaine added with a smile when he squinted at her.

"Locke may be in good physical shape, but I don't see him overpowering two men. Both of them were a good fifteen years younger than him. Woods was not just strong from construction work. The guy used to be an amateur boxer. The other victim looked pretty strong, too. Before the killer or killers got hold of him, that is." Harrison held up a hand. "I don't want to hear theories about supernatural perps."

"Your cops were witnesses at the couple's house when—"

"Neither of them saw ghosts," Harris cut her off, a forefinger pointed at her nose.

"Okay. Sure. Whatever you say," Charmaine drawled.

Jessi returned with two steaming mugs and sat in a third chair. "You can lead the detective to coffee, but you can't make him drink," Jessi said.

Harrison's jaw muscles worked, but he ignored the dig. "Either the killers came back to get whatever they were trying to find, or you surprised looters. We get that at crime scenes sometimes. Vultures figuring the victims won't be needing their big screen TVs anymore."

"You really work hard not believing us after all we've been through together. I'm hurt." Jessi faked a pained expression. The she licked whipped cream from the top of her latte.

"Aside from the insulting skepticism, I agree. Eli has an alibi in at least one of those murders. He's been pretty visible since coming to town." Charmaine frowned at all of the possibilities before her.

"He could have hired out the job," Jessi said. She shrugged when both of them looked at her.

Charmaine turned to Harrison. "Eli is into fine bourbon, beachfront getaways, and being the center of attention at cocktail parties. I don't see him interviewing hired killers. Do you?"

Harrison stood. "I arrested a five-foot-five heiress when I was a uniform. She blew her husband away with a shotgun while he showered. Nothing surprises me after fifteen years on the job."

Jessi sat straight in excitement. "I remember reading about her at the time. I was in high school back then. Tell us everything."

"I've got work to do, and so do you," Harrison replied.

"Oh really?" Jessi snorted.

"Yes. Sort through all the spooky stuff. Somebody is setting up phony hauntings to hide the real crime and killer," Harrison said. He pulled out his cell phone when a ringtone sounded.

"Or killers," Charmaine put in.

"Yeah, okay, I did use the plural. But don't jump on that speculation too fast. One determined man can do a lot of damage."

"Or woman." Charmaine gazed up at him.

Harrison blew out air and looked at a large clock on the wall. "Don't give me heartburn with your brainstorms. Call me when you find something I can believe."

"What if Marie Laveau tells us a group of evil spirits are spreading terror in our good city?" Jessi cocked her head to one side as she looked up at him.

"Glad I keep antacid in my car." Harrison strode off, a hand on his midsection.

Charmaine watched his strong, purposeful gait until he vanished around a corner. She sipped from her mug then set it down. "I'll be chewing those chalk tablets myself in a minute. What a mess."

"We caught ourselves a real doozy for sure. A horror writer who claims his monsters are stalking him. Two jealous women. Four murders. A ghost who hires out to do hits." Jessi laughed. "New Orleans doesn't do crime like anywhere else. I love my city."

"I'm happy you're so happy. And you shouldn't annoy Brian with talk about paranormal urban legends. He's a grouch at times, but he does listen to us. Even if he'd never admit it," Charmaine said.

"I meant what I said about Miss Marie. She wants to talk to us again." Jessi nodded when Charmaine gawked at her, mouth wide open.

"Get ready for another fun night at the cemetery."

"Lord have mercy. Kat invited me to her progressive church. No telling what they'll make of *me*." Charmaine gulped coffee for fortification.

"Keep it simple when they ask you to tell them about yourself. Just sayin'." Jessi winked at her.

Chapter 14

Malicious Intentions

The cool October night looked picture perfect. Moonlight. Magnolia trees. Tombstones. "Quiet as the grave" had a literal meaning here. Jessi and Charmaine followed the well-trodden paths between stone angels, saints, and other memorials to the dearly departed. Traffic sounds even seemed to be muted in respect to St. Louis No. 1, the oldest cemetery in the three hundred-year-old city.

"What do you think the Archdiocese of New Orleans would do if we get caught? Probably throw some holy water on us and hope we burn. Like in those old movies. The witch would sizzle away in puffs of steam. Or smoke." Jessi giggled as she walked along with pep in her step.

"I don't get why you're so jolly," Charmaine muttered. She scanned their surroundings. The beam from their LED flashlights reflected off the bright white of an elaborate monument.

"Because we're going to get answers. I feel it in my bones." Jessi sang the last sentence. She did a few dance moves. "Cheer up, sis. Being summoned by the dead is good news for once."

"I want this case to be over. Now." Charmaine fought off a shiver that threatened to take control of her limbs. She stumbled on a rock. "Damn it! Oh Lord. Sorry."

"You're apologizing to headstones and air. Girl please." Jessi turned a corner.

Charmaine let out a small squeak when Jessi disappeared. She scrambled to catch up. "We're breaking every kinda rule being here. Straight-up disrespectful."

"Look, if anybody living shows we'll just explain that we were invited," Jessi quipped.

"Explaining we RSVP'd spirits will sound great when we're in court for trespassing."

Jessi spun to face Charmaine. "What's really got you on edge?"

"I dunno, Jess. Dead criminals who can kill the living could have me a bit anxious. Or maybe I'm overreacting," Charmaine shot back. Something whished by her head and Charmaine ducked with another curse.

"At this rate you're going to be on your knees asking for forgiveness *a lot*." Jessi chuckled for a few seconds but stopped at Charmaine's frozen evil-eyed stare. Jessi held up her detection apparatus. "Nothing is following us. That was probably just a bat that flew by your head."

"Gee, thanks. I feel a lot better now. Let's get this over with." Charmaine brushed past Jessi to lead the way to Marie Laveau's final resting place.

Jessi jogged until she was by Charmaine's side again. "Seriously. I've seen you scared before but nothing like this."

Charmaine stopped and whirled around. "If we don't figure out who is responsible, how they're calling up ghosts, and figure out a way to stop them more people will die. Still got happy feet?"

"Mission accomplished. You've killed my buzz." Jessi blinked at her.

"I can't." Charmaine resumed her march toward their rendezvous point.

"I get it. The stakes are super high on this one. We're talking a bloodbath, but we've got help," Jessi panted as she raced to keep up with Charmaine. Seconds later, they both skidded to a halt at Miss Marie's Greek Revival final home.

"Yeah. But can we trust them?"

"Ah, we could ask the same question of *you*," came a soft-accented female voice full of unleashed power. Miss Marie's tone held a note of amused censure. Yet made it clear that Charmaine's question had offended her.

"I mean no disrespect, but—"

"And yet you demonstrate it freely," Miss Marie interjected. "In other words, you imply I am a liar, a cheat, someone whose word cannot be relied on."

"I'm sure Ms. Charmaine didn't mean such insults," Lucas put in quickly.

Charmaine blinked at empty air. The words were like whispers that floated around her head. Night sounds seemed to recede as though a force assisted Charmaine in hearing the ghosts. Then nothing while they waited for her defense.

"You heard?" Jessi grinned, delighted to not be alone in talking to the dead.

"Hold off on the celebration. I'm not overjoyed to have more voices in my brain," Charmaine snapped. Then she stiffed her spine.

"Spirits always arrive with their own agendas. We know that from experience. The results can be unpredictable, even disastrous, once they're set free to walk among the living."

Silence dropped like a curtain. Charmaine shuddered at the ominous implications of pissing off Madame Marie Laveau. She sensed that Lucas remained quiet in dreadful anticipation of a supernatural explosion. Jessi's gaze shifted from their ghost companions to Charmaine and back again several times.

"Even if intentions are good, summoning phantoms always have consequences. *Oui*," Miss Marie said. "*Alors*, we understand each other. Our assistance requires a fair exchange."

"And your price is?" Charmaine crossed her arms.

"Hold up. Hold up. We ain't come out here for no negotiation. Lucas?" Jessi looked to the left of where Miss Marie apparently stood.

"I defer to Madame," came the hardly audible soft, deep voice.

Charmaine got the clear message. In whatever pecking order existed in the afterlife, Marie Laveau, aka The Widow Paris, aka Madame Glapion, held a high position. "Agreed."

"Hell no, we don't agree, not without having the terms spelled out first," Jessi yelled.

"There will be more slaughter. Choose," Miss Marie clipped.

"I said we agree," Charmaine said with a side glance at Jessi.

Jessi heaved a sigh. "At least tell us what my sister just got us into."

"An alliance. I will continue to assist you, and you will help me when called on. Don't worry. I won't ask you to break any laws." Miss Marie gave a low laugh.

"We're breaking a law right now meeting you," Charmaine retorted.

"Nonsense. You were invited to my home."

"See? I told you," Jessi put in. She pursed her lips when Charmaine frowned at her.

"We won't do anything that's illegal under *modern* law," Charmaine countered.

"Hmm. You remind me of my oldest Heloise, demanding but smart. *D'accord*, we proceed."

Once again, all became quiet. Charmaine looked to Jessi for answers. Her sister shook her head and shrugged. Then she started what to Charmaine was a one-sided conversation. Without explanation, Charmaine could no longer hear even the faintest murmurings of the ghosts. Jessi gestured in between asking short questions. Jessi yelped, "Say what?" and

"Wow." She waved off Charmaine's attempts to interrupt. Ten minutes went by. Then another five minutes.

"Whoa. Mind about to explode." Jessi huffed a few times. She moved to a nearby grave and perched on a ledge.

"From the look on your face maybe I don't want to know." Charmaine sat as well. Cold seeped from the stone like icy fingers poking her.

"We've got a fight on our hands," Jessi breathed. She stared off into the darkness.

"I figured that out a while ago, what with the poltergeist who can inflict wounds and the Axeman roaming around causing havoc."

"No, I mean for real. Miss Marie and Lucas have gone off to find the powerful *bokor*," Jessi said. All traces of her earlier merriment had faded.

Charmaine jumped to her feet. "A sorcerer?"

Jessi looked at her, nodding slowly. "We have to defeat him. For good."

"No. You can't mean.... We can't." Charmaine's legs felt like mush as she staggered back to lean against a statue. "Kill him."

****

Jessi's equipment sat piled up on her dining room table. Charmaine sorted through her own style of weapons. Diamond sat stunned on the sofa across the room. The enormity of the situation had left her mute. Scotty and Kat moved around, following instructions from Jessi. They took turns stuffing items in a backpack for her.

"I think that's all. Can't afford to be weighed down. Makes me appreciate Logan's work even more," Jessi said to Kat.

"You sure these gizmos gonna work?" Kat held up a device and examined it from all sides before placing it back on the table.

"These have been field-tested. Most of them, at least. Not at this level of strength, though. I hope Logan's tinkering comes through for us." Jessi continued to adjust dials and tap screens as she spoke.

Scotty stood and grabbed Charmaine's arm. "Wait a damn minute. Y'all need more than hope and maybe. There's gotta be another way."

"Ya know, I was all for y'all to screw and get past the whole indecisive thing. I see why

Charmaine resisted." Jessi let out a grunt of annoyance.

"What?" Scotty looked at her with a deep frown.

"Now you're the boyfriend, right? So, you jump to typical masculine crap. Actin' like you're being protective when you want to control her. I got a news flash. Charmaine ain't *that* woman, Scotty." Jessi talked while continuing to examine gadgets.

Scotty's eyes narrowed. "Excuse me?"

"Yeah. Control, you get to hold onto her, mold her into obedience. Next, you'll use the 'It's because I love you' line. Nah, bruh. Control." Jessi turned to Charmaine. "And I didn't have to attend boring grad school or read textbooks."

"Ignore her," Charmaine muttered with a side glance at Scotty.

"She's right, though. Sex workers like us get a PhD on these streets." Diamond shrugged when Scotty transferred his stony gaze to her. "Hey, I'm just sayin'."

"I'm not trying to control you," Scotty said to Charmaine. "I'm trying to reason with you about the risks involved in—"

"Like we haven't done this before. Suddenly you're more of an expert than us," Jessi broke in.

Scotty let out a noisy breath. He rubbed a large hand over his face. Then he watched the others in silence. The women finished packing duffle bags of equipment. Charmaine clipped two compact modified stun guns to a belt around her waist. Jessi and a friend, an ex-hooker who now designed children's clothes, had made two leather belts to be holsters. Diamond moved around with a checklist on Jessi's tablet computer, making sure they had everything.

Jessi glanced at the clock on her phone. She stuffed it into an inside pocket of her jacket. "Cutting it close, but we should be there on time."

"Marie Laveau. You're going to listen to her and not me. Perfect." Scotty shook his head.

"It takes one to know one. Dead people, I mean." Jessi held a gun out as if taking aim. Then she stuck it in her own belt holster.

"Listen, Scotty. I understand you're worried about me." Charmaine stopped when he waved a hand at her.

"Jessi is right. I'm not as much of a male feminist as I thought." Scotty put both hands on Charmaine's shoulders. "You're a pro. I should trust your decisions. It's just... I know how tricky going into battle is."

"Yet you went anyway," Charmaine said in a soft voice.

"Because it was my job at the time. Being a soldier was going to be my career," Scotty replied.

"And this is *my* job." Charmaine gazed into his eyes. They stood close in an intimate conversation.

"Yes." Scotty brushed his lips across hers. Then he let go of her. "You're going in prepared with intel and weapons. Exactly the way my unit went on patrol around Mosul. I finally know what my foster parents and sisters felt when I'd leave on assignment."

Charmaine felt a tingle at the reference to Scotty's two tours in Afghanistan. "You're not used to being the one left behind. I understand."

"Yeah, deal with it so we can get on with business. Let's go." Jessi looped the long strap of her duffle bag over a shoulder.

"Good field trooper. Horrible diplomat," Diamond quipped. She laughed when Jessi muttered an expletive in her direction.

Scotty sighed in resignation. He held up his phone. "At least with the app, I'll have your location in case of an emergency. Meeting up with dead people and an evil sorcerer is bound to go south."

"Only come in with the cavalry if we call for backup," Charmaine said in a firm tone.

"Otherwise, you'll get in the way. We won't have time for trying to rescue nobody," Jessi clipped. She stood at the door with a hand on the knob.

"She means we don't want any normal folks getting hurt," Charmaine put in with a sharp look at her blunt sister. "We know how to deal with supernatural entities and you don't."

"I said what I said," Jessi retorted.

"I wish you could have met them somewhere safe, like in Congo Square. Or even St. Louis No. 1, like before." Scotty looked over the second bag before he zipped it closed.

"In the wooded area off Michoud is perfect, I think. Plus, Miss Marie says the site is where a lot of paranormal activity occurred." Jessi replied. She locked the door.

"There are houses within running distance. Okay, not short runs, but still," Charmaine added when Scotty snorted.

"Miles, a good two-to-three miles if you head deep in," Scotty countered.

"As you observed, my friend, we're prepared. Time to kick ghost booty." Jessi stepped outside. Her Jeep was parked in the driveway near her backdoor. She opened the back of it and dropped her bag on the floor. She repeated the action with the second bag, and then returned. "The plan once again. We're going to drive into the woods so my full arsenal will be close at hand. I've got these to give me time to make a dash." She held up what looked like Roman candles.

"They pop and release gases that scatter certain types of energy waves. Hey, I'm starting to sound like a science geek." Charmaine grinned. She put on glasses. "Check the connection."

Diamond went to the kitchen island where Jessi's laptop was set up. "Looks good."

Jessi and Charmaine had invested in a pair of spyglasses with built-in HD cameras. The accompanying app installed on Jessi's computer recorded images and audio. As much as Jessi complained about Eli, their deep-pockets client had funded more cool gadgets. The downside was how dangerous working for him was proving to be.

"So, we're all set. Tick-tock." Jessi tapped the back of her wrist as if she wore a watch. When Scotty responded by wrapping Charmaine in one last tight hug, she sputtered. "Oh, give me a break. We're not leaving on a deep-space mission."

Scotty released Charmaine and stepped back. He faced Jessi with an impish grin. "Stop hating. You'll find a man one day."

"How you know I don't have one already? Maybe two or three." Jessi snapped her fingers. Then she opened the door and led the way to her Jeep, hips swinging.

"I don't doubt it, baby girl," Scotty called out. He tried to maintain his air of amusement, but the grin faded.

"We'll be fine." Charmaine gave him one last peck on the cheek as she passed him.

Jessi watched while Charmaine climbed into the passenger seat. "Sure we will. As fine as we can be facing a New Orleans version of the Dark Lord."

"Please explain how the hard scientist is addicted to *Lord of the Rings* and African-based fantasy," Charmaine said as she buckled the seat belt.

"At least I know it's not real. Unlike your addiction to an old white guy with a beard who lives in the clouds." Jessi started the engine. "You actually packed spray bottles of holy water and anointed oil. Unbelievable."

"There is documented evidence that herbs and natural substances repel evil forces," Charmaine explained in a patient tone. "Now drive."

"At least if we get thirsty or want to make a salad we'll have plenty of water and olive oil." Jessi chuckled at her own joke. She wheeled the SUV into traffic.

"Extra virgin variety, of course," Charmaine replied with a grin.

They shared a laugh. Their humor served to dispel the anxiety of what they were about to face. Jessi drove to Highway 90 toward Michoud Boulevard. As houses grew farther apart, the night sky grew darker. Fewer streetlights didn't do much to make them feel less isolated. Charmaine fingered the eyeglasses she held in her lap.

"Don't turn the camera on until we're well into the meet. We agreed," Jessi said as if she read her mind.

"I never had anybody worried about me before. Except you, I mean," Charmaine murmured. She gazed out the passenger-side window at the passing scenery.

"Humph. I didn't waste time worrying. Underneath that church-girl shell is a badass. I've seen you in a fight, remember." Jessi glanced at her sideways before looking ahead at the road again.

"We been through some shit, huh?"

Jessi's only response was to nod. They both thought over rough childhoods in even rougher neighborhood streets. Then there was the trouble they faced at home. Their mother, Nola Ray, had made terrible choices in friends and men. Still, she'd done her best. At least Charmaine thought so, in an attempt to give her some credit. She had a long way to go to convince Jessi of that view.

"Don't screw up a good thing because of your past." Jessi said after a while.

"Yeah."

"But if you ain't through banging your way through a pile of fine-ass men and Scotty can't deal? I'll support you." Jessi looked at her with a solemn expression.

"Uh, okay." Charmaine blinked at her.

"I'm straight serious, Char. Look, if you enjoy sex or use it to cope with a crazy world, I'm on your side. Live your life, girl."

"Maybe both. I might want something... special. A long-lasting relationship. And kids, even." Charmaine sighed. "But I don't want to be the mother we had, either."

"You couldn't be. You're wired different," Jessi clipped.

"Thanks." Charmaine squeezed Jessi's arm, then let go.

"I just wanna say one thing, though. I ain't babysitting. Oh. Hell. No." Jessi giggled when Charmaine slapped her shoulder.

"Hey, two minutes ago you promised to have my back. Your vow of support didn't last long," Charmaine quipped.

"Yeah, well you hadn't mentioned rug rats before. Kids are gangster, girl. I'd rather fight a rampaging ghost than be left alone with a mini-you." Jessi gave a snorting laugh at her joke.

"Speaking of which." Charmaine pointed to a sign.

Jessi pulled over so that the Jeep's headlights made it more visible in the dark. On the grass shoulder of the highway, a wooden post had been put up. A placard was nailed to the top. The drawing of a claw-like hand pointed a misshapen finger ahead. The words "Grunch Road - Two Miles" in a deep rusty-red color had been painted below the hand. Jessi and Charmaine exchanged a glance before they stared at the sign again.

"We're expected," Jessi said dryly.

"I don't think it was posted for us. That sign looks like it's been here for decades," Charmaine said. "You know the legend of Grunch Road. Maybe it's a trap."

"I sure as hell hope so. Nothing more fun than spoiling your enemy's surprise party," Jessi said with a hard smile.

She shifted into drive and merged into sparse traffic again. The longer they drove, the darker it became. Other vehicles zoomed by as though eager to get through the empty landscape. Jessi did the opposite. She slowed down to well beneath the speed limit. Both sisters peered hard at the tall vegetation on either side of the highway.

"Hey, we're just over two miles. I didn't see a second sign. Did you?" Charmaine strained forward to scan the shadows beyond their headlights.

"Wait a minute," Jessi said.

She put the Jeep in slow reverse instead of turning around. She kept her gaze on the Jeep's dashboard. The back-up camera had an auto night-vision mode. Their surroundings became a spectral world of gray combined with glowing white, like a vintage film negative. They both studied the screen.

"There," Charmaine blurted and tapped the video display. She jumped out of the Jeep when Jessi hit the brake. "Back up another five or six feet."

"Okay, but you need to be careful," Jessi replied. She eased off the brake as Charmaine gestured for her to keep going. She stopped at a sharp chopping motion from her sister.

Charmaine jogged back and got in the Jeep. "Dirt path. Nothing but a red rag tied around a bunch of weeds marks it. No wonder we didn't see it. So, Grunch Road actually exists."

"You sound surprised. A dirt path is nothing compared to discovering the people behind the myth."

"Truth," Charmaine said.

"Ten dollars says the sign we passed is already gone." Jessi raised an eyebrow as she gazed at her sister.

"Creepy. Dangerous."

Jessi's full mouth curved into a grin. "Hmm. Just the way we *like* it."

Charmaine pulled a stun gun from her belt holster. "Let's not keep 'em waiting."

With a nod, Jessi nosed the SUV off the paved roadway. She switched to four-wheel drive. The dirt and shell road hadn't gotten too uneven, but rain had fallen a few times. No point in risking muddy potholes that could slow them down, even cause the Jeep to get stuck. The path widened the deeper they went. In some sections it was big enough for two vehicles to pass. Then it would narrow before opening up again. Insects bounced off the windshield, drawn by the lights only to end up nothing but splatters. Charmaine couldn't help but wonder if they were like the hapless bugs, following a lure to their downfall.

"Ya know, sis. This might be our worse idea yet. Remind me why we didn't insist on choosing the location," Jessi muttered, an echo to Charmaine's musing.

"We can't control where the supernatural environment is most intense. If we want to stop the bad guys, we sometimes gotta step on their turf." Charmaine cited one of their mentors, a noted paranormal investigator now in his eighties.

"Which really means take the fight to them," Jessi murmured. She squinted at a flash of bright white ahead. It winked off and came on seconds later. Off. On. After twice more, the light glowed steadily.

"Here we go," Charmaine breathed.

Jessi drove the Jeep to the outer edge of a clearing and braked. Tall trees ringed the rough circle. Charmaine looked into the dark. She made out at least three smaller paths that branched on either side. Grunch Road continued down the middle to stretch ahead into woods. A couple of modern tiny houses sat along the side paths. Only the Jeep's headlights provided illumination.

Jessi stepped onto the packed dirt first. Her hiking boots made a soft thud as she did so. Charmaine started to follow but stopped. She grabbed a couple of the Roman candles first. Then she got out of the passenger side. She left the door open a few inches, like Jessi had on the driver's side.

"We ain't out here to play hide and seek with y'all," Jessi called out.

Charmaine flinched at the too-loud sound of her voice in the silent night. She cleared her throat to push the lump that had risen in it. "Miss Marie?"

The Axeman wraith separated from a clump of dense shadows. "Evening, ladies. Am I coming through clear, honey?"

Charmaine nodded in response like a robot programmed to obey. She shook her head to clear away the sensation of being hypnotized. "What do you want?"

"What anybody wants. A good cigar. Some good liquor. A roll in the sheets with a big-hipped babe. Sadly, those days are gone. At least we thought so." He smiled.

Jessi leaned on the Jeep's hood in a casual pose. She pulled out one of her stun guns and pretended to examine it. "Salvatore 'Dirty Sal' Rocca. Armed robber, pimp, and drug pusher."

"So, you know my name. Big deal. At least you got my rap sheet right." Still, his cockiness slipped a notch.

"I know more." Jessi smiled but didn't look up.

"Okay, I'll bite since we got time. Enlighten us," Dirty Sal replied smoothly.

Charmaine looked at Jessi until her sister returned her gaze. She pushed thoughts out, hoping Jessi understood. The Axeman had given them vital information. Whether on purpose or not didn't matter. First, he was waiting for something or someone. Second, he wasn't alone.

"We could use extra hands right about now," Charmaine muttered aside to Jessi.

"We good. Kat ran an errand for me earlier."

Jessi held up what looked like a gray credit card. Charmaine frowned and did a second take. Then she saw yellow buttons on the thing. "The remote from your tabletop wave radio? You really do think this is a party."

"Yeah, boy. Let's boogie." Jessi pushed off the Jeep to stand straight.

"Kat," Charmaine whispered. She resisted the strong urge to look around for their newest contractor. No sense alerting a psychopathic ghost killer he might have a third opponent.

"She's keeping an eye on Rochelle," Jessi replied.

Charmaine hissed in confusion. "What the hell are you—"

The Axeman made a crude farting sound that cut her off. "You know what's gonna happen. The good news is you can join us. We can be a pretty fun gang. The bad news is you'll have to die first."

"Nah, I don't think so. I got other plans. Anyway, like I said, you're an interesting guy. But I don't judge. Guys, girls, it's all cool in these modern times." Jessi walked in a circle as she talked.

"I don't know what you mean." The Axeman squinted at her. He looked to Charmaine as if for clues, then back to Jessi.

"You like the occasional bump session with a cute guy in the rumble seat. Hey, Charmaine. Fun fact. The English called it the *dicky* seat. Get it?" Jessi chuckled deep in her throat. Loud guffaws bounced in the air, and eerie laughter.

"You dirty, lying bitch."

The Axeman kept shouting insults and denials, but the ghostly catcalls continued. Charmaine and Jessi shivered hard. Not because of the creep factor in the sound. They physically felt vibrations from the raucous glee from the great beyond. Jessi glanced down at her smartwatch.

"A spike in EMF," she muttered aside to Charmaine. "Explains why people experience chills. I suspect molecules interact—"

"We don't have time for Spirit Science 101," Charmaine hissed.

"I heard the gossip way back but didn't believe it. Now I'm *hard-pressed* to dismiss it." A female voice, low and throaty, called out. The comment brought on another round of hilarity.

"Shut up!" The Axeman screamed. His high-pitched screech of wrath cut through the night air. Charmaine winced in pain as she clapped hands over her ears. Jess staggered back a few steps from the direction of his voice.

"Dirtbag Sal is right. We ain't here to trade schoolyard jokes. We got a job to do, so let's get to it." A deep voice rolled over them like the first rumbles of a thunderstorm. Silence followed.

"If you're tired of being stuck here, no respect or rest. No earthly pleasures, but no soulful peace either, then listen. I have the method to help you, uh, move on," Jessi said, pushing the words out fast before any of them took action.

"Damn, you sound like a midnight infomercial," Charmaine said.

"Shush, I'm trying to create a distraction. If you got a better idea, then put it in play quick," Jessi shot back.

"Yeah, whatever the sorcerer promised we can do better," Charmaine yelled.

"No, you can't," the Axeman said.

"We ain't in a hurry. It's not like they can get away from us. Let's hear what they have to say," a third voice replied.

"Yeah, slow down. We got all the time in this world," a cultured voice drawled.

"Which is the blasted problem," the female voice chimed in again. "So, what's better than giving us living bodies?"

Charmaine's heart flipped at the question. She imagined the woman, dressed in a tattered dress from a long-gone era, had turned to her. "I—"

"We don't want to cross over. And to what?" The Axeman broke in. "You wanna risk burning for eternity?"

"Hell is real. Think of the things you did in life," Charmaine yelled, seemingly to tall grass and looming trees since she couldn't see anyone.

"Oh, please," Jessi mumbled.

"Not the time for atheism. Putting the fear of God in them might save our asses," Charmaine hissed at her.

Jessi grimaced. "Shit. Keep talkin'."

"I don't know what you think is going to happen, but no one has that kind of power," Charmaine continued.

"Oh yeah? Tell that to Amanda," a voice responded.

"One time, and it didn't last long." Another voice bounced off the trunk of a nearby tree. "Tim said—"

"Shut up, fool!" The Axeman sputtered.

"Tim. You mean Timothy Acker?" Charmaine blinked at Jessi in shock, who shook her head.

"Time's up," Sal said.

The sensation of a giant hand against her back shoved Charmaine to the ground. Surprise, more than force, knocked the wind out of her. Jessi let out a yelp and swung her stun gun in an arc. Deafening pops and hissing like hot metal in water hit them both. Jessi kept up her assault for fifteen seconds, creating chaos in the night. Charmaine grabbed a Roman candle in her pocket. She managed to get it on the ground while still lying flat.

"Damn." Charmaine huffed in frustration.

"Don't tell me. You forgot a lighter." Jessi panted as she fired again. Sparks set a stalk of long grass to smoldering.

"Like you have one," Charmaine yelled back. She rolled away from the useless fireworks. Something pushed her down, like a size thirteen foot on her chest. She grappled with the unseen foe, grabbing at empty air. Mocking laughter pushed her rage to a boiling point, giving her energy. "Bite me, you stinking pile of fart fog."

Charmaine pulled out one of her stunners. She didn't target the ghost, though. Instead, she touched the charge to the Roman candle. Nothing. Jessi yanked a yellow cylinder from a thigh holster. She cracked it in half, which caused it to flash. Smoke shot up from it and then spread. Whoops of anguished surprise came seconds later. Voices winked out until only a few remained.

Jessi clutched at her throat. "Char, use—"

Charmaine scrambled to her feet and sprinted to her sister. "What? Use what?"

A blast of wind knocked her away from Jessi. Charmaine struggled against what felt like a tornado. Pressure made her ears hurt. Tears rolled down her face as she pushed on. Then she remembered the other modified stun gun in her pocket. Her arms felt numb, but Charmaine managed to pull the second weapon from her other holster. She groaned with the effort to recall Jessi's long-winded description of what it could do. Charmaine's head felt ready to explode, as though a giant pair of pliers squeezed her temples.

"Seven eleven," Jessi croaked. She dropped her weapons and clawed harder to get free.

"Oh God. Why is she talking about a convenience store chain?" Charmaine kicked out at something that took hold on her left ankle.

"Setting." The rest of Jessi's speech became garbled.

"I'll show you who's gonna get fucked up tonight," the Axeman growled.

Jessi dropped to her knees with a cry of terror. "Please."

"Oh, now you wanna beg. Feel that? Once I get a real body, I'm gonna spend time with that pretty friend of yours. Then I'll play with her little girl. I like 'em young."

"No, no, don't hurt my godchild," Jessi pleaded, her voice shaking.

Charmaine blinked at her sister. "Setting. Seven, then eleven to reverse the polarity or something. Oh crap, never mind why."

"Even without a live dick, wringing your neck like a chicken is making me horny." The Axeman moaned.

"I got something even more electrifying for ya," Charmaine barked. She aimed. And missed.

Jessi inched across the packed earth and grabbed a stunner. "Dick this, mofo."

Buzz, snap, pop preceded a tortured yowl. Tall weeds nearby bent one way and then another. Charmaine lost her balance as the ground shifted. She'd later swear Jessi had caused an earthquake. She shook her head to clear it and pulled the stun gun trigger. Holding it the way she'd seen TV cops do it, with two hands, Charmaine swept the area around them. She used a thumb to push a dial. The digital display guided her. First seven. Fast or slow. Charmaine had no time for indecision. Fear mixed with anger voted for fast. She toggled back and forth between the settings. Eleven. Seven. Eleven. The scent of burnt grass combined a stench of rotting roadkill.

"Phew-wee!" Charmaine pulled the t-shirt beneath her short jacket over her nose. "What the hell is that stink?"

Jessi sat down hard with a grunt of exhaustion. She heaved in a deep breath and let it out. "That, my sister, is the sweet smell of ghost asses that have been thoroughly kicked."

"I can't move a muscle. Every inch of me aches." Charmaine gasped out. "Like I've been fighting an army of professional wrestlers. Big ones."

"Yeah, well, the night ain't over. Timothy Acker," Jessi said and blew out more air. "We didn't do a deep search on him."

"'Course not. Ruled him out as a minor player." Charmaine looked at Jessi.

Jessi swallowed hard. "We gotta move. Now."

Chapter 15

Triple Cross

Mrs. Grayson sat on her floral sofa. The lounge dress she wore had even bigger daisies. The effect made her look like a floating head and arms buried in a flower bed. She held a cup. When Charmaine and Jessi entered the living room, she stood. Harrison stood in a corner talking into his cell phone. They'd passed Detective Gautier on their way inside.

"Jesus be a fence. I had to brew some lemon balm tea to settle my nerves. All this commotion. You really think they'll come after me? I mean, Penelope has a temper, but attack me? Oh, I have a pot all ready for anyone who wants some." Mrs. Grayson's fingers, rings on each one, fluttered. She seemed more thrilled than frighten.

"Thanks, Mrs. Grayson, but no." Charmaine smiled at her. "Please. Sit down. Detective Harrison has officers searching."

"I'll have a cup. What?" Jessi squinted at Harrison's look of surprise.

"Never saw you as the sipping organic herbal tea hipster type is all." Harrison turned to Mrs. Grayson. "Mrs.—"

"Gladys. Or if you insist on being formal, try Miss Gladys." Mrs. Grayson held up a plate of muffins. "Homemade with real applesauce. Makes 'em so moist."

Harrison gave a slight headshake when Jessi snagged one before he spoke. "No thanks, ma'am. Any odd phone calls like hang-ups recently? Strangers showing up at your house?"

"No. Well, wait. There was a young couple, girl and boy, selling magazine subscriptions. Or was it last week..." Mrs. Grayson blinked rapidly as she frowned in thought. Then her expression cleared. "Anyway, I didn't think anybody sold door-to-door these days with the internet, giggles, and twitters."

"You mean Google and Twitter. Did they ask about your routine or schedule?" Charmaine pressed her lips shut when Harrison gave her an "I'll ask the questions" cop scowl.

"No, we had a nice chat over cookies and iced tea." Mrs. Grayson sat down again.

Charmaine gasped. "Miss Gladys, letting folks you don't know in your house is a bad idea. A really bad idea."

"They were clean-cut and polite as could be. Besides, I have this." Mrs. Grayson pulled a .38 pistol from beneath a sofa cushion. "Smith and Wesson keep me company, dear."

"Whoa, whoa. Put that thing down." Harrison kept his voice level even as he backed up a couple of steps.

"I have a permit, if that's what you're about to ask. Been shooting since I was ten. My granddaddy taught me." Mrs. Grayson held the gun nose down. "I never aim unless I plan to shoot, son."

"Dang, Miss Gladys be packin'. You just impressed the hell outta me." Jessi grinned at the older woman and bit off more muffin.

"Why don't you just let me..." Harrison held out a large hand to Mrs. Grayson. "With all the police presence, you won't be needing it tonight."

"No problem, officer." Mrs. Grayson gave him a grandmotherly smile. She handed it to him with care, butt first. Then she sat on the sofa again. Harrison put the gun in a drawer of an oak side table.

Jessi perched on the sofa cushion next to her. "So, nothing funny going on. As in suspicious."

Mrs. Grayson shook her head. "No, baby. You say an anonymous caller reported a prowler?"

"Ahem, yeah. Call came in an hour ago." Harrison fidgeted under her steady gaze.

"Took your time coming to see about me," Mrs. Grayson said.

"A patrol car was close. They passed by your house and circled the block. Maybe scared 'em off." Harrison started to say more when Gautier stuck his head in the door.

"Sir, a minute."

"Right. Excuse us." Harrison seemed relieved at the reason to escape.

Mrs. Grayson turned her astute scrutiny to the sisters. "You've been meeting with the community after I told you about them. Then an unknown person calls the police to come out and check on me."

"They're very secretive about anyone knowing they exist," Charmaine said.

"I don't blame them. But JoJo and the others aren't bad people. They've been hurt a lot by the world for generations." Mrs. Grayson shook her head.

"Yeah, and that kind of hurt can make people desperate to protect themselves," Jessi replied.

"How do you know them again?" Charmaine leaned forward.

"I went to school with several of them. One girl and I became close in high school." Mrs. Grayson seemed deep in thought for a few moments. "You think they have something to do with what's been in the news? Ghosts all over, folks being murdered."

"We're not sure, but it's best to be safe," Charmaine answered before Jessi could blurt her own take on it.

"I saw that writer being interviewed. Eli Locke. He might be mixed up in the mess. Y'all ought to keep an eye on *him*, if you ask me." Mrs. Grayson wore a sour expression as if saying his name left a bad taste on her tongue.

Charmaine exchanged a look with Jessi. "You know Eli Locke?"

"No, but my friend's daughter got mixed up with him. We lost touch, so I didn't really know the child. Poor Ida didn't even have a body to bury. I called her back then. You know, let Ida know I was praying for the girl. I'm trying to think of her name. Ida had six kids, you know." Mrs. Grayson frowned in concentration.

"Lydia," Jessi said.

Mrs. Grayson blinked at her in surprise. "Yes. But how did you...?"

"Penelope mentioned it after watching the TV reporter interview him," Jessi said smoothly.

"I see. I can't believe he had the nerve to set foot in New Orleans. Now if he'd come up missing, then I'd say the community was involved." Mrs. Grayson looked from Charmaine to Jessi and back again.

"Penelope mentioned he married Lydia," Charmaine said.

"I heard they didn't legally marry but lived together. I heard they was into a lot of kinky stuff. Swapping partners and such. I half-believed she'd run off like he said. Lydia always wanted to get away from the community. Then it was like the girl dropped off the face of the earth."

"Penelope is convinced Lydia is dead," Jessi said.

Mrs. Grayson raised an eyebrow at them. "Really? Guess she's celebrating then. They hated each other. Well, hate might be kinda strong. Fought like crazy.

"They might still have been close. Conflict can bind family, too," Charmaine said with a side-eye at Jessi.

"My grandmother used to swear she knew the exact second one of her sisters died," Mrs. Grayson said.

"Or Lydia might have decided to blend in, cut off all contact," Jessi said, cutting into Charmaine's musings. "But wouldn't she have at least called her mama?"

"Always was selfish. Kinda mean, too, to be honest. Ida gave up looking for her. She didn't have a lot of money to hire private detectives like you two. Hey, maybe y'all can look for Lydia now. Sharp young ladies like you? Bet you'd find her in two snaps." Mrs. Grayson grinned at them.

"We could interview Miss Ida," Jessi said to Charmaine.

"She died in 2006. Lost everything in Hurricane Katrina. Her people say it was the stress. Her husband drowned. They barely got her off that roof before she joined him in heaven. Rest both their souls."

"Too bad," Charmaine murmured.

"No wonder her sister is angry. First Lydia, then her mother," Jessi said.

"The community suffered as much as anybody after Katrina. Anyway, I can take care of myself. I'm tougher than I look." Mrs. Grayson gave a sharp nod.

Jessi looked at her. "You got more firepower up in here, don't you?"

Mrs. Grayson put a forefinger to her lips and winked. "Don't tell that sexy detective."

Harrison appeared as if on cue. "Okay, Mrs. Grayson. We spoke to your neighbors. They haven't seen anything to cause concern. I'll have a marked cruiser circle until daybreak. Preventive measure. But like I said, if there was somebody, they likely won't come back."

"Anybody living, you mean," Jessi mumbled. She winced when Harrison scowled at her.

"I'm all prayed up, put on the *whole* armor of God." Mrs. Grayson sprang up and went to a china cabinet nearby. She rummaged in a draw and held up a small plastic bag. "And just in case, I keeps me some High John the Conqueror Root on hand. Demons can't come against me."

"You pastor wouldn't be pleased, Miss Gladys." Charmaine affected a scandalized expression.

"The Lord made everything. I say he gave it to his children for a reason." Mrs. Grayson winked at her. She slipped the bag in her housecoat pocket and patted it.

Harrison gave Mrs. Grayson an indulgent smile. "Keep the doors locked. If anyone shows up and gives you bad vibes, call us."

"Me and my neighbors on the lookout now, young man. Don't you worry about me," Mrs. Grayson said.

"No shooting," Harrison added in a firm tone.

"I hear ya." Mrs. Grayson returned his smile.

Harrison jerked a thumb at Charmaine and Jessi to follow him. They said their good-byes to Mrs. Grayson. Outside, only one police car remained. Harrison waved to the cop inside. The marked Dodge Charger pulled away from the curb. They watched as she turned off the flashing blue bar on top of the cruiser. Seconds later, the red taillights winked out of sight when the cruiser turned a corner.

Jessi faced Harrison. "Well?"

"Two streets over, a guy swears he saw movement in the woods behind his house. We searched. Flushed out a pack of stray dogs. Animal Control is gonna handle it." Harrison heaved a sigh.

"We didn't overreact." Charmaine crossed her arms.

"Did I say anything? The good thing is, Gautier has nothing to tattle. Well, almost nothing." Harrison raised an eyebrow at them.

"Hey, we can't hide every time the guy shows up," Jessi retorted."

"Mrs. Grayson's neighbor was murdered, so naturally a call about a prowler should be taken seriously," Charmaine put in.

"And she's a key witness." Jessi shrugged.

Harrison shook his head. "For you, not me. Far as my official investigation, Mrs. Grayson reported seeing a *normal human*, possibly. Could have been a shadow. The witness is described as an elderly woman who wears glasses."

"Miss Gladys would set you straight quick if she ever finds out," Jessi said with a laugh.

"My boss would place me on involuntary medical leave if I started talking about supernatural stuff."

"So, what's next?" Charmaine dropped her arms.

"Okay, here's what we do." Harrison drew himself up.

"Yeah?" Charmaine listened with anticipation.

"I'm going home to cuddle with my wife and get some sleep." Harrison ticked off points on his fingers. "You two work hard... at not calling me for at least twenty-four hours or until you have leads that make sense. No ghosts. No voodoo signs pointing the way. Nothing. If it ain't human, I ain't interested."

"Let me let me tell you something." Jessi waved a forefinger at him, winding up for a tirade.

"Goodnight, ladies," Harrison said, authority ringing in his deep voice as he spun away from them.

"You got your best information from us," Jessi yelled after him.

Charmaine jerked her head at a car idling a few yards away. "Gautier is still trolling for dirt. Let's not give it to him."

Jessi huffed. "You're gonna lecture me how Harrison is an ally. Right?"

"He makes it hard to remember, but yeah." Charmaine squinted at the unmarked car. Then she trotted over to it.

Gautier's passenger door window slid down smoothly when she got close. "Evening, Ms. Joliet. I gotta wonder why you showed up. Did my colleague call you?"

"Mrs. Grayson knows us," Charmaine said without missing a beat. "You have any new information on the Rayvon Woods murder here?"

"Not that I'd share with a civilian. One with a sketchy background to boot. I'm not Harrison." Gautier's smile looked stretched with his even teeth showing. He looked like a dog about to bite.

"Your superior, you mean? No. You're definitely *not* Detective Harrison, decorated officer with way more experience."

"Good night," Gautier clipped. He gunned the engine as a warning.

"Nice talking to you, too, Detective Gautier." Charmaine took several steps back.

Jessi came up behind her. "You out here pissing off the po-po. Thought that was my job."

"How did he show up so fast? Harrison didn't call him." Charmaine continued to stare into the night.

"He heard the dispatch call. C'mon. Let's get out of here. I'm starting to see monsters creepin' in every shadow." Jessi yawned.

"Do a background check on him," Charmaine said without moving toward Jessi's Jeep.

Jessi froze in the middle of a stretch. She gawked at Charmaine. "On Gautier? You must be joking."

"I'm wondering how far he'd go to move up the chain of command." Charmaine turned around to face Jessi. They stood without speaking for a few beats.

"Hell, I'm on it, sis." Jessi's expression brightened. The bold new task re-energized her for a long night.

****

The next morning, Charmaine and Jessi had to deal with their regular lives. Day jobs, bills, and other details. They'd both let things slip because of the case. Charmaine sat in her office at the clinic, fighting fatigue. Time crawled by. By ten o'clock she'd two clients. She stifled a yawn for what seemed the tenth time when her desk phone rang. The receptionist announced her next appointment in an annoying cheerful voice. The tapping on her office door came a minutes later. She opened it and put on what she hoped was a bright, yet professional expression.

"Come in Ms. Lirette." Charmaine's smile somehow morphed into a yawn. Her hand flew up to smother it, but not before Theo Dora noticed.

"Partying on a school night, hum? Tsk-tsk." Theo Dora's eyes twinkled with mischief. "Tell me all about it and don't leave out any of the juicy parts."

"You'd be disappointed at how dull my life can be. And we're here to talk about *you*." Charmaine sat down at the same time Theo Dora parked herself in the visitor's chair next to the desk.

"Ha! I pay attention to the news. Though you have to consume what passes for journalism these days with a big saltshaker. Your other vocation is anything but dull. You've been chasing down the grunch. Dangerous business." Theo Dora raised both her auburn penciled-in eyebrows at her.

"Let's talk about you," Charmaine said, determined to do her job.

For the next twenty minutes, Charmaine probed Theo Dora for information. She looked for clues Theo Dora's symptoms had improved. The psychiatrist had monitored her use of the psychoactive meds since Theo Dora's last appointment. Satisfied that Theo Dora was stable, even improving, Charmaine started to wrap up their session.

"Got all you need out of me so I won't be dragged off to the nut house?" Theo Dora beamed at Charmaine.

"I think you're safe to be on the streets for a little while," Charmaine replied with a straight face.

"Whew, what a relief. I keep clean undies in my tote just in case, you know." Theo Dora laughed at her own joke about her frequent past hospitalizations.

"We can revise your wellness plan anytime."

Theo Dora waved off her suggestion. "I'm kidding. Not about the undies. Never can tell with my history. But I'm doing really well."

Charmaine looked at Theo Dora with a critical eye. A client's definition of "doing fine" could be far off the mark. At least what the treatment profession and society considered fine. Still, her appearance gave no telltale sig-

nals of relapse. Her eccentric makeup, cloth-
ing, and mannerisms looked normal for Theo
Dora.

"Good. So, you should have plenty of medication. No need to see the doc. Right?" Charmaine opened the patient records on her
computer.

"Fully stocked for another month or so.
Thanks for letting me be me." Theo Dora gave
Charmaine's hand a pat.

"No one else you can be. You're one of a
kind." Charmaine smiled at her and went back
to tapping notes into the electronic clinic app.

"I've been riding the crazy train for almost
longer than you've been alive, dear. Many of
the medications made me zonk out, a different
person altogether. You and Dr. Vega haven't
tried to erase me, make me act like everyone
else. Not that normal looks the same in New
Orleans as the rest of the USA." Theo Dora
laughed.

"Thank the Lord, right?" Charmaine
grinned back at her.

"And amen. No place like home. Oh, before
I forget." Theo Dora dug into her huge bag.
Decorated in colorful embroidered flowers, it
was stuffed with an odd assortment of items.

"We can always talk about it during our next session," Charmaine replied. A glance at the clock told her the receptionist could call in her next appointment any minute. Last one before lunch and an early day.

"Like I said, I've been following your fascinating case. Got me to remembering more about my Aunt Grace." Theo Dora muttered low as she dug deep into the bag. "I know it was right near the top. Must have slithered down with all that shaking on the streetcar. Or maybe I took the bus. No, no. I called Uber."

Charmaine hoped Theo Dora didn't pull some kind of creature out. She was a devoted animal lover, including reptiles. "It's nice you're connecting with happy family memories. We're almost out of time and—"

"Aha. Here we go. Aunt Grace wore this all the time. She left it to me. It's a Hermes, circa 1961." Theo Dora produced a silk scarf with a flourish worthy of any designer fashion show.

Big enough to be used as a shawl, the scarf floated around Theo Dora's shoulders. She gave a delighted sigh as it draped over her bright orange sweater jacket. The combination of vivid jewel-toned colors worked. Pictures of star-shaped blossoms, ruby-red grapes, and fanciful animals filled the fabric.

Lovely, though it smelled of vintage eau de parfum and dust.

"It's gorgeous." Charmaine stood as a hint the session had ended.

"A gift from a wealthy lover. What am I saying? Most of them were either stinking rich or poor as church mice." Theo Dora smiled as if picturing her late aunt.

Charmaine eased closer to the door. "Interesting."

"Aunt Grace indulged in extremes. She always said middle-class men were fatally dull. She tried a dentist once, according to her. Big mistake." Theo Dora brushed a hand over the silk.

"Wow. Gotta hear that story, but not today." Charmaine tried not to heave a sigh of frustration.

"And here's the extraordinary woman in the flesh, well not exactly. Isn't she elegant?" Theo Dora pulled out a black-and-white photo faded to sepia tones.

Charmaine barely glanced at it. "Yes, lovely. Now if you don't mind—"

"Aunt Grace's Sunday brunches were legendary in society circles. No matter what her latest scandal was, the A-listers wouldn't have dreamed of missing one. Even the invitations were works of art. Here, I have one some-where."

Theo Dora shoved the photo at Charmaine. Startled, Charmaine took it since she didn't have a choice. Theo Dora returned to rummaging in her bag and mumbling under her breath. Charmaine huffed out air and looked at the photo. Aunt Grace appeared to have been a blonde. Whether natural or from a bottle Charmaine couldn't tell. Her high cheekbones and slim figure made her look like a couture model. Nose in the air, Grace showcased the epitome of pampered privilege.

"Seriously, Theo Dora..." Charmaine slipped into informality due to impatience.

"Just another few seconds," Theo Dora said.

She didn't need to beg for more time. Charmaine stood transfixed by the figure the longer she stared. Grace stood against the backdrop of a sumptuous room, but that wasn't what had Charmaine so hypnotized. Rather, it was the line of her jaw. The curve of her mouth. Her heart-shaped face. All so familiar yet different. Charmaine flipped the photo over. "Grace Lindell Simmons, 1939" in faded blue ink was written on the back. Charmaine walked back to her desk and sat down, gaze still on the photo.

"Yes, Auntie Gee, we children nicknamed her that, was a stunner. The camera loved her, as they say. Well, I'll scoot along so you can get on with your important work saving the world." Theo Dora reach out for the photo.

"Um, can I take a picture of this?" Charmaine had already picked up her cell phone.

"I don't mind. I collect vintage photographs, too. Along with my vast collection of other things. What my son and daughter-in-law call piles of junk." Theo Dora clicked her tongue with a frown. "They don't have room to talk. I could tell you a few choice tidbits about their lifestyle."

"Hmm..."

Charmaine heard her voice drone on as background noise. She clicked twice to have more than one copy of the photo just in case. Then she sent the picture to Jessi while she made polite "I see" and "Oh really?" replies to whatever Theo Dora was saying. Still staring at her phone for a reply, she handed the photo back to Theo Dora. Then a snatch of either something said out loud or Theo Dora's thoughts brought her up short.

"Bye, dear. See you next time." Theo Dora's voice echoed from a distance. She had made it halfway down the hall toward the exit back to the clinic lobby.

"Wait. Did you say something about a baby?"

Charmaine scurried to the open door. Theo Dora greeted a male client and launched into a deep conversation. They stood debating the fine points of collecting antique bottle tops when Charmaine approached. After five minutes of gentle prodding, Theo Dora agreed to head back to Charmaine's office. Charmaine's cell phone whistled multiple times in her sweater pocket. A signal that Jessi had replied. The receptionist waved to get Charmaine's attention while pointing at her appointment. She juggled responding to both. First, Charmaine apologized to her other client. He shrugged agreement at waiting another ten minutes. Then she sent a quick text to Jessi. Finally, she managed to extract the information she needed from Theo Dora.

****

"You better cover your ass or you could lose your license," Jessi said in her typical blunt manner. She pulled on her jacket and headed for the door.

They'd met up at Scotty's café and bar. Scotty had let them into his office while he attended to business. The office had a utilitarian look. No family pictures or sentimental decorations. Though his desk did have a military-like neatness. Invoices and other papers were in three neat stacks. A landline cordless phone sat on one corner. His business desktop occupied another corner with a wireless keyboard and mouse.

Charmaine sat in Scotty's executive chair, her tablet computer in front of her. "If push comes to shove, I'll invoke duty to warn."

Kat swung the door open after a quick tap. "Hey y'all. What's up?"

"Details on what Rochelle's been doing," Jessi said as she beckoned at her to come in.

"She's been talking to a Detective Gautier. Know him?" Kat sat in a folding chair.

"Yeah." Charmaine sighed.

"Rochelle was only too happy to give him info. I told you to let me whip her ass," Jessi blurted out to Charmaine.

"If you hadn't gotten into a cat fight with her at a fast food place, Gautier might never had met Rochelle. Ever think of that?" Charmaine shot back. Jessi snorted in reply. "Ro-chelle doesn't know much, or he would have used it against Harrison by now."

"It's the principle," Jessi grumbled. She frowned as if imagining ways to get revenge.

"Rochelle is handled. Her husband got a custody-status hearing pushed up. I helped her see she should focus on her family instead of ways to get back at Scotty. No threats," Kat added before Charmaine could ask.

"Becca is out of the hospital. She's at Locke's house," Charmaine said.

"I'll bet Viola is thrilled to be her personal servant," Jessi drawled.

"Locke hired a private nursing service. He's says Becca is strong enough to talk to us," Charmaine said and stood.

"Hold on. How are you going to handle us finding out about your patient's aunt? You could be in violation of confidentiality laws," Jessi said. "And if a complaint is filed with the social work licensing board..."

"Confidentiality is waived if, during a therapy session, I learn someone might be in danger. Four murders, two people attacked. I'd say the circumstances apply. Come on. Thanks for everything, Kat. We owe you one." Charmaine patted Kat's shoulder as she went past her.

"Had fun helping. Almost considered a career change, but I love cooking too much. Sure you don't want me to come along?"

"Or me?" Scotty stood in the door. He wore a worried frown as he looked at Charmaine.

"Aw, look Kat. They're such a cute couple." Jessi grinned at them.

"Shut up," Charmaine said to her. Then she turned to Scotty. "And you, don't hover."

Scotty raised both hands, palms out. "Message received. Can I at least say be careful without getting my head chopped off?"

"I'm always careful," Charmaine replied, an eyebrow raised. Her smile softened the tart response.

"I can see this relationship is off to an interesting start," Kat whispered aside to Jessi.

Charmaine grimaced, but otherwise ignored the remark. She conceded to a quick peck on the check as she walked by Scotty. "We'll call if we need help."

Ten minutes later they got closer to Locke's Garden District home. Darkness of the early evening had fallen. The dashboard digital clock glowed in soft green, showing it was almost six-thirty. The headlights from other cars flashed around them. Jessi smirked the entire trip as she drove the Jeep.

"Scotty and you gonna have *the talk* soon. I can feel it."

"Stay out of my business and concentrate on what we're about to do," Charmaine said, her tone dry.

Jessi turned onto Locke's street. She parallel parked in front of his house behind a Toyota SUV. "Fine. But you know I'm gone keep teasing you, right?"

Charmaine rolled her eyes and took out a quarter. "Like you had to say. Heads, I'm the bad cop."

"Please. You're too kind-hearted social worker to pull it off." Jessi got out and was up the front walkway in seconds. She'd already rung the doorbell by the time Charmaine caught up. Eli appeared at the door.

"Good evening and tell Becca to get her ass down here," Jessi said. "We need to talk."

Charmaine had little time to seethe about Jessi's preemptive bad cop strike. "Sorry, Eli, but it's kinda urgent we get some answers."

"Rein in your sister. Becca's been through a lot." Locke hurried to get ahead of Jessi before she entered the living room.

"Well, where is she?" Jessi squinted at him.

Viola came in holding a tray with empty dishes on it. "She's upstairs, second bedroom on the right."

"You will not—" Locke blinked hard because Jessi had already climbed three steps. He stomped his way across the floor. "I'll call the police."

"Eli. You really want to call Detective Harrison before you hear what we've found out?" Charmaine raised an eyebrow when Locke spun around.

"You saw how she was after the attack. I don't see how traumatizing the poor woman again will be helpful." Locke glanced up to the second floor.

"Let them go," Lana said in a cool voice. She smiled when Locke, Viola, and Charmaine whirled around to gape at her. "So, Eli. I changed my mind about leaving the city. You didn't hesitate to move your young lover in here."

Chapter 16

It's A Wrap

Locke's mouth worked like a goldfish gulping water for a few seconds before he got words out. "I couldn't leave her with strangers. Rebecca is seriously injured because of me and—"

"More true than you know, sweetie," Lana cut in. Then she glanced up at Jessi and waved a hand. "Go on. Talk to her."

Jessi frowned at Charmaine as if unsure. Then she transferred her scowl to Lana. "Like I need your permission."

"No, but you damn sure don't have mine. This is my home, and Becca is under my care," Locke shouted.

"What's going on?" Becca called as she walked slowly into view. She held onto the arm of a dark-haired young woman in light-green scrubs.

"I can give you something to calm your nerves," the nurse said to her. Then she looked down at them. "I suggest y'all stop arguing, at least so loud that she hears it all. Ms. Hanson needs rest."

"Don't knock her out on drugs before she answers some questions," Jessi said.

"You're not in charge of her medical care," Locke replied. "If Alyssa thinks—"

"My, my. You're already on a first-name basis and the girl's been here barely a day. You work fast," Lana drawled as she gazed at Locke.

"Oh, for God's sake, Lana. Now isn't the time for one of your jealous tantrums. Of course I welcomed Becca into my home. Of course I'm cordial to her nurse." Locke huffed a few times in frustration.

"Relax, darlin'. I care little or nothing about who you screw. The more the merrier, I say." Lana strolled out of sight to the living room.

"Go on," Charmaine said to Jessi and then went to the living room as well.

Locke continued to stammer. He glanced up the staircase and then at the living room. "But I don't... I mean... "

"I'm gonna load the dishwasher. Then I'm going to my 'Won't He Do It' Women's Mission meeting at the church. Count me outta this mess." Viola shook her head as she left for the kitchen.

Finally, Locke decided on the living room. He marched in, twisting his hands together. "I don't know what the hell is happening here."

"I'm not surprised. Have a drink. I don't have to be psychic to know you could use one." Lana grinned at him as she put a tumbler of brandy in his hand. "Your hired help think Rebecca is behind all of the awful events of the past few weeks."

Locke gaped at her and then at Charmaine, eyes wide. "Ridiculous!"

"I agree. Rebecca may be competent at her job, but she's hardly mastermind material." Lana's chuckle was muffled as she drank from the tumbler she held. She went to the bottles of liquor and lifted one.

Charmaine shook her head in refusal. "The most serious attacks on Eli happened when Becca was close by. In fact, those incidents began *after* he hired her."

Lana's smile faded. She put down her half-empty tumbler and turned to Locke. "She's right, Eli. And the girl is possessive."

"You know damn well Becca wouldn't hurt me," Locke protested. He stared at Lana in astonishment.

"I don't know anything of the kind. Ms. Joliet is the professional you hired to uncover the truth. You can't ignore her because it's painful." Lana wore a somber face as she walked over to Charmaine. "I think it's time to call the police. Detective Harrison and Detective Gautier are their names. Right?"

"Lana, stop this nonsense." Locke shook a fist. "I won't have it."

Lana put a hand to her throat as she back away from him. "Why? Because you planned it together? I warned you about those shifty business deals you cut. But I never dreamed you'd try to cover your tracks with murder."

A jingling noise made all three of them turn toward the hallway. The nurse looked at them, holding a set of keys. Her face had drained of color until her white skin looked pasty. She shook her head a few times and swallowed hard.

"Uh, my shift is over. I'll let myself out," the nurse squeaked. She made it out the door and down to the blue Toyota SUV in record time. Seconds later the engine gunned.

Locke whirled back to Lana and Charmaine. "She had another hour and a half at least."

"Wise girl. There's no telling what the other Ms. Joliet stirred to life. I may leave myself." Lana moved to put more distance between them.

"No, you won't," Charmaine said. "You haven't found out how much Jessi and I know yet."

"I don't understand." Locke's puzzled frown pulled his eyebrows into one dark line. He looked at the ceiling when loud thumps echoed. "I better check on Becca."

Charmaine grabbed his arm when he crossed in front of her. "She's going to be fine. You're staying right here."

Locke shook free with force. "Don't order me around in my own home. I should have listened to you, Lana. They're fake psychics and not even good private detectives."

"You've been managing us the whole time, blocking us from finding out the real story. Hiring us gave you alibis and plausible arguments for your innocence," Charmaine said.

"All those horrible deaths. To think I believed your story about ghosts. I'll call the police if you're not willing to do it." Lana crossed to where her expensive handbag lay on a side table. She pulled out her cell phone.

"What are you doing?" Locke glanced sideways at Charmaine and then back to Lana.

"I'm sorry, Eli, but I can't condone the truly terrible things you've done. Ms. Joliet and her sister have it all figured out. The real estate deals, killing the contractor and architect to hide your crimes. I'm sure they've found out about your history in New York, too." Lana looked at Charmaine.

"We did."

"You see, Eli? It's over, dear." Lana wore an expression of regret. "You can't kill everyone who gets in your way."

A strangled cry rang out from upstairs. Jessi shouted as if in fear for her life. What sounded like an angry bull crashing around made the windows rattle. Locke back up until he had flattened himself against a wall. All three of them looked toward the arched entrance as heavy footsteps pounded. Yet no one entered the living room.

"It's happening again. I told you so." Locke swiped away sweat from his forehead. "We have to get out."

"Not yet." Charmaine turned to Lana. "You knew about Eli's crimes, even back in New

York. And his connection to the murder victims. You didn't tell the police anything, but you're willing to turn him in now."

"I trusted the man, even considered accepting his proposal," Lana said, her voice shaking. She squeezed her eyes shut as a tear slid down her cheek. Then she opened them again to stare at Charmaine with a bleak expression. "I loved him... still love him."

Jessi walked in clapping her hands. "And the Oscar for Best Supporting Actress goes to..."

"Lydia Ann Rocca. The Axeman was your grandfather," Charmaine added.

"You have your grandmother Grace's jawline," Jessi said.

"Becca has the dark looks of the Rocca family." Charmaine moved sideways to a position between Locke and Lana.

Lana studied Jessi and Charmaine for a few minutes before she laughed hard. She bent at the waist and then stood straight again, shaking her head. "Do you really think anyone will believe that story?"

"Lydia, who is..." Locke's voice trailed off at the murderous look Lana, aka Lydia, gave him.

"Not that it matters, but yes. The infamous Axeman of New Orleans was indeed my grandfather, curse his name. My slut of a grandmother loved sex more than her reputation. And sex with a dangerous thug thrilled her most of all. One thing I can say for him, though; he believes in family loyalty." Lana's delicate socialite mask fell away. She wore a wicked smile.

Locke cowered into the heavy drapes covering one window. "You didn't—"

"Tell you everything?" Lana laughed again.

"You got a kick out of having an affair with a mother and daughter. Oh, you didn't know at first. But when Lana told you, or should I call you Lydia?" Jessi cocked her head to one side and smiled at Lana.

"Lana is fine, dear. I've been answering to that name for almost thirty-five years." Lana went back to the bar. She picked up her glass of brandy again. "How much do you think you know?"

"Quite a lot. You gave Becca up when she was an infant. A Jewish couple adopted her, moved from here to New York. Becca did a search for her biological parents when she turned eighteen. She found you," Charmaine said.

"Her father was from a 'good family,' old money. I was stupid enough to believe he loved me. He abandoned us," Lana said.

They all turned in surprise to find Becca and Timmy Acker had joined them. Becca leaned on Timmy for support. Yet she didn't look like the frail victim anymore. A sneer marred her smooth, young face. Timmy's gaze flickered around the room like a snake deciding who to sink his fangs into.

"He saw through your good looks, and it scared him. So, he listened to her mother's smart advice," Charmaine said.

"Not to worry. I paid him back in full," Lana clipped with a nasty smile for them all.

"Your grandfather must have passed on his murderous genes. Salvatore Rocca, the Axeman. The police might not have caught him, but an equally nasty rival gangster took him out."

"What is she talking about, mother? You said our people were Irish," Becca said. "Paid my father back how?"

"Be quiet, girl. You're starting to grate on my nerves," Lana hissed.

"They can't leave this house," Timmy hissed.

"Thanks for stating the obvious, sweetie," Lana quipped. She turned to Jessi. "We've removed all your electronic trinkets. But we'll make sure the parts are recycled. We're concerned about the environment."

"And making sure none of your friends reassemble them after you're gone," Timmy said. He stepped away and began to murmur. He lifted his hands as if drawing on air.

"What... What is he doing? Those ghost sightings were fake. Weren't they?" Locke moved to stand next to Lana.

Lana shook her head at him. "Poor Eli. He thought we'd set up equipment to fake the ghosts. That we hired local killers to get rid of everyone who knew about his history. Darlin', nobody cares about your petty crimes. You're as disposal as these two."

"No, mother. You promised Eli wouldn't be hurt." Becca pushed free of Timmy. She tried to stumble toward Eli, but Timmy yanked her back.

Lana laughed. She looked at Jessi and Charmaine. "What a fool. Seems she's inherited her father's weakness. She fell for the pompous ass."

"Those spirits meant to attack Eli. You told them to," Becca shouted. "I could have been killed that night. Look at what they did to me."

"Your fault for following him around like a bitch in heat. Use your brains. Eli is a liability to you, too. You can always find a better lover." Lana nodded to Timmy

"I don't understand. Stop that mumbling, you idiot!" Locke said to Timmy.

"He's a hougan, Eli. A sorcerer." Jessi affected a scared expression. She fingered the weapons in her jacket pocket.

"It was always about covering up *your* past, wasn't it, Lana? Anyone looking into Eli's business dealings would learn you'd been his partner. Then they'd dig into your identity. Maybe it was easy to live a double life in Grace's day, but not in this modern age." Charmaine held onto the fleeting mind impression she got from her. "Eli didn't kill his wife. It was you."

Lana's cool, amused expression turned dark. "Timmy."

"Come forth!" Timmy shouted. He spun in a circle and tossed white dust of some kind as he moved.

Locke clawed at the drapes in an attempt to escape. A flash of bright light made everyone blink except Timmy. Then the room fell dark. Charmaine's eyes adjusted fast. She grabbed at Lana, who batted her hands away. Becca turned from an invalid into a whirlwind of fists. Jessi managed to sidestep the surprise attack.

The Axeman loomed over Jessi. His dark shadow spread like a stain up to the ceiling. "You should have left well enough alone, pretty hips. Now I gotta protect my own."

"You didn't learn from our last fight, huh?"

Jessi aimed and fired her stun gun. The Axeman's silhouette slithered aside. His laughter rumbled liked falling boulders. Charmaine fought off Lana and Becca. She slapped the daughter hard, and Becca went down. Then she shoved Lana away and landed a round-house kick to her stomach. She sent up a silent prayer of gratitude to her self defense teacher at the YMCA. Lana grunted. Becca grabbed at Jessi's ankles and got her hand stomped as a reward.

"Mother, you have to take care of her," Becca shouted.

Jessi took aim at the Axeman with better effect. The arc of electricity made the shadow quiver and shrink. More spirts arrived, chattering like angry hyenas. She pulled out a modified flare, but needed two hands to crack it in half. Three spirits surrounded her, forcing Jessi to continue fire the stun gun. Her eyes widened at the sound of the Axeman's deep chuckle.

"Your toy can't stay charged forever, babe," he said.

"They're outnumbered," Lana managed to gasp.

A musical, contralto female voice responded in a stream of old Creole French. Charmaine only heard a gentle rustle, a few phrases that died away. But Jessi gave a whoop of joy. Charmaine increased the intensity of her attack at the sound of her sister's celebration. Timmy lost much of his swagger. His arms dropped, his mouth hung wide, and he tried to find a voice but couldn't. A force lifted him off the floor a good five inches. He babbled in terror. Seconds later he flew up to the ceiling and came down with a crash. Timmy lay still, a broken heap on Eli's parquet floor. He groaned and tried to stagger to his feet. Chairs spun around the room. One clipped the side of Timmy's head as he crawled toward the front door.

"Eli, stop Timmy. Don't just sit there peeing your pants. Stop him!" Charmaine yelled.

Locke snapped to attention with a glassy stare at the chaos around him. Then he leaped over Timmy like an Olympic hurdler and ran out the door. The leather soles of his designer loafers slapped on concrete as he raced away.

"Damn it," Charmaine screamed.

She landed a final punch to the side of Becca's head. Then she finished off Lana with a series of slaps, kicks, and a knee to her chin. Lana slumped to the floor. The lights blinked on. Jessi and Charmaine faced each other, panting, clothes askew, and bruises already starting to show. Jessi switched her stun gun to full power and went after Timmy, but Charmaine pulled her back.

Jessi scowled when Timmy slithered like a reptile across the threshold. "We'll have to deal with him again. And what if he gets even stronger?"

Charmaine shook her head. "No killing. We'll find another way."

"Maybe, but if he starts shit again and I catch up with him..." Jessi didn't have to finish. She turned off her weapon.

Diamond startled them when she raced in. "We came to help."

Kat bumped into her back. "The doors wouldn't open at first. Windows neither.

Sounded like a hurricane *and* an earthquake up in here."

Jessi picked up her equipment and shoved it into their hands. "Y'all get outta here and take my stuff with you. Put 'em in my bag. Go, go!"

Sirens pushed Charmaine to shake off her stupor. "She's right. Scotty?"

"In his truck outside for a fast getaway. Y'all come with us," Diamond said as she followed Jessi's instructions.

Charmaine sent Scotty a text with directions to drive off as she spoke. "There's an alley to the next street over between the houses. Scotty is gonna meet y'all there. We gotta stay and explain this mess,"

Jessi pushed her friends out when blue lights strobed, lighting up the night. "Go on. Time's up."

Kat and Diamond ran out just as two cops in NOPD uniforms peeked in the windows. Moments later, the officers vanished. Jessi and Charmaine leaned on each other for support. First one, then a second officer entered the room, guns out. Charmaine and Jessi obeyed the order to slowly raise their hands.

****

Jessi and Charmaine sat across from Harrison in his office. Cheerful autumn sunshine painted the morning pale yellow. Police business as usual buzzed just outside. The fantastical events of the night before at Eli Locke's house seemed far away. Charmaine and Jessi's evil versus good battle seemed more like a far-fetched plot in one of his novels. Harrison intended to make that spin official.

"My report is gonna read like this: Eli Locke hired local criminals to kill Rayvon Woods and the couple. Timothy Acker is co-operating. He admits that he helped Locke re-connect with Amanda Morrell but claims he didn't know Locke would kill her. Locke is saying Acker did the killing. Lana—"

"Lydia Rocca," Jessi corrected.

"*Lana Salcedo Reilly*," Harrison rumbled and glared at her, "who changed her name to hide her humble beginnings."

"Nothing about ghosts or Marie Laveau coming to save the day?" Jessi grinned with satisfaction at the result of her poke.

"Aw c'mon, Brian. You'd be a hero for sure. The cop who uncovered the identity of the

Axeman," Charmaine said. "Detective Gautier wouldn't stand a chance at getting your job then."

Harrison's frown turned into a smile. "Yeah, well, I don't have to worry about *him*. Not for a good long while. He's been transferred to the False Alarm Reduction Unit."

Charmaine burst out laughing. "Is that a real NOPD section?"

"Oh yeah. My boss decided he's perfect for the job. He raised plenty of false alarms about me during my investigation. He told the chief I'd 'lost perspective.' He also aligned himself on the butt-kisser team. They let Locke and his fancy friends lead them around by the nose. Those commanders have run for cover."

"And threw Gautier under the bus. I'm having trouble working up sympathy for him," Jessi said with a snort.

"Totally predictable. The DA's office is delighted to have such a high-profile, complicated case. Locke and his girlfriends will likely be tried for murder. And New York is in touch. They're reopening his first wife's missing person case. And they've got forensic accountants looking into his finances," Harrison said.

"Don't forget you have to find who Locke and Lana hired to kill people," Jessi replied.

"Of course, we could help you wrap that up real quick. Miss Marie might even be willing to give testimony from beyond the grave."

Harrison's expression tightened again. He stood. "Ladies, thanks for stopping by, but my calendar is packed today. Let's not keep in touch for a while."

"So ungrateful. We helped take out your backstabbing subordinate. Not to mention position you for a promotion sooner rather than later." Charmaine squinted at him.

"Thank you for forcing me to lie to my bosses and reporters. Enjoy the rest of your day."

Moments later they stood in front of the NOPD District Five building. Traffic zipped by on North Rampart. The natural world ticked along. Yet Jessi and Charmaine hesitated to flow back into their normal routines. Both had taken the day off from their regular jobs. Jessi put on tortoise shell sunglasses and turned to Charmaine.

"You ready to grab the last loose end and tie that bitch up?"

"Let's go." Charmaine put on her own sunglasses.

****

Penelope, JoJo, and two other members of the grunch community sat around the living room. Penelope's cozy décor contrasted with their dismal mood. Cups of tea, a platter of sugar cookies, and another with muffins didn't help.

"Of course, we didn't know. Because of who we are, you're ready to believe the worst," Penelope snapped.

"You knew Lydia wasn't dead. This whole pretense about suspecting Locke killed her was an act. Why shouldn't we think you knew?" Charmaine returned her hostile stare with a frown of condemnation.

Jessi nodded. "Or that you were in on it. Witnesses saw strange—"

"We're human beings, not creatures living in the woods," JoJo rumbled.

"Damn it, people *died*," Charmaine said. She transferred her hard gaze to him until he looked away.

"We didn't think she'd..." JoJo let out a long sigh.

A tall man with a limp entered the room with two others. JoJo stood straight. Penelope's red face of anger turned white. She bit her lower lip. Feeling hemmed in, Jessi and Charmaine stood at the same time. Charmaine touched Jessi's arm. When Jessi looked at her, Charmaine gave a slight shake of her head. Jessi took her hand off the stun gun and out of her jacket pocket.

"Penelope isn't the chairperson of the executive board as of this morning," the tall man said. "We're doing our own investigation, but she didn't break any laws. None of them did. However, it's clear their support allowed Lydia to do harm. We want to protect ourselves from outside persecution, but not at the expense of others. The normal criminal justice system will deal with Lydia and the others."

The people who had been with Penelope before his arrival stood and crossed to stand with the new group. JoJo alone remained on her side of the room. He rested a huge hand on Penelope's shoulder.

"I think it's time to go," Jessi whispered aside to Charmaine.

Five minutes later they were in Jessi's Jeep headed to Charmaine's house. They didn't speak, both thinking their own thoughts. Jessi didn't even turn on her favorite R&B FM station. When she pulled into Charmaine's driveway, neither got out. Instead, they sat staring ahead for a few moments. Then Charmaine let out a slow breath.

"Some case." Charmaine turned to Jessie. "JoJo and Penelope really love each other."

"You mean they're..." Jessi gasped. "Seriously? But she married another man, had kids."

"To clean up the gene pool. They were both scared their kids would be born with deformities. Her late husband suspected all those years. Interesting story." Charmaine sighed a second time.

"You picked all that from JoJo? Wow. You're a powerful witch." Jessi ducked a playful swing aimed at her head. Then an impish twinkle lit up her dark-brown eyes when she saw Scotty open Charmaine's kitchen door. "Speaking of hot love affairs. Guess you'll be spending the rest of the day in bed. And on the floor. Maybe on the sofa, the dining room table, the—"

"Oh, shut up and go home." Charmaine undid her seat belt. She couldn't help but smile, though. "We could both use rest and relaxation."

"First, I'm gonna check on Miss Marie. She's getting help cleaning up all the spirits Timmy boy set loose. Then I've got some legal research to do for my boss. Oh, before I forget, one of his law partners might have some work for us. Her client, a woman in Lafayette, swears an ancestor was the first black female serial killer in the US, and her ghost is—"

"Stop. I don't want to hear one more word." Charmaine got out of the car. She leaned in, still holding the door open. "And Miss Marie and Lucas better leave with you. Yeah, I know they're in the backseat."

"Miss Marie said have fun." Jessi smirked while ghostly giggles joined in the fun.

"Y'all all need to grow up," Charmaine grumbled as she walked away.

ABOUT THE AUTHOR

Mix knowledge of voodoo, Louisiana politics and forensic social work, and you get a snapshot of author Lynn Emery. Lynn has written over twenty novels so far, one of which inspired the BET made-for-television movie AFTER ALL based on her romantic suspense novel of the same name. Holly Robinson Peete and DB Woodside starred as the lead characters.

Her romantic suspense titles have won and been nominated for several awards, including Best Multicultural Mainstream Novel by Romantic Times Magazine.

Learn more at
www.lynnemery.com
www.facebook.com/lynn.emery.author

www.ingramcontent.com/pod-product-compliance
Lightning Source LLC
Chambersburg PA
CBHW030645120726
47905CB00001B/66